PRAISE FOR
SUZANNE BROCKMANN

Gone Too Far

"Sizzling with military intrigue and sexual tension, with characters so vivid they leap right off the page, *Gone Too Far* is a bold, brassy read with a momentum that just doesn't quit."

—TESS GERRITSEN

The Defiant Hero
CHOSEN BY ROMANCE WRITERS OF AMERICA AS THE #2 ROMANCE OF 2001

"A smart, thrilling keeper . . . While heating tension and passion to the boiling point, Brockmann firmly squashes the cliché of military men with hearts of stone and imbues her SEALs with honest emotional courage."

—*Publishers Weekly*

Please turn the page for more reviews. . . .

HEARTTHROB

SUZANNE BROCKMANN

BALLANTINE BOOKS • NEW YORK

A Ballantine Book
Published by The Random House Publishing Group
Copyright © 1999 by Suzanne Brockmann
Excerpt from *Flashpoint* copyright © 2004 by Suzanne Brockmann

All rights reserved under International and Pan-American Copyright Conventions. Published in the United States by The Random House Publishing Group, a division of Random House, Inc., New York.

Ballantine and colophon are registered trademarks of Random House, Inc.

www.ballantinebooks.com

This book contains an excerpt from the forthcoming book *Flashpoint* by Suzanne Brockmann. This excerpt has been set for this edition only and may not reflect the final content of the forthcoming edition.

ISBN 0-345-46608-X

Manufactured in the United States of America

First Fawcett Books Mass Market Edition: March 1999
First Ballantine Books Mass Market Edition: February 2004

OPM   10 9 8 7 6 5 4 3 2 1

For Melanie

One

❧ ❧

JERICHO BEAUMONT USED the pay phone outside the Aardvark Club to call Chaslyn. He automatically hunched his shoulders and turned his face away as a car pulled into the lot and parked, its headlights illuminating him like a follow-spot before being shut off.

As the phone rang, he turned up the collar of his jacket—added protection against being recognized by the college-age kids getting out of the car. But he needn't have bothered.

"Isn't that . . . ?"

"Doesn't he look like . . . ?"

The flurry of whispers were drowned out by a louder voice. "Nah, it's only Jericho Beaumont. Hey, Beaumont, where you been? I keep expecting you to do a guest spot on the new *Loveboat*. Haven't they called you yet?"

Anger flared, but Jed crushed it, stuffing it deep inside, locking it tightly down, ignoring it as completely as the laughter that echoed in the night. And when Chaslyn's roommate Lisa picked up the phone on the fifth ring, his voice was even and perfectly in control.

"Hey, Lisa. It's Jericho. Has Chas left for the wrap party yet?"

Silence. Then Lisa laughed nervously. "Um, Jericho . . . Chaslyn left for London five days ago. She got cast in that Linda McCartney bio-pic, remember?" Her voice became tinged with pity. "Didn't she tell you she was leaving?"

"Yeah," Jed lied. "Yeah, she told me, and I, um . . . I must've forgotten."

"You didn't know she was gone, did you?" Lisa saw right through him. "You know, she told me you wouldn't notice if she suddenly disappeared. And it took you five days just to wonder where she was, didn't it?"

What could he say? It was the truth. "Yeah."

"God," Lisa continued, "and I was about to be mad at *her* for dumping you that way. You're such a loser, Beaumont."

She cut the connection without even saying good-bye, and Jed slowly hung up the phone.

His girlfriend had been gone for five days.

And he hadn't even noticed.

It would've been funny—if it weren't so damn pathetic.

The music inside the club was blaring, and Jed worked his way through the sea of humanity to the bar at the back, where the cast and crew of *Mean Time* were having their farewell bash.

Rhino and T.S. were sitting at the bar, a bottle of Jack Daniel's positioned strategically between them.

"Where's Chaslyn?" Melanie, the makeup head asked as he moved past her table.

Jed didn't stop. "She's not coming. She's already flown to London for her next project."

"Poor Jericho—you're all alone. You must be so sad."

He took the stool next to Rhino, trying to feel sad, trying to care Chaslyn was gone. But the only emotion he could muster up was a vague sense of frustration. And maybe a little envy. Chas had a next project to go to. So far Jed had nothing lined up yet, and the truth was that that hurt worse than her leaving.

He dug deeper, staring into the shot glass filled with golden brown whiskey that Rhino had pushed in front of him, but he still felt nothing more profound than a sense of relief.

Chaslyn had left, which meant he no longer had to worry about hurting her. She had truly cared for him. And he . . . He'd liked the sex.

Bernie O'Hara, the character he'd played in *Mean Time*, had loved Chaslyn's character, Lulu Jerome, with an obsessive passion. It hadn't taken long for the line between reality and make-believe to blur, and five days into the six-week shoot, Jed had wound up in Chaslyn's bed. It should've been no big deal. They were both adults, both unattached.

But Chas didn't realize the heat they generated belonged only to Bernie and Lulu. She didn't realize that underneath Bernie's volatile character, Jed felt damn close to nothing.

That he rarely felt anything at all.

He picked up the glass of whiskey and brought it up to his nose, breathing in the familiar aroma. He closed his eyes, anticipating its smoothness against his tongue, the bite as it hit the back of his throat, the warmth that would rush through him, down to his stomach and outward, all the way to the tips of his fingers and toes.

"You actually gonna drink that this time?"

Jed opened his eyes to see Austin Franz sliding onto the stool on his other side. Franz was a brilliant cinematographer, and one of the meanest sons of bitches in the industry. He'd gotten it into his head that he'd have stood a chance with Chaslyn, had Jericho Beaumont not pushed him out of the running.

Rhino and T.S. shifted in their seats, exchanging a glance.

"Are you?" Franz asked again.

Jed couldn't answer. He never knew for sure if he was

going to drink the whiskey or not—not until he got up and walked out of the bar. So far he'd always walked away.

He sidestepped the question, giving Franz his movie star smile, open, friendly. "I just like to smell it."

"You've been sober . . . how long?" Franz asked.

"It'll be five years next week."

"Shit. That long? You must want to drink that pretty damn badly."

Jed gazed into the shot glass.

"Go away, Austin," Rhino said, his squeaky voice in direct contrast to his girth.

"So what's your next movie gonna be, Jer?" Franz asked.

"Jericho doesn't like nicknames," T.S. supplied helpfully.

Jed's smile was starting to feel decidedly tired. It was public knowledge that he didn't have a next movie yet. He called his agent, Ron Stapleton, twice a day, but apparently, even after being clean and sober for five years, even after showing up every day on time for *Mean Time*, no one wanted to touch him. The best he had was a potential meeting with the producer of another independent feature. He'd have to fly to Boston, even pay for the airline tickets himself, with no guarantee he'd get the part. And until Ron sent him the script, he wasn't even sure he wanted it. Frustration twisted inside of him. "Nothing's lined up yet," he said cheerfully—an Oscar-worthy performance.

"I'm taking a few months off myself," Franz told him, "and then I'm going into preproduction with Stan for this really hot 1930s gangster story. Stan liked you for the lead, but since I'm producing this time around, I talked him out of it."

He was lying. He was trying to piss Jed off—and it was working. Jed turned his smile up a few notches. "It's just as well. I try not to work with the same director twice in a row."

"Come on, Jericho," T.S. said. "I'll challenge you to a game of video downhill skiing."

"I'll challenge you to a different game. You ever play quarters?" Franz stopped Jed with a hand on his arm.

Franz was holding him so tightly, he would have had to really pull to get away. This was the way bar fights started. He knew—he'd been in enough of them in the past.

He briefly closed his eyes. "Austin, I'm sorry about Chaslyn. I honestly didn't know that you were—"

"Screw Chaslyn." Franz laughed harshly. "Well, shit, you already did that, didn't you? Just forget about it, Jerry. She obviously has. This is just a nice, friendly wager."

"I'm not into gambling."

"One game of quarters. That's all."

Quarters was a drinking game where the players took turns bouncing coins off the bar in an attempt to sink one in their opponent's drink. When a quarter was sunk, the opposing player had to drain the glass. Jed had played plenty in his late teens, but usually with beer, not whiskey.

Franz reached for the bottle of Jack, pouring himself a shot. "One game. If you win or tie, I'll let Stan cast you in the gangster project."

"And if I lose?"

"You win anyway, since you really want to drink that shot. I'd just be giving you a good excuse." He pushed a quarter down the bar.

Jed stared into Franz's eyes, feeling . . . what? Anger, yes. The son of a bitch was vindictive and mean-spirited. He wanted to hurt Jed simply for the sake of hurting him and that really pissed him off. But beneath his anger, he also felt . . . interest. A glimmer of excitement, a shadow of possibility.

He *could* win. He used to be good at this. He picked up the quarter.

Rhino clutched at his head. "Jericho—"

"Shut up, Rizinski." Franz was holding another quarter,

and he tossed it onto the bar so that it bounced up. It missed the rim of Jed's glass by a good two inches.

Jed hefted the other quarter in his hand. Last time he'd played, it had been with beer mugs—taller, but wider around. He took a deep breath, feeling the smoky air of the bar fill his lungs. The risk was high, but if he won . . .

He threw. The quarter bounced, clinking as it hit the side of Franz's glass.

Franz threw and missed. Jed threw, the quarter hitting the glass again, but still not going in.

Twice more each, all misses, and Jed knew he could do it. One more shot was all he needed and . . .

Franz's quarter landed dead in the center of Jed's glass with a splash. It settled there, magnified by both the glass and the liquid.

"You got one chance to tie." Franz slid the second quarter down the bar to him.

"Jericho—"

"I can do this, Rhino."

Rhino put his head down on the bar, his meaty arms blocking both his sight and hearing.

Jed picked up the quarter, tracing George Washington's head with his thumb. He knew exactly where to throw it, exactly how much force to use. He *could* do this. He tossed.

The quarter bounced.

And missed.

"Yes!" Franz laughed, smacking the bar with the palm of his hand. "I win."

The reality of what he'd just done came crashing down around Jed. The glimmer of possibility turned to ash, to soul-numbing despair.

He stared at his shot glass, at the quarter at the bottom. He didn't have to lift it to his nose, he could smell the pungent odor from where he was. He knew how good it would taste, how easy it would go down.

And he knew if he drank it, he'd drink another. And another and probably another. Until he was loaded enough not to care. Until he was loaded enough to beat the crap out of Austin Franz.

"You don't have to drink," Franz said generously. "But if you don't, you better believe you'll never work for me, or anyone associated with me, ever again."

Jed lifted the glass.

Kate gazed at the man sitting across from her, nearly giddy with fatigue. "You think I should marry *you* . . . ?"

He was handsome in a bland, spongy, Wonder bread kind of way, with wavy blond hair and very pretty blue eyes. "No, it's not . . ." He closed those eyes and shook his head. "It's not what you think," he said in a soft southern drawl. "I'm not doing this for me." He opened his eyes and gazed at her intently. "I'm doing this for you."

"I don't understand." After five hours, she couldn't put much emotion into it anymore.

He closed his eyes again. "I made a promise to Sarah . . ." The eyes opened again. Another piercing look. Kate clenched her teeth so that she wouldn't laugh out loud and hurt the poor guy's feelings. ". . . that I'd look out for you. If you're married to me, then you won't have to—"

"Thank you," Victor interrupted. "Mister . . ." He searched his clipboard for a name. "Franklin."

"John Franklin," Blue-eyes supplied helpfully. Hopefully. Just like that, the slightly overdone southern accent was replaced by nasal Long Island. "Was that what you wanted? Because I could do it again. Is Laramie supposed to be drunk in this scene, because I can do it more drunk if you want. Or *less* drunk or—"

"Thank you," Victor said again.

"We've got your head shot and résumé, John," Kate told the actor gently as she stood up and escorted him to the door. "Thank you so much for coming." She poked her head out into the crowded waiting room. "Give us five minutes, Annie."

As the door closed behind the man, Kate leaned against it.

"What the hell was he doing with his eyes?" Victor asked. "Where did that guy learn to act?"

"He wasn't *that* bad."

"I wouldn't cast him in a dog food commercial." Victor turned to the casting agent who was manning the video camera. "Erase that," he ordered.

Kate pushed herself up and off the door, resisting the urge to throw herself down on the floor to scream and kick her feet. It wasn't her job to have a hissy fit. It wasn't her job to go insane—at least not visibly so. She was the producer of this movie. She had to be the voice of reason and the oracle of calm even when her blood pressure was 800 over 400, the way it was right now.

She could hear a dull roar in her ears as her blood raced through her veins. Looking on the bright side, if her head actually *did* explode, it was likely that Victor would begin to take what she had to say much more seriously.

Over the past few years—over half a decade now—she'd been the president and CEO of the Supply Closet, an office supply store that she'd built into a multimillion-dollar regional chain. She'd found, in those years, that her normal, soft-spoken delivery didn't always get her the results she wanted, so she'd learned to square her shoulders, raise her voice, and get very, very tough. Most men thought they could steamroll over Kate O'Laughlin, and they probably could. But when she mentally slipped on her Valkyrie maiden breastplate, adjusted the twin horns on her helmet, and let Frau Steinbreaker loose, she could not only make a dent in the roller, but also stop the machine cold.

She hadn't yet felt the need to assume her alter ego with Victor. But she could feel her backbone starting to stiffen—the first sign that the Frau was dying to be unleashed.

"We need to cast this part," she said. That was a simple

enough concept, wasn't it? So why didn't he just do it? "We're scheduled to start shooting this movie in less than a month and a half, and until we find our Virgil Laramie, we're not going to get a commitment from any of the other actors. Maybe it's time to take another look at the five hundred actors you've already rejected out of hand?"

Either that, or maybe it was time for her to start whacking herself on the head with a big stick.

Victor's cell phone trilled, and with an arrogance that still drove her mad, even now, after they'd been divorced for close to seven years, he held up one hand, signaling her to wait as he took the call.

To date, Victor had rejected every hungry young actor in Hollywood for this part. Some of them were rising movie stars. Some were hot and happening TV actors. And they *all* had been willing to take a significant cut in pay—even down to union scale—to do this picture. To take on the meaty role of Virgil Laramie.

Virgil Laramie was a broken, bitter man who returned to South Carolina after a harsh journey to California took the lives of his wife and baby son. He'd returned east and was ready and willing to spend the rest of his life hiding in a bottle of whiskey—until his 14-year-old sister-in law shocked him by asking him to help smuggle a wagon load of runaway slaves out of the county. The girl, Jane, was a conductor on the Underground Railroad, and her fearless passion, along with her deep loyalty and friendship for a young black man, slowly brought Laramie back to the world of the living.

The Promise was going to be a chick flick—a love story, a relationship movie. It was also a period piece. The story took place in the South in the mid-1800s, several years before the American Civil War.

With those two serious strikes against it—the fact that nothing exploded and the characters wore old-fashioned clothing and did a lot of talking—Kate knew that chances of the film being picked up by a major distributor would increase a significant amount if they had a name-brand actor attached to the project. Matthew McConaughey. Matt Damon. Ralph Fiennes.

Kate took a sip of her coffee and felt a jolt of caffeine race through her system, imagining the thrill she'd feel if they could somehow get Ralph Fiennes for the part of Virgil Laramie. At union scale. Yeah, right. Snowball's chance in hell. But Ralph's face was the one she imagined every time she thought of that broodingly dark character. And lately, she was thinking about Laramie far too often.

She'd created the character, and he'd come to life as she'd written the script. He was complex—a swirl of seemingly impenetrable darkness that becomes infused by the bright light of hope. He'd crumbled beneath all the pain that life had hit him with, but then he'd learned to stand and even walk again—carrying more than just his weight.

Kate was more than half in love with him.

As the screenwriter, it mattered that the actor chosen to play Laramie be right for the part. But her practical side knew both she and Victor most likely would have to compromise. If they wanted this movie to get made, they simply could not spend much more time on the casting process. They had their funding now, and those financial backers wouldn't wait forever.

As the producer of this movie, she had four million other things she should be thinking about besides casting. In an effort to cut costs, she was responsible for scouting locations herself. She should be down in South Carolina right now.

Victor ended his call and turned back to her. "Sorry, babe. What were we talking about?"

Kate wanted to scream. Instead she put down her coffee mug and gathered up her briefcase and jacket. "I'll be in South Carolina if you need me."

"Katie—"

"Cast this part, Victor," she told her ex-husband. And then she straightened her shoulders, assuming Frau Steinbreaker's near-militaristic stance as she flexed her producer's muscles. "Or I'll find myself a director who *can*."

She almost ruined the effect by laughing at the look of complete shock on Victor's face as she marched out of the room. It was nearly as effective as having her head explode.

Jed pushed his way into the casting agent's waiting room and stood in line at the desk that held the sign-in sheet.

The crowded room smelled like raw nerves—cold sweat, indigestion, and bad breath. It was silent, too, despite the fact that over thirty men sat in chairs that lined the walls. There was a low table in the center that was covered with magazines, but no one was reading. Some of the men had their eyes closed, others were busy checking out the competition, quickly looking away if anyone else looked up. Eye contact was minimal.

Someone coughed, and Jed heard a sound that had to be teeth grinding. The anxiety level here was off the scale.

It made him feel completely calm in comparison.

Jed filled in the next empty line on the sign-in sheet, taking his time to write his stage name in clear block letters. There was no space on the sheet for him to list his Oscar nominations.

Jed glanced at his watch as he sat down, marking the time as he once again did a quick head count. Thirty-three people. If each man took only two minutes, he was going to be sitting here for an hour. If everyone took five, he'd be here for more than twice that.

He settled back in the folding chair, fighting the annoyance that rose in him, fighting his need for a cigarette, flatly ignoring his need for a drink.

The good news was that no one had seemed to recognize him yet.

"Mister . . . Beaumont?" The mousy young woman who came out to check the many pages of the sign-in sheet was looking around the room.

Jed sat forward. "That's me."

"Did you bring a head shot?"

He stared at her. A head shot. When was the last time he'd needed a photo of himself? When was the last time he'd actually gone to this kind of audition? It had to have been at least ten years. More. "Uh," he said. "No. I, uh, didn't. I'm sorry, I . . ."

The mouse frowned slightly. "Didn't your agent tell you that this was a serious audition? There's a movie director in that back room and—"

Jed reached for the week-old copy of *TV Guide* that was out on the table among the other magazines. One of the networks had run *Kill Zone* last week—was it Tuesday or Wednesday? He leafed through, finding the full-page ad for the movie—a beefcake shot of him, muscles gleaming for his role as a Navy SEAL—assault weapon held loosely in his arms. He tore it out and handed it to the mouse. "Maybe that'll do."

He knew he was being a smart-ass, but he was tired of this. After his agent had sent him the script for *The Promise*, after Jed had read it, and loved it, and realized that Virgil Laramie was the role of a lifetime, the movie's producer, Mary Kate O'Laughlin, had canceled their meeting.

Ron had pressed, and she'd told him flat out that she didn't want to waste Jericho's or her own time. In plain English, she couldn't risk taking a chance with him. She and Vic Strauss were looking for up-and-coming talent, not someone who'd peaked over five years ago. The production was already a high financial risk—their backers might get spooked at the thought of sinking all that cash into a project with an A-list "has been" in the lead role. Beaumont wasn't even C-list these days. He was barely on any list at all.

It was frustrating as hell, especially since Jed knew he could play Laramie better than anyone in the world. It was as if the part had been written with him in mind. It was as if the character had been modeled on his very soul.

Ron called again and again, but O'Laughlin was adamant. She wouldn't even give him a chance.

Over the past three months, Jed had found himself again at the absolute bottom of his personal barrel as he'd fought a bad case of the flu, *and* dealt with the fact that despite being cast in *Mean Time*, Ron's phone wasn't ringing off the hook. Jed had started going to parties, started schmoozing shamelessly in hopes that *some*one would take a chance and cast him in their movie.

But days turned into weeks, weeks into months, and the only call Ron received was from the producers of some bad TV sitcom. Apparently Jed didn't even rate a guest spot on *Loveboat*.

There was only one thing Jed had left to lose by coming to this audition in New York. And he wanted the role of Virgil Laramie more than he wanted to hang onto the remaining worthless shards of his pride.

The mouse's eyes widened as she matched the name on the sign-in sheet with the picture from *TV Guide*, and she looked up at him and swallowed loudly enough for him to hear.

"Oh," she said.

Jed gave her his best smile—the two thousand watt, five billion dollar, movie star version. "What's your name?"

"Annie."

"Do me a favor, Annie, and don't tell Mary Kate and Vic that I'm out here. I want to surprise 'em."

Annie stood staring at him, frozen in place.

"Is that okay?" he asked.

She snapped to. "Kate left about an hour ago. You'll only be reading for Victor Strauss today."

"Really?" Jed turned up his smile even brighter. "In that case, please feel free to let Vic know I'm here."

Ding, dong the witch was dead—or at least safely out of the room. He actually stood a chance.

Jed took a deep breath, careful not to let his hope get out of control. If he let himself get too elated, he'd have much farther to fall if he failed. It was better to feel nothing at all. It was true he'd never soar into the heights, but he'd also never sink into complete despair.

He took a deep breath, firing up the movie star smile again as Annie came out of the back room.

"Mr. Strauss will see you now, Mr. Beaumont."

Two

~~~
∽ ∽
~~~

"**I** FOUND OUR location." Kate sat on the bed in her Columbia, South Carolina hotel room, tucking the phone under her chin so she could reach down to unlace her boots. "A little town called Grady Falls. It's perfect, Victor. It's in the middle of nowhere. There's this little antebellum plantation museum, preserved by the Historical Society that no one ever goes to. They'd let us shoot both exteriors *and* interiors for next to nothing. The town has one motel, with about twenty trailor hookups alongside it. Across the street is this incredible little restaurant—the Morning Glory Grill. It's owned by these two ladies, Edna Rae and Sally, who can cook unlike anything you've ever tasted in your life. I've started preliminary negotiations to take over the Grill instead of setting up a dining tent for food service—we'd save money that way, too."

"I got some good news, too," Victor told her. "I found Laramie."

Kate froze, her boot in her hand. Laramie. She shook herself, tossing it onto the floor. This was good news. This odd feeling of premonition she was having was only due to complete fatigue.

"Did you get the videotape I couriered to you?" Victor asked. "I sent it last night—you should've received it by now."

Kate looked at the package she'd brought up with her from the front desk, the uneasy sensation getting even stronger. "You found our Laramie last night, but you're only calling to tell me about it today?"

"Yeah, well, I know you, and I know until you see this tape you're not going to believe that—"

"Wait." Kate's premonition was growing into a chillingly bad feeling. "Why are you playing games? Why aren't you just telling me the name of the actor you've found?"

"Did you or didn't you get the tape?"

"I got it."

"Play it, Katie. Then call me back." With a click, Victor—the rat—hung up on her.

"I'm hating this." Kate unwrapped the tape and carried it across the room to the VCR. "I'm really, truly hating this, Victor."

She'd spent the entire day either tromping through the South Carolina underbrush or driving to a new location, where she'd tromped through the underbrush some more. Her feet hurt from walking, and her butt hurt from sitting in the car. She was hungry and sweaty, and she wanted a shower and room service and a tall, cold drink—not necessarily in that order.

She was scared to death that the face she was going to see on this tape belonged to an actor who would be absolutely inappropriate for the role of Virgil Laramie. She was scared this face was going to belong to Rod Freeman, who was a fabulous actor but fifteen years too old, or Jamie Layne, who was fifteen years too young. Or, God help her, what if the Internet rumor that she'd heard in Grady Falls hadn't been a rumor after all, and Jericho Beaumont's was the face that would appear on the screen?

Kate turned on the TV and set it so the VCR would play. There was only blue for several long moments. And then the tape gave a visual burp, and a picture came on.

It was a man, and he was sitting in a chair. The lighting was bad, and he was blurry, but she recognized the background as the New York casting office she'd gone AWOL from just yesterday.

The focus improved, and the man in the chair was recognizable, too.

He had shoulder-length dark hair, a long, almost square face that angled suddenly at his jawline, narrowing into a strong, tapered chin, and an exquisite, elegantly shaped mouth. It was the kind of mouth any red-blooded woman would give a good long second glance—and then spend the next ten years dreaming about kissing.

But it was his eyes that truly set him apart. They were hazel—a gorgeous mix of green and light brown with a darker ring at the outer edge of the iris. His eyes were the focal point of his face. They seemed to glow with his intensity, even in the bad lighting of the casting office.

The man in the chair was indeed Jericho Beaumont.

Jericho Beaumont. Nominated for four different Oscars—two in the same year.

Jericho Beaumont. He'd dominated at the box office for close to two years, and then he'd fallen from grace, struck down by his addictions to drugs and alcohol. No one had known that he'd been playing the rehab game for years—or if they'd known, they'd ignored it. He'd dry out, clean up—until the temptation grew too great, and then he'd slip back to his old ways. Apparently, allegedly, he was completely clean now. But in Hollywood, as he attempted to make a come back, there were dozens of bets being made as to exactly how long it would be before he slipped again. Not *if* he slipped again, but *when*.

Jericho Beaumont. Six years ago, he'd been voted *People* magazine's "Sexiest Man Alive." Those six years that had passed had only served to improve him. His face was fuller, with more lines and more character, his dark good looks more broodingly, dangerously intense. He still had that trademark scar just above his left eyebrow. It marred the perfection of his face, somehow making him even more good-looking. The camera still loved him. He was, undoubtedly, the most handsome man she'd ever seen in her life.

Kate pushed a button on the VCR, and the tape stopped.

She picked up the phone to call Victor back, but didn't finish dialing. She cut the connection, cursing Victor, cursing Jericho Beaumont, but mostly cursing herself.

As much as she wanted to, she couldn't use her veto power to exclude Beaumont without watching the tape.

She pushed play and turned up the volume.

Beaumont's voice was smoky and rich, thickened with an outrageously authentic-sounding southern accent. But of course it sounded authentic—Beaumont had been born and raised in some backwoods Alabama town.

"It's not what you think," he said quietly, both his voice and the movement as he very, very slightly shook his head carefully understated. "I'm not doing this for me. I'm doing this for you."

"I don't understand." Victor's voice read the line from offscreen.

Beaumont was silent for a moment, and even though he didn't move a muscle, he succeeded in letting her see everything that Laramie was thinking. Should he tell the truth? Should he say anything at all? Should he just give up and go get another drink?

Kate's heart was in her throat. He was Laramie, her Laramie, come to life before her very eyes. Three lines and one pause, and he *was* Laramie. She couldn't breathe.

"I promised Sarah I'd look out for you," he finally said. "If you're married to me, then you won't have to marry Reg Brooks. I won't touch you, Jane. I swear. This wouldn't be that kind of marriage." He paused, forcing a smile. "Unless you want it to be—I mean, someday, when you're old enough and you decide you want . . . babies. *If* you want babies . . ." He stared down at the floor for a moment, temporarily lost, momentarily slipping into another place or time. After several perfectly timed beats, he looked up. "God knows you're just a girl—you're not ready for anything like that now, and I don't know if I'll ever be, but . . . that's a problem for the future. Right now I'm struggling to find solutions for here and now."

The videotape gave another visual burp, and Beaumont was sitting on the floor now, leaning back against the wall, long legs bent, knees up in front of him. His worn-out jeans were loose-fitting, but the way he sat made the denim hug the powerful muscles of his thighs. He held a coffee mug in his long, graceful fingers and took a sip.

"Tell me your name," Vic said from somewhere off-screen. Kate knew that they were doing an improvised scene.

"Laramie," Beaumont drawled. "Virgil Laramie."

"Isn't it a little early in the day to be drinking, Mr. Laramie?"

Beaumont barely looked up. "It's never too early. 'Sides, this way I'll be totally drunk by dusk. That's my goal in life, you know. Never to be sober when night falls."

"Didn't your wife's sister, Jane, just ask you for help?" Vic asked.

Beaumont's hands tightened slightly on the mug. "Jane. That girl is trying to get us all hung." He laughed, but there wasn't a bit of humor in it. "I don't care what promises I made her sister. There's no way in hell I'm risking my neck to smuggle a wagonload of Negroes past those pattyrollers."

"Pattyrollers?"

"Pattyrollers. Patrollers," he said. "The sheriff thinks he's the law in these parts, but he's wrong. The patrollers run everything. They're judge and jury. Even with a signed pass, they're just as likely to kick the hell out of you as not. And that's riding alone, not with a wagonload of damned runaways."

He was silent for a moment, and again, Kate could see subtle emotion flickering across his face.

He looked up then, directly at where she imagined Vic was sitting. "If I don't help her, Jane is going to take the wagon herself, isn't she?"

"You tell me."

Kate hit the off button and sat down on the edge of the bed. Jericho Beaumont was good. He was beyond good.

He had become Laramie. Without the help of costumes or makeup or lighting, he had quietly slipped into Laramie's tormented soul. He'd done his research, too. Pattyrollers.

She lay back on the bed and stared up at the hotel room ceiling. One minute slid into two as she tried on the idea of letting this movie, her baby, this project of her heart and soul, ride completely on the shoulders of Jericho Beaumont.

Jericho too-drunk-to-remember-his-cue-lines Beaumont. The horror stories she'd heard from the producer of one of his last major studio movies were terrifying. Jericho had shown up late. He'd shown up without his lines learned. He'd shown up drunk. He hadn't shown up at all.

Yes, that had been over five years ago. But the things he'd done were hard to forget.

Her hunger was completely gone—she was nauseous now instead.

The phone rang.

She rolled over and picked it up, not even bothering to say hello. "I can't do it. I can't hire him."

"Come on, babe! Are you nuts?" It was Victor. "He's *brilliant*."

"He is brilliant," she told him. "He's a magnificent, utterly brilliant actor. I'm not disputing that."

"He's starving for this part, Katie. He actually came to an open call."

"So?"

"So he swallowed his pride in order to—"

She cut him off. "No, we're not casting Jericho Beaumont, Victor. No. Absolutely not. Find someone else."

"Katie, watch the tape again."

"I don't need to watch the tape again." She worked to keep her voice from becoming too loud. "Because this isn't about talent. It's about whether or not we can afford to hold production for two days, or two weeks, while Beaumont goes off on some binge."

"Do you want Susie McCoy for the part of Jane, or not?"

Kate blinked at the sudden change of subject. "You told me there was no way we could get Susie. That her father wouldn't agree to less than one and a half million."

"Yeah, well, I just got off the phone with her agent, who told me she's in for union scale."

"What?" Susie McCoy was a fifteen-year-old with a huge amount of talent, who had been underutilized in every one of the ten movies she'd made since she got her first break at age six. Kate had written the part of Jane with the young actor in mind. "That's so amazingly great!"

Victor dropped his bomb. "On the condition that we cast Jericho as Laramie."

She could have Susie McCoy if she took on Jericho Beaumont. Oh, God.

"No," Kate said. "I'm sorry, Victor, but as much as I want Susie, I can't—"

"With two name actors providing box-office draw, we can start shopping for distributors today," Vic said. "We're almost guaranteed success. We could even afford to go over budget—in case Jericho needs drying out halfway through the shoot."

"Oh, God!"

"We don't need to make any decisions now," Vic told her. "Think about this, watch the tape again, kick it around for a few days, and we'll talk when you get back to New York. Love you, babe. Later, okay?"

"No," Kate said. "Not okay. I'm not casting Jericho Beaumont in my movie."

But Victor had already cut the connection. Kate hung up the phone and lay back on the bed again. She stared at the ceiling for all of ninety seconds, and then she sat up, rewound the tape, and, cursing herself soundly, watched it again.

"She's watching it right now," Jed said, telephone tucked beneath his chin as he paced across the New York hotel room. "I know it. I can feel it."

"Why this movie, Jed?" David asked. David Stern's family had moved to Alabama when he was a sophomore in high school. After living in the Deep South for nearly twenty years, he still sounded as if he'd just stepped off of a New York City subway. And he still called Jed by his given name. "And, by the way, have you been to a meeting lately?"

Jed could hear water running in the sink and the clinking sound of dishes. He could picture David Stern in the kitchen of his modest suburban Montgomery house, loading up the dishwasher and helping Alison get dinner on the table. He felt a flash of something similar to envy. Similar, but not quite. The normality of David's life, with his pretty blond wife and his respectable job and his mortgage payments and family-sized car was something that Jed had never expected to achieve. He might have dreamed of it—more so back when he was a kid—but he'd never expected it.

Good thing, because it wasn't going to happen for him now.

"Yeah, I went to a meeting just last week," he told his friend. David had been on his back to keep up with Alcoholics Anonymous's twelve-step program.

"And stayed for only five minutes."

Jed sighed. He'd needed the meetings, two, three, four times a week during the first year or so he'd been out of rehab. But over the past few years, he'd drifted away. He could handle staying sober on his own. But David didn't think so.

David deftly changed the subject back to the movie. "Why is this particular role making you crazy? I can hear it in your voice. You're pacing, right? You sound stressed. Is it really worth putting yourself through this?"

"This character—Laramie—he's . . ." Jed shook his head, unable to explain. "I don't know. I just know that I can play him. I *need* to play him."

David made one of his shrink noises—a cross between hmmm and uh-uh. "So this is not about money. This isn't going to be a big financial windfall, is that what you're telling me?"

Money was something Jed had absolutely no trouble talking about. At least not with David. "Not at first. But I'm hoping to work some sort of percentage deal into my contract, so if it hits big, I'll benefit. And I'll get union scale, which at least will keep the creditors from lighting my house on fire. Oops. I forgot. I don't have a house."

Dave laughed at his pathetic attempt at a joke, but then brought the conversation right back to the place where it chaffed the most. As a psychologist, he was particularly good at doing that. "So if it's not the money, then the need for this part is about artistic fulfillment. Yes? No?"

Jed rubbed the back of his neck as he gazed out the window at the rapidly falling dusk. Lights were going on, and New York City was starting to sparkle. He closed the curtain, blocking out the view. "I guess you could call it that."

"What would *you* call it?"

Jed threw himself down into the room's one easy chair. "I didn't call you to get analyzed."

"This isn't analysis," David pointed out. "If it were, it would come with a bill for a hundred fifty dollars an hour. This movie is some kind of Civil War story, isn't that what you said?"

"No, it takes place in the early 1850s. Prewar. I play a guy who does the California gold rush thing, but his wife and kid die of some kind of fever during the trip west. I come back to South Carolina to find out that my family's plantation house has burned down and my brother was killed in the fire—"

"A comedy, huh?"

"It's not as awful as it sounds. The script is actually a really sweet story about hope. This guy Laramie kind of camps out in his in-laws' barn, does what chores he can manage during the day, and drinks himself into oblivion each night. But he's got this sister-in-law, Jane. She's only fourteen, and the writer, I swear, he caught the perfect mix of woman and child in this character. She works for the Underground Railroad—her family doesn't know it—and she's just so full of life, she manages to breathe some back into Laramie and"—he shook his head— "and Vic Strauss wants Susie McCoy to play her."

"You say that as if that's bad."

Jed exhaled a burst of air. "I don't know what Vic's thinking, but I find it hard to believe Susie McCoy can handle a part with this kind of depth. She's been doing television for the past two years."

"*Uptown Girl* is one of Ken's favorite shows," David pointed out.

"Kenny is six."

"Have you watched it?" he asked.

"I gave up bad sitcoms when I quit drinking."

"This one's pretty good."

Jed wasn't buying that. "There's a hell of a huge difference between playing a spunky sitcom kid and playing a character like Jane Willet," he said. "It was bad enough when she was making movies like *Little Mary Sunshine* and *Slumberparty*. They weren't Shakespeare, but they were better than TV."

"I read somewhere that Susie McCoy took the sitcom part to try to keep her parents from splitting up. All that travel for the movies was taking its toll on their family life."

"That worked really well." Jed stood up and started pacing again. The McCoys most recent divorce settlement battle was making headlines in the tabloids.

"So here's a question for you, Jeddo," David asked. "Suppose they do cast Susie McCoy as Jane. Would you walk away from Laramie? I guess what I'm wondering is, how badly do you want this role?"

"Badly," Jed admitted. He wanted it so badly, his teeth hurt. "I'd do damn near anything to get this—even work with little Susie McCoy."

Her father's face had turned a very dark shade of red. It was so dark, it could almost be described as purple.

But this time he wasn't mad at her—he was mad at her mother.

"Union scale!" Russell McCoy had been shouting those two words as if they were going to starve if she accepted the Screen Actors Guild's minimum wages—wages that were significantly higher than what other fifteen-year-olds earned by working at Taco Bell. "Jesus Christ, Riva! How could you let her do this?"

Her mother was nearly in tears. "Don't shout at me! We're divorced now! You have no right to shout at me!"

"I can shout at you all I want, goddamn it! How long have you known about this?"

Susie sat at the kitchen table, hands tightly clasped in front of her, waiting for this portion of World War III to end. Her agent had made a major mistake by leaving a message on her father's answering machine. She'd been waiting for the perfect time to break the news to her father about her decision to take a role in this low-budget, low-paying, high-quality independent feature film, but the perfect time had never appeared. She'd put it off, and put it off, and now she was paying the price.

She'd told her mother about the movie weeks ago, but all that had done was make her father even angrier today when he found out Riva knew and he didn't.

Susie's stomach hurt, and her head ached. She tried to block out the hateful words that were being fired over her.

Her father looked like an angry bulldog, his jowls nearly shaking. A purple bulldog. The purple-red flush extended up past the receding hairline of his forehead, making him look more than angry. He looked vicious and mean, and Susie could not imagine what her timid, pretty little mother had ever seen in him.

He finally looked at Susie. "Union scale," he said again. "I told them one and a half million—no less—and *you* turn around and say union scale."

"What does it matter how much she gets paid?" Riva asked in an unprecedented show of backbone. "She's got over six million dollars in her bank account, Russell. I think she's going to be able to pay for her own college education. That's how this all started, remember?"

He ignored Riva. "They want you for the next *Slumberparty* movie. You'll get far more than one and a half for that."

"She doesn't want to do *Slumberparty Three*. She wants to do this movie. We've already told the director

Susie's in if he wants her, provided they fulfill the terms of our agreement."

"What terms?" her father exploded. "You've agreed to let her work for slave wages! What kind of mother *are* you?"

Riva's face turned nearly gray.

Susie took a deep breath and stepped in. "Daddy, I asked Mom to stay with me on location this summer because it's going to be a low-budget shoot, and I know how much you hate that."

Her soft words managed to completely shut him up. She'd done ten movies, and Russell had been on set with her every single day of every single picture.

"Susie and I thought it would be nice if I could spend the summer with her," Riva added weakly.

Unfortunately, Russell found his tongue again. "You thought it would be nice, huh? You're the one who moved out. You should've thought in advance how that would impact the time you spent with your daughter."

"Stop," Susie said, and her father turned to look at her in surprise. When was the last time she'd stood up to him? She couldn't remember. But she was doing it now, and even though her knees were shaking, it felt good. "It's already settled. I want this part, and I want Mommy to spend the summer with me."

Her father looked from Riva to Susie and then back. As he walked out of the room, he got in a final dig at his ex-wife. "Better make sure they reserve an extra trailer for you and Jose, the Latin lover. I'd prefer it if you didn't screw his brains out in the same trailer that my daughter is living in."

"His name is Enrico," her mother whispered in the sudden stillness. She turned to Susie. "Are you really sure you want this part?"

Susie nodded. She was in—with a vengeance—provided Jericho Beaumont was cast as Laramie. She'd wanted a chance to work with him for as long as she could remember. She wanted it badly enough to be willing to stand up to her imperious father.

She wanted it more than she'd ever wanted anything.

And after years of doing exactly what her father told her, it was high time she did what *she* wanted.

Kate was in the back room of Victor's New York City office when he returned from lunch.

There was so much for her to discuss with him. They'd received a thumbs-up from the city council of Grady Falls, South Carolina. If Victor approved the location, she would be able to start sending out contracts.

And, of course, there was Jericho Beaumont.

She'd thought long and hard about casting the actor, and she still felt completely uncomfortable about the idea.

But, God, she wanted Susie McCoy to play Jane.

She finished the letter she was writing and was starting a second one when she heard the door buzzer ring.

"Hey," she heard Victor say. "How are ya? Nice to see ya. Thanks for coming over to meet with me."

"I've only got a half an hour."

Whoever had come into the office had a deep, commanding voice—and an attitude that was pure royalty. An actor, Kate decided without even cracking open the door and peeking out at him. Had to be.

"Let's not dick around, Victor. You want me in your movie. My agent wants me in your movie—even though the money you're offering is a joke. Put on your tap shoes and go all out, my man. Give it your best shot. Convince me that spending my entire summer in Crackerville, South Carolina, playing the part of a slave is something I want to do."

Kate gave in to the urge to peek out into the other room, to see who possibly could have read her script and not understood instantly that the part of Moses, the slave, was a part to die for.

The man with attitude was none other than Jamaal Hawkes, one of Hollywood's spiciest flavors of the month. Except Jamaal was more than a tall, young, dark-skinned black man with well-defined muscles and a harshly handsome, impossibly photogenic face. He had true talent. It was yet to be discovered, though, if he had the discipline and drive necessary to shape himself into a major player.

He was wearing what had to be a thousand-dollar designer suit that was tailored to fit. His shirt was crisp and white, and he had on gold cuff links and a matching tie clip. His only other jewelry was a small gold hoop earring in his left ear.

"I'm not going to dance for you, Jamaal," Victor said quietly. "I want you for this movie, because I think you can do justice to this part."

"The slave."

As Kate watched, Victor gestured for Jamaal to sit. The young man hesitated until Victor sat down first. He wasn't as confident as he sounded. But why should he be? Even though he looked and dressed like a grown man, he was only a teenager. Less than three years ago, he'd been living on the bottom edge of the middle class with his social worker mother and two sisters. Now he had a penthouse on Central Park West. He was still new at this game, and learning the rules as he played.

"Moses is the third biggest part in the movie," Victor told him. "Your agent wants you to do it because it's Best Supporting Actor material. And it's different from the roles you've played up to now. That's good for your career."

Jamaal sat down on the very edge of the sofa.

"*I* want you to do it," Victor continued, "because I can't think of another actor who can do justice to this part."

"I'm just not sure I want anything to do with playing a slave."

Victor nodded. "Have you read the script?"

Kate went back to the computer, but she left the door

partly open so she could hear the two men talking. It wasn't eavesdropping. If Victor knew she were here, he'd invite her to join the meeting. But this way she could listen in and still get her work done.

"I've read some of it," Jamaal admitted.

"It's a good script."

"It's a story about a white man."

Victor chuckled. "That's right. Laramie. Your character, the slave, Moses, was friends with Laramie's sister-in-law Jane when they were little. And this girl, Jane, she was really into Moses. Even though he was a slave, he was like her hero, you know? And she had this crazy dream that when she was old enough, she would buy Moses and they'd go out west and she'd set him free."

"Jane's a white girl." It wasn't quite a question.

"Yeah. When the story takes place, she's still very young—only fourteen. And Moses, he's about your age. Eighteen or nineteen."

"And they have a thing going? This little white girl and this slave?"

"It's more complicated than that," Victor told him. "But yeah, there's definitely an attraction between them, along with this long-standing childhood friendship. Anyway, what happens is, at the beginning of the movie, the plantation owner dies and his son inherits—and this son, Reginald Brooks, he's a real bastard. He sells off a whole bunch of the slaves—he doesn't care that he's separating families, he only cares about money. Moses is sold and taken farther south, and Jane doesn't see him for about four years. When she does see him after all that time, he's on the block, being sold again, and he's wearing chains because he's a runaway, right? He's tried to escape to the north, and now they've got to keep him locked up because they know if they don't, he'll run again. And his old owner—the real son of a bitch, Reg Brooks—he buys Moses back and basically kicks the shit out of him for running away. In his warped way he feels responsible—he sold Moses and Moses ran, so now he's going to break him. Brooks has this need to make Moses submit. But Moses would rather die, right? He's got all this pride, see, and he's never going to bow his head and say, 'Yes, master' to any man. And Jane, she still cares very deeply for Moses, and she figures she's got to help him get to freedom before Brooks kills him. She's willing to make all kinds of sacrifices—even sacrificing her own freedom by agreeing to marry Brooks—for Moses. It's a really powerful story."

Jamaal sat for a moment in silence.

Victor just waited for him to speak.

Kate took a sip of her coffee, also waiting. This was it. If Jamaal didn't want in now, after Victor's vivid telling of the part of the movie that dealt with Jane and Moses' complex relationship, there was nothing they could do to convince him.

The young man finally cleared his throat. "Who's, uh, who's playing Jane?"

Victor didn't hesitate. "Susie McCoy." Kate nearly dropped her coffee mug.

"No shit? That cute little kid from *Slumberparty* and *The Thing in the Basement*," Jamaal paused. "She old enough?"

"She's fifteen now. She's got her own sitcom. *Uptown Girl?*"

"Yeah, I've seen promos for that show. That's Susie McCoy? The blonde?"

"That's her."

"Whoa. She's still real cute."

"Uh-huh."

"How about Laramie?" Jamaal asked. "Who you got lined up to play him?"

Kate felt her fingers tighten around the handle of the

mug. Again, Victor spoke as if the contract were already on his desk. "Jericho Beaumont."

"Oh, man, he's great. But he's been off the map for what? Five years? Is he gonna draw? Or will he give this picture a B-list feel?"

"He'll draw. The curiosity factor alone will bring people in. He's a brilliant actor, despite all his personal problems."

"I know," Jamaal said. "I've always wanted to work with him. I never thought I'd have a chance."

"Sign on, and you will."

Kate opened the door and stood there, gazing at Victor. How could he make promises to Jamaal like this? He glanced up at her, and he didn't even have the grace to blush.

"So what do you think?" Victor asked Jamaal.

The young actor wasn't quite convinced. "I'm not sure about being out of the City for the entire summer . . ."

"I know the amount we've offered seems low to you, but both Jericho and Susie have agreed to work for union scale. You'd be the highest-paid actor on the set."

"Yeah?" It was obvious that that idea appealed to Jamaal.

"What d'ya say? You wanna win an Oscar next year? Are you in?"

Jamaal laughed and nodded. "Yeah, sure. Why not? Send whatever you need signed to my agent."

Kate cleared her throat pointedly, and Victor glanced up at her again. "Hey, look, let me introduce you to our producer—Mary Kate O'Laughlin. I'm sorry, Katie, I would've called you to join us when Jamaal first came in, but I didn't realize you were back there."

"No kidding." Kate shot him a look that was meant to burn a hole through him.

Jamaal stood, and Kate met him halfway across the room, reaching out to shake his hand. She forced herself to smile. "It's a pleasure to meet you, Jamaal. But before you—"

"Jamaal's in a hurry." Victor herded the young man toward the door. "I'll send the papers this afternoon."

As the door closed behind Jamaal, Kate glared at Victor. "You lied to him. You sat there, and you *lied* to him."

"Katie, Katie, Katie. It doesn't have to be a lie." Victor's blue eyes danced behind the lenses of his glasses as he came toward her, smiling his most engaging smile.

Her ex-husband was mercurial and ageless, even with the gray in both his hair and his neatly trimmed beard. He was a charming, mischievous boy-man—as innocently, blamelessly egocentric as a two-year-old.

"All I need to do is make two phone calls, and everything I said to Jamaal will be the absolute truth," he told her.

That stopped her. "You're telling me Susie McCoy is ready to sign?"

"Provided Jericho is cast as Virgil Laramie."

There was a sudden sharp pain directly behind her right eye. "We need to talk about this, Victor. I'm not sure you understand exactly—"

He pulled her close. "Great," he murmured, kissing her neck. "Let's talk about Beaumont." He kissed her again, this time expertly catching her mouth with his. His lips were soft and warm, and he tasted faintly of cigarettes and the single glass of wine he must have had at lunch.

And for one one hundredth of a second, Kate let herself enjoy the sensation. God, how long had it been since she'd last had a lover? Three years? Or was it four?

Four. It had been nearly four years since she'd ended her relationship with John Bittler. And what she'd had with John had been so polite and reserved. It had been nothing like the madly passionate wildness she'd shared with Victor seven long years ago.

But Kate knew that her ex-husband, as exciting as he

was, couldn't give her anything more than great sex. And if there was one thing she'd learned by being married to him, it was that she wanted more than that. She wanted a whole lot more.

And she wanted to keep Victor as a friend. She liked having him as a friend.

She shook herself free from his arms. "No," she said. "No, no, no. I'm not going to sleep with you. Consider that a given. An unchangeable, indisputable fact. Two plus two equals four, E equals MC squared, you and I are not going to get it on. Don't you dare try to confuse things."

"Actually, I thought it would bring clarity to the situation." He was grinning at her. "I figured if I could get you to start saying 'oh, baby, yes, baby,' some of that general agreement might carry over into our discussion about Jericho."

Kate couldn't keep from laughing. "Spoken like the absolute, low-down toad you truly are."

"Hey, relax. I was only kidding."

"And I wasn't."

He sat down on the couch and put his feet up on the coffee table. "So. Jericho Beaumont. I want him. You don't. How are we going to deal with this?"

She sat down across from him. "Pistols at dawn?"

"Name your second, babe."

Kate stared at him. He was going with her joke, but there was a certain unnerving seriousness in his eyes. Was it really possible that he wanted Jericho badly enough to walk away from this project?

Victor shifted in his seat. "Not to intentionally change the subject, but as long as I'm airing my grievances, I'm still waiting for you to set up a time for me to meet with the writer—what's-his-name. Nick Chadler."

Kate studied her nails. "He's still out of the country."

He propped his hands up behind his head. "It's been

months, and I still haven't met this guy. I need to discuss some revisions. The ending's not right."

She looked up at him in shock. "Ex*cuse* me? You're planning to change the ending?"

The irony was incredible. The studio that had hired Victor to direct his last project, *Teardrop Twenty*, hadn't liked the way that film had ended. They'd ordered Victor to change it, and when he'd refused, they'd hired someone else to do it for them. And the movie he'd worked on, bled for, slaved over for nearly two years had been completely changed, and he'd had no legal right even to protest.

Teardrop Twenty was the reason Victor had been so eager to move into the realm of independent productions. It was the reason he'd jumped at the chance of directing *The Promise*. Because when an independent film was made, funding came from outside of the Hollywood studio system. The studios were only involved at the very end, after the movie was in the can. At that point, if a studio liked a particular film, they could offer to buy it and distribute it.

But they couldn't change it. Not without permission.

"How could you want to change the ending?" she asked. "I love the ending."

"The bad guy—you know, the plantation owner, Reginald Brooks—comes out ahead in the end. Laramie ends up trading him the land he promised his father he'd never sell. What kind of ending is that? Laramie loses. Where's the justice?"

Kate was practically sputtering. "Laramie doesn't lose—he wins! Jane was ready to give up her future and marry Brooks in return for Moses' freedom. Instead Laramie trades Brooks his family land and saves both Jane and Moses. Laramie wins because his act of humanity helps restore his own life—it helps him come alive again, and you're not listening to a single thing I'm saying, are you?"

"Jericho Beaumont, Susie McCoy, and Jamaal Hawkes." Victor sat up, unable to contain his energy and excitement. "With those names, we could have our pick of distributors, Katie. We could negotiate some control over the promotion—demand a substantial advertising budget. This movie could be huge."

"Provided the movie gets made."

Victor made a face. "What does that mean? Of course the movie will get made."

Kate leaned forward, too. "If you cast Jericho Beaumont, you might be dooming this picture. At the very least, you'd be dooming *me* to nearly three months of intense anxiety."

Victor was unmoved. "You're the producer. Get used to it. Anxiety comes with the territory."

"Somewhere between doom and fear of doom is everything this man could do wrong." She ticked each item off on her fingers. "Late arrivals, slurred speech, inability to remember lines and blocking, erratic behavior, no shows . . . And God help us if your precious Jericho should do something really irresponsible like die. He could start drinking again, Victor. Or using drugs. What substance abuser can ever guarantee that he won't? He could start again, overdose, and die. If it happened any later than the first few weeks of the shoot, this movie will die with him."

"Look, I've talked to some of the directors Jericho has worked with in the past. The key is to control what he uses. Apparently he never used street drugs, only prescription medications—you know, pick-me-ups during the day, sleeping pills at night. We could provide him with small amounts of—"

"Oh!" Kate wanted to close her eyes and plug her ears. "Oh, oh! I can't believe even *you* would have the indecency to stoop that low. Not only is that despicably illegal, but God, Victor! What if Jericho *is* clean? Think about what that might do to him!"

Victor wasn't fazed. He shrugged. "If Jericho's clean, then we don't have a problem."

"But the stress of having to carry a movie might be too much for him to handle. A starring role like Laramie would put pressure on someone who's completely healthy, let alone—" Kate took a deep breath. It was important to keep breathing. Without air, she would just keel over. "Victor, I know you see only the possibility of greatness. You see Jericho's talent. He shines, I'm not arguing about that. It's all over that audition tape. But I'm not convinced that he's going to be able to carry this movie—both physically and mentally. I don't want to gamble all the millions of dollars I've busted my ass finding for this project. I'm not willing to bet all that on someone like Jericho. I can't take that risk—and I can guarantee that the other financial backers won't want to take that risk, either. There's got to be someone else who can play this part."

Victor stood up. "Katie. I hear everything you're saying. And I know what I should do is agree with you and find someone else." He shook his head. "But I can't do it. I can't make this movie knowing that I could have had my number one, absolute, perfect cast. I can't do it knowing that I've got to settle across the board. Because if I don't get Jericho, I don't have Susie. And without the two of them, I won't have Jamaal."

"Victor—"

He held up his hand. "I love you, you know that, and this is the best script I've seen in about ten years, but I *will* walk away from both you and this script if you don't let me cast Jericho. I'm sorry, babe, but it's ultimatum time. I want Jericho. Susie and Jamaal want Jericho. If you want me to stay connected, it's up to you to figure out a way to make the backers want Jericho, too."

Three

❧ ❧

HE'D SEEN HER naked.

Jed paused outside the door to Mary Kate O'Laughlin's production office, and focused for just a moment on that empowering thought.

He *had* seen her naked. And he'd seen her naked just last night, as a matter of fact.

Although *The Promise* was O'Laughlin's first foray into the world of movie producing, Jed had done a little research and found out that although she'd spent most of the past decade building her parent's office supply business into a regional conglomerate, she was no stranger to the Hollywood scene.

And her connection wasn't merely through her short-lived marriage to director Vic Strauss. Mary Kate O'Laughlin had left her suburban Boston home at the tender age of eighteen, another of the many wide-eyed innocents drawn to the glitter and shine of Los Angeles. She'd washed up on the shores of Southern California under the pretense of attending UCLA. And although getting a college degree was one of her goals, it was a secondary goal, for sure. She was really just another moth lured by the Hollywood flame.

She'd met Vic on the set of some low-budget horror movie. He was a second unit director, she was the third victim of the *Hillsdale Horror*, showing up on the credits under the name "Katie Marie." She had three lines of dialogue before she met her demise—all of it spoken breathlessly as she'd danced in firelight, clad only in the barely there lace of her underwear.

She had a body to die for, and Vic had clearly recognized her B-movie potential, because "Katie Marie" had shown up in his next picture as well—*Dead of Night*, another low-budget flick that he'd helmed. The movie had become a cult classic, propelling him to mainstream fame and fortune.

In *Dead of Night*, the underwear had come off. Mary Kate O'Laughlin was only on-screen for a total of seven minutes in that entire movie, but, oh, what a seven minutes it was. She played the part of a college coed who had the misfortune of being picked up in a bar by a serial killer. She brought the man to her apartment, and the sex scene that followed was so steamy, so controversial, and so erotic that, even nearly a decade after the film was made, it was still the main topic of discussion on many internet bulletin boards.

Jed had rented the movie last night, and watched that famous scene. And he'd rewound the tape and watched it again. And again and again.

It was obvious that Katie Marie's alter ego, Mary Kate O'Laughlin, was not eager to cast Jericho as Laramie. Victor had made that much crystal clear. She didn't like him, didn't approve of him, didn't trust him, didn't want him anywhere near this production.

She had only reluctantly agreed to meet with him today, here in Boston.

But he had seen her naked.

Jed took a deep breath, closing his eyes and rolling his head to relax the muscles in his neck as he got into character. Kate O'Laughlin—she'd dropped the "Mary" sometime in the past seven years—wasn't going to meet Jed. She was going to meet Jericho Beaumont, the movie star.

Jericho was smooth. He didn't have any of Jed's insecurities or doubts. He was forthright and funny and friendly. He was going to walk into that office and charm the hell out of that producer.

The fact that he'd seen her naked was really just a bonus, an additional detail to keep him amused.

Fifteen minutes, thirty tops, and he'd have this job in the bag.

Jericho's smile perfectly in place, he knocked on the door.

"Mr. Beaumont," Kate said coolly as she opened the door. "Won't you come in?"

God, he was tall. Movie stars tended to appear so much larger on the big screen, and Kate had found meeting them in real life could be a disappointment. When she'd met Tom and Mel and Jodie, they'd all been much smaller than she'd imagined. But Jericho Beaumont towered over her. He had to be at least six-three, maybe even taller.

And every single hard-muscled inch of him oozed charisma.

He was outrageously good-looking, down to his even white teeth. He was wearing softly faded jeans and a jewel-green poet's shirt with loose, flowing sleeves. His dark hair was long, as if he'd been growing it out for the role, and he wore it pulled back into a ponytail. He wasn't dressed anything like Virgil Laramie, but as Kate looked into his hazel eyes, she saw the character lingering there. She saw Laramie's ghost, and all at once she felt as if she were on an elevator that was falling fast, with her stomach unable to keep up.

Something sparked in his eyes, and she saw a glimmer of sudden heat—and an amused acknowledgment of this sudden rush of odd animal attraction and fictional character overload she was feeling.

He wasn't Laramie. In fact, he was about the farthest thing from Laramie she could possibly find. She straightened her shoulders and let a little Frau Steinbreaker slip into her smile, making it polite, distancing, chilly.

"It's nice to finally get a chance to meet you, Ms. O'Laughlin." His southern drawl was gentler than the accent he'd used on the audition tape, his voice a rich baritone. "And, please, call me Jericho."

He held out his hand, and she shook as briefly as she possibly could before she pulled away. Of course his hand would be warm, his palm slightly work-roughened.

She cleared her throat. "Please come into my office." She purposely didn't tell him that he could call her Kate.

The words she hadn't said seemed to hang in the air between them as she led the way into the room that used to be the old brownstone's front parlor. She felt like a real bitch.

But that was a good thing. Bitch was a good word. Women who were aggressive and strong were tagged as bitches. She should buy herself a T-shirt that read "Proud to be called a bitch."

Jericho was looking around, taking in the bay windows that provided a first-class view of trendy Newbury Street. It was a lovely office—spacious and pleasant. The wood floor gleamed as did the recently cleared top of her desk.

"Nice place," he commented.

"Thank you. Please, have a seat." Kate gestured to one of the leather chairs as she slipped behind her desk. She felt safer back here, separated from this man by four feet of shining wood. *Force field on full power. Frau Steinbreaker on stun.* "May I offer you some coffee or tea? Soda?"

"No, thanks, I'm fine." Jericho sat down. "I didn't realize this meeting was going to be quite so formal."

"We have a lot to discuss." She'd purposely planned this meeting to be painfully formal. She'd made sure it would take place here in Boston, on her turf, even though she knew they'd both been in New York just yesterday. She'd also prepared by wearing her hair combed back severely from her face, and putting on her stiffest, highest-collared business suit. She all but carried a riding crop. Frau Steinbreaker on stun, indeed.

Kate hadn't set up this meeting to make friends with Jericho Beaumont. In fact, it was likely the opposite was going to happen. She'd done quite a bit of thinking, and she'd figured out the only possible way she could cast this man in her movie.

And he wasn't going to like it.

She glanced at her watch. "Victor won't be joining us for at least an hour. I thought it would be better if we had a chance to talk privately first."

He looked up at her, and there was wry amusement in his eyes. "Okay, *Ms. O'Laughlin*. Let's talk. But let's cut the crap and do the long jump down to the bottom line. You don't like me. You don't trust me. You don't want me in your movie. Anything I've left out?"

Kate didn't let herself blink. "You're a walking black cloud of bad publicity, and . . ." Fair was fair, and it *was* part of the bottom line, "I'm not sure there's another actor in the world who could play Virgil Laramie the way you could."

She'd surprised him. Out of everything he'd expected her to say, he hadn't expected that.

"Well, thank you."

"Provided you can stay sober long enough to get the job done," she added bluntly.

He laughed. "Then, there's no problem, because I have

no intention of going on a bender until after the shoot is done."

She stared at him.

"That was a joke."

"A bad one. I'm not laughing."

"I noticed. Look, Kate . . ." He shifted in his seat. "May I please call you Kate? I could sit here and vow that I'll never drink again—not for the rest of my life. But there're no guarantees. I'm going to try my damnedest to die an old man, and never let another drop of alcohol cross my lips. But I can't swear to you that's what'll happen. I'm going to try, that's all I can do."

Kate gazed at him across the wide expanse of her desk. "I'm supposed to be reassured by that? A vague promise to try from a man who was in and out of rehab five different times in half as many years?"

He didn't even look embarrassed. "I only went into rehab once," he said quietly. "The other times I was brought in by other people. I didn't really want to be there, and it doesn't work so well if you don't want to be there."

"And the last time you went in, you wanted to be there?"

He held her gaze steadily. "Yes, ma'am."

He was remarkably charismatic. Kate found herself liking him despite her prejudices. She found herself painfully aware of his intense masculinity as well. God, he was good-looking. She found herself wanting to believe him.

But he was an actor. There was no way she could know for sure that he wasn't simply acting sincere.

"What was different?" she asked.

"The official story is that my brother died and I realized I had to make some changes—but, to tell you the truth, even that wasn't enough to wake me up. I, uh . . ." Jericho smiled ruefully. "This is going to sound really odd, but it's true. There was a picture of me on the front of one of those gossip rags—the *Enquirer* or something, I forget which. But some paparazzi photographer caught me on film during a barroom brawl. I looked . . . I don't know. But the day after that picture was printed, I checked myself into rehab."

Jed stopped talking. Why did he just tell her that? For the past few years he'd let people believe that his brother Tom's death had pushed him into accepting that he'd hit bottom. It was easy to explain—the permanence of death forcing him to examine his own life, and him finding it seriously lacking. The real truth was far more complicated, and he hadn't discussed it at length with anyone besides his private therapist in the rehab center.

So what on earth made him bring it up now?

Mary Kate O'Laughlin was sitting on the other side of that enormous desk, trying as hard as she possibly could to keep him from knowing that she found him attractive. Jed knew damn well she'd noticed the immediate chemistry that had sparked and hummed between them the second she'd opened the office door. And right now he saw she was working overtime to keep from being drawn into their conversation. She didn't want to empathize with him. He knew she didn't want to like him in any way.

She'd done everything humanly possible to hide her goddess-quality body. She was wearing a pantsuit, and although the light-weight fabric flowed pleasantly around her when she walked, her million-dollar legs were completely covered. The cut of her jacket was square instead of tailored. It wasn't unattractive, but it did a great deal in negating the effect of her world-class curves. And the blouse she was wearing underneath—although soft and white—was buttoned nearly all the way up to her throat. Nearly all the way, but not quite. The very last button was left undone, softening the somber effect, but revealing absolutely nothing.

Her face wasn't exceptional. Her nose was unremark-

able, her chin a little too stubborn. Her mouth was too gen-
erous to be called delicate, too graceful to be called lush.
Her eyes were blue, and although they were pretty, they
weren't riveting. Her blond hair was short and combed
back in a style that did nothing to soften her face.

But her skin seemed to glow, making all those not-
quite-perfect features completely beautiful. She had—
without a doubt—the most perfect complexion Jed had
ever seen. It was beyond the legendary milkmaid ideal,
beyond peaches and cream, beyond Ivory girl. At nearly
thirty years old, Mary Kate O'Laughlin had skin like a
baby. And Jed suspected that if he reached across that
mile-wide desk to touch her, her cheek would feel softer
beneath his fingers than the sand-washed silk shirt he was
wearing.

All that soft, perfect skin kept going, down beneath the
collar of her high-necked blouse. It was there even though
he couldn't see it, beneath the spring-weight wool of her
trousers, covering the equal perfection of her incredible
body.

Jed fought his thoughts, refusing to go with the fantasy
of getting busy with this woman right on top of her king-
sized desk. He crossed his legs, too. Mary Kate O'Laughlin
already believed him to be a master of debauchery. All
she'd need to completely convince her was the knowledge
that he couldn't sit and have a conversation with her
without getting turned on.

It wasn't just her perfect complexion that appealed to
him. It was the one stray lock that had escaped from her
severe hair style, curling gently around her ear, under-
mining the entire schoolmarm look. And it was the way
she'd looked him in the eye and had the grace to admit
that—from an artistic viewpoint—he was her first choice
for Laramie.

She was both hot and cold, both sinfully soft and

unswervingly hard as rock. The combination was outrageously sexy, and he wanted to sit back and watch her for a while—try to see if he could figure out what was real and what was an act.

She was talking—something about backers and funding and her responsibility, about how nervous people could get when they put hundreds of thousands of dollars on the line. Her voice was melodic and soft. It had a breathiness to it that worked against her attempt to come across as hard as steel. She stated point-blank that hiring Jericho would be a serious gamble, that her financial backers would first recoil in horror, and then spend the entire summer of the shoot trembling in fear, waiting for him to screw up.

What she was saying was ironic, really. Mary Kate O'Laughlin was a novice when it came to producing a movie. Sure, she'd proven herself competent in the world of paper clips and printer cartridges. But moviemaking was an entirely different banana. It was far more likely if someone were going to screw up, it would be her.

And as much as she seemed to enjoy honest, everything out on the table communication, Jed decided he should probably keep his opinion about that to himself.

"Tell me, Mr. Beaumont, how badly do you want this part?" They were back to titles and formality.

He buried his frustration and shot her his least formal smile, letting himself remember the way she looked naked, draped across a bed. "Just tell me who you want killed." Another joke that she didn't find funny. Jed could have had Dave Letterman's writing staff feeding him material from the waiting room, and she still wouldn't laugh.

She wanted to be Serious, with a capital *S*. Okay. He leaned forward. "You know how badly I want Laramie, Ms. O'Laughlin. Badly enough to go to an open call. Badly enough to come here today and endure your relentless disapproval."

He silently cursed himself. He'd let Jericho slip, and some of Jed's insecurities had come sliding out.

But Kate didn't blink. "You've earned my relentless disapproval."

Frustration flooded through him again, and he bit back the edgy, angry words—Jed's words—that filled his mouth. Her holier-than-thou attitude was crap. She was nothing but a B-grade actress cast for her exceptional breasts who'd gone on to be crowned Queen of Paper Clips.

But he wasn't Jed right now. He was Jericho, and Jericho didn't insult movie producers—at least not until a contract was safely signed.

Five years sober, Jed was still learning how to keep his anger tightly in check without the help of the numbing effects of drugs and alcohol. Somehow he suspected it would be a lifelong endeavor.

"I had no problems at all during a movie called *Mean Time* that I finished shooting about two months ago," Jed told her. "It's not as if *The Promise* would be my first project after five years away. If you want, I can give you the name and number of the director."

"Stan Grogan," Kate said. "I've already spoken to him."

"What did he say?"

"That the total budget for *Mean Time* was under a half million dollars. It's a glorified student film, and there's virtually no use comparing it to this production."

Jed fought another flare of anger. "Except for the fact that I showed up on time and gave my best performance to date."

Kate pulled a file from a drawer and placed it on the desk in front of her. "I hired private investigators to speak to the cast and crew of *Mean Time*. Apparently you spent most of your downtime in a bar called The Aardvark Club?"

Private investigators. Jesus. "I hung out there, mostly

with two of the grips—Rhino and T.S. But I didn't drink." He kept his voice completely calm.

"The bartender said you always had a shot of . . ." She opened the file and glanced through the papers. "Jack Daniel's?"

Shit. There was no way she could possibly understand. "I didn't drink it. I just . . . liked to look at it. Smell it. Sit there with it in front of me."

"Doesn't that strike you as particularly dangerous behavior for an alcoholic?"

He could only be honest. There was no other way to win this fight. "Yes. But I . . . generally don't hang out in bars. It's just . . . we were on location, there was nowhere else to go." He'd been hiding from Chaslyn. Particularly toward the end of the shoot, when she'd begun to start sentences with phrases like, "After the movie is finished shooting."

"There was one incident I'm curious about," she said. "It happened during the production wrap party. Nobody seemed to know the full story, but apparently you got into a dispute with the cinematographer . . ." Another glance into the file. "Austin Franz? Would you care to explain what that was about?"

She was sitting there, on the other side of that enormous desk, one cool, elegant eyebrow slightly raised, and he knew that no matter what he said, she wouldn't understand. She didn't want to understand.

"It was over a woman," he told her. "Chaslyn Ross, my costar in the movie. The disagreement had no basis in reality. She'd already left for London—she didn't want either one of us."

"And Chaslyn's the actress you'd been having an affair with for the previous . . . what was it? Five weeks?"

Damn, that was annoying. She was asking things that were no doubt already written in her file. "It wasn't serious. It was just one of those things that happens sometimes between costars." He leaned forward conspiratorially, ready to see how tough she really was—if the softness of her voice was an attempt to make feminine her balls of steel, or if the steel balls were an attempt to even up her natural softness. "We were rehearsing a love scene, and all of a sudden she had me pinned to the bed. She started going down on me, and for about three seconds I was thinking, wait a minute, *that's* not in the script." He smiled. "But I only thought that for about three seconds."

Kate was blushing. Her cheeks had actually turned pink.

Again, she'd surprised him. It didn't seem possible that someone who had taken off all her clothes and simulated such believably kinky sex on film could still be capable of blushing, but she was definitely doing just that. He'd embarrassed her.

And the fact that she was blushing embarrassed her even further. She cleared her throat, looking down at the file in front of her before she glanced up at him. "Thank you for sharing that with me. I'm sure it was very special."

Jed had to fight to keep from laughing. Maybe she had a sense of humor, after all.

"My point is that it wasn't special," he told her. "We both just got caught up in the moment. Our relationship may have lasted five weeks, but it really wasn't anything to talk about. Like I said, it happens sometimes, you know, when you've got costars trying to create sexual tension."

"Your costar in *The Promise* is only fifteen years old," Kate stated. "If something 'just happened' with her, you'd be facing criminal charges."

"Trust me, I prefer women who are old enough at least to have *parents* who were born before the Beatles broke up."

"I have more questions about this incident with Austin Franz. There's more than one interview with crew members who claim that Franz challenged you to some kind of drinking game? And you accepted?"

She was looking at him as if she'd asked whether or not he bit the heads off small rodents for fun. He opted against shrugging it off, chosing a remorseful wince instead.

"I thought I could win."

"But you lost." She looked through her file. "Both Herman Rizinski and Terry Wimbers left the bar because they didn't want to see you drink that shot of whiskey. Austin Franz refused to speak to the investigator, and no one else was paying attention—at least not at that point."

"In other words, no one witnessed the fact that I didn't drink it."

"Didn't you?"

She looked up at him, and he ditched remorseful and went for flat-out honesty.

"No. I have to tell you—I almost did. Franz told me that I didn't have to drink—but if I didn't, he'd make sure I never worked with him or Stan Grogan ever again. I picked up that glass and . . ." He'd wanted to drink that whiskey more than he'd wanted damn near anything, but he wasn't about to tell Kate that. There was a limit to just how honest he could be. "I looked up, and Franz was watching me, just waiting for me to throw five years of sobriety away. And I knew I hadn't lost. Not yet. Not everything. I'd lost the game, sure. But if I didn't drink that shot, then Franz wouldn't really win. So I put the glass back down, and I walked out of the bar."

Kate was silent for several moments. But then she laughed. "That was good," she said. "That was very good. Whether it's true or *not*, you definitely get points for sincere delivery."

His frustration level rose another notch. She didn't laugh at his jokes, but when he was dead serious, that was when she thought he was funny. "It's true."

She took a deep breath and let it out in a sigh. "Mr. Beaumont, you're an actor. An exceptionally good actor. Your job is to say things and make other people believe they're true." She sighed again. "Are you currently in good health?"

"Yes. I work out every day and—"

"When was the last time you had a complete physical exam?"

Jed resisted the urge to ask why, did she want to play doctor? "It wasn't even a year ago—right before I signed on to *Mean Time*."

Kate nodded, making a note in her file. "Have your agent send copies of that to me."

Jed's pulse kicked into high gear, and he tried to douse his excitement. Still, he had to work to keep his voice even. "Are you offering me Laramie?"

She looked up at him, her eyes carefully bland, her face clear of expression. "I'm sorry, I should have been more clear. I should have said, *if we cast you*, have your agent send copies to me. There are quite a few terms and conditions you've got to agree to before we start talking about signing a contract."

He nodded, each beat of his heart sending blood coursing all the way down to his fingers and toes. He got it. He *got* it. "You might as well get the contract out, because I've already discussed terms of payment with Vic—"

"These conditions don't have anything to do with payment."

"I don't understand."

"Before you sign a contract, I want assurances that you won't jeopardize this project in any way. I want a guarantee that you'll remain alcohol and drug free during the entire course of preproduction, production, and even during postproduction, when we'd be sending you out on the talk-show circuit."

Jed nodded. "I'll give you my word. I'm clean now, and I have every intention of staying clean. I'll go to AA meetings three times a week if I have to—"

"You'll have to," she interrupted. "And, I'm sorry, but as nice as it would be to guarantee a verbal agreement with a handshake, I'm afraid that won't satisfy our financial backers." She opened the file folder again. "So I've taken the liberty of having my lawyer draw up a document—an addendum to the standard Screen Actor's Guild contract—outlining the terms and conditions of your employment."

Jed took the document she held out to him. Damn, it was heavy. There had to be a dozen pieces of legal-sized paper stapled together. The triumphant tom-tom of his pulse skipped a beat.

"You'll want to read that carefully, of course," Kate told him briskly.

"What is this?"

Her blue eyes were expressionless. "Our guarantee that you stay clean, as you so aptly put it. As I said, this document outlines the terms and conditions—"

He still didn't understand. "Such as?"

She opened the file again and took out a second copy of the same agreement, running her finger down the page past all the opening legal mumbo jumbo defining Jericho Beaumont as the party hereafter to be called "the Actor." "The first point, I believe, deals with . . . yes, here it is. Daily urine testing for drugs."

The accelerated dance rhythm of his pulse jerked nearly to a stop, and the euphoria was replaced by nausea.

Jed stared at the packet of paper he held in his hands. Urine tests. This document required him to submit to drug tests—daily. And that was only the first condition. He quickly flipped to the back of the document. Seven. There were six additional conditions he would have to agree to, if he wanted this job. Seven humiliations—of which daily urine testing was only the first.

"The second enables us to conduct unannounced Breathalyzer tests for alcohol. Third, you'll be required to attend AA meetings at least twice a week during the course of the shoot. Fourth, you'll agree to supervision—24/7. O'Laughlin Productions will select your supervisor—"

24/7—twenty-four hours a day, seven days a week. This document, these demands were so outrageous, Jed didn't know whether to laugh or scream. "Don't you mean baby-sitter? Or maybe jail warden?"

Kate pretended not to hear. ". . . and round-the-clock supervision will begin from the moment you step onto the set until the date you're released from production. During preproduction and postproduction you'll be on your own, but if you screw up and embarrass us during postproduction publicity events, you'll lose your right to percentages, providing there are any. If you screw up during the weeks before the shoot begins, you'll lose the job."

Kate flipped another page, scared to death he was going to call her bluff and scared to death he wasn't. "Point five, you'll have two separate trailers on the set. One for sleeping, the other for your use while waiting between shots. According to this agreement, your sleeping trailer will be kept absolutely free and clear of any belongings."

"So I can't smuggle drugs in, inside the cutout pages of a book and use 'em at night when the warden is sleeping, right?" He laughed, but there was no humor in it. "This is outrageous."

She glanced up from the document, praying he couldn't tell she was way over her head. "You can keep personal items in the other trailer, but that trailer will be searched twice daily—more often if deemed necessary. Oh, and your sleeping trailer will be kept locked at night. Your supervisor will have a key, you will not."

"Locked," Jericho echoed, his movie star charm gone. "What you're saying is that I'll be *locked in* at night?"

Kate knew that if she could get him to sign this agreement, her movie would get made with the least possible risks. But it wouldn't be without a price. Jericho Beaumont wasn't going to be her best friend after this, that was certain. She felt the teeniest twinge of regret and quickly quashed it. "Points six and seven deal with the specifics of the percentages deal—the legal working specifying which of your actions would result in what we'd consider a breach of contract."

"Locked in." He couldn't get past point five. "Sweet Jesus, what you're telling me is that I have to agree to be treated like a prisoner in jail for two and a half goddamned months?"

She didn't blink. "I guess you've got to decide how badly you want this part." She stood up, crossing the room and opening her office door as if ready to show him out. "You're welcome to turn it down, of course."

Jed knew what she was doing. She was trying to push him away. She wanted him to walk from this deal. She didn't want him in her movie—she'd said that from the first. He took a deep breath, and somehow his voice was steady and calm. "Okay. All right. I'll agree to the daily drug tests and the AA meetings, but the 24/7 supervision and the locked trailer is completely unacceptable."

"This agreement is not negotiable, Mr. Beaumont. It's all or nothing. I've already spoken to your agent about it. I've faxed him a copy, and he understands that we're willing to take the risk and cast you—but only under the terms and conditions that I've just listed."

Jed sat there. His fingers tingled and his legs felt odd, almost numb. It was as if he were having an out-of-body experience. It was like some kind of bad dream. He could play the part he'd been waiting his entire life to play—provided he subjected himself to this outlined humiliation.

Anger churned through him, and he fought to push it down. "May I . . ." He cleared his throat. "May I please use your phone?"

Kate came back to her desk and slid her telephone within his reach. "Would you like some privacy?"

Jed laughed. "You're kidding, right?" He tossed the legal agreement down onto her desk. "You've worked your ass off to draw up this contract addendum that makes sure I have absolutely no privacy. Why start thinking about things like that now?"

He picked up the phone, but his hands were shaking. For a minute he sat there blankly, unable to remember his agent's name, let alone his phone number. He took a deep breath, and then another. Ron Stapleton. And his number . . . He punched it in.

It was a direct line, and Ron scooped it up after only one ring. "Stapleton."

"It's Jericho Beaumont." His voice sounded harsh, hoarse. "Mary Kate O'Laughlin tells me she faxed you a copy of a contract addendum and—"

"Jeez, I'm sorry, Jericho. I tried to negotiate it down, but the entire thing is a deal breaker. You sign it as is, or you don't get the job."

Jed swore softly.

"Look," Ron said. "I know you're probably mad as hell—I would be, too—but . . . think of it as dues you've got to pay to get back onto the A-list, buddy. Even though it's an indy, it's a Vic Strauss movie. And with Susie McCoy and Jamaal Hawkes ready to make the jump aboard, we're talking high profile."

"But, Ron . . ." He lowered his voice. "Damn it, have you read this thing?"

"Of course I've read it. It stinks. But truth is, you don't exactly have offers piling up right now. And I hate to be the bearer of bad news, but *Mean Time* is having trouble finding distribution—it may never see the light of day. So come on. Suck it up, sign the deal. Do what you have to do to get back on track. And, hey, maybe your supervisor will be a blonde."

Jericho looked over at Kate, who stood in front of an open file cabinet, at least pretending to give him some privacy.

"Call me later and let me know what you've decided," Ron said. "I gotta run."

The connection was cut, and Jed slowly hung up the phone. *Suck it up and sign the deal.* He picked up the agreement and started to read.

It was all there, exactly as Kate had sketched out—right down to the locked trailer door.

When he finished reading, he started over, and read it through again.

He wanted this part.

He wanted it, enough to do anything. Even sign his life away.

It was funny, he'd thought he'd swallowed all that was left of his pride by going to that open call audition, and then again by coming here today. But somehow, he still had some pride left, and it caught in his throat, damn near choking him as he took a pen from the surface of Kate's desk.

He forced his anger and his shame away, and made himself feel nothing as he signed both copies of the agreement, writing the date next to his name. He sensed Kate standing behind him, and as he put the pen down, he turned to her, not bothering to hide the emptiness in his eyes. "Send the contract to my agent."

Considering she'd just won a major victory, she didn't look triumphant. In fact, she looked shaken as she stared down at his signature on both agreements. She looked as if she might have to run to the bathroom at any second to be violently sick.

"Oh, and congratulations," he told her. "You've done what millions of women across America are dying to do."

She looked up at him, confusion on her face.

Jed stepped closer to her, close enough to smell her expensive perfume, close enough so that when he spoke, his breath moved the hair next to her ear.

"You fucked me good," he said softly. And then he walked away.

Four

❧ ❧

"**H**EY, BABE!" VICTOR breezed into the busy Grady Falls production office. "Do me a favor, would ya?"

Kate glanced up from the shoot schedules and housing assignments that were spread across the conference table. She noticed that she wasn't the only one in the suite of rooms who'd responded to Victor's greeting. In the outer office, at least four young women on the production staff had also looked up from their work. Didn't it figure? But, in this case, Kate was indeed the babe he was talking to. He came into the back room they'd labeled the conference area, and shut the door behind him.

"Welcome back," she said. He'd been in L.A. for the better part of the week.

"Get a fax out to that writer pal of yours and see what he can do about beefing up the part of Sarah."

Kate raised an eyebrow. "This is a joke, right?"

Victor sat across from her, stretching his legs out, elbows on the arms of the chair. He used the file folder he was carrying to push up the bill of his baseball cap. "No. I think we've got a chance at getting Naomi Michaelson for Sarah. But as it stands, there's not much of a part."

"That's because Sarah is *dead*."

The character only appeared in a few flashback scenes, and occasionally as a kind of ghostly memory, flitting at the edge of Virgil Laramie's alcohol-sodden consciousness.

"She doesn't have any dialogue, and I'm not sure Naomi'll take the part if we can't throw her at least a few lines. Maybe if we add more flashback scenes—"

Kate put down her pencil. "Victor. Babe. The script is too long as it is. I'm not going to ask for story rewrites and make it even longer—just so you can get into Naomi Michaelson's pants."

He smiled sheepishly. "Am I really that transparent?"

"You're top quality window glass, my friend."

"I met her at a party in L.A. last week," he confessed. "She's unbelievably beautiful. I only had about fifteen minutes to talk to her before she had to leave, but there was a real spark between us, you know? I told her we were still looking for the perfect Sarah. She nearly dropped her drink when she found out we had Beaumont, McCoy, and Hawkes already committed."

Kate gazed at her ex-husband. His beat-up baseball cap was emblazoned with the name of his first feature film, *Dead of Night*. She was struck again by the fact that he'd seemed to have changed so little in the past ten years. Sure, he drove a more expensive car and had a new, pricy address, and his résumé was now filled with an impressive list of both box office and critical hits, but aside from that, he was still a fourteen-year-old when it came to romantic relationships.

And because of that, although she still felt a twinge of remorse for what might've been, she could look at him and feel no jealousy whatsoever when he talked about other women.

He hadn't been the man she'd hoped he was, and she'd grown out of him very quickly. She honestly didn't want him anymore. Not as a life partner, anyway.

Now, if only she could figure out what she *did* want.

Virgil Laramie. She wanted Virgil Laramie. And these days, he was coming to her in a package that looked exactly like Jericho Beaumont.

Kate had been dreaming about an odd mix of both her character and the actor for weeks. In her mind they had begun to blend dangerously into one. And this wasn't good, because although Jericho could *pretend* to be Laramie, he *wasn't* Laramie.

She knew that. She'd been reminding herself of that every chance she got.

But when she closed her eyes, she could smell the slightly sweet, slightly spicy fragrance of Jericho's cologne. He'd stood close enough for her to feel his body heat, close enough to feel his breath against her cheek.

She hadn't really expected him to sign the humiliating agreement she'd drawn up. Yet he had. He'd wanted the part of Laramie badly enough to place all control over his personal life into her hands.

And after the initial shock had worn off, Kate had started to get excited about the possibilities. With 24/7 supervision, it was extremely unlikely that Jericho was going to fall back into his old habits. Even if he wanted to stray, he was going to be watched virtually all the time.

The man Kate had hired to watch Jericho was a former marine named Bobby Hollander. Hollander was a huge, hulking, unfriendly looking bear of a man with an impressive set of credentials. It hadn't been easy to find someone she could trust completely, but Hollander's last job had been similar. He'd been hired to supervise the nineteen-year-old son of a Fortune 500 Company CEO. The kid had been through rehab but needed a little extra help staying sober once out of the hospital. She'd spoken with the CEO, and he'd given Hollander a glowing reference.

Somehow, she got the feeling that Jericho Beaumont wasn't going to like Hollander quite so much.

Across the room Victor was still talking about Naomi—about how she looked enough like Susie McCoy to play the part of her older sister. Her hair was the same shade of golden blonde, and her mouth and chin had a remarkably similar shape. He was almost certain they could throw some extra lines of dialogue in for her without increasing the running time of the movie by more than a few minutes.

He was smitten and ready to do just about anything to get close to this woman. There was no doubt about it. But it wasn't necessary.

"Whatever you said to Naomi," she told him, "it made an impression. Her agent called two days ago, and I expressed them a copy of the script. I got a fax this morning—Naomi's our Sarah. We don't have to add a single line of dialogue."

Victor sat up. "Why didn't you tell me that when I came in?"

"Because I didn't realize it would matter so much to you," Kate told him. "Then, when you started talking, I wanted to see how far you were willing to go to get this girl." She smiled at him. "You didn't disappoint me. You're obviously willing to compromise artistic integrity for a cheap thrill."

He grinned at her. "I'd compromise nothing. If the scenes didn't work, they'd hit the cutting room floor, no question."

"So it would be a very *expensive* thrill. All that extra shoot time, all that extra film . . ."

Victor stood up. "The point is now moot. Reserve a private trailer for Naomi for the entire month of June."

"Like hell I will. We need her for two days of shooting—maybe three, tops."

"Katie. Babe—"

"You'll have three days, Victor. After that, it's up to you to figure out a way to get her to stay on the set as your guest."

Undaunted, Victor pushed himself up out of the chair.

"Make a note on the schedule to send me a reminder memo the day before Naomi's due to arrive."

"I've already done that," she told him. "You'll get memos in advance of all of the talents' arrival and departure dates. In fact"—she shuffled through the papers on her desk—"I might as well save Annie a trip and give you this one now."

Victor glanced at the sheet of paper she handed him. "Both Jericho and Jamaal arrive tomorrow."

"And Susie'll be here the day after."

He looked up at her, all teasing gone from his eyes. "Are you ready for Jericho Beaumont?"

Kate smiled grimly. God, she hoped so. "As ready as I'll ever be."

Jed stepped inside of one of the two trailers that were to be his home for the next two and a half months.

It was . . . a trailer. It was neat and clean, if not particularly luxurious. There was a refrigerator and a tiny cookstove and sink, along with a small table with bench seats. The refrigerator was well stocked with bottled water, cans of soda, orange juice, and milk. There were cabinets filled with dishes and glasses, and a drawer full of silverware. Another cabinet held a wide selection of junk food. A third held dozens of drug test kits. Jed closed that door quickly.

This was the trailer he'd be spending his days in.

On the other side of the room, a couch lined one wall. There was a TV setup, with a VCR and a cheap boom box. The bathroom was a claustrophobic's nightmare, with a shower stall about the size of a phone booth, a tiny sink, and a toilet. Farther down the hall—if it was long enough to qualify as a hall—was a bedroom in which the bed had been replaced with another couch and a table.

With the exception of the main entrance, there were no doors anywhere. The back room didn't have one. The *bathroom* didn't have one.

Jed had hoped that the addendum to the contract he'd signed had been merely a threat, a "here's what we'll do to you if . . ." kind of deal. Or maybe he'd just been hiding from the truth, hopefully wishing that Mary Kate O'Laughlin wouldn't really take such extreme measures.

He should have known better.

He set his duffel bag on the couch and went to check out the other trailer—the one that had been designated for sleeping only.

It was the same size, but the cabinets in this one were empty. And instead of a couch in the main room, there was a bed. Another bed was in the back room as well. Both were unmade, their mattresses bare, with sheets and blankets neatly folded on top of them.

This trailer would remain empty to keep him from hiding his stash anywhere—nevermind the fact that he was clean and he didn't have a stash anymore.

There were no inside doors in this trailer, either. Welcome to privacy hell.

The screen door opened with a squeak, and Jed turned to see Kate step inside. "I'm sorry I wasn't here to greet you when you arrived," she said in her deceptively breathless, helpless-little-girl voice. "Welcome to Grady Falls."

She looked incredible. Her blond hair was feathered loosely around her face, and she was wearing a sleeveless white silk blouse and a slim-fitting khaki skirt that ended many inches above her knees. She was wearing high-heeled sandals and natural-colored hose that made her legs seem to shine. She looked gracefully elegant and cool—as if she'd stepped out of a Paris fashion show-room, rather than a film production office in some backwoods, stickily humid, South Carolina swamp of a town.

Her bare arms were slim, the muscles of her shoulders and triceps very slightly defined. Her skin was smooth— and probably as soft to the touch as he'd imagined. Her arms were nearly as sexy as her legs—and her legs were off the chart.

Unlike the first time they'd met, she wasn't trying to hide her drop-dead body behind starchy clothes. She was dressed to impress—and it was working.

He fought it, refusing to acknowledge anything about her but the fact she'd forced him to sign that agreement from hell. She was the devil to whom he'd sold his soul. He was supposed to despise her, not *want* her.

He shut himself down. He refused to feel anything. "I'd appreciate it if you'd knock next time you want to come in." His voice was flat and cold.

She didn't miss a beat. "I'm sorry. I certainly will. Please forgive me—most of the cast and crew don't stand on ceremony, and I thought—"

"You thought wrong, Ms. O'Laughlin."

He had to hand it to her, she wasn't about to let herself be intimidated. And she didn't try to sidestep the issue. She came at it, head-on. "I know you must still be very angry with me."

Jed leaned against the door frame, crossing his arms. "I've been watching your death scene in *Dead of Night* over and over again in an attempt to handle my intense feelings of hostility."

Her death scene was preceded by that notoriously blazing hot sex scene.

Kate's cheeks flushed. Still, she managed to put a smile on her face. "I'm glad someone's finally been able to put that movie to good use."

Jed laughed, wanting to see her squirm. "From what I've read, *Dead of Night*—and that scene with you in particular—has been put to extremely good use, particularly since it came out on video. Of course, I suppose it all depends on your definition of *good use*."

She knew what was coming. He saw it in her eyes, and in the darkening tinge of pink on her cheeks.

He continued ruthlessly. "I read in *Details* magazine—"

She tried to brush it off and avoid having the conversation go any further. "Yeah, I read that, too. It's old news."

He didn't stop. ". . . that *Dead of Night* was voted hottest movie of the decade, coming in number one with a record 86 percent of all men polled. And, according to their statistics, something like one third have used that particular scene as fantasy enhancement while . . . shall we say . . . flying solo. And that's not including the huge percentage who are unwilling to admit they've ever taken that particular flight."

Her cheeks were pink, but she held his gaze. "And what percentage do you fall into?"

She would not be intimidated. She would not be embarrassed. She could take what he dished out in this game of implications and underlying sexual tension, and serve it right back to him. But she hated it. The pink tinge to her cheeks gave that much away.

"Actually"—Jed gave her a tight, flat smile that he knew didn't touch the chill in his eyes—"my only interesting experience with that scene also included a young woman named Carla. The combination of you and me and Carla was . . . memorable."

Her flush deepened, but she stood her ground. "How lovely for you. I'm so glad I was able to give you the help you needed."

Ouch. That comment had teeth. While it didn't quite even things up, she had certainly scored a point.

She turned toward the door, her demeanor much cooler than when she'd come in. "I've got a desk piled high with paperwork. I'll just introduce you to your supervisor before I leave. I'm sure you're looking forward to getting acquainted with Bob Hollander."

"Gee, I sure am," Jed said. "As I was flying out here from L.A., I was just sitting on the plane, thinking, wow, I am really looking forward to a total lack of privacy over the next two and a half months."

Kate pushed open the screen door, and a mountain came into the trailer.

The man was seriously a giant. He had to twist his body sideways to fit his shoulders in through the door. He stood only about an inch or two above Jed's own six feet four, but he was built like something that had escaped from Jurassic Park.

He was not going to win any beauty contests, either, with a mouth that was set in a permanent scowl and small eyes that were surrounded by folds of flesh. His hair was military short and flecked with gray.

But just because he looked like a humorless, completely non-compassionate, tough-as-nails son of a bitch didn't mean he actually was one.

"Hey," Jed drawled, holding out his hand and giving the man Jericho's best "let's be buddies" smile. "Bob. How's it hanging, man? Nice to meet ya."

Hollander crossed his arms, making sure Jed knew he had no intention of shaking hands. "Here's how it works," he said in a gravelly voice that spoke of too many packs of cigarettes. "We're not gonna be friends, Mr. Beaumont. I'm not going to sit around and be a sounding board for your overinflated ego. What I *am* going to be is your shadow. What I *am* going to do is watch your every move, at all times. Everywhere you go, I go. Including into the bathroom."

Dear, sweet Lord, this was worse than his wildest imaginings.

"You better call me Jericho," he told Hollander, praying that he'd see a flicker of humor in the big man's eyes. "Because have you seen that bathroom? If we're going to be in there together, we might as well be on a first name basis. In fact, we might have to start calling each other 'honey.'"

Nothing. No humor, no amusement, nothing. This guy wasn't just soulless, he was an automaton. There was, quite possibly, no humanity in him at all. Or at least none he cared to show.

There was a rap on the door, and a friendly-faced man stuck his head in the trailer. "Miz O'Laughlin? Annie said you might be over here."

"Nate, come on in."

"Ethan's here, too." He pulled back the screen all the way and came into the trailer, followed by another man. They were both wearing security guard uniforms.

"Nate and Ethan will be responsible for conducting the searches in your trailers," Kate told Jericho.

Nate leaned forward to shake his hand. "How d'ya do?"

Ethan just waved. "Howdy." The two men looked as if they might be brothers. "It's a pleasure to meet you. I loved you in *Die Hard*."

Nate elbowed Ethan. "That wasn't Jericho Beaumont in *Die Hard*. Jericho did the *Kill Zone* movies."

"That's right. I loved you in *Kill Zone*."

"Thanks," Jericho said.

"Well, we just stopped in to say howdy," Nate told him. "We better get back to it." They trooped back outside.

To follow them out, Kate was going to have to squeeze past the mountain. "If you'll excuse me. I know you and Bob have some business to take care of."

"Wait!" It came out sounding a little too panicked, and Jed took a deep breath and forced a smile. "Before you go, I have to talk to you."

Her eyes were innocently wide. "Was there something else you needed?"

She was enjoying this. Even though she wasn't laughing, even though she wasn't even smiling, he could tell that she was having a grand old time at his expense.

Jed felt anger slice through him, and he wanted . . . he

wanted . . . Perfect. Every single one of his revenge fantasies involved her willing and eager participation. What were the odds of that ever happening?

He forced his anger away and turned to Hollander. "Would you please wait outside?"

Hollander looked to Kate, who nodded.

Jed waited until the screen door closed behind Monsterman. Kate was watching him, her face carefully expressionless. He knew he had to be equally careful, or everything he was trying so desperately to suppress—all the rage and frustration—would burst out of him and splatter against the walls like emotional roadkill.

He knew he should be deciding how to talk to her. He knew he had to figure out the best approach to use to make his appeal, but his mind had gone completely blank. He pulled Jericho out at the last minute, biting back Jed's acerbic "Are you friggin' nuts . . . ?" and instead saying, remarkably calmly, "I really don't think this is going to work out."

She crossed her arms and tilted her head slightly to one side. "These *are* the conditions of our agreement."

Jed wanted to scream, but Jericho managed a weak smile. "Somehow I didn't expect you to hire a former marine drill sergeant to be my baby-sitter. I mean, come on, Kate. Have a heart."

"Bob Hollander comes highly recommended. His credentials are impeccable and—"

"You don't really expect me to spend the next two and a half months, 24/7, with Gigantor breathing down my neck?"

She didn't blink. "I expect you to follow the terms of our agreement."

"The man has no sense of humor."

"Like he said, he's not here to be your friend."

Jed ran his hands down his face, and when he turned

back to Kate, he did the only thing he could do. He begged.

"Please," he said quietly. His words were like ashes in his mouth, but she had him by the balls. Again. "You've got me where you want me with this setup—two trailers, baby-sitter, the drug tests . . . You've won. I'm completely humiliated. But please don't rub my face in it this way. Hire someone I at least have a *prayer* of getting along with. How about one of those security guards? Nate or Ethan? They seemed human at least."

"They have jobs with the town bank. They'll be searching your trailers during their breaks. They're also both married and unavailable during evenings or nights."

"There's got to be somebody else."

Kate shook her head. "I'm sorry," she said. "I know you don't think so, but I am sorry. And I'm even more sorry that I can't take anything you say at face value. I can't, and I don't think you can blame me. I've got to think there's some other reason you don't want Bob Hollander around. Maybe it's not just a personality issue. Maybe you're upset because you know that Bob will never let you get away with anything. Maybe you know Bob will never let you cheat the rules. I know for a fact that Bob will never let you go into a bar, order a shot of Jack Daniel's, and sit there *smelling* it. And that makes me think I've made a good choice in selecting him."

"That's not what this is about."

"Of course, that's what I'd expect you to say."

Jed's control slipped. "Christ, why did you even hire me?"

She didn't hesitate. "Because Victor wanted you. I never would have cast you—not in a million years, but Victor threatened to walk. I had to cast you to keep him happy."

"I guess spreading your legs for him doesn't do it anymore, huh?"

She flushed, this time with anger. And then she raised her voice. "Bob, you can come back in now." She didn't add the rest of her sentence, but her eyes said it for her: *and beat the crap out of Jericho Beaumont.*

Jed sat down at the kitchen table, disgusted with her, disgusted with himself. God, he needed a drink. He closed his eyes, imagining the soothing warmth, the blessed numbness.

When he opened his eyes, Kate was gone. Bob Hollander stood in front of him, setting a urine specimen cup down on the table with a thump.

"First thing we do," Hollander said, "is verify that you are indeed as clean as you claim to be."

Perfect. Absolutely perfect.

Jed took the cup and stood up. And his six and a half feet tall, two-hundred-seventy-pound baby-sitter followed him into the bathroom, just as he'd promised he would.

Jericho Beaumont was incredible.

Susie lurked near the producer, Kate O'Laughlin, watching as Jericho collapsed out in the middle of a field.

Even from way back here, he was amazing.

Today they were filming a scene from early in the movie. His character, Laramie, had drunk himself into unconsciousness.

In a few weeks, when they started shooting at night, the crew would bring special equipment back to this very field. And Jericho would lie exactly as he'd fallen, and she—playing Jane—would come searching with a lantern, and she'd find him here. The wind would be picking up, and it would start to rain, and she'd pull him to his feet and half drag him back to the shelter of the barn.

Edited together, it would be very dramatic—nevermind the fact that they would have shot the entire sequence disjointedly over a period of two or three weeks.

"Ready for this afternoon?" Kate asked her.

Susie liked Kate. And it had nothing to do with the fact that the producer told her this script was written with Susie in mind for the part of Jane. Well . . . Maybe some of it had to do with that. Most people wrote movies called *The Dog Ate My Homework* or *Baby-sitter's Nightmare* with Susie McCoy in mind.

"I'm always ready," Susie said, then cringed. "I didn't mean for that to sound so . . . pompous or egotistical. I just meant I love it so much, you know?"

Kate nodded. It was amazing how she always managed to look so cool and composed, even on a day like today where the temperature was climbing toward ninety-five degrees. She never wore ratty old clothes like the rest of the crew. Even when she wore shorts, they were dressy. And she wore them with sandals that had heels.

Susie looked down at her own T-shirt and cutoffs. Her feet were bare. "I've been walking around barefoot for the past two months—trying to toughen up my feet."

"That's right—Jane is barefoot in almost every scene," Kate said. "Gee, I never really thought about how that would affect you as an actor."

"It's not a problem." Susie smiled. "It actually helps me get into character."

Kate's attention was temporarily caught by the lighting crew's movement of some large reflective sheets out near Jericho, but then she turned back to Susie. "Has Victor had a chance to talk to you yet about the scene you'll be shooting after lunch?"

Susie shrugged. "Not really. But I don't think it's going to be that big a deal."

Later this afternoon, the cameras would remain set up in this very field. Susie would race across the open expanse, running full speed—barefoot—with her skirts hiked up and tucked into her belt. It wouldn't take much time— it was a wide shot, encompassing the entire field and the huge blue sky.

They'd then move the cameras and set up in the woods, where Susie as Jane would run down a trail, leaping over rocks and roots. She would stop to collect a few pretty, shiny rocks, and scramble up into the branches of a tree to hang upside down.

"I know these scenes might not seem very important," Kate told her, "but they really are."

"Oh," Susie said, "I didn't mean they wouldn't be a big deal in importance—just that they wouldn't be hard to do."

Yesterday they'd shot scenes of a very reserved and serious Jane using her training as an herbalist to take care of slaves who were sick or injured. Today's scenes of her playing in the woods—of letting herself still be a kid—would contrast with that, leaving the audience a little confused about the character. Who was she? A woman or a child? Jane existed in both worlds, but didn't quite belong in either.

Susie could really relate.

"Settle!" someone yelled from the set. It was the command to be quiet—for watchers to get into a position that was comfortable, where they wouldn't feel the need to shift around and make noise.

"Rolling," someone else shouted. "Speed!"

"Action!"

Out in the field, Jericho fell to his knees. Susie suspected that he was able to relate to Laramie—just as she was able to relate to Jane. She'd been living a double life as both a child and an adult since she could remember.

She'd been six years old when she got her first movie role. And she'd gone onto the set, memorized her lines, and performed like a professional right from the first day. She'd been six, and she'd done a job that many adults had difficulty doing. She'd played with dolls in her trailer, but when it was required, she'd met the producers and backers, shaken hands, and carried on conversations as if she were twenty-six years old.

She had no problem when it came to speaking to studio suits. It was her father she couldn't talk to.

But her father—with all of his disapproval and disappointment—wasn't on set with her this time. And that was good, since there was quite a bit in this script he would've disapproved off. Along with a scene where Jane stumbles across plantation owner Reginald Brooks brutally forcing himself on a female slave, there was another scene, at the very end of the film, in which Susie would share her first on-screen kiss with Jericho Beaumont.

If he knew, her father would totally have a cow.

Susie, on the other hand, was looking forward to it.

Not that she had any ideas of an actual real-life romantic relationship developing. After all, she was fifteen, and Jericho was something ancient like thirty-four or thirty-five.

Well, okay. Maybe she *did* entertain fantasies of Jericho pulling up to her house when she turned eighteen and announcing—now that she was finally of age—that he hadn't been able to forget her ever since that kiss they'd shared as Laramie and Jane.

In her fantasy he would take her hand and help her into his car and . . .

And this was the point where the fantasy got a little foggy. Sometimes—actually, most of the time—this was where Leonardo DiCaprio pulled up in *his* car and refused to let her run off with Jericho.

Susie smiled. It was ridiculously, wonderfully silly.

Still, she wasn't going to have trouble getting into character on the day they filmed that kiss.

"Cut!"

Beside her, Kate started breathing again. "They'll only have time to do one more take before the crew mutinies and demands lunch."

Susie cleared her throat. "Kate, will you do me a favor?"

"Sure, what do you need?"

"Will you introduce me to Jericho?"

Susie had been on set for nearly four days, and she hadn't managed to come face-to-face with him yet. Although she'd had rehearsals with some of the other actors, Victor Strauss had decided Jericho would play these early scenes unrehearsed. His character, Laramie, was drunk most of the time, and Victor thought it best if Jericho were allowed spontaneity. Later on, though, Laramie would discover that Jane worked for the Underground Railroad. After that, and after they shot a scene in which he sobered up during a harrowing trip north with a wagonload of run-aways, *then* Victor would schedule full rehearsals with all of the cast for the remaining scenes.

"You haven't met Jericho yet?" Kate asked.

Susie shook her head. She'd seen Jericho laughing and talking in the restaurant used as a dining hall, but every time she headed toward him through the crowd, he'd vanished. If she were at all paranoid, she would think he was avoiding her. But if there was one thing she was sure of on set, it was that time was often in short supply. People frequently relaxed until the last split second, and then hurried away.

"Settle!"

"As soon as they're done here, I'll introduce you to him," Kate whispered.

"Action!"

Out in the field, Jericho fell to his knees. Susie was too far away to hear his dialogue, but he said his lines and then slowly toppled forward onto his face.

"Cut!"

There was silence, then several of the crew applauded. Jericho stood, bowing grandly as he dusted himself off.

"Come on," Kate said. "They're going to call lunch in about ten seconds. Let's catch him before he escapes."

Susie followed the producer out onto the field. "Jericho!" Kate called.

He turned and saw them coming. He'd been laughing, but now his smile faded.

"Susie tells me you haven't been introduced," Kate continued. "She wanted a chance to say hello before tomorrow."

"Tomorrow?"

"We do our first scene together tomorrow." Susie held out her hand. "Hi, I'm Susie McCoy."

As soon as the words were out of her mouth, she cringed. Susie. Why had she called herself Susie? She'd decided that the credits on this movie would read "Susannah McCoy." Susie McCoy made cute, fluffy movies like *Slumberparty*. Susannah McCoy appeared in movies with great depth and intensity.

"Nice to meet you." Jericho's hand was warm as he briefly shook hers. But it was the only thing that was warm. There was absolutely none of his legendary friendliness in his eyes.

But maybe that was because he looked so dreadful. Hungover. Whoever was doing his makeup had really done it right.

"Excuse me," he said, scratching the stubble of beard on his chin. "I'm really hungry—I've got to get some lunch."

Susie bolstered her courage. "Maybe—if you don't mind—I could join you? I don't have to be in makeup until two o'clock. I'd love to get a chance to talk about the scenes we're shooting tomorrow."

"Oh," he said. "Well"—he glanced from Susie to Kate and back—"actually, I was gonna have lunch in my trailer. I need to run some lines and . . . take a nap if I have time, so. . . . Today's probably not the best day to do that. Sorry."

Jericho hated her.

Beside her, Kate had stiffened, and Susie knew that she'd picked up on all the negative energy, too.

He absolutely hated her.

He couldn't see beyond the corny movies and the hokey TV sitcom. He didn't bother to look into her eyes. He'd already decided that she wasn't good enough, that she wouldn't be able to give the kind of dramatic performance necessary for this role.

Susie forced her mouth into a smile. "Sure," she said. "No problem. Some other time, maybe."

Jericho nodded. "Yeah. Maybe." He walked away.

Kate was furious. But she, too, managed to smile as she turned to Susie. "I'd love to have lunch with you."

Susie shook her head. "I think I'm going to hang out in my trailer, too. You know, get focused for this afternoon?"

Kate watched Jericho, who was still walking toward the cars that would take him back into town. "I don't think he realized how rude he sounded."

"It's not a big deal," she lied. "He's probably decided to keep his distance from me while these opening scenes are shot. I mean, our characters don't really know each other, so it makes sense for us to start out as strangers and . . ." She shrugged.

Kate nodded. "Do you want a ride back into town?"

Susie shook her head. "No, thanks. I've got my bike."

"You ride your bike barefoot?"

Susie smiled. "My feet are really tough."

She wished the rest of her skin was as thick.

Five

"**W**HAT?" KATE CLUTCHED her towel as her wet hair dripped onto the telephone. "Jericho is *where*?"

"That's just it. We're not sure." Annie sounded as if she were going to faint. "He's already a half an hour late for call.

"A half an hour?" Kate's voice went up an octave as she gripped the telephone receiver. "Oh, my God, Annie! I was supposed to get a call if he was ever more than ten minutes late!"

"I'm sorry." Now Annie sounded as if she were going to cry. "I didn't notice until ten minutes ago. I know I should have called you right away, but I thought maybe he was running late. I thought I could take care of it without having to bother you. Your blood pressure's high enough these days."

Kate tucked the receiver under her chin and started drying herself in earnest. "I assume you called his trailer?"

"No one picked up. So I went over there and banged on the door. Still no response. The door's locked, and I don't have a key. Victor remembers seeing Jericho at dinner last night, but no one's seen him since."

Kate felt a flash of hot and then cold. It was happening. Her worst nightmare was finally happening. Despite all of her precautions, Jericho had gone AWOL. "I've got a key to his trailer. I'll be right there."

She hung up the phone as she fumbled for the day's shooting schedule. The shorts and T-shirt she'd worn the night before were still on the floor. She pulled them on as she scanned the schedule and read what she already knew by heart.

The cameras were being set up to shoot exteriors at the location they were using for the Willet farm. The first scene scheduled for the morning was one where Jane's brothers inform her that Reginald Brooks, the brutal plantation owner thirty years her senior, has asked to marry her. The money he's offered as a dowry will solve their financial woes. Jane has no choice, they tell her, as Jericho's character Laramie looks on in barely disguised horror. She must accept Brooks for the sake of her family.

Although Jericho had no lines in that scene, his presence was necessary.

Victor could compensate for Jericho's absence by shooting close-ups of Susie McCoy and the actors playing her brothers first. But Jericho would be needed within a few hours at best.

And it was up to Kate to find him.

Jericho had been a royal pain in the ass since he'd arrived on set. There were troubles with his trailer. The refrigerator was stocked with too many diet sodas one day, not enough diet soda the next. His mattress was too soft. The replacement Kate had had shipped in was too hard. The window blinds let in too much light, but shades made the room too dark.

Jericho's single-most goal in life seemed to be driving Kate mad. Or at least to run her ragged with his relentless demands.

But this was the first time he'd ever been late to the set.

Kate slipped her feet into her sneakers and, raking her fingers quickly through her still wet hair, she grabbed her keys and headed for Jericho's trailer at a run.

The sun had only been up a very short while, but it was clear that the day was going to be another steam bath.

Annie was waiting for her outside of Jericho's trailer, her freckles standing out against the ghostly paleness of her thin face. "I just realized Bob Hollander's car is gone."

Kate unlocked the door, then handed Annie her keys. "Go into my office and find the file on Hollander. Leave a message on his answering machine—I know he checks it regularly. Tell him to call in immediately. Oh, and I think he's got a pager number. Find it and page him. I want to know what the hell is going on."

Annie ran back toward the production office as Kate pushed open the door to the trailer.

It was dark and cool inside with the shades drawn.

"Hello?" she called, not expecting an answer.

"Back here."

Kate nearly hit her head on the door frame in surprise. "Jericho?"

He spoke again, each word distinctly enunciated. "I'm back here."

Kate turned on the light and headed down the tiny corridor to the back bedroom, her annoyance making her voice sharp. "You're over a half hour late for your call and—"

The light from the main room lit the bedroom enough for her to see Jericho through the open doorway.

He was sitting on the bare mattress of his bed, his legs outstretched and casually crossed at the ankles as he leaned back against the headboard.

He was naked. Completely naked.

Kate found herself staring, her mouth all but hanging open in surprise.

Some men looked better with their clothes on, but

Jericho was not one of them. In fact, the "hero without a shirt" scene was a requirement for almost every Jericho Beaumont movie. And seeing him without his shirt, in person, Kate now knew precisely why.

The man was in outrageously good shape. He wasn't quite as built up and muscular as he'd been for the *Kill Zone* movies. But his arms, shoulders, and chest had a definite female drool factor of about twelve on a scale from one to ten, and his stomach was enough of a washboard to garner the male audience members' admiration.

But not only was he shirtless, he wasn't wearing pants, either. And as for the rest of him . . . She forced her eyes back to his face.

"What are you doing?" It was an inane question, but it was the best one she could come up with. "Where's Bob?"

He shifted slightly under her gaze, and the light from the hallway reflected off the shiny metal of handcuffs and . . .

*Hand*cuffs?

"Is this some kind of joke?" she asked sharply.

He held up his hands for her to get a better look. Yes, he was definitely wearing handcuffs. And a thick metal chain connected those handcuffs to some sort of bracket that was attached to the wall.

"Does this look like a joke?"

"Oh, my God," Kate breathed.

"Yeah," Jericho said. "Oh, my God."

"Where's Bob Hollander?" she asked again.

"Good fucking question. Do you mind uncuffing me? I have to pee. Badly."

Kate stood frozen, completely unable to move. "I don't . . . I don't have a key. Why did Bob lock you up? *Did* Bob lock you up?"

"Well, it sure as hell wasn't the Easter Bunny who left me here like this."

"Kate?"

It was Annie's voice, calling from outside. Kate heard the squeak as her assistant opened the trailer's screen door.

Jericho nearly dove off the bed, but there was nowhere for him to go. The chain kept him from being able to hide. "For Christsake," he said from between clenched teeth, "will you lock the door? This isn't a goddamned zoo!"

Kate moved fast. And with the movement of her feet, her brain kicked back in. "Annie." She stopped the young woman from coming all the way inside the trailer. "I need a bucket or a pail, and I need it fast. And a yellow pages— I'm going to need a locksmith. Leave 'em both right here, outside the door. Oh, and give me back my keys."

Annie was confused. "Is Jericho in there? Is he sick?"

"He's here, he's fine. *Go.*" Kate pushed her assistant out the door with her, locking it tightly behind her.

She ran to Jericho's other trailer and fumbled with the keys in the lock, dropping them twice before opening the door.

Once inside, she took a quick look around. With just a glance, she could see that Jericho had claimed the bedroom in an attempt to have something of a private area. She grabbed a pair of shorts from his closet, then ran back to the other trailer.

She went inside, locking the door securely behind her.

Jericho was sitting on the edge of the bed. His elbows were on his knees, and his head was down, resting in his hands.

And Kate knew the truth. The way he'd been sitting there when she'd first come in had been an act. He'd had a choice between showing his embarrassment or acting arrogant upon being discovered chained up like some kind of animal. He'd chosen arrogance, but she knew what he was truly feeling was beyond embarrassment.

This must be impossibly humiliating. Kate tried for a second to put herself in his place, but the thought of him walking into her bedroom to find *her* naked and in chains was too awful to dwell on.

"Annie's gone to get a bucket to use as, um, as a temporary chamber pot, and a yellow pages. I'll call a locksmith and—"

He looked up at her. "That's not a very good idea." His hair was a mess, and he had a heavy growth of stubble on his face. His eyes were bleary and red-rimmed from lack of sleep, but his gaze was still sharp. "You don't want news getting out that Jericho Beaumont was found naked and handcuffed to his bed." His mouth twisted in a near approximation of a smile. "Now, if I'd been found naked and handcuffed to *your* bed, that would be a whole 'nother story entirely."

Kate let out a burst of air that in any other situation might have been called laughter. "I can't believe you can joke about this."

"That wasn't a joke."

But it had been. He had every right to be mad as hell, but he was able to find humor in the situation. Kate felt humbled. She wasn't sure she would have been able to do the same.

She held out his shorts. "Here. I got you . . . Here."

He reached, but the chain didn't go very far. She had to step forward, much closer, to put them in his hands. She then turned away.

"I'm sorry," he said. "I think I'm going to . . ." He cleared his throat. "I'm gonna need some help."

The chain that attached his handcuffs to the wall was only about three feet long. As Kate turned back, she saw that it kept him from bending down to step into the shorts. He was too tall, and the chain was too short.

He was mortified to have to ask for help. She could see embarrassment and shame darkening his cheeks.

The best thing to do in a situation like this was move quickly. Get it over with. Kate reached for his shorts, kneeling in front of him so that he could step into them easily.

"Hollander got a call a little after midnight," he told her. She wondered if he were talking to distract her or himself. She kept her eyes firmly on his feet as she pulled the shorts up his legs. He had remarkably nice feet—long and elegant-looking, with nicely shaped toes and neatly trimmed nails.

"I was already asleep," he continued, "but he woke me up. He said he had to go out, but he'd be back long before I had to be on set in the morning."

As soon as his fingers could reach the waistband of the shorts, Kate stepped back and turned away.

"I asked, but he wouldn't say where he was going. I thought he was kidding when he got out the handcuffs, but he wasn't." The sound of his zipper being pulled up seemed to echo in the room. "He took my clothes and the bed linens, too, in case I somehow pulled a houdini and got free." Jericho laughed harshly. "As if fear of being seen naked would keep me in this trailer if handcuffs couldn't hold me . . ."

Kate didn't know what to say as she turned to face him again. "I'm so sorry."

He glanced at her. "Yeah, I know you are."

The screen door opened with a screech, followed by the sound of the trailer door being unlocked.

Kate moved quickly, intending to run interference. She didn't know who else had a key to this trailer but—

The door opened, and Bob Hollander stepped inside.

He had returned.

He was sweaty and rumpled—as if he'd jogged several miles in his suit in the already scorching morning heat.

"Sorry," he said shortly. "Car broke down."

Kate waited, but that was it. He didn't volunteer any further explanation.

"Is that Hollander?" Jericho asked from the other room. "Did he actually have the balls to come back here?"

"Where were you?" Kate demanded.

"I had some business I had to take care of. Again, I apologize for the inconvenience."

"Incon*ven*ience?" Kate couldn't believe the man's nerve. "You locked Jericho in handcuffs—"

"Actually, that's standard operating procedure, particularly when the client has an obvious lack of respect for authority. I've found it helps clear up any misunderstanding in regard to who is actually in charge."

"That would be me, Mr. Hollander," Kate said coldly. She didn't need Frau Steinbreaker today. She was mad enough to pull it off entirely on her own. "*I* am in charge. And at no time, during any of our conversations did the subject of handcuffs ever come up."

"Excuse me," Jericho called from the back. "Can I get these goddamn things off now?"

Hollander ignored him. "If you'll look at our agreement, you'll see that you granted me the authority to—"

"Do you have the key?" Kate interrupted.

"Of course—"

"Give it to me."

Hollander dug into his pocket. "I'll unlock him."

"Oh, good idea. Send Bobby on in here, Kate." Jericho's voice was tight. "Please. I'm looking forward to kicking the shit out of him. Or wait. I know—maybe I'll wrap this goddamn chain around his neck."

Kate blocked Hollander's way, holding out her hand. "I'll do it. You better wait outside."

Hollander didn't blink. "I can handle him."

She stood her ground. "I don't want you to handle him."

The ex-marine shrugged and dropped the key into her palm.

Kate heard the screen door screech open and closed as she went back to Jericho.

He was sitting on the edge of the bed again, breathing hard as if he had just run a race. "He doesn't think he did anything wrong, does he? The son of a bitch. *Son* of a bitch!"

She sat down next to him, aching for him. "I don't think he does, no."

Jericho was holding onto the chain so tightly his knuckles were white. "I'm not going to kill him. As much as I want to, I'm not going to. This isn't good. This doesn't help me."

He was trying to control his anger. As Kate watched, he closed his eyes and took several deep breaths.

She reached for him, putting her hands over his, tugging his fingers free from the chain. "It's okay for you to be angry, Jericho. But it's not okay for you to kick the shit out of Bob Hollander."

He looked up at that. "So how else do you suggest I release all this hostility?" He glanced down at their hands, still tightly clasped, and when he looked back at her, the entire room seemed to tilt. This wasn't just a room, it was a bedroom. And not even five minutes ago, this man had been sitting here completely naked.

Kate could see a reflection of her own sudden hyper-awareness in his eyes. Hyperawareness—and attraction.

She was sitting on Jericho Beaumont's bed, holding his hands. And despite the fact that he'd been trying his best to make her life as difficult as possible over the past week, there was a light in his eyes that told her he would not be adverse to fanning this spark between them into flames. Searing, consuming, white-hot flames.

Or maybe that light was just a reflection of her own attraction. God, she'd practically had to wipe the drool from her chin when she'd first come in and found him here.

Kate pulled her hands away, feeling her cheeks heat

with embarrassment. She fumbled for the key, and dropped it once before getting it into the lock. The cuffs sprang open, and he was free.

"Jericho, I'm so sorry about this," she said again.

His wrists looked red and sore, but he didn't seem to notice. He just stood up and went right into the bathroom. Kate didn't move, well aware that there was no door. No privacy. She heard him relieve himself, heard the toilet flush, then the sound of water running in the sink. And then . . . She heard the metallic shriek of the opening screen door.

She dropped the handcuffs, and they hit the wall with a rattle as she ran for the door.

Sure enough, as she stepped out of the trailer, Jericho was heading directly for Bob Hollander.

She caught up, and he glanced at her. "Don't worry, I'm not going to kill him."

"That's not what I'm worried about," she said, stepping in front of him and forcing him to stop. "Hollander's a former hand-to-hand combat instructor. It would be crazy for you to start anything with him. He'll chew you up and spit you out. You should be running in the opposite direction!"

His eyes were no longer hot with anger. In fact, they were oddly devoid of any emotion. He looked almost empty, as if part of him were no longer there.

He shook his head. "Aw, hell. Now I've got to." He stepped around her.

Kate looked across the dusty driveway to Bob Hollander. "Bob . . ."

The former marine looked as exhausted as Jericho, but he didn't try to move away. "You don't want to do this," he warned.

"You're right," Jericho admitted. "But if I don't, Kate's going to think I'm a coward." He circled the bigger man, who turned warily to keep facing him.

"I will not," Kate called. "I'll think you've finally got a few of your brain cells working. I'll think you're behaving as a professional—considering the impact a black eye and bruised face will have on our shooting schedule."

"Don't worry. I'm not going to let him touch my face." There was something about the flat matter-of-factness of Jericho's voice and his total lack of expression that was unnerving.

"There's no way you could win." Hollander was sounding less certain of that.

"Are you sure?" Jericho's eyes were oddly devoid of emotion. "You don't have a clue where I've been, Bobby. You don't know where I came from—who I've had to fight in my life, just to survive."

A crowd was starting to gather. The members of the cast and crew who weren't busy preparing for the morning's shoot were filtering out of the Morning Glory Grill to see what was going on.

Kate moved toward Jericho and Bob Hollander. "All right," she said. "I think this has gone—"

Hollander swung first, throwing a punch at Jericho, moving incredibly fast for such an enormous man. But Jericho had spun out of the way with the grace and speed of a dancer, easily dodging what could well have been a teeth-rattling blow. Hollander lunged for him again, but it seemed as if Jericho had eyes in the back of his head, and again he moved out of reach. And as Hollander was off balance, Jericho feinted with his right hand, then followed quickly by a hard left.

It all happened so fast, Kate didn't even have time to shout for them to stop. Bob Hollander blocked Jericho's punch, but his movement left the rest of him wide open, which Kate realized was Jericho's plan. Because while Hollander was open, Jericho kicked him—hard—in the groin.

And Hollander fell, face first, into the dusty street.

"Stop!" Kate shouted. "Stop this right now!" She moved between them. "Back away," she ordered Jericho. "Get back—*now*!"

His gaze had been glued to Hollander, as if he expected the bigger man to leap to his feet and come after him, but now he glanced up at Kate.

His eyes were empty. There was nothing there. No anger, but also no exhilaration, no triumph. It was like looking into the frozen void of outer space.

"Back away," she said again, her voice little more than a whisper.

To her relief, Jericho obeyed.

But Hollander managed to push himself to his knees. He'd also found his voice. "Come back here, you little piece of shit and finish what you started!"

Jericho obeyed him, too, and again, Kate stepped between them.

"You!" Kate bellowed. "Hollander! I want to see you in my office in twenty seconds!" She turned to Jericho. "And you. You're late for the set. Get your butt down to make-up, on the double." She pointed at one of the gofers who was standing in the crowd, watching wide-eyed. "You, Tony! Go with Jericho and *stay* with Jericho until I tell you otherwise. The rest of you get back to work. Now, *move* it!"

The crowd scattered.

Susie McCoy's father was so pissed, Jamaal wouldn't have been surprised if he started shooting firecrackers out of his butt.

Speaking of butts, the man was butt-ugly to start with, and it didn't help matters one bit when he started shouting and great big, gross purple veins began sticking out from his forehead and neck.

Jamaal sat back behind the line of cameras, settling in to watch the show. He'd come down here to check out both Susie and Jericho as they worked. He had today off, but there wasn't much to do in Grady Falls, South Carolina. He snorted. Now that was the understatement of the year. There was *less* than nothing to do in this cultural wasteland.

So he'd thrown on a pair of shorts and a T-shirt, and wandered over to the set to see what was going on.

The truth was, the action on set intrigued him—even when he wasn't one of the people in front of the cameras. He hadn't been involved with that many movies for it to have become mundane—at least not yet.

As far as what was going on right this moment— Jamaal honestly hadn't expected to find himself watching an episode of the McCoy's Private Freak Show and Circus. Still, checking out the amazing purple-necked man wasn't without *some* entertainment value.

Russell McCoy had come raging into town behind the wheel of some pretentious rental car. It had been obvious two seconds after he'd arrived that he wasn't here as a loving father paying a visit to his daughter.

No, Susie McCoy's moms seemed to be the lucky winner of the Russell McCoy shouting sweepstakes. She was the target of all the noise, and she looked as if she were literally being hammered into the ground. She seemed to get smaller and smaller with each of ol' Russ's harsh words.

Production assistants hovered around them nervously, like flies. Vic Strauss kept looking in Russell's direction, as if he were milliseconds away from having someone turn a fire hose on the entire pack of 'em.

"What were you thinking?" Russell was bellowing. "How could you possibly allow her to be in a movie with him?"

The *her* he was referring to was Susie, and the *him* was Jericho Beaumont.

Jericho was lying back in a lounge chair, waiting for the

camera to be set for the next shot. His eyes were closed, as if the war raging around him had nothing to do with him.

Susie, though, was looking as if she were praying for God to open the sky and smite her with a bolt of lightning.

Jamaal couldn't blame the girl.

"Have you read this script?" Russell had more than a passing resemblance to Jabba the Hut in this light. "There's no way Susie is ready for this."

Susie's moms said something Jamaal couldn't hear.

"I saw the last few takes," Russell told his ex—and everyone else in a five-mile radius. "She was awful."

Susie cringed, and Jamaal cringed along with her. Susie's moms spoke again, and again Jamaal couldn't hear what she'd said.

"I don't give a damn!" Susie's father had not yet run out of things to say—too bad for them all. "Let them wait! They're going to have to put the production on hold anyway, because they're going to have to recast Susie's part."

Jericho's eyes opened at that, and Jamaal knew that the negative energy he'd picked up from the man during the last series of shots hadn't been his imagination. Jericho was less than impressed with Susie's performance.

And, yeah, Jamaal had to admit that after Jericho made the scene, Susie *had* tightened up. She got stiff—self-conscious. But who could blame her? If she was anything like Jamaal, Jericho had been her hero since the beginning of time. It wasn't easy to drop that sense of awe and suddenly become peers with your own personal God. And Jericho, the fool—he had really let the ball drop. He'd done absolutely nothing to make the girl feel more comfortable. In fact, as far as Jamaal could see, he'd done his damnedest to make Susie even more uptight.

So she blew some lines. Big deal. Everyone blew lines now and then. But with Jericho looking as if she were intentionally wasting his own personal stockpile of time . . .

So, yeah, Susie's performance over the past few hours had been less than perfect. But what Jericho and her father hadn't seen was how she'd breezed through the close-ups they'd done before either of them had arrived on set. She was just a kid, but when she was relaxed and comfortable, she was a complete pro. And she was damn good. Shit, she was beyond good. She had Jamaal completely believing she was Jane Willet.

Susie stood up now and faced her father, looking for all the world as if she were going mano a mano with a fire-breathing dragon. She knew she was going to be burned to a crisp, but she was gonna do it with her head held high.

"They're not going to recast my part," she told him. "I've signed a contract. Even if I wanted to back out now, there'd be a lawsuit."

A car pulled up, and the producer, Kate O'Laughlin, got out. She came charging onto the scene like the cavalry to the rescue.

Up until this morning, Jamaal had figured she was pure window dressing. She was Vic Strauss's ex—he'd thought for sure she'd only been given a title and a desk to play office with. Kind of like, "Yeah, sure, honey—you can be producer. Don't hurt yourself with that stapler, babe . . ."

But this morning, Kate had stuck herself directly in the middle of what was looking to be a very bloody fight between Jericho and his warden, Hollander. She'd diffused a rather huge bomb. And afterward, when Jamaal had made discreet inquiries, he'd found out she was indeed the producer in responsibilities as well as title. The woman had a brain to go inside that Maserati-style, performance-ready body.

And as far as today's early morning fight went, most folks on the set didn't know who Hollander was or his connection to Jericho. There was even some speculation that the two men were longtime companions—although anyone with eyes in their head could see how completely foolish an idea that was.

It hadn't taken Jamaal long to figure out Hollander was Jericho's very own personal, live-in prison guard. And something had happened this morning in cell block thirteen that had pushed Jericho too far.

But Queen Kate had taken command, raising that wispy little voice of hers to a lion's roar, until everyone's ears damn near rang.

Jamaal had never been on a movie set where so much of the shouting had gone on behind the cameras.

Right now, as Kate approached the battling McCoys from the rear, Jericho pushed himself to his feet and sauntered toward them from the front.

This was going to be good. Because even though Kate had managed to break up the fight earlier, and even though it seemed—by the lack of Hollander's presence here this morning—that she'd jettisoned the man, Hollander *had* been her minion. And Jamaal was willing to bet that Jericho had a thing or two to shout at Kate himself.

But Jericho didn't shout. And he didn't address Kate; he spoke to Russell McCoy. "You know," he said in his good ol' boy drawl, "it wouldn't be a contract violation if both you and the creative staff came to the mutual decision that Susie's not quite right for this part. I mean, it happens sometimes. Actors take parts that they're not able to handle, but they don't find that out until after the filming starts."

The look on Susie's face was heartbreaking. She turned away, tried to hide it, but Jamaal saw her pain, clear as day. Jericho had just announced that he believed Susie was not up to playing the part of Jane. Jamaal respected the man as a fellow actor, but what he had said was *way* harsh. And way unnecessary—because it wasn't even remotely true.

Kate's voice was sharp. "Excuse me," she said to

Jericho. "I thought this was an issue between Mr. McCoy and Ms. Turner. I'm not sure why you're involved."

"I was just suggesting—"

"There's no way I'm going to allow my daughter to spend the next two months with some junkie," Russell interrupted. He turned and fired a shot at his ex. "Are you some kind of mental deficient? What were you thinking to let Susie near *him*?"

Susie wasn't anywhere near Jericho. In fact, Susie was gone.

Jamaal turned to look for her and saw her drifting toward the craft table that had been set up in the shade. She looked at the collection of snacks and fruit that were laid out there, but didn't take anything. As he watched, she bent down to open a cooler filled with cans of soda, but again didn't take one out. She let the lid fall closed as she just crouched there, unmoving, her head bowed.

Jamaal started toward her. He whistled as he approached, but even then, she didn't seem to hear him coming.

"Hey," he said, and she jerked her head up, startled.

The kid was crying. Jamaal's stomach tightened. With her wide blue eyes filled with tears, she looked about eleven years old. Two tears escaped, making tracks down her cheeks.

"You're messing up your makeup."

"They're all out of root beer," she told him.

He frowned. "Really?" He lifted the lid of the cooler and reached in, pushing the icy water and cans around. There was definitely no more root beer. But there was one last can of cream soda. He took it out, letting the water drip off of it before he handed it to her. "Give this a try. It's not root beer, but it's kinda like a distant second cousin."

She straightened up, no longer eleven years old, but suddenly much older—cool, efficient, and ageless. "Would you mind getting Mindy for me? She's one of the makeup assistants. Usually I can cry without ruining my makeup, but this time it got away from me."

Jamaal took the soda from her and opened the top. "How do you cry without ruining your makeup?"

"You kind of tip your head forward and let the tears fall out of your eyes." She demonstrated.

"You, uh, cry much?"

She forced a smile. "Only when there's no root beer."

Jamaal nodded. "Uh-huh." He held out his hand. "I'm Jamaal Hawkes."

"I know."

"And you're Susie McCoy."

Her hands were tiny, her nails bitten down nearly to the quick.

"*Susannah* McCoy," she corrected him.

"Susannah. Okay. That's . . . that's a very pretty name. I can see why you wouldn't want anyone to shorten it."

She took a sip of the cream soda and made a face. "God, this is sweet."

"Yeah," he said. "Great, huh?" He reached for the can. "May I?" She handed the soda to him, and he paused before drinking. "You sure you weren't crying because you have some deadly disease that's passed by sharing cans of soda?"

Her smile still held a trace of Hollywood fake. "No. Would you mind finding Mindy? She's the really pretty black woman who's around here somewhere . . ."

"No problem." Jamaal took a long drink of the soda. "I happen to be a magnet for really pretty black women. Just . . . If you don't mind, can I say something first?"

Her shoulders narrowed as if she were preparing for him to hit her, and again something shifted in his stomach.

"Look, Susie—Susannah. What Jericho and your father said . . . About you not being up for this part? They're both completely full of shit."

She wasn't expecting him to say that, and it caught her off guard. "Thanks, but—"

"No buts. They're wrong. Don't you lose your self-confidence. And don't you dare let Jericho intimidate you into getting all tight. He walked in here thinking he knows you. I know it's not fair, but now you've got a job to do—you've got to prove him wrong. And cut the SOB some slack at the same time. This is the first big picture he's done sober in years. He's probably carrying around a trunkload of his own self-doubt." He handed her back the can. "Okay?"

She nodded. She was so serious. Dear Lord, who ever would've guessed he'd be standing here giving advice to Susie McCoy? The thought made him grin. "You know, I've been a big fan of yours since *The Thing in the Basement*."

"That was my first movie."

Jamaal sat down on the cooler. "Yeah, I know. I've seen 'em all."

Her eyebrows rose. "*Slumberparty*?"

"Shit, yeah. I even saw *Slumberparty Two*. Well, okay, I waited for the video. But I saw it. You were good."

She rolled her eyes. "Too bad the rest of the movie sucked."

"No sequels. Repeat after me. No sequels. Come on."

"No sequels," she said with a smile that didn't look as if it were about to break. When it was real, she had a knockout, killer smile.

"Good girl. Now when Vic and Kate come knocking at our doors with an offer of two mill each to do the sequel to this movie—after it sweeps the Oscars, of course—"

"Of course." She giggled.

"What are we going to say?"

"No sequels."

"What are you *nuts*? You're really going to turn down two million *dollars* for a picture that's probably going to be great despite the fact that it'll be a sequel?"

Susannah McCoy laughed aloud.

Mission accomplished. Jamaal stood up. "I'll go find Mindy for you now."

"Jamaal."

He turned to look back at her.

"Thanks for the soda." Her smile was shy now. "I'll, um, see you around?"

Holy shit. He'd done more than make her laugh. He'd made her have a crush on him. Susie McCoy had a crush on *him*. Jamaal smiled back at her. "Yeah, sure. I'm not going anywhere."

Six

THIS TIME SHE had seen *him* naked.

Naked and in chains.

Christ.

Jed took a moment outside of Kate's office, and took a deep breath.

How exactly should one go about greeting the woman—the impossibly attractive woman—who had witnessed the single-most humiliating moment of one's life?

Hell, she didn't just witness it—she was responsible for the whole bloody scenario by making him sign that damned seven-point addendum to the contract.

He sat down on the bench outside the production office door, bone weary and desperate for a drink. Not only had Kate forced him to have 24/7 supervision, but she'd gone and hired Hollander without realizing the man's standard MO involved locking his clients in chains and handcuffs while he ran errands at night. No, Mary Kate O'Laughlin may not have intended to subject Jed to such relentless humiliation, but she *was* responsible.

She had done this to him, and Jed wanted . . . something.

He wasn't sure exactly what he wanted besides a tumbler-sized glass of whiskey. But he knew he couldn't have that, so he figured he'd grab himself some retribution instead.

Jericho didn't usually subscribe to the concept of revenge, but he wanted—he really wanted—to look into Kate's eyes and know that *she* knew he'd gotten the best of her.

It was petty. It was childish. He knew that. But he didn't care. It would taste almost as smooth as that whiskey he was denying himself.

And he knew the exact way he was going to extract his pound of flesh, so to speak.

He was going to make her want him. Instead of looking at him and seeing the loser she currently imagined him to be, she was going to see the perfect man of her dreams.

And he was going to seduce her. Slowly, patiently. Until she invited him into her bed, until they were moments away from complete sexual fulfillment, until she was begging him to make love to her. And then he'd laugh and walk away.

Or . . . maybe not.

Maybe he'd make love to her and then laugh and walk away. Or maybe he'd make love to her for the remaining weeks of the shoot and *then* he'd laugh and walk away.

Jed knew the laugh-and-walk-away part was essential to his plan—he just wasn't sure exactly where it would best fit in.

Seducing Kate was going to be a piece of cake. She was lonely, she was single, she was hot-blooded—and she was already experiencing an intensely powerful physical attraction to him.

He'd seen her eyes when she'd first come into his trailer and found him sitting naked on his bed. She'd taken one look and nearly fallen over.

Jed knew exactly what he looked like. He saw himself in the bathroom mirror every time he took a shower. He knew for a fact that he was physically quite beautiful, and he could say that honestly without any ego involved. It had nothing to do with him—nothing to do with who he was, with his achievements, at any rate.

His looks were the result of a genetic crapshoot. God knows his sister Louise hadn't gotten the genes he had— his brother Leroy, either, for that matter. Tom had, though. His eldest brother had had both the looks as well as blond hair, though no one knew where *that* had come from.

No, Jed's striking looks were simply another tool at his disposal. He'd used his handsome face and lean body to get noticed when he'd first tried to break in as an actor. God knows he was using it now as he attempted this comeback. Having such assets certainly didn't hurt when it came to popular appeal.

He didn't take it seriously, but other people sure as hell did.

People like Mary Kate O'Laughlin.

He'd looked into her eyes, and he knew that she was not unaffected by him. Hell, there was one point this morning, right before she uncuffed him, where she'd told him with body language that she wanted him to kiss her.

Now maybe that had been purely a message from her subconscious, but it didn't matter. There was a part of her that wanted something sexual from him.

And he was going to deliver.

Yeah, he was going to get even indeed, and he was going to enjoy it on more than one level.

But there was a long road between here and there, and he didn't just want her body. He wanted a piece of her soul. And the first thing he needed to do was figure out what kind of man she was attracted to, so he could form a character and take on that part.

Kate O'Laughlin struck him as the kind of woman who would go for blunt honesty in a big way. God knows she'd jumped right into the fray with Russell McCoy and his ex, and read them the riot act with no holds barred. So he'd start with blunt honesty.

Jed stood up. He opened the door and walked into the production office, as ready for this as he'd ever be.

Kate's private office was directly in front of the main entrance. Even though she was on the phone, her door was open and she saw him arrive. With a practiced, somewhat tense smile, she waved him in, pointing toward a seat.

It was amazing she could smile at all, considering the morning she'd had. First the deal with him, and then Russell McCoy . . .

"Yes," she said into the phone as Jed sat down. Unlike her office in Boston, this place was purely functional. A gray metal desk, several beat-up file cabinets. A table that was cluttered with files and papers. Several corkboards and white erasable marker boards filled with information about the production.

Even though there was an air conditioner chugging away in one of the windows, Kate had a small fan on her desk. It swiveled slowly, and when the air hit her, it gently ruffled her hair.

"Yep," she said, still into the phone. "Got it. Look, I've got to go. I've got an important meeting and—" She laughed. "All right, then. Later."

She dropped the phone into the cradle and turned to Jed. "Sorry about that."

"I'm really embarrassed about this morning," Jed said. "I'm trying hard not to be, but I'm pretty much completely mortified." It was weird. By taking this approach, he was forced to actually be blunt and honest. And as a result, for the first time since he could remember, he was standing in front of an industry peer without attempting to hide behind his Hollywood charm. In a way, he felt nearly as naked as he had that morning.

Kate stood up and quietly closed her office door. "Thank God," she said. "I was afraid we were going to have to play a game where you pretended it was no big deal, and I pretended it was no big deal and . . . It *was* a big deal, and I'm embarrassed, too. Thank you for bringing the issue into the open."

Jed realized she'd changed out of the shorts and T-shirt she had on this morning. She was back to her usual somewhat dressy, professional career-woman clothes—a tan skirt that ended too few inches above her knees for his tastes, high-heeled sandals, and a white blouse.

Kate's closet had to be packed with different varieties of white blouses—and she looked damn good in every one of them. Today's version was soft and long-sleeved, made from some kind of silky material that flowed around her and was just not possible to see through.

Although not from a lack of trying on his part. Yeah, he was definitely going to enjoy these next few weeks.

She sat down behind her desk, folding her arms somewhat awkwardly in front of her. Now, wasn't that interesting? She didn't like being looked at—despite the nonconservative, attention-seeking style of her clothes. Or maybe it was only *him* she didn't like looking.

"Here's what I figure." Jed kept his gaze focused on her face. He was here to make friends—at first, anyway. "You know, to make it fair and all, you should go into my trailer, take off your clothes, put on the handcuffs, and wait for me to find *you*."

Kate stared at him.

Uh-oh. That may have been a touch too direct. It was pure Jed Beaumont. And one thing he'd already determined was that Kate didn't fully appreciate Jed's twisted sense of humor.

But then she laughed. What do you know? She blushed, too, which he still found intriguing. "I don't think that's the solution."

"Works for me. All will be forgiven—I guarantee it."

She leaned forward slightly, holding his gaze. "Jericho,

I can't tell you how sorry I am about what happened. I want you to know that Bob Hollander has left and he won't be coming back."

Jed nodded, noting with satisfaction the way her blush deepened as he purposely didn't break eye contact. Oh, yeah. They were practically best friends already. "That's a relief. It occurred to me as he was landing face first in the street that I'd probably armed him with everything he needed to negotiate a second chance. You know, kinda like, "I won't press assault charges against Beaumont if you overlook my little mistake.'"

Kate shook her head. "That was no little mistake. He shouldn't have left you locked up for five minutes—let alone more than five hours. Can you imagine what might've happened if there'd been a fire? I feel sick just thinking about it."

She wasn't kidding. She was really upset by this. It was a shame her desk was too wide for him to reach across and take her hand. "Yeah, well, it's over now. It's behind us."

This was going really well. On Monday, he'd ask her to have dinner with him. Until then, he'd have three days to cement this friendly rapport they'd established through his newfound blunt honesty and Kate's sense of guilt. By Monday, she'd be ready for him to introduce a hint of romance and . . .

"It does leave me in something of a jam," Kate admitted. "It took me four weeks to find Hollander and get his background checked. I'm not sure even where to look to find a replacement."

He stared at her. "What?" A replacement? For Hollander?

"I really don't want to make the same mistake. On the other hand, this isn't a position I'm willing to entrust to one of the gofers—as if they didn't already have enough to do."

Jed pushed both Monday and dinner completely out of

his thoughts. "Wait, you're not serious, are you? God, you *are*."

She looked confused. "Serious about . . . ?"

"Hiring a replacement for Bob Hollander!" Jed couldn't keep his volume down. It was all he could do to keep the four-letter adjectives out.

She recoiled slightly from the force of his words, but otherwise stood her ground. "Oh, Jericho, you didn't honestly think I wouldn't replace him?"

"Yes, I did. After last night's disaster—"

"Our funding is based on the terms of the agreement you signed," Kate told him. "Production would be shut down so fast if word got out—"

"Word wouldn't get out. For christsake, half of the crew thought Hollander was my lover."

Kate laughed—a burst of uncontrolled emotion. "Oh, my God. They did?"

"No one knew why he was sharing my trailer, and *I* sure as hell didn't tell 'em the truth." Jed ran his hands down his face as he took a deep breath. Shouting about this was going to get him nowhere. "Look. Kate. What do I have to do to convince you that I'm not going to put this film into jeopardy?"

She was already shaking her head.

"How about we make a deal? How about you waive my twenty-four-hour supervision for the remainder of the shoot, and I won't press charges against O'Laughlin Productions for last night's incident?"

It was her turn to be shocked. "Press charges?" She laughed in disbelief. "Weren't you just the one who said everything that happened is over now? It's behind us?"

"Obviously it's not behind us if you're gonna insist on hiring another Nazi to follow me into the bathroom whenever I have to take a crap."

Kate was watching him as if she were trying to figure out the best way to crawl into his head and read his thoughts. "You don't want this story playing on CNN's Headline News any more than *I* do." She pushed her telephone across her desk toward him. "I'm calling your bluff, Beaumont," she said, her velvet voice in direct contrast to her steely words. "Go ahead. File charges. And in case you haven't thought it through, you should probably be aware that the media feeding frenzy and all the negative attention that will follow violates terms six and seven of our agreement. You'll be in breach of your contract, and you *will* lose this role."

Jed didn't let himself blink. He didn't let anything he was thinking show as he reached for the phone and dialed. "So I'll lose the role. I'm past the point where I give a damn," he lied smoothly. "Hell, I'll earn far more than union scale in the settlement. And you know there *will* be a settlement."

Out in California, his agent picked up the phone. "Stapleton."

"Yeah, hi, Ron, it's Jericho. Sorry to call you so early, but we've run into a little problem out here that I thought you should know about and—"

On the other side of the desk, Kate couldn't stand it any longer. She jumped up and grabbed the telephone receiver away from him. "Ron, Jericho's going to have to call you back."

Breathing hard, she hung up the phone, then turned to glare at Jed. "God *damn* you." For one long, stretched-out moment, Jed thought she would pick up the phone and throw it at him. "You're an actor. You're probably the best actor I've ever met. And that really sucks when it comes time to negotiate with you, because I never know when you're acting and when it's real." Her eyes narrowed. "But it's not real, is it? I jumped the gun, didn't I? You might've told Ron about what happened, but you weren't going to do anything about it."

She pointed her finger at him. "I know you're not doing

this for the money. I know you're here because you want
this part. You know and I know that you could kill this entire movie right here and right now. You can call your
agent, and yes, we'll probably settle out of court. And you
can get even more revenge, because the legal fees'll wipe
us out. You'll shut this production down. Except—as long
as we're threatening each other here—be assured that if
you were to do this, the entire world would find out that
you signed a contract admitting that you required around-
the-clock supervision—"

"I didn't admit anything by signing that—"

Kate didn't stop, she just got louder, shouting over him.
"And the producer of your next project—assuming that
there is a next project—will think, Gee, that's a good idea,
and he'll cover his ass the way I covered mine, and you'll
find yourself right back where you started, peeing into a
cup every morning and having your trailer searched every
night. Except next time around, who knows what lousy
role you'll have to suck up and take? All I know is that it
won't be a role like Laramie."

She shoved the telephone closer to him. "You're not going
to call Ron back. And if you *do* call him, you're not going to
have him call your lawyer and press charges. You fooled me
for a minute, Beaumont. Your acting is brilliant, but I know
too much about you. You'd sell your soul to the devil for this
role, if you had to. You're not going to throw it away now.
You love Laramie as much as I do."

So now what? She had him pegged. Hell, she had him
nailed to the wall. For a half a second, Jed actually considered picking up the phone and calling Ron. For a half a
second, he considered taking the money—if only to prove
to Kate O'Laughlin that she was wrong.

But she wasn't wrong. She was right. Playing Laramie
meant more to him than money. It meant more to him than
his pride.

Jed sat there as she glared across her desk at him. She

was leaning slightly forward, supporting herself with both hands, fingers splayed across her desk. He'd pissed her off, and now she was ready to do battle. She'd fight him to the death, if need be.

Perfect. He'd come in here planning to win her over, soften her up, make friends. Instead he'd managed to completely alienate her. Now she looked at him, and she didn't just see a loser. Now she saw the loser who had threatened the existence of her movie, the sorry-assed loser whose threats were nothing but an empty bluff.

He knew the smartest thing he could do was apologize and get the hell out of there.

But he couldn't do it. Because although she had won, her position had been considerably weakened. If he had any chance at all of negotiating, it was going to happen now.

"I want doors on both of my bathrooms," Jed said quietly, fighting the anger that licked through him at the thought that such a thing would have to be negotiated. "And I want 'em there before I go to bed tonight."

Kate nodded tersely. "All right."

He looked her in the eye and didn't try to hide his distaste for this entire situation. "I also want veto power in regards to Hollander's replacement. And don't even think about hiring someone from an ad in the back pages of *Mercenary* magazine."

Kate sat down as if her knees had suddenly given out. She, too, spoke quietly, as if she'd had more than enough shouting for the day. "I was thinking about trying to find someone who'd worked in a rehab center. Someone who would know what the issues are, without the drill-sergeant attitude and the handcuffs."

"Handcuffs are no problem—as long as my supervisor is named Trixie and wears high-heeled boots and carries a whip. Do we have a deal regarding my veto power?"

"No. I'll certainly make arrangements for you to meet the candidates, but ultimately the choice will be mine."

"Yeah, why stop when you're on a roll? You did so well with your last pick." Jed couldn't keep his mouth shut.

She straightened a pile of papers and files that were on her desk. "Win the Oscar, Mr. Beaumont," she said tightly. "You'll be in a far better negotiating position then."

"Better than lying naked on my back with my hands cuffed and chained to the wall?" Jed stopped himself and stood up. It was probably time to leave—before he got even more blunt and honest. But then it occurred to him: "What's going to happen until the replacement shows up?"

She looked up at him and spread her hands in a shrug. "I don't know. I haven't gotten that far yet. I'm going to have to talk to Victor. Until then, maybe one of the gofers would want to earn some overtime."

"Yeah, the average age of the gofers is what? Twenty-two? I don't know whether to laugh or be insulted that you're considering letting one of them be my baby-sitter. You know Tony offered me dope and a hit from his hip flask three different times this morning."

Kate shot out of her chair as if her underpants were on fire. "He *what*?"

Jed backed toward the door. "Hey, it's not a big deal. I think he didn't know what to say around me, so he offered what he considered to be a refreshment. He's not a bad kid. It wasn't as if he was trying to mess me up."

Kate picked up her phone and dialed. "Hi, Annie. You know the gofer named Tony?" She paused. "Tony Evans. That's him. Give him his walking papers, please."

"Whoa," Jed said. "Wait a minute."

But Kate wasn't listening. "Yeah, that's right, and you can tell him that this is a drug-free set. Tell him he's welcome to come and talk to me, but that's not going to change anything."

"Kate, I didn't tell you that so you'd fire the kid!" He might as well have been invisible for all of the attention she paid him.

"Yeah," she said into the telephone, to her assistant, "and find a replacement. We had a bunch of applications come in from people who live here in town. Stress the fact that there will be no drugs on my set. And then come to my office, please." Kate hung up the phone.

Jed stared at her. "I can't believe you did that."

"Why?" she said. "You want him around to be your supplier?"

"That's not funny."

"It's at least as funny as most of the things that come out of your mouth." She reached into the bottom drawer of her desk and took out a urine test kit. "I think you know what to do with this."

"I know what I'd *like* to do with it."

"See what I mean?" She pushed it across her desk, closer to him. "You're a real laugh riot, too."

He pushed the urine collector back toward her. "This isn't necessary. I told you about Tony. I'm not trying to hide anything. I'd have to be pretty stupid to use what Tony offered and then tell you about it."

Kate picked up the plastic-wrapped urine test kit and put it down—very firmly—on the edge of the desk near Jed. "Here are some facts. I'm sorry for what happened to you last night, but I don't trust you. I do trust the lab. As far as how stupid you are—I suppose that could be countered by asking how stupid I would be *not* to test you."

Jed sat there.

Kate came around her desk, picked up the test kit, and placed it into his hands. "Get busy." She breezed toward the door. "I'll have Annie escort you to the men's room. By default, she'll be spending the rest of the day with you while I figure out what to do about tonight. In the meantime, try not to act too much like a snake, will you? She's really shy, and if you scare her, I swear, I'll break your knees."

Jed stood up. "Sorry, you can't break my knees. According to my contract, the only thing you're entitled to break are my balls."

She didn't blink, but her telltale blush gave her away. "Oh, and one more thing. I want to see you this evening at the dailies."

No way. Jed had a policy of never watching footage shot during the day. All of the mistakes glared without the gloss of editing and musical score. The few times he'd watched dailies, he'd gotten the king of all tension headaches. "Sorry, I've got an AA meeting tonight, and according to my contract, I can't miss it."

"I'll write you a permission slip," she said. "I want you at the dailies."

"I don't watch 'em," he told her. "I can barely bring myself to watch a movie's final cut."

"Well, tonight you're going to have to get tough. There's something I need you to see. Be there at seven-thirty."

"Gee, sorry, you left the mandatory viewing of dailies clause off that contract addendum. I'm not going."

Kate smiled. It was far too sweet a smile. "It also doesn't say anywhere in the addendum that I have to put the door back on your bathroom."

Jed stopped short.

"If you show up at seven-thirty, I'll give the work order. If not . . ." She shrugged and opened the office door.

Her ghostly assistant, Annie, was standing there, about to knock.

"Good," Kate said briskly. "You're here. Please escort Mr. Beaumont to the men's room and then to the Grill for lunch. Stay with him until I tell you otherwise. And call me if he gives you any trouble." She turned to Jed. "Don't make her call me."

Kate closed the door behind him, leaving him standing

in the outer office with Annie, who looked as if she were going to faint.

"Wow," he said. "I think Kate's starting to like me."

Victor didn't hesitate. "No."

Kate took a step backward. "No? Just . . . no? Automatically no? Can't you at least pretend to think about it?"

"I don't need to think about it." Victor leaned over and started taking off his boots. "I'm not the one who's got a problem with Beaumont, remember? You are."

"Victor, please. Just for tonight? I've asked everyone else I could think of. I'd trust Nate or Ethan, but both their wives work nights as nurses over at the hospital. They need to be home to watch their kids. Talking about desperate—I even called Harlan Kincaid."

"Who?"

"*Pastor* Kincaid?"

"Why can't he do it?" Victor tossed his boots into the corner of the motel room, and started stripping off his T-shirt.

"He's busy. He's got a life of his own. I don't know. He didn't tell me specifically, and I didn't think it was appropriate to demand why. He said he'd be available to stay with Jericho during the day every now and then. And he gave me a good lead on a permanent replacement for Hollander but . . ." Kate took a deep breath. "Victor. I'm asking you to do me a favor. If you don't help me, *I'm* going to have to stay with Laramie—I mean, Jericho—tonight, and will you please stop taking off your clothes?"

He took off his glasses and set them down on top of the television set. "I have to get into the shower. I'm running really late. Naomi came to town early, and I'm supposed to meet her for dinner in five minutes."

Naomi Michaelson. "Oh," Kate said, the last of her hope dying.

"Look, Katie, I know I'm being a selfish son of a bitch,

but I can't help you out tonight. This girl came here because she wanted to see me. And if things go according to plan, I won't be able to help you out tomorrow or the next night, either. In fact, let's be optimistic here and cross me off your baby-sitter list for the entire month of June and half of July. I'm planning to be very busy at night for the next few weeks. Thank God."

It was going to have to be her. Kate felt sick. *She* was going to have to spend the night with Jericho in his trailer. Not just tonight, but tomorrow night, and the next night, and on and on—until she found a permanent replacement.

Even the lead Harlan Kincaid had given her—a Grady Falls man who was teaching high school up in New York City—wouldn't be available until school let out at the end of June.

"How about asking Russell McCoy to stay with Jericho?" Victor laughed at his joke. "We could get a betting pool going as to which one of 'em would still be alive when we unlocked the trailer door in the morning."

Kate put her head in her hands.

"You know, Jericho put in a performance today that was off the scale," Victor told her. "And this was *after* he'd spent most of a sleepless night in chains. He's going to make this movie *sing*. I know you're still skeptical, but I'm telling you, he's fabulous. He knows what I want before *I* know what I want."

He started taking off his Bermuda shorts, and Kate stood up and turned away. "This is going to be a great movie, right?" she asked him. "And all these problems I'm dealing with—it's all going to be worth it?"

Victor didn't answer. He was already in the shower.

Seven

❦──❦

"**O**KAY, HERE'S THE deal," Kate said as she slipped into the restaurant booth across from Jericho. "I'm it."

Jericho didn't stop eating his salad. He didn't even look up. "Are we playing tag or something?"

"No," she said. "I wish this was a game, but it's not. The gofers need supervision themselves, the crew is all union, the actors have enough to worry about, and I wouldn't trust any of the PA's farther than I could throw them—except for Annie, who would go into cardiac arrest if she had to camp out in your trailer all night."

He was looking up at her now, realization dawning in his eyes. Realization and something else. Amusement, maybe. Or some kind of perverse pleasure. A slow smile spread across his face. "*You're* going to be my supervisor?"

Kate nodded briskly, looking everywhere but at his face. Smiles like that should be illegal. "Yes. Until I can find a permanent replacement, it looks like we're stuck with this . . . somewhat awkward situation."

She glanced up at him and saw that his smile had turned into laughter. He had lines at the corners of his eyes that deepened when he laughed, making him somehow—

impossibly—even more good-looking, damn him. He wasn't Virgil Laramie. He *wasn't*.

"It's hardly funny," she said tightly. "We can't spend more than five minutes together without fighting. We're both going to need to cooperate—extensively—to make this work."

"If you cooperate by playing out my female warden fantasy, I can guarantee you the fighting will be a lot more fun."

"There," she said, pointing at him. "That—in the name of cooperation—is exactly what you need to stop doing. Always making suggestive comments thinly veiled as jokes. Saying stuff like that is not going to help this situation."

"Yeah, but it makes you blush. How old are you, anyway? Don't you know the average American woman stops blushing when she reaches seventeen?"

God, she was ten times more tense than she'd ever been in her life, and he was sitting there, lolling back on the padded bench seat of the booth, completely relaxed as if he didn't give a damn about any of this.

Everything about him—right down to the arm he had up along the back of the seat—oozed nonchalant charm. The painfully honest man who'd walked into her office and admitted that he was dreadfully embarrassed was nowhere in sight. Nor was the man who was so angry that his hands shook. And the man with the empty eyes who could have beaten the crap out of enormous Bob Hollander was gone as well.

But that wasn't surprising. Jericho Beaumont was an actor. And right now, he had slipped into his laid-back, easygoing, Hollywood movie star persona. She'd seen it before, on her TV, when he'd appeared on Jay Leno and David Letterman—and when he'd walked into her office that very first time they'd met.

"So, in other words," she said, "you're admitting that

you say all those rude things because you enjoy offend-ing me."

Jericho ate some more of his salad thoughtfully. "Yeah, I guess I am admitting that."

What would it take to make him drop character? She'd done it before, she realized. She'd taken him by surprise, and the easygoing movie star had morphed into someone else. Someone with a hot temper, a sharp tongue, and a truckload of anger buried deep down inside. Someone who was not at all easygoing and relaxed. Someone with the rather frightening ability to shut himself down and feel nothing at all.

Someone she suspected was quite possibly the real Jericho Beaumont.

If there *was* such a thing as real when it came to Jericho.

Kate wanted to see if she could make that person appear.

"Let's make a deal," she said sweetly. "Right here—right now. You stop pushing my buttons with your sleazy innuendos, and I won't kill you. And, as a bonus, I won't rub your nose in the fact that you're arrogant, ignorant, and rude when I prove you wrong—which I'm sure will happen repeatedly as we spend time together."

She watched for his facade to dissolve, wanting to see it when it happened.

Jericho laughed, but there was an edge of disbelief to it. "Well, *that* wasn't at all hostile, was it?" he said. "Shit—aren't you supposed to get some kind of tiara after you're crowned the Queen of the Bitches?"

Jackpot.

There he was, the real man, gritting his teeth and holding onto his salad fork so tightly it seemed all too likely he was going to bend it in half.

"Okay," Kate said. "Now that we're both here, let's cut the crap, shall we?"

He was silent for several long moments, but then he

blinked and laughed. He put down his fork and leaned back, his eyes narrowing slightly as he studied her. "Okay," he said. "Let's."

She studied him just as carefully, wishing she could get inside his head. She would give nearly anything to know, just once, what he was really thinking. Because it was entirely possible that this, too, was nothing more than an act.

"I've come up empty-handed in my search for a replacement for Hollander," she told him. "So far the only candidate's not available for another three weeks. And even if I find someone tomorrow, I'll have to run reference checks. And he'll be required to submit to drug and alcohol testing as well, and it'll take several days to get *those* results back from the lab, so. . . ."

"So in other words, you're going to be bringing more than just an overnight bag to my trailer."

Kate nodded.

"You know, it occurs to me this is going to be your big opportunity," Jericho said quietly. "I know you don't like me and you don't trust me—you haven't exactly tried to hide that. If you really want me off the set so badly, what's to stop you from saying you caught me with a bottle of Jack Daniel's? Where that bottle came from would be my word against yours."

"I'd *never* do that. That would be lying." Kate was shocked.

"My God," Jericho said slowly. "The blushing-good-girl thing isn't an act, is it?"

Kate raised her chin. "Look. If you slip up, then you're gone," she said heatedly. "It's that simple. I'm not actively seeking ways to get rid of you. If I were, I would've had Bob Hollander tie you up, toss you into his trunk, and take you with him when he left."

Jericho lifted his hands in mock surrender. "All right. I just wanted to point out if you were thinking of doing something like that, you should remember I'm carrying a trump card." He rested his arms on the table. His wrists were still red and sore, as if he'd rubbed them raw trying to get free last night. He shifted, turning his arms over to examine them ruefully. "Now the makeup head thinks I'm into B&D. You should've seen what she had to do to cover this up."

"I *am* sorry."

"But not sorry enough."

Kate was silent.

He glanced down at his wrists again. "You know, my old man had this ugly yellow dog—some kind of big, mean mixed-breed, chained up in the corner of our yard. He had a doghouse, but he only used it in the winter. The rest of the time he just lay down and slept in the dust. But during the day, when he wasn't sleeping, he was tugging on the end of that chain. He'd worn the grass away in a big, dry circle around the tree he was chained to."

Jericho paused. "I remember—I must've been around nine years old—my brother Leroy threw a book report I'd written for school into the back of that doghouse, and I knew, I just *knew* I was screwed. That dog was nearly as mean as my daddy. He snarled at me every time I tried to get close.

"I didn't have time to do the assignment over. It was only about twenty minutes before school started, and I just stood there staring into that dog's eyes, knowing he was going to enjoy biting me if I got close enough, and wondering what the hell it was made a dog—or man—turn pure mean like that."

Jericho looked down at his wrists again, smiling tightly. "Last night I found out." He looked away. "You must be hungry. You haven't had dinner yet, have you?"

Kate glanced at her watch, wishing it weren't so late, wishing he had told her the end of his story. Had he gotten into trouble for the missed assignment? Had he gotten a failing grade? If his father was as mean as that dog had been, how had he dealt with that bad grade? Had he hit Jericho? Or worse . . . ?

But the dailies were going to start in ten minutes. There was no time to sit and talk. Or eat. "I'm going to have to grab something later," she told him, sliding out of the booth. "We need to go."

"I hate to break it to you," Jericho said, purposely not moving, "but someone voided your dire threat by putting the door on my bathroom before I even left for dinner."

"Actually," Kate informed him, "I told the crew to go ahead and do the work so they could be done for the night. It didn't seem fair they should just stand around on hold until seven-thirty. And I figured the doors could just as easily come off again tomorrow. So I'm sorry, but my threat stands."

Jericho still didn't budge. He just sat there, gazing up at her, and Kate felt uncertainty slither through her. If he were smart—and she knew he was very smart—it wouldn't take much for him to realize that since she was going to be sharing his trailer at night, *she* would probably appreciate the privacy provided by having a door on the bathroom even more than he would. In fact, she would find sharing a trailer damn near impossible without a bathroom door. Jericho could make things extremely difficult by refusing to watch the dailies and forcing her to carry through with her threat.

And she'd have to carry through. She would lose what little authority she had if she didn't.

"Let's go," she said, adding quietly, "please."

Finally, *finally* he put down his napkin and stood up. He headed for the door, and Kate tried not to collapse from relief. Dear God, this had been one hell of a trying day.

Jericho actually held the door for her as they left the Grill.

They walked in silence for a few moments, heading

down Main Street toward the VFW Hall that was serving as a screening room.

Kate couldn't hold her question in any longer. "So did you get in trouble for not handing in that book report?"

He glanced at her, as if surprised she was still thinking about that. "Actually, I handed it in," he told her. "It was wrinkled and smelled bad, and the teacher made me copy it over during recess, but I got the assignment in on time."

Kate studied his face in the lingering twilight. "How on earth did you get it out of the doghouse?"

He gazed back at her for several long moments before answering. "I made the dog chase me around and around the tree until he'd wound his chain so tight, he couldn't move. He wasn't the smartest animal on the planet. And then while he was straining against about four inches of chain, I went into the doghouse, grabbed my report, and ran like hell."

"Pretty resourceful thinking—especially for a nine-year-old."

Jericho's smile was crooked—a far cry from the toothy movie star grins he'd been flashing her in the Grill. "You had to keep on your toes, living in my house. I learned to be pretty resourceful—if you can call it that—early on."

"Did you have just that one brother—Leroy?" Kate asked.

"Two brothers and a sister—Tom, Leroy, and Louise. All older by at least five years. We were a textbook example of a dysfunctional family—Tom was the golden boy, straight A's, sports hero; Leroy was the scapegoat; Louise the clown. And me, I just learned to disappear."

The lost child. The one most likely to follow in the footsteps of an alcoholic parent. Kate cleared her throat. "I read somewhere you left home when you were sixteen."

"That's right." He gave her another half smile. "I'd had just about all I could take by then. Tom was living in San Francisco at the time, so I headed west and—" He stopped himself abruptly. "Anyway, what I should have done with that dog was get a sledgehammer from the shed, break that chain, and set him free." He gave a snort of laughter. "And then go after Leroy with the sledgehammer."

Kate looked at him. His words were obviously meant to be a joke, but she had to wonder. She remembered the way he'd gone after Bob Hollander, remembered the flatness in his eyes.

Jericho still made himself disappear, nowadays by distancing himself from his anger and emotions. Shutting himself off like that couldn't possibly be a good thing. What did he do with all his rage? Did he force it deep inside of him to fester and ferment? And if so, what would happen when the pressure built to the point where he couldn't hold it in any longer?

Yes, he'd learned to be resourceful living in that house as a child. But she had to wonder just what else he might've learned as well.

Kate smelled like sunblock.

Jed sat down next to her in the VFW Hall as the lights went out and the dailies began.

One of the production assistants was passing out popcorn, and the scent of it combined with the slightly sweet smell of Kate's sun lotion pulled him rather effectively back to his early days in L.A. It brought him back to a time when he was working as a waiter to pay his rent, a time when he used most of his earnings to pay for his head shots and résumés. He'd always scrounged together enough cash to get into the movies, though, and he'd also always managed to find some suntanned, sweet-smelling beach bunny willing to accompany him. However, in those days dinner and a movie meant getting a bag of popcorn at the show.

Kate passed him some of the popcorn, and he automatically put his arm around the back of her chair.

He realized what he'd done as she leaned closer to whisper, "Okay, now, watch this."

Her attention was on the screen, thank God, and not on the fact that he'd gone into autopilot and made a move on her. But before he could pull his arm away, he, too, found himself captivated by the rough footage on the screen.

There was no music, the foley guys hadn't yet added any sharpened sounds, and the edit of the scene was extremely rough. But the camera had focused on the face of a young girl, and for several long seconds, Jed didn't recognize that the girl was Susie McCoy.

She seemed so completely natural, he felt almost as if he were watching *Candid Camera*.

Jed turned to find Kate gazing at him instead of the screen. "But . . ." He shook his head. What had happened? Whatever Susie was doing when this particular scene was shot, she'd stopped doing it when he'd arrived on set.

"Just watch," Kate whispered.

The footage continued. Contrary to what Jed had believed this afternoon, everything he saw was usable. In fact, it was going to be a challenge for Victor Strauss and his editor to decide which of Susie's takes were the best.

And then, there he was. God, he hated seeing himself on the screen before the movie was fully put together. Jed squinted, watching himself through the haze of his eyelashes.

Kate leaned over toward him again. "Don't watch yourself," she told him. The words "you idiot," weren't said aloud, but they were certainly implied from the tone of her voice. "Watch Susie McCoy."

He saw almost instantly why she had been so intent on him watching this footage. He'd have to be completely blind not to see that Susie was scared to death of him. From this side of the camera, it was more than obvious. She'd been intimidated by him, and that had made her choke.

On the screen, she blew a line, and he could see his own reaction. His body language made it clear he was exasperated as well as completely disgusted. He couldn't have done more damage to the girl if he'd gone up and slapped her across the face.

He remembered the way she'd approached him several days ago and introduced herself. He'd been so into his own agenda that he hadn't even taken the time to give her a smile.

She was a kid, and he'd been treating her like the spawn of Satan. He'd helped cause a tense situation, and the things he'd said and done this morning on set had exacerbated it a thousandfold.

He swore softly.

Susie McCoy was perfect for this part—or at least she would be if he didn't undermine her efforts with every breath he took.

Kate was silent. She didn't say anything at all.

The rest of the dailies were too painful to watch. His attitude toward this girl—whose performance before he'd arrived on set had been truly exceptional—was embarrassing. Jed sat with his eyes closed, rubbing his forehead with one hand, trying to relieve his sudden splitting headache.

It would have been one thing if he'd done this while he was drinking. But he'd been completely, unquestionably sober.

God, he needed a drink. . . .

He felt Kate lightly touch his leg. "I think we can probably go," she leaned close to whisper.

Jed opened his eyes and found himself looking directly at Kate. His arm was still around the back of her chair, and for a moment, she was close enough to kiss.

And he really wanted to kiss her.

Even more than he wanted that drink.

For the briefest moment, he could have sworn he'd

seen an answering yearning in her eyes. But then she stood up, instantly businesslike. Jed followed her out, ducking underneath the light from the projector.

She was silent as they went up the stairs and out onto the sidewalk. She was silent as they headed back down Main Street. True to her word, she had proved him wrong, and she wasn't rubbing his nose in it. She didn't even utter one single "I told you so."

God knew he deserved it.

Kate looked nearly as exhausted as he felt, and he had another twinge of guilt for keeping her running over the past few days, adding his petty and unnecessary demands to her lengthy list of duties as this movie's producer. The mattress, the window shades, the soda in the fridge . . .

She glanced up as if she felt him watching her, and somehow shook off her fatigue. She straightened her shoulders and held her head high, and instantly looked as cool and collected as she always did. And she always *did* look perfectly composed, even in running shorts and a T-shirt, with her hair still damp from her shower, the way it had been that morning.

Jed tried to picture her caught in a rainstorm, soaking wet, bedraggled, but he couldn't do it. Somehow the cloud would know not to rain on her. Or maybe she simply wouldn't do something as inefficient or uncalculated as going out without an umbrella on a potentially rainy day.

He tried to picture her in bed, waking up in the morning, clean of makeup, hair mussed from sleep. That image didn't come easily, either. He had no problem picturing her naked, though, draped across satin sheets—he had *Dead of Night* to thank for that. But sleepy-eyed and warm, ready to snuggle underneath the coziness of bedcovers . . . No, that picture simply didn't come.

She struck him as the kind of woman who would shower after making love, dress, and then drive herself home. Or expect him to do the same if they happened to be in her apartment.

But what would she expect him to do if they were sharing the same trailer for the night?

Jed had to laugh at himself. He was thinking way ahead of this game. Kate didn't even like him. There was no way she was going to climb into bed with him tonight. Thinking along those lines was only going to get him into trouble.

Besides, he had something else he had to do before he could focus on his game of one-on-one with Kate O'Laughlin. Someone else he had to talk to.

They were approaching the Grill, and he could see many of the cast and crew inside, still hanging out. Jamaal Hawkes was there, sitting at a window booth with one of the makeup assistants. Kate's assistant Annie was surrounded by other female members of the crew. A table of male crew members sat nearby, watching them.

Riva Turner and Russell McCoy were off to the side, at a table in a corner of the room. Russell's posture was aggressive, and Riva looked as if her shoulders were about to cave in.

And several tables away, Susie McCoy was by herself, unenthusiastically toying with a piece of blueberry pie.

Jed stopped outside the front door and turned toward Kate. "We should go in and get you something to eat."

Kate shook her head. "I can have one of the gofers bring something to your trailer. I know you have things you probably want to do. Lines to learn for tomorrow."

"Actually," he told her. "I'd prefer it if we'd stop. There's someone I have to talk to."

He held the door for her again, and Kate went inside first. Everyone looked up as Jericho followed her, and she realized that over the next few days the two of them were going to be virtually inseparable. To those of the cast and crew who weren't aware of the additional contract stipulations, it was going to look as if they had something going on.

As uncomfortable as that made her feel, she knew Jericho would be far more unhappy if word went out that she was his contract-enforced baby-sitter.

Kate went to the buffet table. Dinner had been cleaned up, but there was a small pile of freshly made, wrapped sandwiches. Kate found one that looked to be chicken salad, and grabbed a cola. She was going to need a little caffeine to get all her work done tonight.

There was pie out on the table, wrapped up and ready to go as well, and she turned to see if Jericho wanted a piece.

But Jericho had crossed the room.

He stood next to Susie McCoy's table. "Mind if I sit for a sec?" he asked in a voice that carried back to Kate.

Susie shook her head, looking for all the world as if she were bracing herself, about to be hit.

Jericho pulled out a chair and sat, as across the room Jamaal Hawkes slid out of his booth. The young actor started to move closer.

"I owe you an apology," Jericho told Susie, still loudly enough for everyone in the Grill to hear. Jamaal stopped moving. "I came into this project with some preconceived ideas about you, and I was way off base." The room was dead silent. Even those who at first had been pretending not to pay attention were now listening. "I thought you couldn't handle this role, but I was wrong. You've got Jane down cold. I'm truly sorry for my inexcusable rudeness. I hope you'll find it in your heart to forgive me."

Susie looked about as dazed as Kate felt. She murmured something that Kate couldn't hear. It seemed to satisfy Jericho, though, because he nodded and stood up. "I'm looking forward to working with you," he told Susie.

And then he was moving back across the room, toward Kate, toward the door. She grabbed her sandwich and soda and followed him outside, hurrying to catch up.

"That was . . ." She was speechless. "Above and beyond the call of duty," she finally managed. "You know, you could have pulled her aside and apologized quietly."

"I insulted the kid in public," Jericho said matter-of-factly. "It's only fair I apologize in public."

Bemused, Kate followed him toward the trailers. Dear God, this had been the longest day of her life. Starting when she walked in on Jericho Beaumont chained and naked in his trailer, she'd seen more facets to him than she'd ever dreamed existed.

He slowed his stride as he realized she was struggling to keep up, and in the evening shadows, he was suddenly Laramie.

His voice was as soft as the night around them. "Thanks for making me sit through the dailies." He smiled then, Laramie's smile, crooked and slightly self-mocking. "Believe it or not, the word thanks *is* in my working vocabulary."

Kate forced herself to stop gaping at him and start walking again, determined not to give herself away. Lord knew, she could hold her own against Jericho Beaumont. But when he started acting human, when he started acting like Laramie, she was in big trouble.

Eight

ᕫᕫ ᕬ

WHEN KATE WAS thirteen, she often baby-sat at
night for a young couple who lived down the street. They
both sang in a community chorus, and every Tuesday evening she would bring her homework over to their house.
She'd sit at their dining room table and work after she'd
put their two-year-old daughter, Laura, to bed. It was one
of the *good* memories she had of her early teenage years—
a time she tried hard not to think too much about.

She now sat with her papers and files scattered across
the table in the main room of Jericho's trailer, wishing that
Jericho would be as quietly obedient as Laura had been.

She'd sat, trying to work, while he reviewed pages of
dialogue. He'd muttered and tried different inflections
even while taking a shower. She'd kept her gaze carefully
on all of the day's reports and tried not to think about the
water sluicing down over his perfect body. She hadn't
dared do more than glance up as the bathroom door—the
one she'd ordered installed just a few hours ago—had
opened, as he'd gone, still muttering, into the back room
with only a towel tied loosely around his hips.

God forbid he should give her another one of those

melting looks he'd sent her way right before they left the dailies.

For one split second, she'd imagined that he was going to lean forward and kiss her.

And she'd sat there like an idiot, half hoping that he'd do it. God, what a mess *that* would be. She was nervous enough about spending the night in his trailer. She could not—*could not*—let sex play any part in their working relationship. It would blur the lines between supervisor and supervisee—which, of course, would be exactly what Jericho wanted.

The telephone rang, and Kate picked it up, grateful for a legitimate distraction. "Hello?"

There was silence on the other end. "I'm sorry," a male voice finally said. "I must have the wrong number. I was looking for Jed?"

"Who?"

"Jericho. Sorry. *Jericho* Beaumont. I'm sorry if I have the wrong number. I wrote it on a piece of paper, but then spilled some coffee and . . ." The voice had a distinctly New York accent. "I'm having a little trouble reading it."

"You got it right—he's here. Whom shall I say is calling?"

"It's David. Look, I know it's late. I can call tomorrow. I mean, if this is an inconvenient time . . ." His voice trailed off tactfully.

He thought she and Jericho were . . .

Kate nearly jumped out of her seat. "No! No, this is fine. Let me call Jericho. He's in the other room," she made a point to tell him. "Jericho—David's on the phone?"

Jericho came out of the back room wearing only a pair of running shorts. His hair was wet from his shower and slicked back from his face, his tanned skin still moist.

He glanced down at all her work spread out on the table as he took the phone. It was a wall phone, and there was nowhere he could go for privacy. Still, it was clear that he thought the idea of her moving her stuff into the other room was ludicrous. So he stood directly beside her as he spoke. "Hey, how's it going? You checking up on me?"

Jericho was standing so close, Kate could hear David's voice, scratchy and thin through the cheap phone speaker. "You didn't call. I always figure when you don't call it's either going really well or really badly. And right now I'm betting it's really excellent. Who is she? Some impossibly hot actress?"

Jericho sat down across from her, on the other side of the booth, lifting the curled phone cord up and over her head. It stretched, quivering, across the table.

"Her name is Kate, and she's my producer."

Kate waited for Jericho to say more—to explain that although it was after ten o'clock at night, she was there on business.

Instead he added, "My impossibly hot producer." He gave her a smile that would melt a mastodon. It was one hundred and fifty percent Jericho Beaumont, and completely resistible.

Kate focused her attention on her work. She really didn't care if he wanted his friend to think they were involved.

David spoke, but now that Jericho had moved, she could only hear the timbre of his voice. She could no longer make out his words. Not that she cared.

Whatever David had said, Jericho smiled again. "Yes, she's blond and beautiful."

Kate glanced up to find him watching her. His eyes were warm, his gaze skimming her body. She felt herself tense, and had to hold tightly to her pencil to keep herself from crossing her arms. God help her if he found out how uncomfortable his wandering gaze made her feel. She could handle being looked at out on the street, out in a crowd. But one-on-one like this made her feel twelve years old again.

He smiled. "And, yes, I happen to find her incredibly

attractive." His words were more for her than for David's ears.

"It's the price you have to pay for being a movie star," he continued. "Beautiful women throwing themselves at you, day and night. And every now and then one comes along that you just can't ignore."

She put down her pencil and gave him her best Frau Steinbreaker look. But she knew it would do little good, considering the blush that was heating her cheeks.

His smile widened into a grin. "Hey, you're a shrink," he said into the phone. "What's your take on a twenty-nine-year-old who blushes?" He laughed at whatever David said. "He offers his condolences. I don't know where he gets the idea, but he seems to think that you're—in his words—dead meat with me around. And, yeah, I have to admit I enjoy watching you react." He pulled the receiver closer to his mouth. "Not you. *Kate*. I meant, it's fun to make her blush."

He picked up the pencil she had put down, saw that it had her name printed on it in shiny gold letters, and glanced up at her again, lifting an eyebrow.

"David, here's another clue in the incredible Kate mystery. She has pencils with her name on 'em. What's your take on *that*?" He paused, listening for a moment, then again directed his conversation to Kate. "He says, in his esteemed professional opinion, it probably means that you have a close personal relationship with a six-year-old."

"She's seven," Kate said. "But close enough. My niece, Kerrie, gave me those for Christmas."

"Did you hear that?" Jericho said into the phone. "Uh-huh . . . He says the fact that you actually use 'em is extremely telling. He says I should—" He stopped himself. "No way. He's insane. In a sad twist of fate, the psychologist has finally lost his mind."

He laughed again, and Kate had to look away. She could resist Jericho Beaumont, it was true, but this was

Jericho Beaumont set on heavy stun. She longed for a pair of protective goggles.

"Yeah, why *did* you call?" he asked his friend. At least she thought this David was a friend. Although Jericho's lighthearted, best-friend–style banter could be just another act. God knows he'd stopped well short of telling the truth as to why she was in his trailer at this time of night.

Kate tried to focus on the cameraman's report.

Jericho laughed. "No kidding!" He tugged at the papers Kate was holding. "Hey, David and his wife, Alison, are going to have another baby in . . . when's the date?" He paused. "In October. Man, that's great news!"

He stood up, flipping the phone cord back over her head as he pulled it to the little sink and refrigerator. It made it, but just barely. Kate scrunched back into the corner of the booth to avoid being bumped by the cord.

She tried not to watch the muscles in Jericho's back as he stood at the tiny counter and fixed himself something to eat. She tried not to pay any attention at all to his legs. God, he had nice legs.

He was *not* Laramie. *Not Laramie*.

But he looked just like Laramie, smiled just like Laramie. And the way he'd apologized to Susie McCoy—that was something Laramie might've done.

He was mostly silent now, letting David talk. From what Kate could glean from the few words he spoke, David and his wife had been trying to have a second child for quite a number of years. Jericho asked about Alison, asked about a project David was running at the state penitentiary—apparently Alison wasn't thrilled to have him up there counseling prisoners three times a week, but at least a funding grant he'd applied for had come in.

Finally the conversation ended. Jericho turned to hang up the phone, and Kate glued her gaze back onto her papers.

"Want some salad?" He was off the phone, and there was only one person he could be talking to.

"No thanks." She answered automatically, but then did a double take. Did he say . . . "Salad?"

Sure enough, the man who'd once been known as the unofficial spokesperson for the Hostess Twinkie had fixed a large bowl of garden greens for himself. As she watched, he added dressing and, picking up the bowl, leaned back against the counter and began to eat.

"Yeah, my late-night snack used to be pure sugar," he said between mouthfuls of lettuce. "Back in the bad old days."

"I remember. I read somewhere that your movie contracts included demands for name-brand junk food. In astonishing quantities."

Jericho rolled his eyes. "I learned about nutrition in rehab. Most alcoholics—and recovering alcoholics—suffer sugar imbalances. Lots of 'em—us—are hypoglycemic, and I'm no exception. Hypoglycemics crave sugar. You should've seen me—I used to eat an entire half gallon of ice cream in one sitting. Complete overload. I sucked down anything sweet that crossed my path. I always carried M&M's. And alcohol. Alcohol turns straight to sugar in your system, you know."

"I didn't."

"While I was in rehab, I was put on this low-sugar diet. I had small meals—things like salads, with high vegetable content. Small amounts, served often. Not just three times a day but maybe even six or seven.

"Nowadays, I don't eat ice cream. I stay away from all kinds of sugar and high starches that turn to sugar easily. And I've stuck with the lots-of-small-meals concept—I think it really works. It seems to help curb my craving for sugar—and for alcohol."

Kate couldn't keep the question in. "Do you still crave alcohol?"

Jericho was quiet for a long moment. Then he laughed ruefully. "Hell, I don't know how to answer that. I guess since you're my producer you might get scared if I answered it truthfully, so maybe we should just change the subject. Or maybe I should lie and say no. Nope, not me. No, ma'am, I don't crave a drink. Not anymore. I'm completely beyond that." He looked up at her. "How'd I do?"

Kate shook her head.

"Yeah." He stabbed more salad onto his fork. "That's a tough one to swallow. You know, if you weren't my producer, I'd tell you that for some people, the craving never goes away. It's always back there, lurking, day after day. And if I *really* wanted to scare you to death, I might even tell you that there hasn't been one single day in the past five years, four months, and twenty-two days, that I haven't wished for a drink. And that's why some very smart person made up that slogan, one day at a time. See, instead of saying that I've got to stay sober another five years— which sounds pretty impossible—all I have to do is make it through today. Hell, all I have to do is get through the next few hours without taking a drink. And then I have to get through the *next* few hours until another day is done. I can handle a few hours, and even if I can't, I know I can handle a few minutes. And when you add all those minutes and hours together, presto change-o, what do you know? They become five years, four months, and twenty-two days. And you've got yourself a real life instead of a blur of binges and hangovers."

He ate more of his salad before looking up at her again. "So. Now you know. Kind of makes you want to call for ol' Bob and his handcuffs, huh?"

He was trying to make a joke out of it, but she could see some of the vulnerability he used for playing Laramie in his eyes. But this time it was real. He'd opted to tell her the truth, and Kate knew that it was a truth some people would disapprove of.

It was funny, actually. Jericho covered himself with his movie star persona to bluff his way through life, thinking his laid-back, friendly, good-old-boy self-confidence and control would make others perceive him to be strong. Yet when he admitted he was weak, when he bypassed the glitter and theatrics and tossed the naked, ugly truth out onto the floor, whether it was telling her this now, or admitting to Susie McCoy that he'd been wrong, *that* was when he showed his real strength.

Kate could only imagine the courage it must've taken him to get through . . . what had he said? Five years, four months, and twenty-two days.

Calling back Bob Hollander was the last thing she wanted to do. What she really wanted was to give him a hug.

But Kate had no doubt in her mind that he would take that absolutely the wrong way.

Instead she cleared her throat and let a little of Frau Steinbreaker slip into her voice—but only because he was expecting her to. "You know, I've done my research, and frankly, if you'd told me you *didn't* crave alcohol, *then* I would've been worried.

"I've heard that recovering alcoholics often are vulnerable at the five-year mark of their sobriety," she continued. "If people are going to slip, they're more likely to do it then."

"Yeah, I've heard that, too." Jericho shrugged. "But I'm doing fine."

"You're not really into AA, are you?" she asked. "Some people I know go to meetings all the time."

He shrugged again. "I was in the program while I was in rehab, of course, and then for the first year and a half after I got out. But it takes a lot of time, and there's so many rules and . . . I found I did just as well white-knuckling it—you know, staying clean on my own."

"That sounds pretty risky."

He nodded. "Yeah. But I make a point to know when the local meetings are. If I feel like I need some help, I stop in."

Jericho smiled, but it was Laramie's smile, and for several dizzying moments, Kate experienced the odd sensation of looking into the eyes of a man that she'd created. Her perfect man. Broken, but beginning to heal, battered, but not completely defeated. Strong enough to reach up from the pits of despair and grab hold of a thread of hope.

Her heart flipped, and she had to look away.

"Don't you ever change into comfortable clothes at night?" he asked. She could feel him still watching her. "It's after ten, and you're still wearing work clothes."

Kate purposely didn't look up. "That's because I'm still working."

Jericho laughed ruefully. "O-kay. So much for pretending that we're actually enjoying each other's company."

He turned toward the sink, and as she watched beneath lowered lashes, he washed his salad bowl and the fork, and set them in the dish drain to dry. He stood there for a moment, until she glanced up again.

"Do you have a lot left to do?" He added apologetically, "because I didn't get a whole hell of a lot of sleep last night, and I've got maybe three minutes left in me before I crash."

Kate swept up her papers, evened off the edges, and put them in her briefcase. "I've been done for a while," she admitted, gathering up her purse and the gym bag into which she'd stuffed pajamas, her toothbrush, and clothes for the next morning. "Do you need to bring anything over with you?"

"No, I'm all set." It was freaky—this stilted, too-politeness that they'd suddenly fallen into. They were going to go into the other trailer now, and sleep in virtually the same room. It was unavoidably uncomfortable, and they were both playing it as if it were completely normal.

But then, Jericho neatly broke the odd mood. "Unless . . ." he said. "You've got the condoms in your bag, right?"

Kate dropped her keys.

He laughed at the look on her face. "Just kidding."

"Very funny." She turned off the light to hide the color that was rising in her cheeks.

Kate followed him out of the trailer. The night was like a blanket, solid and damp and hot after the air-conditioned coolness inside.

"You've got to admit, there's something about this that feels, well . . . really naughty."

Kate laughed nervously. "Naughty. Now, there's a word I haven't heard in a long time."

"But it kind of fits, doesn't it? You don't happen to sleepwalk, do you?" He stood back to let her go up the steps to the other trailer.

"Nope."

"Too bad."

Finally she got the key into the lock and the door open. She gestured for Jericho to go inside first.

"Do you snore? Hollander snored. First time I heard it, I thought someone was using a chain saw outside the trailer."

It seemed impossible, and Kate knew Jericho would never admit it, but he was nervous, too.

She locked the door behind her and turned on the light. "I don't snore," she told him. "Of course, it's been years since I've slept in the same room with . . ." She cut herself off. God, why was she telling him that?

"Really?" Too late. "Years?"

She turned toward him briskly. "Why don't you use the bathroom first?"

Jed lay in the dark, just listening as Kate got ready for bed. She turned off the light before she opened the bathroom door, and he heard her move quietly through the other room, heard the rustle of sheets as she climbed into bed.

And then there was silence.

One minute became two, and he tried not to think about her, lying there, mere yards away from him, wearing . . . what? Definitely not an oversized T-shirt. She wasn't the type. And it was too hot for flannel pajamas. That left . . . some kind of cotton nightie? Or maybe a transparent baby-doll with a matching G-string . . . yeah, right. Dream on.

He tried to think about something else, and found himself focusing on the way he and Kate had had to wait outside the other trailer tonight as Nate and Ethan searched it. After they'd stopped at the Grill and he'd apologized to Susie, he'd come back to find *that* magic.

It was damned unsettling to have all of his belongings and clothing constantly rifled through. Nothing was ever in the same position. Everything he owned was handled and examined. It set his teeth on edge.

But thinking about it wasn't going to help him fall asleep. His thoughts of Kate weren't going to put him to sleep, either, but at least they weren't unpleasant.

He tried to picture exactly how she was lying, out there in the other room. As nine minutes became ten, Jed couldn't stand it another second. "Kate. Are you awake?"

He heard her shift slightly. "No."

"Do you sleep on your back or on your side?"

Silence. It stretched on far too long. But then she laughed and asked incredulously, "Why?"

"I'm curious."

"Did you ask Bob that, when he was sleeping in here with you?"

Jed laughed. "Not a chance. I just lay here and prayed that he wouldn't start dreaming he was back in 'Nam, sleepwalk, mistake me for one of the VC, and slice me into little pieces."

He was quiet for a moment. "I *did* ask him if he was gay. That didn't go over too well."

She was trying her damnedest not to laugh. "I thought you were exhausted, Beaumont."

"I am. I'm just . . ." What? Restless? If he told her he was restless, she would interpret it to mean horny. Of course, he was that, too. "I stayed with my brother Tom back when I first came to California, and he always had three or four people camped out in his living room. I'm not sure if they just didn't feel like going home at night, or if they had nowhere else to go—not that it mattered to Tom. But I had to stake out the couch early or I'd end up on the floor. His friends were all talented conversationalists, and sometimes the discussions would go on until three or four in the morning."

"Tom was your brother who died of AIDS?"

Just like that, Jed lost the urge to talk. "You do your research, don't you?" he said. Tom's death still made him feel sick. Not over the fact that he'd died—he'd been ill for years, and it seemed inevitable that sooner or later he'd lose the fight. But when Tom died, it had been more than two months since Jed had last gone to see him. He'd cared more for his own stupid reputation, and purposely stayed away.

Out of all the low moments in his less than exemplary life, it was one of the most shameful, one of which he was least proud.

"That must've been really hard for you," Kate said quietly.

He made a sleepy sounding noise that might've been agreement.

"Good night, Jed," she said after another moment of silence.

Despite everything, he had to smile at that. "David told you, huh?"

"When he called, he asked for Jed Beaumont. I guess I always figured that Jericho wasn't your given name. But I didn't know what it really was."

His name wasn't usually something Jed talked about, either, but coming off of the topic of Tom's death, it suddenly seemed very safe. "When I got cast in my first movie, I had to join the Screen Actor's Guild," he told her. "And you know, they have that rule—no two people can have the same name in the organization. Like, Michael J. Fox had to add the J. to his name because when he joined SAG there already was a Michael Fox. When I joined, there already was a Jed Beaumont. I wanted to use my full name, but my agent vetoed that. Tom came up with Jericho, and it stuck."

"What's Jed short for?" Kate asked. Her voice was relaxed, sleepy. Jed closed his eyes, imagining her in this bed instead of that one. She'd curl around him, all soft and warm and . . . "Jedidiah?"

"Nope—Jeddo."

She laughed.

"I'm not kidding—and it's sure as hell not funny," Still, he couldn't keep from laughing, either. "My daddy insisted it's an old family name. I was always of the mind-set that old family names were okay if they were something like Washington or Vanderbilt. But when the ancestral fold were illiterate, no-account moonshiners, well, maybe it's time to go with something new."

Kate's soft laughter wound its way around him in the darkness. He liked the way it felt. He liked the sensation of being on the same side, rather than going head-to-head as adversaries. He liked the thought that the more he made her laugh, the sooner she'd be inviting him into her bed. The sooner she'd be opening her arms—and her legs—to him.

"I think it's cute," she said. "Jeddo Beaumont."

"Promise you won't tell anyone?"

"I won't," she said, "Jeddo." She snickered. "Good night."

"What do you mean, good night? Now you have to tell me one of your deepest darkest secrets."

"My real name is . . ." she paused dramatically. "Mary Katharine." She laughed again.

"No fair."

Kate lay in the darkness, crossed her fingers, and avoided lying by evasion. "I'm pretty boring."

"Everyone has secrets."

The fact was, she was a ball of secrets. She had so many, she couldn't keep track of them anymore. She had the secrets she kept from her family. Her parents still didn't know she'd done that nude scene in *Dead of Night*. And she'd never told about that incident at Nancy Breaker's party in eighth grade, not even to Mickey, her youngest brother.

She had secrets she kept from Victor, too. The fact that she wrote the script they were shooting was pretty high on that list—never mind the details of that one awful, hazy month right before she filed for divorce, when she started playing *his* game, using *his* rules.

And now she had secrets she was keeping from Jericho, too. And she would keep those secrets from him. There was no way in hell she would ever let him know that the mere thought of spending the night in his trailer was so unnerving that all hope of getting a restful night's sleep had flown straight out the window. She'd never reveal she had to work to remember to call him Jericho instead of Laramie. And she'd never let him know that she spent almost every night lying in bed, imagining Laramie was there with her.

"Okay," she said. "Okay. How about . . . when I was ten, I went to Girl Scout sleep-away camp, and I stood trial for stealing another girl's bracelet, based on the circumstantial evidence that I was seen walking through the woods past that girl's tent the day before the bracelet turned up missing. I've never told anyone about that—not my parents, not my brothers, no one."

"Did you do it?"

"No!" Kate sat up in bed. "But when I told the other girls that, they didn't believe me. It was the first time that ever happened to me—my introduction to the real world. Up to that point, it never occurred to me there might be someone who wouldn't simply take my word at face value. I wasn't completely naive—I knew there were kids who told lies, and I knew enough not to believe everything anyone told me. But *I* wasn't a liar, and I guess I always just assumed I had some kind of non-liar's aura or something everyone would be able to see. Boy, was I wrong."

It had happened B.B. Before Breasts. At the time those accusations had been the end of the world. A year later, she'd looked back on it and wished her life could be that simple again.

"God," Jericho said. "When *I* was ten . . ."

Kate waited, but he didn't continue. "What?" she asked.

"Just that . . . we come from two really different worlds."

"I was so ashamed those girls actually thought I would steal. I spent the entire final week of camp in a daze. It really shook me up."

"I learned to lie early." Jericho's soft southern drawl was warmer than ever in the darkness. "We learned to tell the neighbors that Daddy's back was acting up, when, in truth, he'd drunk himself into a stupor again. And I don't know *how* many times I told the school nurse that my lip was split or my eye was black because I walked into a door or a tree or fell off my bike. Hell, I didn't even have a bike, but I figured she wouldn't know that. I liked telling the lies, because in order to convince her that what I was saying was true, I had to believe it myself. And I liked believing I had a bike I could fall off of. I liked being this other kid whose father really did have a bad back."

Kate didn't know what to say.

"You would've been scared to death of me if we'd met when we were both ten," he said with a short laugh.

She was scared to death of him *now*. Another secret to

keep from him. And yet, her fear had mutated. In the course of a single day, it had softened. Jericho was far from perfect, but his problems had had their causes.

Kate could picture Jeddo Beaumont, age ten, forced to create a fictional life and a make-believe family not just to get by, but also to give himself hope.

God knows without hope, very few could survive. And the jury was still out on Jericho. Had he made it? Would he continue to survive?

From the back room came the sound of his breathing—steady and slow. He'd fallen asleep just like that, all of his senses shutting abruptly down, as if someone had turned a switch.

Jericho had gotten through another day. Against all odds, five years, four months, and twenty-two days had become five years, four months, and twenty-*three* days.

"Good night, Jed," Kate whispered, staring up at the darkened ceiling, willing sleep to come, but knowing it probably wouldn't.

"Hey!"

Susie—Susannah—McCoy paused, turning to look back, and Jamaal ran to catch up.

It wasn't quite nine a.m., and already the heat of the day was pressing in on him relentlessly. Even running just a little was enough to make him sweat.

"Heading over to breakfast?" he asked her as they walked toward the Grill.

"Yeah. My call's not till late this afternoon."

"I've got about an hour before they need me," he told her.

Susie was wearing cutoff shorts and a baggy cotton T-shirt. Her hair was unwashed, and she looked every inch a sort of pretty but very grubby kid.

"I've already been in makeup—this is how they want my hair today," she told him self-consciously.

"It's looking . . . pretty authentic." Jamaal wiped his face with the bottom edge of his T-shirt. "Hey, that was some show last night, huh? Jericho coming into the Grill and apologizing that way." He poked her in the side. "Told you you were a good actor."

She giggled, pushing his hands away. For a fraction of a second, their fingers were entangled, and she looked up, directly into his eyes.

His stomach did a triple lutz. It was the oddest thing. He couldn't remember the last time that had happened.

He *could* remember going to see *The Thing in the Basement* when he was eleven or twelve years old. He remembered staring up at the screen, into Susie McCoy's big, innocent blue eyes, as Bunny, her character in the thriller was used as a pawn in her screen parents' bitter divorce. Their self-absorption put her in dire danger from a psychotic killer.

He could remember watching Susie on-screen, and thinking he would take care of her. If he only had a chance, *he* would keep that little girl safe.

It must've been a residual of those feelings making his stomach do a funky dance. Remnants of being a longtime fan rearing up and biting him on the ass. Had to be. It was okay for her to have a crush on him, but the other way around was a little bit demeaning. He was eighteen, and she was a kid, just fifteen years old.

He jammed his hands into the front pockets of his shorts. "So how come you didn't sit with me and Mindy last night?" He'd caught her eye when she'd first come into the Grill, but when he'd waved for her to join them, she'd shaken her head.

As she did now, again. "I had some lines to study. I'm sorry, I was . . . feeling a little antisocial."

Yeah, and that pit bull of a father of hers had been sitting there, ready to bite the heads off of anyone who got too close to his daughter.

They stopped outside of the doors leading into the Grill, and he leaned back on the top edge of a bicycle rack. "How long is your dad planning to visit?" he asked.

She tensed. Jamaal didn't so much see it as sense it. She was strung pretty tight to start with, but everything about her got that much more so.

"Actually," she said, her voice giving away none of her tension, "he's here for the duration. My mother left this morning."

"Oh, *shit*."

"He's not that bad," she said quickly, obviously lying through her teeth. "Besides, my mother had . . . she had, you know, business she had to take care of back in California. It came up suddenly, and . . ."

She trailed off, as if she realized how completely lame she sounded.

Jamaal clenched his teeth, not wanting to say anything that would dis her mother, but knowing full well that the lady had flat out deserted Susie. She hadn't been able to deal with Pit Bull Man, so she'd split—never mind what her kid wanted or needed.

"Shit," he said again, more softly this time.

Susie sat down next to him. "You know I was thinking about what you said—about winning an Oscar for this movie."

"Yeah?" He let her change the subject. "You one of those Oscar crazies who run around putting a full-page ad in *Variety* two months before the nominations— 'For Your Consideration?'"

She stretched out her legs to touch the front bar of the bike rack with her bare toes. She may have been fifteen, but she had eighteen-year-old legs—no doubt about it. "I've never been in a movie that's even come close to winning an Oscar," she admitted.

"A lot of it's political," he said. "The nominations, the awards . . ."

"There's a scene in *this* movie," she said, "that's going to get us all nominated—I know it. The scene where Jane and Laramie see Moses being sold. Up on the block."

It was a scene that Jamaal was not looking forward to doing. Even though it took place early on chronologically, they wouldn't be filming it until the end of the shoot, thank God.

"I'm supposed to be nearly naked in that scene," he told her. "And you think *that's* gonna get us the Oscar nod? I can just see the list of nominations. Susannah McCoy for Best Actress, Jericho Beaumont, Best Actor, and up for Best Supporting Actor, Jamaal Hawkes's big bare ass."

Susie laughed, and Jamaal grinned back at her, feeling his stomach do another gold-medal-winning leap.

The door to the Grill opened.

"Susie."

Just like that her laughter dried up. Her shoulders tightened, and something odd flashed across her face as she turned to her father, who was standing just inside the Grill.

"Aren't you having breakfast?" Pit Bull Man said pointedly.

"Yes, I'm—"

"I've ordered you French toast. Hurry up. It's getting cold."

Susie's French toast wasn't the only thing chilling. Jamaal could feel the icy blast of the arctic tundra as Susie's father looked right through him.

"I better go," Susie said. "See you around."

"Right," Jamaal said.

And as he watched her go into the Grill, he knew where he'd seen that odd look in Susie's eyes before. He'd seen it frequently in his old neighborhood—on the faces of kids he knew were scared to death of their parents. It was a haunted and haunting look. And it was one he'd never forget.

He'd assumed Pit Bull Man's bark was worse than his bite. But now he had to wonder.

"So how long were you and Victor married?"

Kate had just taken a bite of her sandwich, and rather than answer with her mouth full, she held up four fingers.

"Four years," Jed answered for her.

She was wearing a light-weight, short-sleeved white cotton sweater that didn't quite cling to her full breasts. But it didn't matter that it wasn't skintight. With her body, she could've worn a caftan two sizes too large and still looked unbelievably sexy.

She shifted in her seat, looping her arms loosely in front of her, blocking his view. "It wasn't quite four years," she told him, "but it was close."

"I think it's great that you can still work together."

"I knew after just a few months that we would've been better off as friends," Kate admitted. "But I couldn't just give up on an entire marriage without at least trying."

"I'm assuming—with his reputation—that he cheated on you."

She pushed her half-eaten sandwich aside. "You're also assuming that I'm going to talk about something that's very, very private."

She was smiling, but her mouth looked strained. It had been another tough day. This baby-sitting thing was really taking its toll on her.

It was taking its toll on him, too. Two days in, and he was taking cold showers at every opportunity. But as overwhelming as his attraction for her was, Jed knew that she was at least a week away from willingly climbing into his bed. And she had to be completely willing. He didn't want to have to talk her into anything. Hell, he wanted her to beg.

"I'm sorry," he said, giving her one of Laramie's crooked smiles. "I didn't mean to pry."

She was definitely affected when he let little bits and pieces of the character he was playing slip out, Jed noted with satisfaction as she looked away from him, her cheeks turning slightly pink. Yeah, she liked Laramie. A lot.

Jed liked Laramie, too. And he liked him even more knowing that the character was going to help him get this woman into bed. But even with Laramie's help, it was going to take time.

"How would you like it if I started asking you a bunch of personal questions?" she asked. "Details about your alleged drug habit?"

"I wouldn't mind." He answered quietly, with Laramie's risen-from-the-dead matter-of-factness. "What do you want to know?"

She blinked at him for a moment. "I heard that most of the money you made on the *Kill Zone* movies went up your nose."

He shook his head. "Not true. I've never even tried cocaine." He smiled. "I have a tendency toward sinus infections, and the thought of putting something up my nose that doesn't belong there completely freaks me out. In all honesty, I wasn't opposed to the rush, just the method of getting it."

"But I heard that the worst of your addictions started while you were making *Kill Zone II*."

Kate took another bite of her sandwich, and a little bit of mustard clung to her lower lip. As Jed watched, she caught it with the tip of her tongue. And just like that, he was instantly aroused. He forced his gaze away from her mouth, and found himself staring directly at her breasts. He closed his eyes briefly, trying to remember what she had just asked him. *Kill Zone II*. Addiction. Right.

He cleared his throat. "Up to then, I was only drinking—heavily, yes, but never while I was working. But during *KZ Two*, I did some of my own stunts. They were just easy jumps, no big deal, one of those rope-across-a-stream, Tarzan leaps, you know? But I landed wrong, and totally jammed my ankle. It wasn't broken, but it might as well have been, considering the pain."

She bit her sandwich again, and Jed nearly laughed aloud. It was absurd. The woman was only eating her dinner, yet it was so erotic, it was tying him into knots.

"The production was already behind schedule," he told her. "They couldn't afford to give me any downtime. So the doctor gave me a prescription for a painkiller. It worked. I could walk—I could even run on the damn thing, but it made me pretty sluggish. So at the director's request, the good doctor prescribed me something else to pick me up. It only took days before I was completely dependent. A few months later, I was still taking the pills, pretending that my ankle was giving me trouble. It wasn't, though."

Jed laughed. "I made *Mr. O'Rourke*—a movie with an antidrug message—completely under the influence. I used to wash those pills down with Jack Daniel's, take a hip flask with me onto the set for a hit between takes." He paused. "It's not a time of my life that I'm particularly proud of."

She was watching him with a soft look in her eyes.

He wanted to reach across the table and take her hand, but he didn't. Touching her would only make him want to kiss her, and if he kissed her, he'd be lost. And he knew the last thing he should do was rush her. No matter how badly he wanted her, no matter how badly he wanted to take off her clothes and feel all that incredibly soft skin against him, tonight was too soon.

For now, he had to settle for undressing Kate with his eyes. In his mind, he peeled her sweater back, revealing lingerie made of satin. Satin and lace. Yeah, definitely lace in the front, allowing him tantalizing glimpses of the dark pink peaks of her nipples, and . . .

"Hello." Her voice was tinged with annoyance. "I'm up here."

He lifted his gaze to her face. God, he'd been staring at her breasts again. Her eyes were no longer soft.

"You do that all the time, you know." Her voice shook slightly.

Damn, he'd gone and pissed her off again. And after she'd been looking at him so warmly. "I'm sorry."

"I *hate* it when men like you do that. When you carry on entire conversations with my chest."

She was lumping him in with the lowlifes, and indignation stirred. "I wasn't doing that. I was just . . ." No matter how he put it, it sounded bad. He gave her one of Laramie's weak smiles.

It only made her eyes narrow. "What? You were just . . . what?"

"Looking," he told her. "Just enjoying the view. You're a very attractive woman, and I happen to like looking at you."

"At my breasts," she qualified.

"Among other things, yeah."

The look she was giving him implied that his answer had not pulled him out of the low-life pile. And that annoyed *him*. "It's not as if you don't want men to look at you. I mean, considering the way you dress."

Wrong. Wrong, wrong, wrong.

It was the absolute wrong thing to say.

Her eyes flashed, and the breasts in question strained against the cotton of her sweater as she leaned forward. "That's bullshit and you know it. Look at this sweater I'm wearing. Does it have a neckline down to my naval? No! Is it tight? No. Goddamn it, stop staring at me!"

Jed purposely let his gaze linger. "You just told me to look at your sweater."

"Perfect." Her voice shook so much, for one unnerving moment, Jed thought that she was crying. She wasn't, but she was dangerously close. "I've just given you all the ammunition you need to completely push my buttons. I do something you don't like, now you can stare at my breasts. That's just perfect."

She put her head on her arms, down on top of the table. When she spoke again, her voice was muffled. "You know, when I was in fifth grade, I had to wear a bra. I was only eleven years old, and I had this grown woman's body. It was awful, the way the other kids teased me, but then, when I went to middle school, it got worse. Then it wasn't just teasing. Then I was elbowed in the hall. Touched, grabbed, squeezed. Except when I turned around to see who'd done it, there was always just a crowd of boys standing there, none of 'em even looking at me. It got to the point where I felt violated every time I walked down the hall. If they weren't touching, they were looking, and they weren't at all subtle." She lifted her head. "I know that you didn't mean to insult me by looking at me that way. I can even take it as a compliment some of the time. God knows, it got to be so that I liked it—the looks, I mean, not the touching. I never liked that. But now when I walk down a street, I start to feel bad if I *don't* get any whistles—how's that for being really screwed up, huh?"

Jed nearly reached for her hand. "Kate, I'm really sorry. I didn't mean to—"

"I don't know why it bothers me when *you* look at me. I expect it from a lot of men, and sometimes I even play into it." Her eyes were filled with tears, but she was fighting to keep them from escaping. "Just . . . don't use it as a weapon, please? I know you've got plenty of reasons to be mad at me, but just . . . don't get back at me that way, okay?"

"Okay." Jed nodded. "Although I can't promise I'll be

able to stop, you know, looking. I mean, you're nice to look at, and I'm a guy and . . ." He covered his eyes. "Oh, God, now I'm afraid to look at you."

Kate laughed, but it sounded decidedly damp. Jed purposely didn't watch, in case she was wiping her eyes.

"I've got to do these camera reports. Why don't you go into the other room and learn your lines," she said.

Jed stood up. "Good idea."

The morning dawned, and Kate understood why sleep deprivation was used as torture.

It was particularly galling how easily Jericho dropped off to sleep at night. They would be in the middle of a conversation about *some*thing that was guaranteed to drive Kate's blood pressure sky high, and then, just like that, he'd be asleep. And she'd be staring at the ceiling.

Kate peeled her face off her pillow and struggled into her bathrobe as she heard the shower shut off.

Jericho Beaumont was *not* a morning person. It was a good thing. She wasn't, either, and she wasn't sure she would've been able to stand his relentless attempts at conversation so early in the morning. For the past few mornings, he'd crawled out of the shower, thrown on some clothes, and staggered over to the Grill for coffee before he barely said a single word.

But this morning the phone rang.

Kate picked it up, sliding into the bench seat of the tiny table so that she wouldn't have to stand. "O'Laughlin." Her voice sounded as if she'd started smoking five packs of cigarettes a day. Or as if she hadn't slept in three days . . .

"Katie." It was Victor. "*C'est moi*. A change in the morning's plans, babe. Naomi's not up to speed."

"What's wrong with her?" Kate flipped opened her file. The entire morning's schedule was all Jericho and Naomi—scenes of Laramie, haunted by Sarah, his dead wife, along with a flashback scene of a younger, happier, clean and shiny Laramie, at his wedding to Sarah.

"We think it was food poisoning. We went out to dinner last night—a place that had grilled catfish. She was up all night yuking her guts out."

Kate winced. "Poor thing."

"Yeah, she's literally green. FYI, she was up for sticking to the shoot schedule. I'm the one who opted to rearrange. She's supposed to look beautiful and unearthly. She got the un-earthly part down—she looks as if she's just been exhumed."

"So what's the plan?" Kate asked.

"Colin and Sharlee are ready to do their scene," Victor told her. "I've already spoken to both of them. We'll just flip-flop this morning's schedule with tomorrow morning's. After lunch, we'll go back to our regularly scheduled program."

Colin Adams was the actor playing the villainous Reginald Brooks. And Sharlee Sherman was the actress playing a slave Brooks forced himself on. Jane was to stumble across the violent sexual act, watching in horror from the loft of the slave quarters. But her reaction shots would be filmed separately, on a different day. For Sharlee's sake, since nudity was involved, the set today would be closed, with as few people as possible on hand.

Kate ran down the list of shots scheduled for the after-noon. Jericho wouldn't be needed until late in the day. "It's okay with me," she said. "Are you absolutely positive it's all right with Sharlee?"

"She said she'd be relieved to get it over with."

"Okay, then," Kate said. "Tell Naomi I hope she feels better."

She hung up the phone and looked up to see Jericho standing in the doorway of his room, still wearing only a towel. "What's up?" he asked.

"Want to go back to bed?"

It was the wrong thing to ask. Kate started to blush even before he responded.

And he didn't hesitate, flashing her his best movie star smile—a real effort for him at that early hour. "With you? In a heartbeat."

She put her head down on the table. "It's 4:48 in the morning. I have absolutely no sense of humor at 4:48 in the morning. I have no patience at 4:48 in the morning. You know damn well what I meant. Naomi's got food poisoning; we're switching this morning's schedule with tomorrow morning's—which means your day is clear for the next eleven hours and change. Let's get crazy and sleep—separately—until six-thirty at least." She opened one eye and turned her head so that she could look up at him. "Please."

Jericho came toward her, and gently pulled her up and out of her seat. Before she could protest, he'd unfastened her belt and peeled her bathrobe back off her shoulders. "Cute pj's," he added. "At least the bottoms are cute anyway, because remember, I'm no longer allowed to even glance at any shirt you might be wearing. Although if I *did* happen to look, I'd definitely approve. In a completely nonthreatening, nonsexually harrassing way, of course."

Kate looked down at the little yellow roses that decked the cotton shorts and barely there sleeveless top of her pajamas and closed her eyes. "Oh, God. How can you make jokes at 4:48 in the morning?"

"Your problem is that you always assume I'm joking." He tossed her robe over a chair, pulled back the bedcovers, and pushed her down onto the bed. As he pulled the covers over her, he leaned down and kissed her on the cheek, right on the corner of her mouth.

"My problem," he told her, with one of Laramie's rueful smiles, the kind that could make her heart miss a beat, "is that you haven't figured out I'm dead serious."

He turned off the light and vanished back into the other room.

And Kate lay in the darkness of the early morning, suddenly wide awake.

Nine

ꙮ ꙮ

"**S**O HOW *DID* you know you wanted to be an actor?"

Kate glanced at Jericho, interested in hearing the answer to Susie McCoy's question.

They were heading north on the state road. She was behind the wheel of one of the production minivans, with Jericho in the passenger seat, and Susie McCoy and Jamaal Hawkes in the back.

With the set closed to any unnecessary personnel for the morning, and with all three of the actors not needed until the late afternoon, Susie McCoy had come up with a plan to visit Brandall Hall—the museum and former working plantation where the movie crew would be shooting later in the month.

Kate had been urging Jamaal to take a drive over to the historic site. He was struggling with playing Moses, and she thought it might give him some perspective to see the carefully preserved buildings—including a row of brick slave quarters that still stood along the drive in front of the big house.

Jamaal had hemmed and hawed until Susie expressed

an interest in going. And Jericho completely surprised Kate by inviting himself along.

With Kate as chaperone, Susie's father seemed content to stay behind, thank goodness. While there was room for him in the van, there wasn't any room for him in Kate's brain. Too much was going on in there already even to consider taking on the additional angry baggage that Russell McCoy brought with him.

She glanced at Jericho again, waiting for his reply, wondering for the four thousandth time that morning how she should interpret the words he'd spoken earlier.

My problem, he'd said, is that you haven't figured out I'm dead serious.

Had it been just another line, orchestrated to get a rise out of her? Or had he actually meant what he said? And how serious could dead serious possibly be? It hadn't been that many days since Kate had been convinced Jericho hated her.

What kind of game was he playing?

"Actually, why I decided to become an actor is a long story," Jericho said, answering Susie's question.

"We've got until four o'clock," Jamaal pointed out.

Jericho laughed. "It's not that long a story." He turned in his seat so that he was facing the back of the van. "I guess I knew when I was about nine years old. I used to spend entire days pretending I was someone else. My home life wasn't very structured, and I could disappear for a day or two without anyone noticing. So I would go camping, or I'd hitch a ride into the city, and I'd pick a character and *be* that character for an afternoon or a weekend. I had some favorites that I came back to again and again, but for the most part, I created an entirely new life for myself each time. And I'd set myself a time limit, and for that entire time, I'd stay in character—I didn't know it was called that at the time, but that's what I'd do. Didn't matter who I met and talked to. Whatever I did, I had to do it as this other person—and I had to stay true to that character's personality.

"I remember one time, I was probably around thirteen, and I was playing a kind of a prince-and-the-pauper-type game—you guys know that story? A prince trades places with a poor kid who looks just like him, and it's fun for an afternoon. Only it turns out it's not easy to make the switch back, and the prince is stuck out on the streets for far longer than he wants to be."

Kate glanced in the rearview mirror. Both Susie and Jamaal were nodding, paying rapt attention. Hey, it was Jericho Beaumont talking to them, telling them about his childhood. He'd given interviews to magazines like *Premiere* and *Rolling Stone*, and he'd never answered any questions about his childhood.

Susie looked as if she had won the lottery. It was clear Jericho had meant every word of that apology he'd given her in the Grill.

"Well," Jericho continued, "I'd decided I was going to be that prince for a weekend, and pretend that I was stuck in this crappy little Alabama town, unable to find my way back to London." He laughed. "I took a bus into the city, and I spoke in a very proper British accent. I even had tea with my burger for lunch. I had just enough money to take the bus home—I'd saved it for weeks just for this game—because I figured Prince Harry wouldn't know how to hitchhike. But I missed the last bus that night. And instead of breaking character and hitching home, I stayed in the bus station all night, waiting for the first morning bus."

Kate could picture him, thirteen years old, sitting in a bus station, trapped by his own strict game rules.

"I was *so* hungry, but I knew if I spent any of my money on food, I wouldn't have enough for the trip home. I remember sitting near this lady who was waiting on the 11:23 to Nashville, and she had a box of crackers in one of her bags. And, probably because I'd dressed myself so neatly and even slicked back my hair, she asked me to watch her stuff while she took her kid into the bathroom. I sat there, wanting those crackers more than I'd wanted just about anything in my life, but I didn't nick 'em, because even though it was something *I* might've done, Prince Harry had too much honor to steal. And for that night, I *was* Harry."

Susie leaned forward. "But how did you get from playing games to knowing that you wanted to go to Hollywood? Didn't I read somewhere that you just left for California when you were sixteen?"

"Yeah, you know, if I could live my life all over again, I'd do it differently," Jericho told her. "I'd leave home a whole hell of a lot sooner."

Kate glanced at him, sure he'd been about to say the exact opposite.

"And when I left, I'd make sure I took my mother with me. You guys know what a dysfunctional family is?" he asked, then answered for them. "Of course you do. Dumb question."

"We've both played characters that come from really messed-up families," Susie said.

"Played it, and lived it," Jamaal added. "My father died when I was eight. It took my mother awhile to get back on track."

"Yeah, well, my father was a raging alcoholic," Jericho admitted, "and I mean that pretty literally. My mother was the queen of all enablers, and she drank too much, too. My older brother Tom was my father's pride and joy, until one day he announced, 'Oh, by the way, Dad, I'm gay.' Tom left home, Dad drank himself into a stupor, beat the hell out of my mother, and I escaped to the movies.

"My other brother Leroy was a real party animal, and one night he got drunk and didn't back off when a girl said no. She claimed date rape, Leroy conveniently didn't remember anything, and the charges were eventually dropped due to insufficient evidence. I remember getting the sense from my father that it would be okay with him even if Leroy *did* end up going to jail, because at least it proved he wasn't gay. Ol' Lee eventually got sent down to the state facility for his fourth DUI offense. He left to put in his eight months, Dad drank himself into a stupor, beat the hell out of Mom, and I escaped to the movies.

"A few months after that, my sister Louise got herself pregnant. She was seventeen, and I still remember her wedding pictures. They'd be laughable if it weren't so tragic. The bride and groom both looked doomed, the wedding party are children, and both sets of parents look like they're auditioning for roles as Nazi death camp commanders. I didn't even bother going to the wedding. I just went to the movies."

"I'm starting to pick up a pattern here," Jamaal said.

"I started sneaking into the West Park Double Cinema when I was five," Jericho said as Kate turned into the Brandall Plantation parking lot. "By the time I was ten, I was determined to find my way up there onto that screen. And when I was fourteen, there was a national casting call in Birmingham for one of the *Bad News Bears* sequels—remember those movies?"

As Kate glanced into the rearview mirror, she saw Susie look at Jamaal and grin.

"No sequels," they said in unison, then both laughed, breaking the somber mood that Jericho's grim story had cast.

"Yeah, good. You practice saying that. *Kill Zone II*—what a mistake," Jericho told them with a smile. "But if I didn't know that at age twenty-six, I sure as hell didn't have a clue at fourteen. All I knew was they were casting for a movie in Birmingham on Saturday. My mother had to work, and I didn't dare ask my dad for a ride. Tom had already left home, so I ended up hitchhiking on the interstate. I left before dawn, and made it to the casting office just before three."

Kate parked the van, but didn't turn off the engine. She put it into park and left the air conditioner running. She turned to watch Jericho's face as he told his story. He was a very good storyteller, but that didn't surprise her at all.

"Turns out the audition was a scam," Jericho said. "Oh, sure, they had us read lines from a script. And they took videotape they said they'd send to Hollywood. But the people running this particular open casting call also ran a talent management agency that made most of their money selling head-shot packages and acting classes. And when all those mamas brought their pretty little boys and girls in for the 'national' audition, that agency talked an awful lot of 'em into dishing out some serious cash to get a 'Hollywood quality' head shot."

He paused, and Kate could see an echo of anger in his eyes, even after all those years. "I was counting on that audition to be my salvation, and at the time, I was too young to recognize it for the con game that it was. All I saw was the hope. ➤

"I didn't have two hundred dollars to invest in a head shot, and that worried me. Hell, I didn't even have two dollars to buy myself lunch. But still, I waited my turn—probably for around two hours—and I went in and read, and they said 'thank you.' And I didn't understand that meant they wanted me to leave. Thank you. You guys both know that means you're done. Go away. Don't call us.

"So I just stood there. I mean, this was when they were supposed to tell me I'd gotten the part, right?"

Kate wanted to cry, but she laughed softly instead.

Jericho laughed, too. "So one of the assistants hustles me out of there. Then I'm just standing in the waiting room, thinking maybe I should put a new name down on the sign-in list, wait another two hours and take another crack at it. And then one of the agents comes out of the back room in a big hurry, and he comes up to me and says, thank God, you haven't left yet. And I'm thinking, this is it. I got the part. And he says, I need to talk to your mama.

"And like a good little liar, I tell him my mama's waiting out in the car with the baby—I figure I'd throw a baby in there, make it sound more real. And he goes, come on, I'll walk you out, cause I really want to talk to her. And I figure there's probably going to be hell to pay, but I haven't got a choice now, and I have to tell him the truth— that I came to the audition by myself.

"And he kind of sizes me up, and asks me what were the chances of my parents coughing up the two hundred bucks to pay for head shots? And I basically tell him devil's chance in heaven, and what do those pictures have to do with me getting this part? And he just stands there, kind of staring at me for a really long time.

"I'm starting to get a little nervous, you know. I just told this weirdo that I was on my own, seventy-five miles from home. And he tells me no, sorry, I didn't get the part. I wasn't gonna get the part. But he's got this other job—a modeling job—and he knows I'll be perfect for it."

Kate held her breath, afraid of what was coming next. Pornography? Something illegal?

"But I'm like, screw modeling. I want to be in a movie. But he tells me lots of movie stars got their start modeling. And then he says this job pays thirty-five bucks an hour.

"And after I scrape myself up off the floor, he tells me he'll make a deal with me. He'll front me the money for the head shots. He's a photographer himself—it'll only cost about fifty bucks without him taking any profit—and after only two hours of work, I'll be able to pay him back. In fact, there's a job he knows about next Wednesday, posing for a newsprint ad for a Birmingham sporting goods store. It'll only be about an hour of work, but it's a start.

"We make a plan for me to meet him at his office next Wednesday. He gives me his business card—his name's Danny Pierce, and I give him my name and phone number, and we shake hands."

"He was legitimate?" Kate had to ask. "He wasn't just some creep who wanted to take pictures of you without your clothes on?"

Jericho glanced at her. "No, it was a real job."

"Oh, my God," Susie said. "Do you still have the ads?"

"No, I didn't get the job. I made the mistake of going home and telling my father. I thought he would think thirty-five bucks an hour was cool. I thought he'd be proud of me, but he went ballistic. He called modeling sissy work. He told me modeling and acting was for fags. He asked me if this was Tom's influence.

"I stood tall, told him this had nothing to do with Tom. This was something I wanted. I told him about the sporting goods job on Wednesday. And I told him I didn't give a damn what he thought. I was going to do it.

"So he kicked the crap out of me," Jericho said matter-of-factly. "He broke my nose and nearly broke my jaw as well—he hit me so hard, his wedding ring cut me open." He fingered the scar above his eyebrow. "It took the doctor twelve stitches to sew me up."

Susie and Jamaal were dead silent. As Kate watched, Jericho smiled, but it was a grim smile that didn't touch his eyes.

"The son of a bitch did it on purpose. He purposely messed up my face. When I went back to Birmingham on Wednesday, my nose was taped and I had two black eyes, a swollen lip, and that big Frankenstein cut on my fore-head. And when Danny Pierce saw me, he nearly cried.

"I was green enough to think I could still do the job, but he set me straight. He told me to come back in six months or a year—maybe by then the scar I was going to have on my forehead would've started to fade. He told me in the meantime to take as many acting classes as I could—or to get involved in whatever drama programs were available at my school.

"I did," Jericho said. "And about a year later, I went back to see him, but his entire office was gone. There was a copy shop there instead, and no one inside had ever heard of Danny Pierce, let alone knew where he'd gone.

"But that day, that Wednesday I didn't get a chance to earn thirty-five dollars an hour . . . I went home, and I stood in the bathroom, and I looked at myself in the mirror, and I made a vow. I was going to succeed. That was the day I started planning my escape. From that moment on, my entire focus was on getting to Hollywood and being successful once I got there. From that moment on, I was determined that someday I'd win an Oscar, and as I stood there on that stage, I would spit in my father's eye. So there you go. End of story."

Kate suspected it was only the beginning.

The tour of the plantation house was conducted by a young woman in a hoop skirt. She looked as if she might give way to the vapors when she realized her customers were none other than Susie McCoy and Jamaal Hawkes.

Forget about Jericho Beaumont. He might as well have been invisible.

He was quiet as they went first into the front parlor, and then into the lavishly furnished dining room. They'd be filming the scene where Jane had dinner with Reginald Brooks and his family right here.

Jericho hung back to look out the window at a beautifully maintained flower garden as the tour guide led the way into the kitchen.

And Kate hung back to wait for him.

He looked particularly good today, refreshed and healthy, despite the stubble of beard—Laramie's beard— on his chin. He wore a Hawaiian-print shirt, a pair of khaki shorts, and Teva sandals, his long hair back in a ponytail because of the heat. With his sunglasses on, he seemed ready to play the part of a beach bum in some retro, early 1970's movie.

It was possible that the tour guide simply hadn't recognized him. He'd worn his hair extremely short in his most recent movies. And of course his most recent movie had been out five years ago—a lifetime by Hollywood standards.

Jericho turned to see Kate standing there, and managed to read her mind.

"It's my fault for not having a movie out in years." He smiled crookedly. "Completely my fault. It took longer than I thought to get clean. And once I was ready to come back, I'd been out of the public's mind for too long. I was no longer a guaranteed box-office draw and that—combined with how I'd burned my bridges on the way to hitting bottom—has made me uncastable." He held out his hands in a gesture of amused resignation so like one Laramie would make. "I stand before you—a has-been at age thirty-four."

She stepped around the dining table. "You're not a has-been."

"Yes," he said. "I am. I'm counting on this movie to hit big. And bring me back to life."

"But if it doesn't?" Her voice sounded very small in the high-ceilinged room.

Jericho turned back to the window, but not before she caught a glimpse of the sudden bleakness in his eyes. "I don't know. Damn, if I go through this, and I'm still considered uncastable . . ." He laughed, but there wasn't any humor in it. "Hell, I might as well go through life stinking drunk. What's the point in torturing myself to stay sober if no one's going to hire me anyway?"

Kate took another step toward him. "You can't really mean that."

His voice was tight. "You have no idea how hard it is. *No* idea."

She touched his back. She couldn't resist. "And you seriously believe that it wouldn't be any easier if you got back into some kind of twelve-step program?"

"Yeah, great, *that's* all I need—to go around trying to make amends with everyone I hurt because I was a drunk? Well, most of 'em are dead. Nothing will get resolved, and I'll just end up feeling like shit. No thanks."

"You *know* there's more to those programs than that." Beneath her hand his muscles were tight, his shoulders tense. "Jed, you need to learn to relax."

"Whiskey relaxes me just fine." He turned to look at her. "Sex does the trick, too."

She lifted her hand from him and started backing away. "We better catch up with the others."

He caught her by the wrist. "I'm sorry. Damn, I'm always apologizing to you, aren't I? It's just . . . I can't figure you out. How could somebody so uptight do a movie like *Dead of Night*? I hate to tell you, babe, but half the men in the country have spent quite a bit of time staring at your breasts. And you sure as hell weren't wearing a high-necked sweater at the time."

Kate felt herself flush, but she held his gaze steadily as she pulled her hand free. "You're right. I wasn't." She took a deep breath. "I wanted to be an actress. And *Dead of Night* was a movie. I talked myself into believing that I wouldn't care that I had to take my clothes off. I convinced myself that because people had been staring at my body since I was eleven, I might as well use it to launch my career. But I was wrong—I *did* care. That was something I should have learned back in seventh grade, courtesy of my brothers and their classmates."

He was silent, waiting for her to go on, but she turned away. "They're probably wondering where we are."

"I'd like to be your friend," Jericho said suddenly.

She turned back to look at him. He hadn't moved an inch, but he had become Laramie. God, somehow she must've given herself away. Somehow he knew exactly how to get under her skin.

He smiled slightly. "I'd also like to jump your bones, but I figure that's pretty much understood, whereas the friend thing might not be."

It was her turn to stand there, silently staring at him.

"What happened in seventh grade? And I'm praying that you're not going to tell me that one of 'em touched you when you were what? Thirteen years old?"

"I was twelve. And no. They didn't try that until I was in eighth grade."

Jericho swore.

"But in seventh grade, my brothers always had this steady stream of friends coming over to the house, always at the same time, after dinner. I thought they were coming over to do homework, or to play games. Timothy and Stephen were heavily into Dungeons and Dragons, and Jack was really good at chess. Mickey liked basketball, so he always had a few friends out in the driveway, shooting hoops. He wasn't a part of it, though. It was Jack and the twins."

"Part of what?" Laramie asked. She could tell from his eyes that he knew what she was going to say before she said it.

"My brothers had a nifty little business going. They charged guys a dollar to watch me get ready for bed at night. Jack's room was directly over mine, and they drilled a bunch of peepholes in the floor. When I found out about it, I was beyond mortified. God knows what those boys saw. I was twelve, and I had the body of a seventeen-year-old. I was alone in my room with the door locked and the shades pulled down. I thought I was safe."

The memory was still enough to make her heart pound with anger. "When I found out," she continued, "Timothy gave me half of the money they'd made, hoping I wouldn't tell on them. I took it, and I didn't tell, but only because I was so embarrassed. It sure wasn't the money that kept me from talking. There was enough there to buy a new tape player, but I never spent it. I couldn't—it made me feel sick just to look at it, and I knew I'd feel the same about the tape player. The money's still hidden in my parents' house. In the closet in my old room, under a loose board."

"I have this overpowering urge to go and kick the crap out of your brothers," Laramie said. Laramie? *Jericho*. Jesus.

"Who are you kidding?" Kate asked, angry at herself for slipping that way. He wasn't anything like Laramie. "You would've been standing in line with your dollar in your hand."

"You're wrong."

When he said it like that, with Laramie's conviction in his voice, she could almost believe him. But he wasn't Laramie. He was only a very talented actor who could sometimes make her believe he was someone special. It was not the same thing.

"I'm afraid to ask what happened when you were in eighth grade," he said.

"Then don't."

Jericho reached for her. "Kate—"

She moved out of his grasp. "We need to find Susie and Jamaal."

As if on cue, Susie burst into the room. "Kate, you've got to see the slave quarters!"

Kate slapped a smile on her face. "Hey, I was just coming to find you." Jericho was still standing there, wearing Laramie's concern. She looked at him pointedly. "Want to go see the slave quarters?" In other words, conversation over.

To her relief, he nodded.

"This is amazing," Susie said. "Do you realize that right here, right in this very spot, people who were *owned* by other people lived and walked and probably even died? Children played right here in this yard. Women gave birth to babies—babies that would be sold away from them on their master's whim. For more than *sixty years* this was all there was for these people. This was the beginning and end."

The slave cabins were made of brick. An entire row of them, about ten altogether, ran down the driveway in a neat line, outside of the main gates of Brandall Hall.

Jed could feel Jamaal's tension as he stood in the yard and looked past the brick structure, up toward the gleaming white splendor of the big house. He motioned toward it with his chin.

"Imagine having that view every day of your life," he said quietly to the younger man. "Living down here, like animals, looking up at that. And you know, these brick houses were the quarters for the domestic slaves—the *civilized* ones—the men and women who worked as servants up in the main house. They were allowed to live at least a little bit like human beings."

Jamaal turned away, and Jed followed him. "On this plantation, the field slaves were stabled in wooden shacks. They had a separate house for the men, a separate one for the women, and another one for the children. The strongest men were used as studs, sent to lie with women at the foreman's command. And babies were taken from the women shortly after birth and raised in a group, like animals. There was no sense of family, no hope for love."

Jamaal clearly didn't like what he was hearing. "How do you know so much about this?"

"I did research," Jed told him. "This was the world Laramie lived in. A world where the people you love most can die from a common fever in a matter of days. One day they're there, the next day they're gone. It was a crapshoot. It was also a world where people treated other people worse than dogs—where men could kill other human beings that he owned, and not be thought a murderer, but merely a poor businessman."

Jamaal looked up at Brandall Hall, and when he spoke, his voice was tight. "I can't imagine living here," he said. "And that's my problem with playing Moses. I can't imagine ever being another man's possession. I can't stand wearing those chains—and have you seen that costume? Shit, I know I'm an actor and supposed to be beyond that, but every time I put on those rags, I feel—I don't know—humiliated and completely pissed off."

"But that's exactly what Moses is feeling," Jed told him. "Humiliation and anger. He can't imagine being a slave, either—that's why he runs. Most of the slaves who ran away were caught and killed. Moses knows that, he's an intelligent man, but he'd rather face a brutal death than live his life in chains."

He could feel Kate watching him, sense her listening. This was why she'd wanted Jamaal to come to the plantation, so that he could see and really begin to understand the desperation that was Moses' life.

She had no idea the story he'd told in the van had been for her benefit. He'd wanted her to know where he'd come from, but years of being completely private prevented him from being comfortable just sitting down and starting a conversation. "Hey, got a minute? Thought you might want to know about the pond scum from which I evolved."

If she'd asked, he would've told her—provided she didn't ask about things that were still too tough to think about, like Tom or his mother. Or that phone call from his sister Louise that prompted him to pack his bag and check himself securely into rehab.

So far his plan was working. She was starting to like him. At least, he hoped she was. If he could just be patient, he could use Laramie to wear her down, and he'd find himself in her bed soon enough.

But right now, all he really wanted was to pull her into his arms and hold her.

It was the strangest thing, this tenderness that had stirred to life within him.

Jed was still feeling a little light-headed from all that Kate had told him about her brothers' 'business' deal. That must've been a nightmare for a twelve-year-old girl. He could remember how body conscious and embarrassed he'd been at that age. He ached for her, and for the little girl she'd been.

He wished they hadn't been interrupted. He wanted to know what had happened in eighth grade. He wanted a chance to apologize to her—for all boys and men, everywhere. He wanted to find out more about her.

She'd told him she'd taken that part in *Dead of Night* to further her acting career, but after that one movie, she'd dropped off the face of the earth. She'd married Victor Strauss shortly after, but as far as he knew, she hadn't acted again. And he wanted to know why.

Maybe it was because he could use that information to convince her they should be lovers. That was his goal here, he reminded himself. Revenge, with some hot sex as a bonus.

A very large bonus.

But he had to take his time, make sure he didn't scare her away.

Of course, what he'd said about wanting to jump her didn't fall under the heading "taking his time." He definitely had to take a deep breath and back off. There was no way she was ready for a direct assault. Unless . . .

He was going to Alabama in a few days—to appear as the guest of honor at a fund-raiser David was throwing for the Rehab Center. If he could make sure she came along . . .

"It's just so different from anything I've ever experienced," Jamaal said, breaking into his thoughts.

"Moses is a great character," Jed told the kid. "And

you've got way more in common with him than you think. Neither of you can imagine living your lives in chains. Wearing that costume makes you feel humiliated? Hell, that's a good thing. Use it. Use your own humiliation to give real depth to Moses' anger. When you play Moses, it's going to come across as being completely real— because so much of it is real. So much of it is your own."

"Is that what you do?" Susie dared to interrupt. "Take your own emotions and channel them into the character you're playing?"

Jed thought about that. "Yeah, that's one way of describing it. I'm not . . . really very good at expressing myself," he admitted carefully. Man, was that the understatement of the year, or what? "I think I have a need to be an actor not just because I like slipping on other people's lives, but because it gives me a chance to vent some of the emotions I might—in my own life—have trouble venting. I can allow myself to get angry, and really feel angry, but it's in a very controlled environment because I'm acting. It's safe."

He turned away, suddenly uncomfortable, aware that he'd stripped himself down, nearly to the bone, in front of Kate O'Laughlin, of all people. Or maybe this was something else he'd wanted her to know, too.

"But we're not talking about me—we're talking about Moses, here," he said, gesturing toward Jamaal.

"I'm not Moses. I don't want to be Moses. Shit, *that's* the problem."

Jed moved toward the cabin's open door, motioning for Jamaal to follow him. "Come here. Come inside."

Jamaal hesitated in the doorway.

"All the way in," Jed ordered him. There was a huge fireplace smack in the center of the back wall. Windows with a single swinging shutter were cut only into the front of the building. The walls were rough brick, and the floor was hard-packed dirt. It was dark and damp and reminiscent of a prison cell.

Jamaal inched in a little farther.

"Sit on the hearth," Jed ordered, sitting on the bricks that extended out two or three feet into the room. Jamaal slowly sat next to him. "Close your eyes."

Before he shut his own eyes, Jed caught a glimpse of Susie and Kate, peeking in through the open windows. Kate was wearing a baseball cap to protect herself from the screamingly hot sun. She'd worn hiking shorts and clunky boots for this outing, with a slightly clingy T-shirt that defied description. Lord, what a body. He'd had to turn and face the back of the van during the ride over, because there was no way in hell he could look in her direction and keep his gaze from traveling southward.

Having her as his baby-sitter was both his salvation and his punishment. She was driving him mad, but at the same time, he didn't want her to find a replacement.

Luckily she was having trouble finding anyone. She'd thought she'd found someone yesterday—a man named Simon Nealy—only to discover this morning that he had a police record. He'd served time for armed robbery. So long, Simon. Currently, Pastor Harlan's teacher friend was her only hope. And he wasn't due back in Grady Falls until June 26.

If Jed's luck held, Kate would be stuck with him for another few weeks.

"Take a deep breath," he told Jamaal, taking one himself and attempting to exorcise Kate from his mind as he exhaled. Kate and her demure little yellow-flowered, innocent-looking cotton pajamas that covered a body that was pure sin. Kate, her face scrubbed clean of makeup, looking sleepily up at him and innocently asking if he wanted to go back to bed . . .

"Now," Jed told Jamaal, "open your eyes really slowly and . . . listen."

As he opened his own eyes, Kate pulled Susie down with her, beneath the windows, out of sight.

The silence was complete, and very spooky. After only about thirty seconds, Jamaal shifted. "Listen to *what*?"

"Shhh." Jed motioned the younger man to be silent.

Outside the cabin, nothing moved. There was no wind, no life to the oppressively hot South Carolina day. And there, in the dimness of that cabin, even the stony silence of all the years since emancipation couldn't suppress the voices of the past. Generations of African American men, women, and children had lived in this building. They had lived in oppression, and they had lived in fear because their lives were not their own.

Jamaal was sitting with his head down, elbows on his knees, his hands locked behind his neck, staring at the dirt floor.

"God knows how many young men just like Moses lived in this very cabin," Jed said softly. "God knows how many of them ran, and were caught and beaten to death. Moses is fictional, but they're not. Even though there's no record of them, they lived and they died." He paused, listening again to the silence. "You know what amazes me the most?"

Jamaal shook his head, still staring down at the floor.

"They were born into this backward, fucked-up world, and they were told right from the first moment they could understand that this was the way things were. And you know that their mothers and fathers—out of love and fear—taught them to bow their heads and say 'yes, master,' because if you bowed your head, you wouldn't be beaten. If you bowed your head, chances were, you wouldn't be killed. But some of these little black boys and little black girls grew into men and women who took everything they'd been taught and threw it away. Because they knew in their hearts that it *was not right*. And somehow they could see past the oppression and fear, and they could hope. They took that hope and that belief that slavery was wrong, and they sought to escape. And that's Moses. Smart enough to see through the lies. Strong enough to stand tall despite the fear. So proud that he'd rather die than bow his head to another man. So full of hope."

Jamaal looked up at him, understanding finally glistening in his eyes. "Shit."

Jed nodded, meeting his gaze. "Yeah."

Kate turned off the light and climbed into bed.

"I was wondering what happened to you in eighth grade . . ." Jericho's warm voice slipped quietly through the darkness. "You never got around to telling me."

Kate wanted to scream. She didn't want to lie here in the dark, talking quietly with this man. She didn't want this deceptive sense of intimacy.

She wanted to watch him act, and to cut his paychecks. Period, the end. She didn't want him to smile at her, she didn't want him to talk to her. She didn't want to follow him around and supervise him.

And most of all, she didn't want to feel him watching her, to know that he wanted more.

He wanted sex.

He'd said as much to her today at Brandall Hall.

And if she were the kind of woman who had casual relationships—well, then, she'd want it, too. But she wasn't. At least not anymore.

But every now and then, like this morning when he'd brought Jamaal into the cabin and spoke so eloquently about slavery, like in the van when he'd told them the way his father had purposely scarred his face, like when he went in front of the camera and transformed himself into Laramie, like when he caught her eye and smiled—not one of his movie star smiles, but that little rueful lifting of one side of his mouth . . . At those times, Kate caught herself watching him. And wanting him.

She didn't want Jericho, she corrected herself. She wanted Laramie. And those were two very different things.

It was stupid to want him, no matter who he was pretending to be. Yes, he was sexy. There were few who disputed that. But Kate refused to want him simply because of the way he looked. She refused to be that shallow. She'd engaged in casual sex only one dreadful two-week period of her life, and it had been awful, terrible, miserable. She'd felt bad for months after. Years. She wasn't going to do it again.

Especially not with a recovering alcoholic and substance abuser. True, Jed had been clean for more than five years, but he'd told her today that staying sober was painfully difficult. Who in their right mind would want to deal with *that* on an ongoing basis?

Add into the equation all that she'd learned about his childhood—his abusive, alcoholic father, and the fact that lying and stealing were not against his moral code. At least it hadn't been when he was young.

And while she could certainly forgive Jed Beaumont for his "survival at all costs" mentality, and while she could even admire his determination and endurance, she would be insane to even consider starting a romantic relationship with him. Because he wasn't Laramie. He wasn't some fictional character who could be saved by the power of love.

So why was she lying here, thinking about him, dwelling upon the possibilities, and—God help her—considering giving in to the subtle sexual pressure he gave her simply by looking in her direction?

"Kate, are you awake?" he asked quietly.

She breathed slowly and steadily, praying that he'd think she was already asleep.

She heard him sigh, heard him start muttering to himself—tomorrow's lines, she realized, recognizing a word here and there.

Finally, after what seemed like forever, he fell silent, the way he'd done every night, sleep coming instantly, as if someone had pulled his plug.

And then Kate lay in the darkness, listening to him breathe, tired to the bone and knowing that when she finally *did* fall asleep, a curious mix of Jed Beaumont and Virgil Laramie would haunt her dreams.

Ten

❧❧

"I'M SORRY, *WHAT* are you doing?"

Jed looked at Kate, who was standing in the doorway, and repeated himself. "I'm packing for my trip to Alabama."

"Oh," she said. "Oh, no . . ."

He zipped his overnight bag closed as he glanced up at her again. She was completely dismayed. "David's fund-raiser for the Center is tonight. I made arrangements to have tonight and tomorrow off, weeks before shooting started."

Jed could tell from her face that she remembered. "But that was before Bob Hollander left. He was supposed to go with you. I'm sorry, Jericho, I can't possibly leave the set."

"I promised David I'd be there. I'm the guest of honor. Believe it or not, people are paying a hundred bucks a plate to eat dinner in the same room as me."

She slumped against the door frame, covering her face with her hand. "Oh, God."

Jed held his breath. He wanted her to come to Alabama with him. He was counting on it, in fact.

Of course the alternative—letting him go all by himself, like the responsible grown-up that he was—would be nice. While it wouldn't be as much fun, it would mean that she trusted him enough to let him go.

Since Bob Hollander had been fired, since Kate had been providing his supervision, 24/7, the daily urine tests had stopped. Maybe Kate figured there was no point to the tests, since the results had come up consistently clean. Or maybe she figured to cut back on lab costs, since she could see with her own eyes that he'd had no opportunity to obtain or ingest any chemical substances.

Or maybe—dare he believe—one tiny part of her was starting to trust him. It was funny. He was starting to want her trust almost as much as he wanted her to sleep with him.

Kate turned and went into the other room. He heard her pick up the phone, heard her dial. She made at least eight calls, but each time she hung up she was no closer to finding a replacement baby-sitter than before.

She came back down the hall, and Jed pretended to be engrossed with organizing his script, making sure he had the scenes they'd be filming upon his return—lines he was planning to review during the flight to Alabama. And for one sudden, nearly paralyzing moment, he didn't want to look up at her. Because he knew he'd be able to tell with one look whether or not she trusted him to go by himself. And suddenly, it was *so* important that she trust him.

"Any luck?" he kept his voice light.

"No."

"How about if I promise to be good?"

Kate sighed, and when he turned to face her, she looked as if she were going to cry. "I'd love to let you go by yourself."

"But you can't."

"I'm sorry, Jed." She was, that much was obvious.

So okay. Back to his original plan. She was going to have to come along. He may not have had Kate's trust, but he was going to have *her*—tonight. "I can't miss this," he told her, pulling out a little Laramie and adding it to the apology in his voice. "I've got to go."

She took a deep breath. "What time's the flight?"

"A little after three."

She looked so miserable, Jed took his plan, and took Laramie and threw them both out the window. "Look, I was going to visit David for a few days," he said, "but maybe we can make arrangements to fly back tonight—after the dinner. We can take a red-eye."

Her face brightened. "You'd do that?"

He had to laugh. "No. I just thought I'd suggest it and then refuse—you know, to torment you."

She laughed, too. And then she crossed the room and hugged him. "Thank you."

A hug was the last thing Jed had expected, and he was caught completely off guard. She smelled sweet, her perfume so enticingly faint, he wanted to bury his face in her neck. And her body—with her soft breasts and firm stomach and thighs—was a completely perfect fit against his. Her hair was like silk against his cheek.

But she pulled away before he could capture her in his arms, before he could find his voice and beg her to stay right where she was for the next four years, before he could seek the softness of her mouth with his own.

She was blushing. "Sorry. That was inappropriate."

"Yeah," he said, "I mean, no—I mean . . ." Whoa. Slow down. Get a grip. It was only a hug. "We're starting to be friends, so . . ." Christ, what was *that* supposed to mean?

Kate nodded as if she knew. "I'm glad you feel that way, too. I'll call the airline."

"The party's formal. Do you have a dress?"

She gave him a look. "Do I have a dress? What kind of a question is that for a producer who raised millions of dollars through schmoozing?"

"A valid one." His heart rate was finally returning to normal. "I didn't bring my tux on this shoot—I figured there wouldn't be much occasion for black tie. David's getting me a rental for tonight."

"I have a dress," she reassured him.

"It would be great if it was something that'll make you look like you come from Hollywood."

Kate crossed her arms and lifted an eyebrow. "You want skintight silver sequins or cleavage?"

So much for his heart rate. And so much for his thinking he was finally starting to figure her out, too. "You have a dress that . . ." She'd made him so afraid of offending her, he couldn't even say the word *cleavage*.

"For a Hollywood-type party, absolutely." She shrugged. "I guess I figure as long as people are going to stare, I might as well give them something to look at."

"So wait a minute. Let me get this straight. It's okay if hundreds of people check you out, but *I'm* not allowed to look?"

Kate nodded, suddenly completely serious. "It *is* a contradiction, isn't it? I can't explain it. I like dressing up. I even like having people look at me. Sometimes. I guess it's the closest I come to acting these days. But when someone looks at me maliciously—"

"Whoa. I was never being malicious."

She made a face. "Bad word choice. I mean . . ." She shook her head. "I'm not sure there's a word for what I mean. But when a man looks at a woman's body with the intention of trying to intimidate, or somehow put her in her place, to imply she's nothing more than a pair of breasts, even if it's not intentional—"

"The other night—I wasn't trying to intimidate you."

"Weren't you?" Her eyes were such a heavenly shade of blue.

It would've been like trying to lie to God. "At one point I was, yeah," he admitted. "But most of the time I was just . . . I don't know. Fantasizing? If I was implying anything, it was that I really like what I see when I look at you."

"My body," she said quietly. "There's more to me than my body, Jed. And if you don't stop staring at my breasts, you might never see that."

She turned away, as if assuming he would be unable to come up with a rebuttal to that. She was right. "I'm going to go pack," she continued. "Don't go anywhere. I'll meet you back here in fifteen minutes, okay?"

If he wasn't speechless before, he was now. She was leaving him alone? Unguarded? For fifteen whole minutes?

It was stupid how happy that made him. So she trusted him to stay out of trouble for fifteen lousy minutes. Big friggin' deal.

But it was.

It was a very big deal.

Jed turned away, afraid he was going to do something *really* stupid, like burst into tears.

He made himself frown, made himself remember Kate O'Laughlin was the woman who had forced him to sign away his freedom for a part in her movie. He should be feeling angry that she didn't trust him for more than fifteen minutes on his own. He should be mad as hell that she treated him like a troublesome child, telling him not to go anywhere. Where the hell did she think he'd go? Across the street to the bar?

Jed let himself get good and angry.

Anger was far more familiar than happiness. It was easier to push down and negate.

Happiness scared him to death.

Kate fastened her seat belt as the jet started its approach into Montgomery.

She couldn't believe she was here, hundreds of miles from the action, with only her cell phone and her laptop to connect her to her multimillion-dollar movie. She'd never been particularly good at delegating, and even though Annie had reassured her that the world would continue to spin even if Kate weren't available to orchestrate the sunrise and sunset, she had her doubts.

It wouldn't be so bad if she'd been able to get a return flight to South Carolina at eleven P.M., or even midnight. But the next available flight wasn't until tomorrow morning. It wouldn't get them back into Grady Falls until mid-afternoon at the earliest and—

"Kate."

She looked up from her view of the clouds outside of the aircraft and into Jed's gorgeous hazel eyes.

"I've been wondering. Why did you come back, you know, to Hollywood? If there ever was a place where people are judged by their looks, it's in this business."

"Why did *you* come back?" she countered.

He looked past her, out the window, at the tops of the clouds. "Because all I've ever wanted to do was act. It's something I need to do." His eyes shifted, and he met her gaze for the briefest of instants before looking away. "I feel safe when I get inside a character. I don't have to worry about . . ."

He was speaking so softly, she leaned forward to hear him. "What?"

He glanced at her and smiled. "No fair. I asked about you."

"You don't have to worry about what?"

"I'll tell you, if you tell me what happened to you in eighth grade."

This time, the clouds outside the window caught *her* attention.

Jed laughed softly. "Yeah, that's what I thought. So why did you come back? You were making a fortune selling paper clips."

"That's exactly why. I was making a fortune selling *paper clips*," Kate told him. "I wanted to do something creative—to make a movie. If I couldn't be in front of the cameras, I wanted to be behind them. With the money from the stores, I finally had a chance. Of course, if *The Promise* fails, I'll be out a lot of cash. So I'll go back, focus on The Supply Closet stores for a few years—until I get the funds I need to get back into the game again."

He tried to stretch out his legs, but they were flying coach, and there wasn't enough room. "It just seems funny to me that you'd want to be involved in a business that's so exploitative. Didn't it bother you to have to dress up and, well, virtually sell yourself to raise money to fund your project?"

A man across the aisle had been saving a little bottle of whiskey for the descent. He opened it carefully now, and poured it into a plastic cup. Jed was trying not to watch.

What would he do if someone handed him a glass? He'd told her he'd gone into a bar while filming *Mean Time*, held a shot of whiskey to his nose, but didn't drink. How many times could he do that before his willpower crumbled?

He turned and looked at her now, waiting for her response to his question. She wondered if he even knew that for several long seconds, his complete focus had been on that whiskey across the aisle.

"It did bother me," she answered him. "It does bother me. You know, every time someone new comes onto the set, they come into the production office, and I have to watch them look at my name and my title of coproducer on the office door, and then look at me. I know their first impression is that I'm some kind of bimbo. They think I'm there only because I'm Victor Strauss's ex-wife, and that I couldn't possibly have anything to do with the actual production of this movie. If Victor's not around, they go to Annie to get their questions answered because she looks more like what a smart professional woman should look like—at least in their miserable, narrow-minded perception. But don't think I didn't run into that while I was acting CEO of The Supply Closet. It's not a stereotype that's confined solely to Hollywood, believe me."

Kate snorted. "Show me the scientific studies that prove that a woman's IQ is directly disproportionate to her bra size. It's only a myth, but it's one we're all guilty of perpetuating. God knows I've done it myself—I've used the 'little ol' me' strategy to catch a business opponent off guard, to fool them into thinking I was harmless."

She looked directly into his eyes. "Tell me honestly. When we first met, was your initial thought 'Wow, I bet she's a card-carrying member of Mensa,' or 'Wow, I bet she'd look great jumping topless out of a cake?'"

Jed laughed. "How can I possibly answer that?"

"Honestly," she replied. "But you don't need to answer, I already know."

He nodded. "Cake." He held her gaze, and for several long, dizzying moments, she was unable to look away. "I'm guilty," he admitted. "And I'm really sorry."

"I forgive you," she whispered. "Do you forgive me for doing whatever I could to protect my movie?"

He leaned toward her, and for one heart-stopping moment, she was certain he was going to kiss her. "Cut my leash, and I'll forget it ever happened."

Once again, she was trapped by his gaze. "I'm sorry, Jed, I can't do that."

"Sure you can. If you wanted to, you could."

"Maybe," she said. "But I don't want to."

He looked away, but not before she saw a flare of anger in his eyes. As she watched, he glanced again at the now-empty cup of the man sitting across the aisle.

"You didn't actually think I'd say yes, did you?" she asked.

"Yeah, I guess maybe I did," he told her. "I mean, now that you're starting to know me . . ."

But she didn't know him at all. She knew only what he

wanted her to know. She knew that while he'd success-fully fought his urge to drink for five years, his hold on his addiction was tenuous at best. And slipping fast.

She was scared of him, but mostly scared *for* him.

No way in hell would she trust him on his own.

"I guess then I need to ask you a favor," he said. He cleared his throat. "See, I haven't exactly made the stipulations of my contract public knowledge, and I'd prefer it if people didn't find out about the round-the-clock supervision thing." He took a deep breath. "I was hoping you could help me save face tonight, and pretend to be my . . . well, girlfriend, I guess. Significant other. Lover. Whatever you want to call it. I mean, why else would you have come along, right?"

Kate stared at him.

"Please? Just do me a favor and pretend you like me."

He actually looked as if he were afraid she'd turn him down. With uncertainty glinting in his eyes, he looked so much like Laramie.

"All right," she found herself telling him.

His smile of relief was genuine.

At least she thought it was genuine.

He was, however, the best actor she'd ever met in her life.

Jericho didn't need clothes to make him attractive. Kate knew that firsthand. But the sight of Jericho Beaumont in a tuxedo was undeniably breathtaking.

The tux was a rental, but despite that, it looked as if five tailors had slaved for hours to fit it exactly to Jericho's precise measurements.

He wore his long, dark hair slicked back into a ponytail, and because of that, he looked almost stern. Except when he smiled. Which he was doing quite often. In fact, he was smiling almost continuously down into her eyes as he held her close, out on the dance floor.

It was like being in the middle of an A-list Hollywood movie.

Kate could barely even remember what David and his wife Alison looked like. Traffic had been heavy, and the limo they'd taken from the airport to the Stern's suburban house had been delayed. There'd been little time to do more than say hello before Kate had been shown to a guest room to change into her evening clothes.

Alison was a pretty blonde. David was short and thin— pure energy in human form. His hair was dark—at least she thought it was. And he hadn't stood still long enough for her to see the color of his eyes behind his glasses.

They'd taken the same limo to the hotel where the dinner was being held, and Kate knew she'd made small talk with her host and hostess, but she couldn't remember what the conversation had been about, or what she'd said.

All she knew was that from the moment she'd stepped out of the guest room dressed in what she called her "mermaid" dress, all she was aware of was the glint of heat in Jericho's eyes.

She'd gone with sequins, not cleavage, but her dress was no less sexy despite that. Silver and glittery, the neckline may have been cut just above her collarbone, but nothing about it was conservative. The sequin-covered fabric was stretchy, and the sleeveless dress fit like a second skin, molding itself to her breasts, leaving very little to the imagination. It hugged her body all the way down past her knees, flaunting her figure, and then tapering out slightly at the bottom, reminiscent of a mermaid's tail.

It was absolutely nothing like the starched-shirt suit she'd worn when Jericho had first come to her office. And back then—had it only been just a few weeks ago?—she never would have believed it possible if someone had told her she'd be wearing her mermaid dress tonight—and actually enjoying the appreciation in Jericho's green eyes.

More than enjoying.

She was hopeless. Just a few days ago, she'd lit into him for looking at her. Tonight, she wanted him to look. Something had changed. Or maybe it was because the look in his eyes wasn't predatory. He wasn't trying to intimidate. On the contrary.

"Thank you for doing this," he said as the band finished its song.

Kate knew exactly what he was talking about. The fact that she was pretending to be involved with him. Pretending to be his *lover*. Touching his arm, brushing her lips across his cheek, giving him long, lingering looks . . .

Go ahead, a voice in her head taunted. Say what you're thinking. Say, *it's completely my pleasure*. "It's been awhile since I've had an opportunity to do any acting," she murmured instead.

Yeah, right. Deny that you are enjoying this, five hundred percent. Deny that the sensation of this man's arms around you while you dance isn't quite possibly the nicest thing you've ever felt in your entire life. Deny that you're not getting off on your own little fantasy here, pretending that this man isn't Jericho, but rather Virgil Laramie and—

Kate tried to shut down the noisy little voice in her head as Jericho took his arms from around her and they both applauded the swing band.

"All the men are looking at me and wondering what I did to get you to come here with me." His eyes crinkled at the edges as he smiled. "What they don't know, huh?"

"Just think about how they'd be looking at you if I were Bob Hollander."

He laughed as the band kicked into another song—a slow, romantic version of "Harlem Nocturne"—and Kate tried desperately not to want his arms around her again.

"Are you thirsty?" he asked. "You know, it's okay with me if you want to have a real drink. I mean, alcohol. Wine. A martini. I don't know—whatever you like."

She had to laugh at that. "You don't really think I drink martinis?"

He leaned back slightly, studying her eyes. "Whiskey sours, or maybe strawberry daiquiris?"

"Candy drinks," she said. "Pah. Not even close."

"Hey, I'm out of practice."

"Good," she said. "Stay that way."

"Are you going to tell me what you *do* drink?"

"Actually, I was hoping for another dance." Her voice came out sounding breathy and far too eager. It was one of the first honest things she'd said all night, and as soon as the words left her lips, she regretted saying them.

But just like that, Jericho's arms were around her again, holding her close—closer even than he had before, and her regret vanished.

"Do you remember how to do a screen kiss?" he breathed in her ear.

As he moved, she could feel his thighs brushing against hers. She looked up at him. "I—"

He kissed her, softly, sweetly, brushing his lips against hers.

He pulled back, looking into her eyes, and she tried to protest. "Jericho—"

"Shhh," he said softly. "Stay in character. You like me, remember?"

He was going to kiss her again. She could see it in his eyes as his gaze lingered on her lips, as he seemed to memorize every inch of her face.

And Kate couldn't breathe, let alone speak. She was about to be kissed again by Jericho Beaumont. She couldn't remember how many times she'd watched one of his movies and dreamed of what it would be like for that gorgeous mouth to claim her own.

He lowered his head slowly, giving her plenty of time to escape.

She almost did. Kissing in public wasn't part of their deal.

But then she saw it. In his eyes. A spark of uncertainty—a faint vulnerability. He wasn't sure if she was going to let him kiss her. And he wanted to kiss her. He wanted it, bad.

And Kate couldn't back away. She didn't want to back away.

Instead she lifted her mouth, closing the last fraction of an inch that gapped between them.

His lips were soft, his mouth sweet, tasting faintly of coffee. She felt him sigh, felt herself melt with him, felt him taste her, touch her lips with his tongue. She opened her mouth to him, and he kissed her so slowly, so deeply, so completely.

It was not just a kiss, it was a communion. It was sheer ecstasy, complete delight.

And it was a million times better than she'd ever imagined.

He wasn't even pretending to dance anymore. And Kate clung to him as if she would fall without his arms around her. She was pressed against him from her breasts to her thighs, and she couldn't help but notice his arousal.

Jericho pulled away first. "My God," he breathed into her ear. "Do you know how long I've wanted to do that?"

Kate's heart was pounding so hard, she almost couldn't hear him over the roaring in her ears. Realization of where they were, and of how completely she'd surrendered to him made her cheeks begin to heat. "Jed, it was only acting."

He lifted his head to look at her again. "The hell it was. You couldn't act your way out of an open window." He touched her cheek. "Look at you. You're blushing because you know everyone who saw that kiss knows damn well that I'm dying to get inside you—and that you're dying for me to be there." He laughed, a brief burst of air. "Hell, we can't even look at each other without giving that away."

Kate shook her head. "You asked me to pretend . . ."

"Imagine how good it could be."

She didn't have to think hard to imagine that. "We hardly even know each other."

"We've been sharing a trailer for more than a week now," he said. "I think we know each other plenty well enough."

Jed gazed down into Kate's upturned face, knowing damn well that she wasn't going to agree with him. Yes, Jericho, I definitely think we should have sex tonight. No, those words weren't going to come out of Kate's mouth here at David's party. But maybe back at the house . . .

"Hey," he said, knowing he would get farther ahead by backing away. "No pressure." Of course, his message would've been a little more convincing if he weren't pressing a hard-on the size of a sawed-off shotgun into the softness of her belly. God, he wanted her. Taking a deep breath, he willed his attraction and arousal to diminish. He tried to push the heat he was feeling far, far away.

It worked. For about three seconds. But then she looked up at him and moistened her lips with the very tip of her tongue, and his desire slammed back into him so hard he was dizzy.

He kissed her again. He couldn't stop himself. And she only hesitated for half a second before kissing him back.

He ached to fill his palms with the fullness of her breasts, to pull down the zipper that ran the length of her back, and to slowly peel this incredible dress from her body. He tried to imagine her underwear, all smooth satin and lace against her equally smooth skin, then imagined himself removing it from her, pictured her draped back on the bed in David's guest room.

"You can't kiss me like that and then deny that there's something intense between us. You know if we *did* have sex, it would be the best either of us have had. *Ever.*" Wrong approach. Jed knew the instant the words were out of his mouth. He'd put her on the defensive. He should've apologized. Whispered that he couldn't resist her. Begged her to help him stay in control . . .

Kate started backing away. "Jericho, we work together. Starting something between us would be *insane*—"

He'd been Jed just a few minutes ago, but now she was calling him Jericho again. That wasn't good. Still, he didn't let her go. "So let's not start something. Let's just take tonight and get this out of our systems. We're hundreds of miles from the set. No one would ever have to know."

"Do you really think we could just . . . get it out of our systems?" she asked softly.

Jackpot. She was admitting there *was* something between them. One of her hands was cupped at the back of his neck, and he could feel her fingers in his hair. It was a sensation beyond description, and he wanted her to leave her hand there forever. Her eyes were so blue and wide, for a moment Jed felt as if he were in danger of falling in and drowning.

"Do you?" she asked again.

He was playing to win, but he had to answer honestly. "No."

She nodded. "I don't think so either."

"Okay," he said. "So we set aside the next two weeks— or however long you think it'll last—and every time we go into my trailer and shut the door, I take you right on the table. We order all of our lunches and dinners in, and spread food on our bodies so that we can at least get a little nourishment when we take turns licking each other all over and—"

Kate laughed. "Stop," she said. "The fact that I'm even remotely considering this means I've completely lost my mind." She took a deep breath, exhaling in a burst, like an athlete preparing to run a marathon. "Tell me how you met David."

"You're changing the subject."

"Brilliant deduction."

"I'm not done telling you all the different ways I want to make love to you."

"You told me no pressure."

"Yeah, but I didn't really mean it."

"Just . . . tell me how you met David."

Jed considered kissing her again, but instead told her what she wanted to know. "It was in high school. I was a freshman, he was a senior. He'd moved to town a few years earlier, but we didn't exactly run in the same circles. At least not until after I went into the city for that audition—and my father . . . did what he did. Rearranged my face."

She nodded. "I remember."

"Danny Pierce—he was that agent who was going to find me modeling jobs—one of the things he told me to do until my face healed was to get involved in the school drama program. 'Course only the nerds like David Stern did drama at my high school. But I auditioned for the spring play anyway—they were doing *Streetcar*. I was only a ninth grader, but I went out for the part of Stanley. I figured, go big or stay home."

"You must've blown the director away."

Jed smiled. Kate had such faith in his ability as an actor. Her conviction made him feel warm, and he realized with bemusement that that warmth was happiness. Imagine that. Happiness, twice in one day. Hell, how long had it been since he'd allowed himself to feel happy about some stupid little insignificant thing? The stakes had been too high for too long.

"Actually, the director thought I was there as a joke," he told her. "To mock the other students, or maybe screw things up by being cast and then bailing a week before the show. So he cast David as Stanley. I was a spear carrier—an extra. I didn't even have any lines."

"*David* was Stanley . . . ?" Kate tried not to laugh. "Oh, dear."

"He wasn't that bad," Jed said. "But . . . he wasn't that good, either. He drove me insane at the time—he didn't do even a quarter of what he could've with that part. I used to grit my teeth to keep from telling him what to do with his body—how to move, how to stand . . ."

"But somehow you and he became friends."

"Um. Not exactly."

"Why do I get the feeling that this is going to be good?"

"David got mono three days before the show opened," Jed told her.

"Ah. And you were the understudy, right?"

"Wrong. The understudy was some geek who hadn't even bothered to learn the part. But I had. I'd memorized all the lines and even worked out better blocking. Still, the director, Mr. Howe, didn't believe me when I told him I was ready to go—that the show could go on as scheduled. I had to coerce Emily Pratt—the girl who was playing Blanche, who also happened to be David's girlfriend— into playing a scene in the hall outside of Mr. Howe's classroom. It worked. The show opened on schedule. I played Stanley, blew everyone away, and stole Emily Pratt away from David in the process."

"Oh, ouch."

"Needless to say, he didn't like me very much after that."

Kate was watching him, amusement dancing in her eyes. Had he really once thought her eyes were nothing special? How could he have failed to notice all the different flecks of color combined with the vivid blue, changing hue with her mood. He wondered what color her eyes would become when she lay looking up at him from her bed, as he slowly filled her. . . .

"So what happened to make him change his mind?" she asked.

God, he wanted to kiss her again. Her lips were slightly parted as she gazed up at him.

"I'm not sure." He had to clear his throat. "He gradu-ated, and a few years later, I left town, too. I didn't see him for more than ten years. But my sister used to send me clippings from the local paper—you know, news about people I'd known from school. So when David was ap-pointed the head of the Rehab Center, I knew about it. And when I was trying to find a place to go—somewhere I could be sure I wouldn't get VIP treatment, I remembered him. I figured he'd enjoy watching me suffer. He'd make damn sure I didn't get anything special to take the edge off my pain when I was going cold turkey."

"So you've only been friends with him for the past few years?"

"Five years," Jed said, "four months, twenty-nine days."

Kate was silent for a moment as they danced. But then she looked up at him. "I don't do casual sex," she said qui-etly. "Sex without love is . . . belittling something very special. I feel very strongly about this."

Jed held his breath, praying that a "but" was coming.

"But," she said, "I have to be honest—both with you and with myself. I wish I could jettison my beliefs and just go for sex for the sake of sex, because I also believe that you are completely right. You and me?" She shook her head. "It would be better than anything I've ever known."

"I'm with you on that," Jed murmured, unable to resist brushing the softness of her neck with his lips.

Her breath caught. "And then I start thinking, if casual sex is so awful, then how come I'm feeling this way?"

"Good question." He kissed her again.

"Oh, God," she said. "We never should have left the movie set. How are we going to go back to sharing that trailer now? It was hard enough lying there with you in the next room before this."

Jed lifted his head. "Really?"

Kate started to blush. "Yes," she said. "All right? Are you happy that you know?"

He was. Extremely happy. So much so that he almost didn't mind when she pulled out of his arms. He followed her off the dance floor and over to the bar.

"Whiskey," she told the bartender. "Straight up." She glanced at Jed as if daring him to comment.

"And a ginger ale," he ordered.

The whiskey came first, and as Kate reached for it, Jed put his hand down, over the top of the glass. "Don't," he said. "I know I told you that I didn't mind. And I wouldn't mind if you just wanted to have a drink, but I know what you're doing, even if you don't."

She lifted one eyebrow, giving him that cool, appraising warrior-queen look that he'd come to know so well. "Really? Just what, then, am I doing?"

He didn't move his hand. "You want to break your rules," he told her. "And this way, you can have something other than yourself to blame. You can make love to me tonight, and wake up in the morning and say, oh, my God, I shouldn't have had all that whiskey last night. I wasn't thinking clearly, and look what happened." He shook his head. "It takes the edge off the responsibility and the guilt. But it's cheating if you do it this way, Kate. Believe me, all you'll end up feeling is worse."

Kate reached up to touch his face, her eyes filled with a mixture of emotions. Confusion, amusement, disbelief, and something warmer, something sweeter.

Her fingers were cool, and Jed closed his eyes, turning his head to kiss the palm of her hand.

She shivered. "Just when I think I've got you pegged, you pull something like this. I would've thought you'd want me to take a little of the edge off my sense of responsibility."

Jed looked down at the whiskey. "Not this way," he said. He let go of the glass, and pushed the ginger ale he'd ordered in front of her.

"I want you," she whispered, and something in his chest squeezed tight. "And you're right. I was going to get a little tanked, so I could be with you."

"Hey, Jed, there you are." David appeared at his elbow. "Mind if I steal your date for a minute or two?" he asked Kate. "I've got somebody I want him to meet. It'll be quick—I promise."

Kate forced a smile. "Take your time."

"Actually, David," Jed started, "now's not the—"

"It's all right," Kate interrupted. She pulled him forward and kissed him lightly on the lips. "Thanks for ordering me a ginger ale." She smiled. "Go get your ass grabbed by some rich old lady."

Jed laughed as David pulled him away. But then he broke free. "Wait a sec," he told his friend as he went back to Kate.

He kissed her again, a slow, lingering kiss that made the room seem to spin. And it affected her as much as it did him. He could see it in her eyes. "I'm starting to think it's not casual," he said softly. "Maybe you should give that some thought, huh?"

She didn't answer. She just stared at him.

"I'll be back in a minute," he told her, then went to join David.

When he glanced back, she was still watching him.

Kate came out of the bathroom wearing only a towel.

There'd been no more time to talk to Jericho during the party, and after returning to the Stern's house, she'd excused herself as quickly as possible. She'd escaped to the guest room to take a long, hot shower, and had stood in the little attached bathroom for close to fifteen minutes, just letting the water drum down on the back of her neck.

She had absolutely no clue what she was going to do about Jericho. *I'm starting to think it's not casual.* What was *that* supposed to mean? That their relationship could be serious? That she was supposed to think she had a future with this man? Having a long-term, serious relationship with Jericho Beaumont was just as foolish an idea as having a casual one-night stand.

She'd left her pajamas in her bag, and as she reached for them, she let the towel drop.

"Um, you don't know I'm in here, do you?"

Kate looked up and directly into Jericho's eyes then dropped behind the edge of the bed, hiding herself from his gaze.

"God!" she said. "What are you doing in my room?" She wrapped her towel back around her, but still didn't stand up. Even the towel didn't offer enough cover from his eyes.

"It's my room, too," he told her.

"What?" She peeked over the mattress to look at him. He was sitting on the sofa on the other side of the spacious guest room.

"David and Allie assumed we were . . . together," he said with a shrug. "It was either this or have me bunk in with Kenny. I think they probably thought as far as roommates go, I'd prefer you to a six-year-old."

"Yeah, well, I'd prefer you to have Kenny."

Kate reached up and pulled her bag down next to her and found her pj's. She slipped the cotton shorts and sleeveless shift on, and then found her robe. Fastening her belt, she finally stood up.

"So," she said, coolly trying to ignore the fact that she was still blushing. "Lucky you. You got to see me naked."

"I've seen you naked before." Jericho had unbuttoned the top button of his shirt and released his hair from his ponytail. He'd taken off his tuxedo jacket as well, and the picture he made sitting there, with his sleeves rolled up and his bow tie undone, was one of relaxed elegance. "But only in the movies," he added.

He was drinking soda directly from a bottle, and he held it out, silently offering it to her.

There was no way in hell she was going to get close enough to him to take that bottle from his hand. She shook her head, folding her arms across her chest.

"Real life was much more fun." He took another sip of soda, his gaze warm. "You look good naked." He smiled. "I suppose I have to apologize for looking, although you better believe that intimidation was the last thing on my mind."

She wasn't going to move toward him, but she sure wouldn't be able to stop him from coming toward her. And if he were to come toward her and put his arms around her, she'd have to tell him that was probably a bad idea. And if he kissed her . . .

If he kissed her, she wouldn't be able to say much of anything, because she'd be kissing him.

Oh, God, she wanted him to kiss her. She wanted him to wrap her in his arms and force this burning physical attraction she was feeling to fog over all of her beliefs, all of her convictions, until the only thing she cared about was the pleasure he could bring.

What kind of an awful person was she?

Kate turned to the bed, briskly pulling the covers back on one side only. "I'm exhausted. We have to be up by seven to get to the airport on time." She turned to look directly at him. "If you want a bed, find Kenny. Otherwise, you're on the couch."

That was good. That was what she was supposed to say. It would keep him from coming any closer much more effectively than saying something like *kiss me now*.

Jericho set his bottle on the windowsill behind him. He stood up in one fluid motion and moved toward the bed. "Kate—"

She backed away. "Jed, please don't. I'm not strong enough to deal with this."

"All evening long, all I could think of was—"

"Stop," she said, her back hitting the wall. "Don't say it!"

"You and me. In here. Alone. Kate, make love to me tonight."

"Oh, God, you said it!"

"Please."

"I didn't have anything to drink," she told him. "I have no excuses."

"I know." He was close enough for her to feel his body heat. But instead of leaning forward and covering her mouth with his, he slowly sank to his knees. He looked up at her from the floor, this beautiful, tuxedo-clad man with dark hair cascading down his back, and the most all-consuming fire glowing in his eyes. "Please," he whispered again.

Kate couldn't move.

He reached up and slowly took hold of the overlapped front of her robe, separating it to reveal her legs to his hungry eyes. He touched her then, first with his gaze and then with his mouth, kissing the inside of her knee, then higher, wending his sensuous way up her thigh.

She was trembling. She was actually shaking.

She knew what she should do. She should slip away, out of his grasp, walk to the other side of the room and tell him no. No, she didn't want this.

But if she did, she'd be lying.

Kate could feel his hands at her waist, his fingers slipped up underneath her pajama top, warm against her bare skin. And then she felt him kiss her intimately, right through her pajamas. Softly at first, but then harder, deeper. She could feel his tongue, feel the wetness of his mouth through the thin cotton, feel him kissing and exploring as his hands slid down beneath her shorts to cup her derriere and hold her more securely against him.

It was shockingly intimate. She'd never known a man bold enough to think he could do such a thing. She waited for a moment, listening for herself to tell him to stop, but all she could say was his name.

She was lost.

She felt her body arch, felt herself opening and moving toward him, wanting more. She laced her fingers through his hair, holding him in place, afraid that he would stop, afraid . . .

Then he did stop, pushing her legs together, but only to sweep her shorts down, off her body. And then he was kissing her, really kissing her, with nothing between them.

It didn't seem fair that something so wrong could feel so right. But he didn't love her, and she . . . No, she didn't love him. She couldn't love him.

But, oh, Lord, she loved the way he was making her feel. And she wanted more.

"Please." Her voice was hoarse, barely more than a whisper.

He lifted his head, looking up at her, and she sank down on the carpeting and kissed him.

He met her mouth with passion, kissing her harder, deeper, even more completely than he had earlier, out on the dance floor. The room seemed to spin around her as she tasted herself on his lips, as he pulled her onto his lap to straddle him, exploring with his fingers where his mouth had been mere moments before.

Then he pulled her robe off her shoulders, and she helped him, shaking it free from her arms. He broke free from their kisses to tug her pajama top over her head, groaning as he filled his hands with her breasts.

He drew her into his mouth, tugging and tasting, drawing harder and harder, until she, too, cried out.

Kate found his hardness through his pants, pressing herself against him shamelessly. She searched for the button, fumbled for the zipper, and he was there, reaching between them, freeing, and then covering himself with a condom he must've been carrying in his pocket.

The fact that he was so well prepared didn't give her pause. She was only grateful as she felt him shift her hips, pressing her down, ensheathing him in one smooth move.

"Oh, *yeah*," he breathed.

He pulled back then to look into her eyes, and what he saw must've been enough to let him know that she didn't want to think, she didn't want to stop, she only wanted to feel.

He rolled her over onto her back, setting a primitive rhythm right there on the floor as she tried to unbutton his shirt. She wanted to touch those incredible muscles he'd paraded in front of her for the past week. With one hand he yanked his shirt over his head, and she pulled him down on top of her, finally skin to skin.

He filled her deliciously hard and fast, plunging into her again and again, and she clung to him, her body straining to take more of him, *all* of him. He kissed her just as hard, taking her mouth just as possessively.

He pulled free from her, and he swung her into his arms, carrying her to the bed. She reached for him, but again he pulled back, quickly pushing his pants down and off his legs as he gazed at her, his eyes dark with need.

Kate propped herself up on her elbows, watching him just as hungrily.

He smiled then, a quick fierce smile that lit his face. "Look at you," he said. "I'm living my fantasy."

"Please," she said, opening her legs to him, near delirious with desire.

He covered her with his body, filling her again with a single thrust, and she moaned her pleasure. Having him there, between her legs, the solid weight of his body against hers felt so right, so perfect.

Her fantasy would be to stay like this, right in this very moment, forever. Her fantasy would be to never have to wake up and face reality.

Her fantasy would be for Jed to kiss her—one of those

deep, soul-touching kisses that he did so marvelously well—and gaze into her eyes and tell her . . . what? That he loved her? That was ridiculous. What they were doing here had nothing to do with love.

Jed was moving more slowly now, each long, sensuous stroke sending waves of scorching pleasure rocketing through her. It was quite possibly the most exquisite sensation she'd ever felt in her life, but it was too beautiful, too intense. And it allowed her too much time to think.

She moved beneath him, and he picked up instantly on her harder, faster tempo, changing his rhythm, giving her exactly what she wanted.

Pure, mindless, deliciously frantic sex.

It was savage, it was wild, it was more passionate than anything she'd ever known. And her release was on a similarly grand scale—a raging storm of thunderous proportions, wave upon wave so intense that the pleasure was almost pain.

Almost.

She took him with her—felt him tighten, heard her name wrenched from his lips.

Ears still roaring, heart racing, her breath still coming in sobs, Kate clung to him. She didn't want it to end. She didn't want to have to open her eyes, didn't want to have to look into his eyes, didn't want to have to talk about it— or worse yet, not talk about it.

She felt Jed shift his weight off of her. He settled himself on the bed beside her, pulling her close—her back to his front. She felt him pull the bedcovers up over them, felt him reach for the lamp on the bedside table, heard the click.

When she opened her eyes, the room was dark.

It was as if he somehow knew.

He sighed deeply, possessively wrapping one arm around her, cupping her breast as he nestled close. He kissed her gently just below her ear and sighed again.

"Best night of my life," he murmured.

His soft words made her heart leap. She knew it was foolish. She knew they were just words. And she knew what she and Jed had just shared was only sex. Nothing more.

But she closed her eyes, letting herself relax.

The dawn, with its harsh light and cold reality, would come soon enough.

Eleven

⤸ ⤸

"**Y**OU'RE UP EARLY."

Kate looked up from her coffee to see Jericho standing in the kitchen door, a towel wrapped around his hips. She blushed, remembering the night before, remembering the way that she'd let him touch her, kiss her . . . Remembering, and wanting him to do it again, God help her.

She took a deep breath and forced a smile. "It's not that early."

"Are you okay?" he asked. The look in his eyes was almost funny. She could see his concern mingling with that heartbreakingly sweet vulnerability that she thought of as belonging to Laramie. He lowered his voice. "I didn't . . . hurt you, did I?"

"I'm fine," she assured him, certain that she was about to be immediately arrested by the understatement police. She was so much better than fine. She was amazing. She was ecstatic. Physically, that was.

Mentally, she was a wreck.

What had she done?

Last night, she'd made love to a man she knew she should've stayed far away from.

She had no excuses. She hadn't been drinking. She couldn't even claim to have been swept away by her fantasies of Laramie. She hadn't even thought of Laramie once, all night long.

No, she'd made love to Jericho Beaumont, and she'd done it with her eyes wide open.

"I don't suppose I can talk you into coming back to bed . . . ?" He looked incredible standing there, six feet three and all hard muscles, with the roguishly dark stubble of beard on his face.

Kate took a steadying sip of her coffee. "Not unless you want to risk missing our flight back to South Carolina. You've got just enough time to shower and grab some breakfast."

"How long before we have to leave?"

"Thirty minutes."

Jericho shook his head. "No, that's not enough. Next time we make love, I want to take my time. I want to spend thirty minutes just looking at you."

Kate felt a rush of heat. God help her . . . "Is there really going to be a next time?" Her voice shook very slightly as she looked up at him.

"I thought—" He broke off, laughing softly. "I'm sorry. I guess I just assumed—God, I hope so." His voice shook, too.

But he was an actor. He could control those things.

"I guess maybe we should set aside some time to talk," Kate said carefully. She was going to have to be upfront with him. She was going to have to tell him she was in danger of becoming emotionally involved. He'd hinted that might be okay with him, but she suspected he would have said damn near anything last night to convince her to make love to him.

"Can we talk on the plane?" he asked quietly. "You know, if it's not too crowded? As long as we're not sitting next to a nun?"

Kate couldn't keep her lips from curving up into the be-

ginnings of a smile. "All right." They could start there. If it
wasn't too crowded—and there were no nuns in sight.

"Good." He turned away, but then turned back. "Last
night was . . ." He couldn't find the words.

Kate's smile grew. "Yeah," she said huskily. "It was."

He grinned then—pure sunshine.

"You better hurry," Kate told him.

"Let me guess—Jed hasn't even taken a shower yet.
That boy is the original procrastinator." David breezed
into the room, setting a paper bag down on the counter. He
took a mug from the cabinet and poured himself some
coffee.

"He just left. I think he must've heard you coming."

David opened the refrigerator and added a healthy
helping of half-and-half to his coffee. "I got bagels and
cream cheese. They're nothing like New York bagels, but
that's okay. I consider their mere existence in Alabama
something of a miracle. Want one?"

"Thanks." Kate stood up and crossed to the counter,
taking a still warm bagel from the bag.

"So you and Jed met recently, huh?" David handed her
a huge knife. "Working together on this movie, right?"

"Yeah." Kate focused on cutting the bagel in half, pre-
ferring not to discuss her brand-new, almost nonexistent
relationship with a man who was not only Jericho's best
friend, but also a licensed psychologist.

"At the risk of sticking my nose in where it's not
wanted," David said, "there's a couple things you should
know about Jed."

Kate looked up. "I'm not sure—"

"It's nothing terrible," David assured her, watching as
she spread cream cheese on half of the bagel. "I'm not
giving away any deep dark secrets here. That's for Jed to
do. But it sure can't hurt if you go into this knowing that
he's one of the most private people I've ever met. And it's
not that he won't talk about himself, because he will. He's

also one of the best storytellers I've ever met, and he'll give you the facts in a heartbeat. And he tells his stories in such a way that you get all wrapped up in 'em, and you don't notice—at least not right away—that he keeps his own distance. He never talks about how he feels, or even how he felt—past tense. He talks about things his father did to him, but he never talks about his own anger. I'm not sure he's ever really let himself feel it.

"I'll tell you one thing, though, Jed's childhood was very tough. If anyone has a right to be angry, *he* does."

"I know," Kate said. "He's told me some things . . ."

"Even if only a quarter of the rumors I've heard about his father were true, Jed lived through a nightmare as a kid. I guess it makes sense he'd learn to hide inside of himself. It makes perfect sense he'd have his own intense struggle with alcohol, too."

Kate washed a bite of bagel down with a sip of coffee. "What are the chances, really, that he'll manage to live the rest of his life without taking another drink?"

David laughed. "I wish I had the answer to that one, but I don't. I wish he'd get back into a twelve-step program, though. Until he does, I can't help but feel that he's at risk. He truly wants his career back, though, and that's good."

"But how can anyone ever really trust him? How can he trust himself?"

"I can't answer that one, either," David told her. "Jeez, what good am I, anyway? One thing I can tell you—and this is really important for you to remember: It's okay for you not to trust him. Jed's earned every little last drop of mistrust that he has to face. I know he's probably given you a whole lot of crap about the around-the-clock supervision, but personally, I think the humbling experience is going to be really good for him perspective-wise and—"

"Wait," Kate said. "Back up. You know about the twenty-four-hour supervision?" She set her coffee mug on the counter, afraid that she was going to drop it. Her fingers were tingling. In fact, her entire body suddenly felt numb.

"Yeah," David said. "Sure. Jed told me about it, spitting fire, after he signed the contract. What he didn't tell me was that his supervisor was going to be you."

Kate sat down at the kitchen table. It was all she could do not to drop her head between her knees. She was both faint and nauseous.

Jericho had lied to her. He had asked her to pretend to be his lover in order to fool David—to keep him from finding out that he needed a baby-sitter. But David had known, and she was the one who had been fooled. She'd played right into Jericho's hands, putting herself exactly where he'd wanted her—in his room last night.

Dear God, last night had been a planned seduction, right from the start.

It had been nothing but a game to him.

Like the acting games he'd played as a child, he'd set the rules and goals for this one. Make her trust him. Make her want him. Score.

Kate looked at David. "I'm not actually his supervisor," she told him. "I'm just filling in, temporarily. In fact, I'm looking for someone who can come onto the set for the next two weeks and take over the job until the permanent replacement arrives. I don't suppose I could talk you into doing it?"

"No, thanks."

She tried her damnedest not to sound as desperate as she felt. "Spending a little vacation with your friend on a movie set? A paid vacation? Jericho's told me you're something of an actor yourself. There're still a couple of small roles—two or three lines—we were planning to fill from our local extras. I could see that you get one."

David laughed. "You make it sound tempting, but, I've gotta say no. This is a busy time of year at the Center, and—I don't know if Jed told you—I also work a few nights a week up at the state prison. I just received a grant to implement a new program with the prisoners, and the next few months are going to be crazy."

Kate resisted the urge to burst into tears. "Do you know *someone—any*one—you could recommend for this position?"

David looked at her oddly. "Did I miss something here? You suddenly seem very upset."

Kate forced a smile. "I'm fine," she insisted. And she would be fine. She just needed a little time. It wasn't as if Jericho had broken her heart or anything. It wasn't. She stood up. "It's time to go—I'll get Jericho."

Kate was on the phone.

Again.

As Jed came out of the shower, he glanced into the main room of the trailer, but Kate didn't look up.

Something was definitely going on. She'd seemed a little tense this morning in David's kitchen, and for several heart-stopping moments, Jed had been afraid that she was going to tell him that last night was a one-shot deal. But then she'd given him hope by admitting how damned good it had been for her, too, and by telling him that she wanted to talk.

Except ever since then, she seemed to be making every effort humanly possible *not* to talk.

The flight from Montgomery back to South Carolina had been nearly empty, but she'd told him that something had come up—she had to make some calls. It was vitally important.

Kate had moved to the other side of the plane, and he'd sat there, staring at his script without really seeing it, wondering why she was no longer looking him in the eye.

He knew something was wrong, but there on the plane wasn't the right time or place to confront her.

And it wasn't the right time after they'd hit Columbia,

either, with one of the gofers driving the van. Kate had spent the entire ride into Grady Falls on her cell phone. And Jed had focused on not wanting a drink.

And then, back on set, he'd had to go to work.

It had not been his best performance ever. He'd been distracted. It was a real clock-watcher of an afternoon and evening as he counted the minutes until he and Kate could go back to his trailer and talk.

Just talk. All he wanted to do was talk. And rid himself of the damned insecurities that were clogging his throat and making his heart beat too fast.

It was crazy and stupid. He'd planned to seduce her and then laugh and walk away.

Laugh and walk away. It was the essential part of his plan for revenge. Except sometime between its moment of conception and today, his needs had taken a sharp left turn.

And now the last thing he wanted to do was walk away.

So now they were here. Kate O'Laughlin. In the trailer. With the telephone.

Kate had jumped on the phone the second they'd walked in, and Jed opted against pulling out his hair in frustration. He'd taken a shower instead. He now finished drying himself off and pulled on a pair of running shorts. On second thought, he took a T-shirt from his drawer, suddenly self-conscious about walking around half naked the way he usually did. Taking a deep breath, he went out into the kitchen to make his usual late-night salad, even though what he really wanted was a shot of tequila.

The best he could hope for was a worm in the produce.

As he got the lettuce from the refrigerator, he heard Kate hang up the phone. He turned to face her and found her sitting at the table with her head in her hands.

Jed sat across from her, his heart suddenly beating much too fast as he reached out to touch her gently on the arm. "Hey, you all right?"

"Go to hell," she said wearily, shaking him off. "You're not any kind of a friend, so quit pretending that you are."

Whoa. Jed gripped the edge of the table. "Kate, what's going on?"

"Oh, *stop*." She looked up at him, real contempt in her eyes. "Just . . . do yourself a favor and shut the hell up."

"What did I do?"

She crossed her arms, the contempt turning to brightly burning anger. "Let's see if I can refresh your memory. You. Fucking me. Last night?"

Jed sat back slightly at her vehemence and her uncharacteristically harsh language. "Okay. I remember that. I also remember that it was still pretty much okay with you this morning." He was trying desperately to remain calm. She was on the verge of a pressure-cooker explosion, and whatever confusion was happening here wasn't likely to get cleared up if they both hit the ceiling. "You said you wanted to talk—"

"That was before I got hit in the face with the truth."

"*Which* truth?"

She laughed in disdain, shaking her head. "Most people only have one version of the truth, Jed—the true one. I could see, though, how *you* might get confused."

"Kate, will you please just tell me what I did so I can apologize and we can get this over with?"

The anger in her eyes flared. "Why? You wanna fuck me again?"

"Well . . . yeah. But that's not—"

"Oh, Jesus, help me!" She swung herself out of her seat and started to pace across the tiny room.

"I'm trying to be honest here! What do you want me to say? *No?* No, I don't want to re-create the best sex of my entire life? Last night was mind-blowing."

"Last night was nothing but a game to you!"

"And you've figured this out by . . . reading my mind?" He took a deep breath. Cool. He had to stay cool.

Kate spun to face him. "No, I figured it out after David accidentally spilled the beans." She gripped her cell phone as if she were going to throw it at him. "You went out of your way to convince me to pretend to be your adoring lover, so your good friend David wouldn't find out something that he already knew! He knew about the contract stipulation—you told him about needing round-the-clock supervision yourself."

"Oh, shit." Jed briefly closed his eyes.

"Yeah," she said. "Oh, shit. You asked me to do you a favor and you sounded so embarrassed, so apologetic, and—stupid me—I believed you. But you're an actor. What was I thinking? You probably planned the whole thing before we even left Grady Falls yesterday, and I just followed along, willingly. God, what an easy target. I practically begged you to sweep me off my feet."

She started pacing again, raking her hands through her hair. "But it's not entirely your fault. I should've been able to resist you. I should have said no, no, no—don't put your tongue there. I should have said, okay, so what if you are the sexiest man in the friggin' galaxy—I have my rules and my number-one rule is no casual sex—especially not with a *jerk!*"

She fought back tears of anger. "God*damn* you. I compromised one of my strongest beliefs, and you were just playing a game!"

"Kate, I—"

"Look me in the eye, you bastard, and swear that when we were on that plane heading for Montgomery, you didn't have a clear vision of exactly how last night was going to end."

Jed took a deep breath. "Okay. You're right. I was hoping we'd end up in bed together—but Christ, Kate, I've been hoping that every day since the shoot started! I thought it was a good opportunity to face up to this attraction between us." He looked up at her, praying that she would understand. "I didn't know how else to do it. I thought if I could just get you in my arms . . ."

"And the hell with integrity," she said sharply. "Get me in your arms any way you possibly can. Lie if you have to, right?"

"It didn't start as a lie," he told her. "I thought what I asked was for you to pretend to be my lover at the *party*. When we got to David's, I realized you assumed what I meant was for you to pretend in front of him and Alison. I was going to tell you the truth, I swear, but . . ." He took another steadying breath. "But then you kissed me before you went in to change. And I thought . . . what harm will it do? And then, in the limo, you were sitting so close and . . . I should have told you. You're right, I was wrong not to tell you that you'd misunderstood. But I couldn't do it. I . . . couldn't. I wanted you too much."

Kate sat down on the couch as if all of the life had been deflated from her. "Your number-one goal in your career is to win an Oscar so that you can stand there, on national television, and tell your father to go to hell. I was wondering why you felt you needed to lie to get me in bed, and it occurred to me that you seduced me as some kind of revenge." She looked up at him. "I fucked you with that contract—that's what you said, your word. So you figure you can get back at me by doing it to me—literally—in return."

Something must've flickered in his eyes, because she looked away from him. "Oh, God. I'm right, aren't I?" She exhaled sharply, as if she were suddenly having trouble getting enough air. "Well, isn't that perfect?"

Jed realized that what he said right here, right now, in these next nanoseconds was either going to save this relationship or kill it for good. "It might've started out that way—me wanting to get back at you—"

"Might've?"

"All right. The truth. It *did* start out that way. And for

maybe a day or two, that's where I was coming from. But then everything changed. I started to like you."

"Great. So then you didn't want to fuck me—as you so elegantly put it—because you hated me. Then you wanted to do it because you *liked* me, right?" Kate stood up. "Maybe you should just shut your mouth before you make things worse." She dug into her briefcase and pulled out the familiar plastic-wrapped urine test kit. She threw it at him. "Fill it."

Jed caught the container, then stood, too, feeling sick to his stomach. "Kate, I don't want our friendship to end."

She was already dialing her cell phone. "What friendship?" She turned away from him speaking into the phone. "I need Jim in carpentry. I know it's late, but I need a door installed, and I need it now."

Jamaal ran one finger lightly over the screen in the back room of Susie's trailer.

The curtain moved, and her face appeared—a pale blur temporarily catching the dim streetlight. And then slowly, achingly slowly, and very quietly, she pushed open the window and took out the screen.

"Catch me?" she whispered.

He nodded, checking to make sure that, in the darkness, no one was watching.

Jamaal always caught her. It was one of the two parts of the evening that made his mouth dry and his heart pound. And it wasn't just because Daddy Pit Bull might hear his baby daughter sneaking out. It was because for about thirty seconds, Jamaal got a chance to hold this girl in his arms.

She came out of the window feetfirst as usual, and he helped her by taking hold of her legs and giving her something to cling to as she shimmied the rest of her out. She was such a little thing, it was hardly a workout.

He held her, trying not to think about the way she locked her legs around his waist as she pulled the curtain closed and carefully reshut the window. He tried not to think about how smooth her legs felt, how firm the tush was he held in his hands. And he definitely didn't focus on the fact that, as she strained to shut the window without making a single noise, she'd leaned forward slightly and managed to stick her breast directly in his eye.

He was learning quite a bit about himself this summer, and one of the things he was learning was he had will-power and restraint unlike any other human male on earth.

He'd also learned he was completely out of his mind because he had a serious jones for a fifteen-year-old girl.

He was Jamaal Freakin' Hawkes, and he had grown women, seriously mature women, throwing themselves at him all the time. Mindy the makeup woman. Tara the PA. Gloria the script supervisor. Mindy, Tara, and Gloria all wanted some. Mindy, Tara, and Gloria all had made that more than clear.

Yet here he was, six nights in a row, risking certain death from Pit Bull bite, just to hang with this scrawny little underage child that he dare not so much as touch.

Except for the times he helped her out of, or back into, her trailer through the window.

"Got it," Susie whispered.

He made himself let go of her butt, and she slid down him as if he were a fire pole. Damn, he was starting to live for that sensation.

They moved quickly, heading away from the trailers and the town, heading down a path through the nearby woods, toward a small pond. And once there, surrounded by the shadows, away from the lights of the tiny town, lit only by the hazy light from the moon, Susie relaxed.

"One of these days, I'm going to have a heart attack from doing that," she told him.

"Ditto." Although his was going to be for an entirely different reason.

"You were great today, by the way." She picked up a

rock and skipped it across the surface of the water. "I saw the dailies. You rocked."

Jamaal picked up a rock and threw it. It sank to the bottom. "Shit."

She laughed. "You've got to think lighter."

"I can't skip stones because my thoughts are too heavy, is that what you're saying?" Jamaal smacked the back of his neck. The mosquito that had been feeding on him was the size of a bird. He peered at his hand in the dim light. "Oh, man, would you look at this? This thing has fangs."

Susie took a bottle from her back pocket. "I brought some of that bug repellent I was telling you about. Wanna try it?"

He took the bottle from her. "What, I smear this stuff on myself and then I die of cancer in ten years?"

"I'm wearing it. Do you see any bugs bothering me?" She twirled around, doing a graceful dance at the edge of the water.

He let himself watch her. "That wasn't what I asked. I didn't ask if it worked—I asked if your ass was going to be *dead* in ten years."

"If I am, sue them for me."

Another mosquito took up where the first had left off. Jamaal opened the bottle and squeezed a minuscule amount of the lotion into his hand.

"Do you have another project lined up, after this one?" Susie asked, coming back to watch him gingerly apply the lotion to his arms.

"Actually, my agent's been calling. Said there's a couple scripts I need to read. He's sending 'em down, but I'm feeling kind of . . . I don't know."

"Kind of ambivalent?" She took the bottle from him and squeezed out a healthy blob into her own palm. "Lean over, I'll get the back of your neck."

"Yeah," he said. "Ambivalent. That's the word."

He leaned over, closing his eyes as she gently rubbed

the lotion into his neck. She had no idea what her touch did to him, and because she had no idea, it wasn't a bad thing, right? She was being a friend. *He* was the one who needed therapy. What did she just say? *Think lighter.* He was the one who needed to start thinking way lighter.

She was just a girl who had no clue that she set his world completely on fire. But he wasn't going to be the one to tell her. No way. And he sure as hell wasn't going to touch her, no matter how badly he wanted to. He liked her too much to start something she couldn't possibly be ready for.

"If you could do anything in the world, what would it be?" she asked, slipping her fingers under the collar of his T-shirt and rubbing in the lotion.

It took him a minute to realize that she was talking about movies. Acting projects. "Shit, I don't know. It's not like I've got a really huge choice. I mean, I'm not Harrison Ford, you know."

"Oh, my God, you're not?" She wiped her hands on her shorts as he straightened up.

"No, smart-ass. I'm not. Basically I choose between movies where I play an addict stuck in the ghetto, and movies where I play a member of a gang, stuck in the ghetto."

"You need to do a Will Smith."

He snorted. "What, become a rapper on the side?"

"He was a rapper first. But no. Think about *ID4* and *Men in Black*. In both of those movies, Will didn't play a black man. He played a man who just happened to be black. Both of those movies would've worked with a white actor playing those parts. Yeah, the dialogue would've had to be reworked for a white guy, and the movies probably wouldn't've been so funny—but that's just because Will's so good. Anyway, that's what *you've* got to do next," Susie decided. "Don't take a movie unless the part that you're offered could be played by someone white."

"Yeah, right," he scoffed. "Those kinds of offers are just rolling in."

"Get your agent to work for you," she told him. "That's what he's supposed to be doing. Tell him what you want, and tell him to go find it. Or go after the scripts yourself. Make friends with someone huge like Leo DiCaprio and ask him to pass anything your way that he likes but doesn't have time for."

Jamaal sent another stone straight to the bottom of the pond. "All right," he said. "I'll call my agent later tonight. I love waking him up." He turned toward her, brushing the dirt off his hands. "So now are you going to let *me* pick *your* next project?"

She skipped another rock. "I think I'm going to have to do *Slumberparty Three* next, just to keep my father from having an aneurysm."

Jamaal laughed. But then he realized that she was serious. "Oh, no way!"

Susie was pretending to be engrossed with finding the perfect skipping stone in the hazy moonlight. "Here, try this one. It's perfect." She held it out to him.

Jamaal didn't move. "You can't honestly go from *this* movie to—"

"Yes, I can. It's not that big a deal." She stood up and reached for his hand, positioning the stone between his thumb and first finger. "Now, throw it kind of like a Frisbee."

But he didn't throw the stone. He just looked at her.

"I had to promise him I'd do it," she said quietly. "I thought it would help get him off my back."

"Did it?"

She turned away, slapping her arm. "These bugs are really getting bad."

"What's he do to you?" Jamaal asked. He'd asked her about her father before, but never point-blank like this. She was always evasive, never giving him a straight answer. But the thought of that man hurting this girl made his blood boil. "Does he hit you?"

"No." She answered too fast. "Jamaal, I don't want to talk about him, okay?" She slipped the plastic bottle of lotion into the back pocket of her shorts. "We better get back."

Jamaal caught her hand. He'd vowed never to touch her unless it was necessary, but this was definitely necessary. "Susannah, we're friends, right?"

She nodded, staring down at her feet.

He tipped her chin up so that she had to look him in the eye. In the moonlight, she looked like some kind of angel. A tense angel. She was strung so tight, he was afraid she was going to snap in half. He lowered his voice, trying hard to sound as gentle as he possibly could. "You can trust me enough to tell me anything, you know. There's nothing you can say that would stop me from being your friend."

"It's not what you think," she said, but her eyes filled with tears.

"What *do* I think?" he asked quietly.

Again, she didn't answer him directly. "He loves me," she said, her mouth trembling. "He just . . . forgets sometimes."

"No," Jamaal said. "It doesn't work that way, baby. When you love someone, you don't ever 'forget.' There's no exception to that rule."

Susie was watching him with those big, wide eyes, listening to what he was saying. He liked being with her, because she listened. She listened to what he had to say, and she thought about it, and she discussed it as if it had merit. She was smart, and she made him feel smart, too. She made him feel as if every word out of his mouth was a precious gem to examine and treasure. He prayed that she would listen double hard to the words he was saying now.

"If he's touching you," he continued, "it's wrong. If

he's hitting you, it's wrong. And if he's using words to hit and hurt, that's wrong, too."

She was silent, just gazing up at him. "We better get back," she said again, finally pulling away.

Jamaal followed her into the woods, along the trail to town. She didn't say much, and then as he helped her back into her trailer, she couldn't say much. They both had to be quiet. He boosted her up, then waited until she gave him the all-clear signal.

Still, he waited even longer, as had become his custom. He sat there in the darkness alongside Susie's trailer, and he waited to make sure that her father hadn't discovered she was gone. He waited to make sure that if the Pit Bull *had* found her out, he didn't attack her in his rage.

He waited until the light went off in Susie's room, and then he waited a little bit longer.

And then he went to his own trailer, and picked up the phone. It was after midnight, but this was one call that couldn't wait.

"You're lucky I'm a fan of 'Politically Incorrect.' What's *your* excuse for being up this late?"

Jamaal smiled, just the sound of her voice gave him faith that this was going to be all right. "No excuse. I'm definitely up past my bedtime."

His mother could read him like a book, and her voice softened. "Baby, are you okay?"

"I'm fine." He took a deep breath. His mother was a social worker who dealt with stuff like this all the time. He'd grown up with books on physical, emotional, and sexual abuse all over the house. His mom had made him read some of them, too. "But I've got a friend, and I think she's being abused. Except she won't talk to me about it. I'm not sure how hard I should push this."

She sighed. "Do you think her life is in danger?"

"No. But I think she's miserable, and I *know* she's scared."

"And you've confronted her about this?"

Jamaal sat down on his couch and rubbed the back of his neck. "Just tonight. She says nothing's going on. But I know that even if her father's not touching her, he's breaking her with his words."

"Give her time," his mother told him. "You may have frightened her by asking her what's happening. If her father *is* abusing her—and I assume you believe it's sexual abuse . . . ?"

Jamaal closed his eyes. "I don't believe it—I'm just afraid that's what it is."

"If that *is* going on, you better believe she's working overtime to keep anyone from finding out. And then *you* come along and essentially say to her 'I see through your disguise.' That's got to be pretty shocking to her. Give her time. But don't let her distance herself from you. Give her the hotline number. Make sure she knows that she doesn't have to talk to you about it—but she *does* have to talk to someone."

"All right."

"You want me to come down there?"

Jamaal smiled. "With your busy schedule?"

"If you want me to come, just tell me, and I'll come."

"Thanks, Mommy, I know. And I might take you up on that. But right now . . ." He sat up. "I'll call you later in the week."

"You want to talk more about this now?"

"No, I got an early makeup call."

"I'm glad you phoned. I'm proud of you, and I love you," she told him.

"Back at you, babe."

"Sleep well, smart-ass."

Jed lay in the dark, listening to Kate pretend she wasn't crying.

She'd had her team of builders come in several hours ago and install a door down at the end of the hall, offering her a small amount of privacy. But the door was flimsy, and try as she might, she couldn't control the raggedness of her breathing.

After hustling all day to find a replacement, she'd actually called the other financial backers, recommending that they let the 24/7 supervision requirement drop. She'd been *that* anxious to get away from him.

But much to her dismay, the backers had insisted Jed continue to be supervised, that she protect their investment.

Short of letting one of the gofers baby-sit him, she was stuck.

He got up and stood next to the door that now separated his half of the trailer from hers. He leaned his forehead against it, then tried the knob. Locked.

"Kate."

She was suddenly absolutely silent—it was as if she'd even stopped breathing.

"I'm sorry," he said through the door.

And he was. He was tremendously sorry. He couldn't remember the last time he'd felt this bad.

Just yesterday, he'd let himself dare to feel happy for the first time in forever. And now he was facedown in the flip side of it.

This was why he always tried his damnedest not to feel anything at all. It was better to skip the happiness entirely than feel this way.

He tried to push all he was feeling away from him, to vaporize this persistent sense of loss. What had he lost? The chance for something unattainable. It wasn't as if anything lasting would've come from a relationship with Kate. It was absurd to think that was a possibility. He'd lost the opportunity for great sex. It was regretful, but nothing to cry over.

So why couldn't he shake this feeling of despair?

Nearly an entire minute passed, and Kate finally spoke.

"Go to sleep, Jericho. Wasn't last night enough of a win for you?"

He pressed the palm of his hand against the door. "What's it going to take to convince you that it wasn't a game to me?" His voice came out sounding husky, his accent a little thicker. It was Laramie's voice. If anyone could get through to her, it would be Laramie. And if Laramie couldn't win her trust, Jed himself didn't stand a chance.

"Probably years of therapy." He heard her draw in a deep breath. "Just . . . leave me alone. Back off, all right? I'm not going to sleep with you ever again—not for as long as I live, so you might as well make things easier on both of us and just accept that."

So much for Laramie. Jed's stomach hurt. "Okay," he said. "What if I *do* accept that? Can we be friends again?"

She was silent.

"Can we?" he asked again.

"I don't think I want to be your friend."

Jed closed his eyes. God, he wanted a drink. "I'm sorry," he said again.

"Me, too."

Twelve

❦

THE HEAT WAS driving Kate insane.

And she wasn't the only one. Tempers were on edge all over. Even Naomi and Victor had taken opposite sides in the set-wide argument over the ending of the script. Two of the production assistants had even come to blows over whether or not a rewrite was needed.

Kate heard the shower shut off and braced herself for Jericho to come out into the trailer.

The air conditioner was positioned at its coolest setting, but even working overtime, the lowest the thermostat went in this heat was seventy-five. Still, when Jericho came into the room, it felt a whole hell of a lot hotter.

Kate had the TV on, tuned to the Weather Channel, and she focused on it as she heard him come out of the bathroom. It seemed impossible that she'd managed to survive the past five days since they'd returned from Alabama. But she had. And she was going to survive three more. But only three more. Because in three days, a social worker named Joe Boren was flying in from Alabama to take over as Jericho's supervisor.

The good news had come in that afternoon.

She could feel Jericho watching the TV over her shoulder. "Lord," he said. "More rain?"

The current environmental condition was one of the few topics she'd discuss with him. Everything else seemed way too personal.

But summer had arrived with a vengeance, and the heat had gone from hellish to unbearable. And with the heat had come torrential rainfall. And with the rain, the mosquitoes swarmed.

There was plenty to talk about.

The rain was pounding on the roof of the trailer, and the thought of having to go out in it to get to the other trailer was exhausting. But the thought of just about everything was exhausting these days.

Kate was trapped 24/7 with a man who—simply by existing, simply by breathing—repeatedly reminded her of the hottest, most explosive sex she'd ever had in her life.

But it was also among the cheapest, and least meaningful. It wasn't worthy of such extensive thought, such shallow obsessing. It had been nothing more than a one-night stand—a point that shamed her beyond belief. She'd sworn to herself she'd never do that again.

And the fact that she still wanted him was even more mortifying. It was bad enough to be duped, but for her to know full well the kind of man he was and still yearn for his touch . . .

Lightning flashed and thunder boomed almost immediately, and Kate jumped. God, she was on edge.

"Kate, what's this?" There was a note of something in Jericho's voice that was more than mere curiosity.

She glanced up.

He was standing by the table, where two glasses of iced tea had been set, complete with lemon wedges, sugar cubes, and long-handled stirring spoons. One of the glasses was empty.

"It's really great iced tea," she said. "It was there when we came in. Didn't you call and ask Edna to send it over?"

"No." He picked something up from the table. "Oh, Christ. Did you drink this?"

"Yeah." Kate stood up. "Why? What's that?"

There was some kind of card—the kind with a little envelope that florists sent with flower arrangements. He held it up for her to see. "This was under the glass."

" 'Have a nice trip,' " Kate read aloud. "What does that mean? I'm not going anywhere."

He reached for the phone and quickly dialed. "Hey, Edna. Yeah, it's Jericho. A question—do you ever use sugar cubes at the Grill—you know, those little squares of . . ."

Kate crossed her arms. "What are you—"

He held up his hand. "I didn't think so. All right. Thanks." He hung up the phone and turned to Kate. "The Grill uses those little packets of sugar. How many of those cubes did you put in your tea?"

She stared at him. "Jericho, you're scaring me."

"Kate, I ran into Tony today. Remember Tony? The kid you fired for drugs? You were on the phone, and I went over to craft services to get a soda. He came over to me—I don't know how he got on the set. He was really wasted, and he wanted to know if I was interested in scoring some really top-notch acid. He told me I wouldn't have to worry about getting caught—that I could keep my stash in the kitchen, in plain view because it was in sugar-cube form."

Sugar cubes. Kate felt all of her blood drain from her hands and feet. It was the oddest sensation and, despite the heat, she suddenly felt cold. "And you think those sugar cubes I put in my iced tea . . . ?" She couldn't even say it.

"I told him to get off the set, to go somewhere and decompress, and then get out of town. I gave him a hundred bucks to pay for his gas—I guess because I felt bad about getting him fired. He got mad at me and started making all kinds of threats."

"Why didn't you tell someone?"

"I should have. But I thought it was just the drugs talking. I didn't think he was serious." Jericho grimly shook his head. "Kate, I don't mean to scare you, but you need to tell me how many of those sugar cubes you used."

"Two. Actually, I only used one and a half in the tea, but then I . . . I ate the other half."

"Shit."

Lightning flashed again, and the power in the trailer flickered and went out.

"No," Kate said. "God, no. Not now, please . . ."

She heard Jericho moving around, saw lightning flash again as he peeked through the blinds. "Looks like this entire part of town lost power." He picked up the phone and swore again. "The line's dead. Look, Kate, go into the bathroom and try to make yourself throw up, all right? But first give me your cell phone. I'm going to call David. He'll be able to tell us how long we've got until this stuff kicks in."

Kate's hands were shaking as she dug through her purse and found her phone. She handed it to him. "Jed, find a candle, please? I'm afraid of the dark."

He dialed David's number by touch, then started searching through the kitchen drawers. "I'm on it."

"David said if there was LSD in the sugar, you'll definitely start experiencing its effects within twenty minutes."

"It's been at least fifteen since I had the tea." Kate looked up at him from the bathroom floor. She was sitting, leaning back against the wall, holding her knees close to her chest. She looked scared to death, her eyes wide in the flickering light from the candle he'd found in the bathroom cabinet, of all places.

"It's occurred to me that Tony might've just wanted to

scare us," Jed said, sitting down next to her. "He may not have laced the sugar cubes with anything at all."

She sat up slightly, such hope in her eyes. "You think?"

"Yeah," he lied, smiling at her. "Yeah, definitely."

David had told him quite a bit about LSD—the most important fact being that if she *had* ingested it, there was not much anyone could do for her, except stay with her over the next few hours while the hallucinogenic drug ran its course. If she became too agitated, he could take her to the hospital and she could be given Valium to calm her down. But David had suggested staying away from the hospital—simply being in a hospital often created extra fear in most people, and fear and negative emotions were often the cause of what was known as "a bad trip."

The first thing Jed had to do was get Kate to relax, to try to override that fear.

"It's hot in here," she whispered.

"No power equals no air conditioning. I called Annie—apparently a car hit a telephone pole over on the state road. The electric company's giving it a repair priority, but best case scenario doesn't have it fixed until tomorrow morning."

"We can't get another day behind schedule," she said worriedly.

"Oh, no way. We won't. We're shooting up at Brandall Hall tomorrow, remember? For the next few days, we're working all those scenes with Susie and Jamaal in the slave quarters, so we're okay, even if it keeps raining. I had Annie call up there and check, and as of right now, they've still got power. We're good to go."

"You had Annie call . . . ?" She was looking at him with such surprise.

"Yeah. I thought you might be worried about tomorrow, and I didn't want you to have to . . . you know. Worry. About tomorrow."

"Oh, my God, am I going to die?"

Jed laughed. But then he realized that she was serious.
"Oh, Kate, no." He put his arms out, and when she came
willingly into his embrace, he realized that she was even
more terrified than she was letting on. "You're going to be
fine."

She tilted her head to look up at him. "So why are you
being so nice to me?"

"Believe it or not, I, um . . ." He cleared his throat. "I
like you. A lot. And—"

She was still looking up at him. "And you think maybe
if you act really sweet and nice, I'll have sex with you
again."

He smiled down into her eyes. "And then there's that,
yeah."

She actually smiled back at him. "I like it when you're
honest."

Jed nodded. "Yeah, I'm trying to remember that."

"So you really don't think Tony actually put any LSD
in those sugar cubes?" she asked, searching his eyes.

Um. "I think it's entirely possible that he didn't, no."
There, that wasn't a lie, was it?

"So maybe I made myself throw up for nothing." She
rested her head against his shoulder, and he stroked her
hair, amazed that the tide had turned so completely. An
hour ago, he never would've believed he could be sitting
here with Kate in his arms. Still, he wished this hadn't
happened—that it wasn't happening this way.

"Bulimics must be insane," she mused. "I will never do
that again, as long as I live. Ack." She sighed. "Maybe I
should just go to bed. Maybe if I just go to sleep, then even
if there was LDS in those sugar cubes—oops I said LDS. I
meant LSD. That's funny—but maybe even if it *was* in
there, I can just go to sleep and then when I wake up, it'll
be gone and—"

"I don't think you're going to be able to sleep."

She didn't seem to hear him. "God, it's hot in here. Will

you help me open the windows? Hmm. Do these windows even open, I wonder? I mean, I'm so used to having the air-conditioning on—I don't even know if the windows in this trailer have screens and—" She stopped cold. "Jericho. The walls are moving. Like they're breathing. They're . . . Oh, God. It *was* in there, wasn't it?"

"Yeah," Jed said, quietly. "Now I pretty much think that it was."

She held him tighter, closing her eyes. When she spoke, her voice was very, very small. "Please don't leave me."

"I'm here with you," he told her. "All the way."

"I don't want the walls to move," she whispered. "Can we go outside—where there aren't any walls?"

"It's raining."

"I don't care."

She'd had a late-afternoon interview with an editor from *Premiere* magazine, and she was still wearing a sleeveless white silk shell and a slim-fitting linen skirt. She'd kicked her high-heeled sandals off, and they lay on the bathroom floor. "You've got on really nice clothes," he reminded her.

She struggled to her feet. "Please, I just want to get outside." She put her hands around her eyes like blinders. "Oh, God. Oh, God. Oh, God . . ."

"Close your eyes." Jed picked her up and carried her out of the bathroom and toward the door. He opened the door, and they were instantly hit with a blast of rain, right through the screen. "You sure?"

"Yes!"

He pushed the screen open, and they were outside. As he set Kate down, the rain soaked them to the skin almost instantly, sticking Kate's hair to her head, and plastering her blouse to her incredible body.

"Better?" He had to lean close and speak right into her ear to be heard over the roar of the rain.

She was staring down at the grass. "No." He still had

his arms around her, and he could feel her start to take short, sharp, panicked breaths. "Jed . . ."

"I'm right here."

"There's something out there!" She practically leapt up and into his arms. "I don't like this, I don't like this!"

"Okay," he said, trying to sound calm. "Let's go back inside, and get the candle and the cell phone, and then go into the other trailer."

She didn't want to go back inside, but she didn't want to stay outside, either. He grabbed her gym bag with her pajamas and the cell phone, keeping Kate in his arms, and the candle lit until right before they stepped out the door.

The candle went out, and Kate closed her eyes as he carried her into the rain.

Inside the other trailer, Jed put everything down—including Kate—and relit the candle.

"Kate, look at me."

She opened her eyes.

"This is the trailer where we sleep at night," he told her, praying that this was going to work. "There's nothing in here. You know there's nothing in here but our beds and our pillows and our blankets and sheets. Other than that, this place is clean. You know that. So if you see something weird, it's only the drug talking. It's not real. And if you have your doubts, ask me. I swear to you, I will only tell you the truth tonight, all right? I swear on my mother's grave."

Her eyes widened. "Your mother has a grave?"

Damn. Poor choice of expression. "She died a long time ago."

"I'm sorry." She made an incredible picture standing there, her hair plastered to her head, her skirt misshapen and dripping wet. But it was her silk blouse that truly did him in. It was glued to her breasts and completely see-through. Her bra had been made transparent by the soaking rain as well, and she looked like a knockout grand-prize-winning contestant in a wet T-shirt contest. Absolutely nothing was left to the imagination—her dark pink nipples standing out, clearly outlined in sharp relief. It was as if she were completely topless.

Jed tried his best not to look, but failed. Miserably.

She looked down at herself, following his gaze, and didn't try to cover herself, for once didn't even seem to mind. She just stood there, letting him look. "I see you're admiring my Hollywood résumé—the two great big reasons I was cast in *Hillsdale Horror* and *Dead of Night.* You're also looking at the reason Victor married me." She put her hands on her hips and thrust her chest out even farther. "Pretty nifty, huh? The not-so-secret to my success." Her laughter was giddy, and on the verge of hysterical.

"But not after this year," she continued. "After *The*—" She stopped, blinking. "What is this movie we're making called?"

"The Promise."

"Right. *Right.* After *The Promise* comes out, I'm not just going to be some B-list bimbo with big boobs. I'm going to be the B-list bimbo with big boobs who won two Oscars—best picture and best screenplay." She laughed again. "One for each boob."

Best screenplay . . . ? *"You* wrote this script?"

"Oops. That was a secret. Do you mind if I take off my skirt?"

"No." Jed was completely bemused. "You really wrote—"

"You were right about this trailer." She shimmied out of her skirt. "It's a little hot, but so far the walls are behaving. Do you mind if I lie down?"

"No." Sweet God, she was wearing thong panties. Jed opened her bag. "Maybe you should put on your pajamas . . ."

She went down the hall and climbed into his bed. "Did you know I spent three years working as a body double?"

He followed, still carrying her pajamas, and the candle as well. "No, I didn't. God, three *years*?"

Body doubles took off their clothes for the camera. They suffered all the indignities of movie love scenes and nude scenes—having to work naked in a crowded room—without any of the star recognition and glory. Still, at the same time, he could see why she would have gotten quite a lot of work as a double. She had a body to die for.

She stretched languidly. His mouth went dry, and he had to look away, setting the candle down on the floor in the corner of the room.

"It was right after *Dead of Night*," she told him. "Right after Victor and I got married. He finally got a chance to direct a studio movie, and I figured it was finally *my* chance, too, to have a part that didn't involve my taking my shirt off. But Victor didn't cast me. My own husband didn't think I was good enough. But you better believe when the time came to shoot the love scenes, I was brought in as a body double. The first time it happened, Victor had a double cancel on him and he was desperate. Or so the story goes."

She looked up at him, suddenly remarkably lucid. David had told him that might happen, but that Jed shouldn't leave her alone. She might come across as completely together one minute and then completely lose it the next.

"You know, I cried for four days after filming *Dead of Night*," she told him. "I never told Victor, but I hated every minute of it. But I couldn't tell him that, I never told anyone. I just pretended to be this sophisticated actress who walked around naked on the set and didn't give a damn about anything. Inside, I was sick to my stomach. Inside, I was twelve years old again, only this time I *knew* those boys were watching me undress. This time I was keeping the money. It was awful. And as bad as *Dead of Night* was, being a body double was ten times worse."

She closed her eyes and stretched again, and Jed let

himself look at her. He hadn't had a real chance to do that at David's. He'd been right about her skin. It looked as smooth and impossibly silky as he knew it to be. He would have given damn near anything to be able to touch her again. She wasn't one of those women who worked out four hours a day, with a washboard stomach and sinewy arms. She was curvy in all the right places—completely, thoroughly feminine with gracefully shaped arms and legs, and a softly rounded, impossibly sexy stomach.

"I wasn't even a person," she said, her eyes still closed. "I was a collection of attractive body parts."

"Why did you do it for three years?"

She opened her eyes and looked up at him. Damn, she was beautiful, even with her hair wet and her makeup smeared. Her eyes were so blue and so sad, he wanted to sit down next to her and take her into his arms. But he knew that would be asking for trouble. Once he started touching her, he damn well wouldn't want to stop.

"At first I pretended it was acting." She laughed, a tinge of hysteria in her voice. "But then my marriage started falling apart—which it did pretty early on, since Victor apparently was absent from school the day the word 'fidelity' was added to the vocabulary list. And I . . . I guess I kept taking work as a double to punish myself. Or him. Or both of us, I don't know. Probably mostly to punish myself. I grew up Catholic, you know."

Jed had to smile. "I know."

She sat up, motioning him to come closer. He leaned down, and she whispered into his ear. "I was bad back then. I had sex with the boom operator, and I didn't even like him." Her eyes filled with sudden tears. "He didn't even know me. He said, 'Want a beer?' And I said okay, and I was already so drunk, the next thing I knew, we were in his truck, doing it. I didn't even know his name." She put her head in her hands. "Oh, God . . ."

Jed sat down on the bed, next to her. "Don't think about

that," he told her. "Those aren't good thoughts. Besides, it doesn't matter. You're not that person anymore."

She thought about that for a moment, but shook her head. "Yes, I am. If I were different now, I wouldn't have had sex with you."

"We weren't strangers in the back of a truck. We were clearheaded adults who liked each other enough to become lovers and—"

She scuttled back on the bed, hitting the wall with a thump. "Jed! The walls!"

He took her hands, pulling her so that she was facing him. "Look at me, Kate. *Look* at me. The walls are fine. It's just the candle flickering."

She was starting to breathe hard again. "There's something coming out from underneath the sheet," she whispered. "I think it might be a snake."

"I swear to you, there's nothing here." Still holding on to her with one hand, he swept the sheets back and off the bed with his other, leaving no hiding places for snakes—real or imaginary.

"Something's on me!" She was about to hyperventilate. "Get it off, get it *off*!" She pulled away from him, yanking her shirt up and over her head and flinging it across the room. But even that wasn't enough. Her bra and panties followed, along with all of the pillows on the bed.

And then Kate started wiping herself, as if there was something on her skin. But then she wasn't wiping, she was scratching, and Jed grabbed her, holding her hands and pulling her close against his body. She was shaking, straining against him, sobbing, trying to get free.

"There's nothing there," he told her. "Kate, there's nothing on you. Remember, I promised I'd tell you the truth—that I'd take care of you? I'm telling you right now, there's nothing there!"

"But I see them!"

"Close your eyes," he commanded her. "Close your eyes and trust me!"

"Jed!" She was crying now, great huge, tears that made his own eyes start to fill. "I can't close my eyes! When I do, I see all the dark corners of my brain!"

He turned her so that they were nose to nose. He repositioned her arms up over her head so that he held both of her wrists in one hand as he pinned her with his body. "Look into my eyes, then," he said. "I'm going to tell you a story, okay? Just keep looking into my eyes, all right? I'm going to tell you . . ." In desperation, he reached for the one thing he thought might hold her attention and distract her. "I'm going to tell you a secret. I'm going to tell you something I've never told anyone before in my life— the real reason I checked myself into rehab. I sort of told you part of this before, but not the whole story."

She held onto his gaze as if it were a grappling line. "The *real* reason?"

"Yeah." She was calmer now, and he started to pull back, aware that his full weight was on top of her, painfully aware that she was naked beneath him.

"Don't," she begged, clinging to him. "Please, don't leave me."

"I'm not going to leave," he promised. "But I don't want to crush you."

"I like it," she whispered. "You make me feel safe."

Jed didn't know what to say. No one had ever told him that before. "Well, shoot. So much for taking advantage of the fact that you're naked and in my bed. Now I have to be responsible and upstanding and all that crap, so that you don't stop feeling safe."

She laced her fingers through his hair. "I would feel very safe if you kissed me."

"Wow, that's a really bad idea." He was completely aroused but trying his damnedest not to be. And although he'd joked about it, he'd been dead serious. There was no way in hell he was going to take advantage of her while she was so out of it.

"Jed, something's moving in the corner of the room." The panic was back in her voice.

"Don't look over there. Don't look anywhere but into my eyes."

"Talk to me. Please."

"I'll tell you what happened, but first you've got to promise me you'll never tell anyone."

"I promise."

Jed took a deep breath. "After my brother Tom died, I did a slow spiral downward as far as my drinking went. I was pretty heavily hooked on prescription drugs by that time, and things got really bad. I started missing call times, started phoning in my work until I finally got fired."

"That's not a secret," she told him.

Jed had to laugh. "No kidding. I'm getting to the secret part, all right?"

She nodded.

"I remember thinking, okay, the director—Hank Anton—he couldn't be serious about this. This was just a scare tactic to get me back in line. Anton wouldn't really *fire* me, no way. Because, hey, I was Jericho Beaumont, right? Everybody wanted me to be in their movie. So I got sober, and I went back in to work, expecting little more than a scolding. But to my complete shock, Andy Garcia was in my trailer. I'd been replaced by someone more reliable." He could still taste the complete shock, still see the embarrassed look in Garcia's eyes. He'd been badly embarrassed *for* Jed.

"I went on a binge that lasted more than two weeks. And one of the last things I did was get into a bar fight."

Kate was playing with his hair, running her fingers through it in a way that felt too damn good. And every now and then, her gaze lingered on his mouth. Under normal circumstances, he would have taken that as a direct invitation to kiss her. But there was nothing even remotely normal about any of this.

"Paparazzi were there," he told her, "and one of 'em got this picture of me in action, beating the crap out of some cowboy I don't remember for some reason I don't remember. But I was mad as hell, and it showed in my eyes and on my face—my teeth were bared. It was a really awful picture—I looked completely insane. And the next week, that picture ran on the front page of one of the supermarket tabloids. And my sister Louise called me up. She'd seen it. Seen me. And you know what she said to me?" He paused.

"I really love your hair."

Jed laughed. "Are you listening to any of this?"

"I can listen and love your hair at the same time. And I can't guess what your sister said to you, because, really, there's just too many possibilities. I mean, she could have said, 'Hi, Jed, this is Louise. Did you watch *Ally McBeal* last night?' Unless it was a Friday, in which case she might've asked if you'd watched *Friends* or—"

"I completely get your point and immediately retract my question."

"You should probably just tell me what she said. It'll save time."

"She said 'You look just like Daddy.' "

"Uh-oh."

"My heart stopped," Jed told Kate. "I went down to the store on the corner, and I bought that paper and I looked at that picture, and she was right. That wasn't me in that photograph. That was my father's face.

"I went into the bathroom, and I looked into the mirror, and my God, I saw my father looking back at me. With my eyes red and my skin gray, with the pathetic 'it's not my fault' attitude I'd been carrying around since I got fired, I looked exactly like my old man."

Kate had tears in her eyes again.

"After I finished crying," Jed said, "I dumped every bottle of booze that I owned into the kitchen sink, and I flushed all of my pills down the john. I packed some of my clothes, and I called David Stern at the Montgomery Rehab Center, and asked him if I could have one of his empty beds.

"And ever since then, I've been working really hard to keep my father's face out of my bathroom mirror."

Jed took a deep breath and exhaled loudly. "Pretty terrible secret, huh?"

"Your voice keeps the bugs and snakes away. Talk to me some more. Tell me another secret."

"I think it's your turn to tell me something." He didn't stop looking into her eyes, but he was aware of her body, so soft beneath his.

"I'm naked," Kate said.

Jed laughed. "Yes, ma'am. But I'm afraid that's not exactly a secret."

"I do have a secret—I want to make love to you," she said, still gazing up at him.

Jed nearly choked. "That's . . . that's great," he said, "but you know what? I think we should wait and see if you still feel the same way tomorrow, okay?"

"But I really liked making love to you, and I want to do it again. Don't you?" She bit her lower lip, holding it between her teeth as she looked up at him.

"Yes. Yes, I definitely do, but now's not the right time."

"Why not?"

"Well, gee, let's see? How about . . . because you're *tripping*. There's been a whole lot of really crazy things coming out of your mouth tonight, and I've got to assume that your wanting to make love with me right now is about as real as one of those snakes you keep thinking you see."

She moved beneath him, and the weight of his body settled more completely between her legs. Still holding his gaze, she pressed herself up against him. "Please, Jed?"

"Oh, God, Kate! I'm not really very experienced when it comes to doing the right thing, but I'm trying really hard here." He rolled off of her, releasing her hands. But that was almost worse, because now he couldn't help but look at her lying there, all that beautiful, smooth skin just begging to be touched.

She stretched, and he forced himself to look away. "I'm very warm—I'd like to go out in the rain again." She frowned. "Except I didn't like the things in the grass. Do you think we could have it rain in here?"

Jed gave up and let himself look at her. God, she was perfect. "I think we could, but then we'd probably get into a lot of trouble for tearing a hole in the roof of the trailer."

Kate smiled, turning toward him and lacing her arms around his neck. "I think I love you."

Jed's heart was in his throat. Truth or snake? "That's . . . very nice." She snuggled closer, and he put his arms around her. It was a reflex, but once his arms were there, he didn't want to let her go. Her skin was so soft beneath his fingers.

"Are you sure we can't go out in the rain again?" she asked.

"Yeah, if you really want to, I'll carry you. You don't have to worry about the grass." He'd do anything to get them out of this bedroom—even go stand in the pouring rain.

"You'd do that for me?"

"Your wish is my command."

"In that case, I wish that you would make love—"

"Rain, yes. Sex, no." Jed swung her up and into his arms. "Stop driving me nuts."

Kate was hot. Hot and sweaty and thirsty, and in the snake room of the Sarasota Jungle Gardens—a nature park her parents had taken her to during vacations in Florida, back when she was a child. The snake room was always hot and smelled faintly, evilly reptilian, even though the snakes were kept securely behind glass.

There was something inherently sinister about creatures who could move without any legs or feet. Kate had always been fascinated by this part of the museum, particularly the snakes whose labels read "Danger: Extremely Poisonous."

She gazed through the glass at one of them now. A cottonmouth—native to the South. It slid toward the glass, toward her, its entire body rippling and rolling seductively, its beady little eyes watching her unblinkingly.

And then it lunged, striking out at her, white mouth opened obscenely wide, fangs dripping venom.

The glass broke, shattering as easily as if it were sugar candy, and the cottonmouth seemed to fly toward her face.

Kate jerked wildly back, the sudden movement pulling her from her dream and leaving her gasping, heart pounding—and staring directly into Jericho's green eyes.

"You okay?" he asked, his voice raspy from sleep.

He was holding her, his arms tightly around her. Kate looked past him, up at the ceiling, around at the room, which was dimly lit by the hazy light coming in from behind the window shades. Jericho's room. She was in Jericho's room. In Jericho's bed. And she was . . .

Dear mother of God, she was naked.

She reached down, wildly searching for the sheet, and Jericho was there, helping her pull it up, helping her cover herself.

"Do you remember any of last night?" he asked quietly. "Do you remember drinking the iced tea?"

Iced tea . . .

She turned to look back into his eyes as it all came crashing back. LSD in the sugar cubes. The walls undulating like belly dancers' stomachs. Jed beside her, always beside her, promising her he'd stay with her, carrying her so she wouldn't have to walk on a floor covered with snakes, talking to her nonstop to keep the demons at bay.

His voice wasn't raspy—it was flat-out hoarse because he'd talked to her all night long.

She remembered taking off her clothes—remembered that awful sensation of ants crawling all over her body.

And she remembered begging him to make love to her again.

Rain, yes. Sex, no.

He still had his shorts on.

"Kate?" There was real concern in his eyes. "Are you okay? Are you back with me? Say something—you're scaring me a little here."

"I was wrong about you," she whispered. "You *are* my friend."

He'd taken an impossible situation—a situation where she was made completely vulnerable in every possible way—and he'd made himself vulnerable in return. That story he'd told her about hitting bottom . . . He'd purposely shared with her one of his darkest moments, because somehow he knew this morning would dawn. Somehow he knew that after the night was over, Kate would feel even more vulnerable by the memories of all he'd seen, all she'd said and done.

This way, she wasn't the only one who'd bared her soul—and a whole lot more—last night. He looked exhausted, his eyes rimmed with red, fatigue lining his face.

Last night she'd told him she thought she loved him. This morning, she didn't just think it. She felt her eyes fill with tears. "I was so wrong about you."

"You may not have been that wrong," he admitted. "I'm kind of . . . still stumbling around in the dark, trying to figure out exactly who's looking back at me from the bathroom mirror."

She ran her fingers through his beautiful long hair, pushing it back behind his ear. "Not your father."

"Uh-oh, you remember that, huh?" He shifted so that he was lying down next to her, propping his head up with one hand, leaning on his elbow. He looked as bone-weary as she felt.

"I remember everything," she admitted.

"An Oscar for each breast?"

Kate laughed in surprise, and her tears overflowed. She wasn't sad—she was just so emotional. "Did I really say that?"

"You sure did."

"Oh, my God, I told you I wrote the script, didn't I?"

He gently touched her cheek. "I won't tell. I promise. Although it's so damn good, I can't figure out why you don't want everyone to know."

"Victor wouldn't have even read it if he knew I wrote it. I'm not supposed to be able to write well, because of the boobs-to-brain ratio, remember?"

"If you told him the truth, Victor might have a better understanding of why you don't want to change the ending," Jed pointed out. "He doesn't realize that it's *your* story."

"I think it's more likely he'd call William Goldman and order a complete page-one rewrite." Kate rolled her eyes. "No, Victor's better off thinking Nick Chadler wrote it. I'm going to keep it like that for now."

"Who's Nick Chadler?"

"A friend of mine. A manager from my Natick, Massachusetts, store. Whenever Victor wants to meet him, I tell him he's out of the country—I say that Nick'll fax whatever changes Victor wants. Then I make the revisions, fax 'em to Nick, who faxes 'em back."

His eyes searched her face. "That's one hell of a lie for a nice girl like you."

Kate felt herself go very still. She wasn't any kind of a nice girl, and he knew it now, too. Last night, she'd told him about those awful two weeks before she'd left Victor, left California. Oh, God, she'd actually told him about that nameless, nearly faceless boom operator she'd had a one-night stand with on the bench seat of his truck.

Jed was watching her, and he knew exactly what she was thinking. "Nothing you told me last night will ever leave this room."

"I'm so ashamed of what I did."

"You were drunk."

"Being drunk is no excuse—you've said so yourself." She closed her eyes. "God, it's been seven years, and it still makes me feel sick."

"There you go," Jed said. "Proof you're a nice girl. It's when you don't care—that's when you have to worry."

"It's just . . . It's the most awful thing I've ever done. I broke my marriage vows. The fact that Victor was cheating on me was no excuse, either."

"Everybody's done something they're ashamed of. Hell, my list's a mile long, but there's one thing that tops it." He lay back on the bed, hands propped behind his head, elbows out as he gazed up at the ceiling. "You know my brother Tom died of AIDS, right?"

She nodded, turning slightly to look at him. "Yes."

"He was sick for a long time, but when he finally died, I wasn't with him," Jed told her quietly. "I hadn't been to see him or even returned his calls for over two months, and I will regret that until the day I die."

"Were you busy making a movie?"

"No. I mean, yeah, I probably was, but it was out in L.A. I could've taken a few days to go up to San Francisco. But I didn't." He turned and looked at her. "I knew Tom was dying. He'd had AIDS for four years. He was my best friend—he and his lover, Ian, and all his other friends were the closest thing to a real family that I'd ever known. But, see, they were all gay. Blatantly, openly, flamboyantly out.

"And one day, I was being interviewed for some magazine, and the reporter asked how I'd pulled off getting all these real macho Hollywood roles, since I was so obviously homosexual. At first I just laughed, but he was serious. And when I told him I wasn't gay, he told me he knew I was lying—he had proof that I was. And he showed me some photos of me with Tom and his friends. So I explained. I told him this was my brother, and my brother was gay. All these guys were gay, sure—not that you could particularly tell that from the photos—but they were my friends. I told him it was possible for me to be straight and be friends with men who were gay—which seemed a pretty basic, easy to understand concept to me. But the reporter didn't believe me—and neither did the producer of *Kill Zone*."

Jed laughed. "I thought it was pretty funny, until the producer paid nearly eighty thousand dollars to keep the article and pictures from being run. The producer was afraid if the story was printed, no one would come to see his movie. And he told me that although coming out was very PC, if I let slip my ugly little 'secret,' my career would be over.

"I told him again that he was wrong, that I adored women, that I was about as heterosexual as I could possibly be—in fact, it frequently got me into trouble, but he didn't believe me. He told me to stay away from my 'little friends' in San Francisco or I could kiss my career good-bye.

"And when I told my agent about it—and Ron knew I wasn't gay—he told me that even a rumor about being gay could seriously damage my image as an action/adventure star.

"And I believed them both." Jed turned to look at her again, and his eyes were bleak. "I let myself be bullied into worrying what people would think. I stopped returning my brother's phone calls, and I wasn't there for him when he died. How's *that* for something to be ashamed of?"

Kate couldn't speak. What an awful burden to carry around.

"So, see—I'm not much of a friend," he told her. "I don't stick around when the going gets tough."

Kate wanted to cry. She wanted to tell him, on the contrary, that he was a very good friend, indeed. Because she knew what he had done.

He'd taken out this still-raw, emotionally charged piece of his soul and put it on display for her to see, in a gallant, selfless attempt to even things up. He'd orchestrated a hostage exchange of sorts. She'd told him her darkest most shameful secret last night, so he'd now told her his.

"Thank you," she whispered.

He knew exactly what she was talking about. "I wanted you to know."

She had to laugh. "Like hell you did."

He turned on his side, head propped on one arm. "No," he said. "I honestly did. I think I'm probably looking for some kind of forgiveness, or absolution." He smiled crookedly. "And despite what you think, you *are* a nice girl. In fact, you're probably the closest I'll ever get to an angel."

Kate laughed, a burst of disbelieving air. "That's a *terrible* line."

"It's not a line," he told her. "It's the way I . . . feel. When you smile at me, I'm . . . I'm okay."

Those were words from her script. "Laramie says that to Jane."

Jed nodded. "I know. It's such a good line—and it really seemed to fit."

He was silent then, just gazing at her.

"I'm naked," Kate said suddenly, fighting a fresh flood of tears to her eyes. "And I'm in your bed. Can't we do something with our mouths besides talk?"

Something flickered in his eyes. Uncertainty. It made him look desperately sweet and impossibly young. She could actually see him deciding just how to answer her. He chose humor. "You mean, like make farting noises?"

She laughed. "I'm inviting you to kiss me," she said. "You now have two choices here. You could either continue to be an idiot, or you could accept my invitation."

"I'm sorry. It's been a long night, and it's been filled with many really long hours that that—individually—would have been enough to override the three miracles needed for my sainthood application."

"You're still not kissing me."

Jed leaned forward and brushed his lips against hers.

Her mouth was as soft as he remembered, but salty from both her tears and the night's heat.

He lifted his head to look into her eyes. "This is not why I did it," he said. "Last night . . . It wasn't just because I wanted this."

"I know," she whispered, touching his face, his hair.

He caught her hand and kissed her fingertips, trying to identify this odd sensation in his chest and behind his eyes. It was the strangest thing. He knew that before the morning was through, he was going to make love to Kate again. He was already almost entirely aroused—he'd spent the entire night in that state—so maybe that was why other parts of him were starting to swell.

Of course, a far more likely explanation was that he was going to cry.

It was absurd, but he felt so completely, impossibly, goddamn amazingly happy. He felt a barrage of emotions, each one more complex and gut-wrenching than the last. Elation. Relief. Hope. Inspiration. Triumph.

He had to stop and analyze. He had to rein in everything he was feeling, to catalog and file it for further use.

Because God help him if he just let loose. He'd scare Kate to death, maybe even scare her off. And he'd scare himself as well. He didn't want to feel this way, so raw and open and exposed. Emotional highs were usually followed by emotional lows—he'd experienced that just last week—and he needed to maintain a more middle ground.

Always.

Jed took a deep breath. And he grabbed hard onto his control.

He took everything he was feeling, and he squeezed it all together until it could fit neatly and safely into a mental container the size of a shoe box. And he managed to smile at her instead of pulling her into his arms and bursting into tears.

But when he leaned forward to kiss her again, as he searched her eyes and found anticipation and desire and such sweet warmth, the shoe box expanded and for a moment the lid popped off. And instead of kissing her, he pulled her close, burying his face in the softness of her neck, breathing in her sweet perfume, holding her next to his heart.

"Everything in my life has been leading up to this," he whispered. "Everything that's happened, everything I've done has been worth it because it's brought me here."

Sweet Christ, what was he saying? What was he *feeling*? He mentally stomped the lid back on that box, and kissed her, hard, if only to shut himself up.

But her lips were soft, her mouth welcoming and gentle. And he knew that this time, she didn't want a frantic, near-savage joining. This time, she wanted to be loved slowly, tenderly.

He could do that. These days he was the king of self-control.

He kissed her deeply, forcing his own pulse to even out, pushing all of his ping-ponging emotions even further away.

Jed tugged at the sheet, and it fell away from her, like the unveiling of some incredible work of art. He allowed himself only the briefest surge of wonder and elation. She was his. At least for now, she belonged to him.

He touched her then, skimming his hands across the softness of her skin, leaning down to touch each tip of her perfect breasts with his tongue.

Kate shivered. "You said the next time we made love, you were going to spend thirty minutes just looking."

Jed had to laugh at that. "I got my thirty minutes in last night," he told her. "About twelve times over. If you don't mind, I'd like to move on to tasting and touching." He lowered his head, forcing himself to move one hundred times more slowly than he wanted. He oh-so-gently kissed her breast, tasting her incredible sweetness until she moaned aloud.

But then she spoke. Her voice was even more breathy than usual. "No fair. I didn't get my thirty minutes to look at *you*."

She was serious. "But . . . I'm not as much fun to look at as you are."

"Wanna bet?" She smiled. "Take off the shorts, pal. And make it good."

Jed grinned back at her. "Good, huh? You want me to do my Full Monty imitation? It won't be as effective without music."

"You want music?" She started to sing.

He laughed, and another firecracker of joy escaped from his box of emotions. "I can't strip to a Garth Brooks song."

"Why not? I could."

She gave him a very innocent look, and his heart nearly stopped beating as he pictured exactly what her words implied. Dear, *dear* Lord. Kate. Wearing one of her cool professional producer outfits. Doing a slow striptease for his eyes only . . .

Even more heart-stopping was the thought that she'd consider doing that for him—knowing her past.

"I'll remember that." His voice was even more hoarse. "But maybe for now, we should just go without music."

He took a deep breath as he climbed off the bed and positioned himself in the middle of the room with his back to her. He looked at her over his shoulder. "Ready?"

She shook her head. "Jed, I was just kidding. I wouldn't really make you do this, I mean . . . Unless you wanted to . . ."

"Oh, I want to. I like it when you look at me. But you better get it straight—I wouldn't do this for anyone but you."

She was kneeling on the bed, and the sight of her so beautifully naked made his heart race again. She had total bed head—her hair had been wet from the rain, and it had dried going every which way. The effect was completely charming. Even though she still looked tired, and every bit of makeup she'd had on had long since worn off, she was gorgeous. And, God, she was *his*. She smiled, her eyes alight with anticipation.

It was her eyes he truly loved to look at. As beautiful as her body was, her eyes never failed to captivate him.

"Ready," she said.

Jed closed his eyes for a moment, centering himself. He could do this funny. He knew she would like funny. She loved to laugh—his initial impression of her being humorless was completely wrong.

But right now he didn't want to make her laugh. He wanted to make her burn. He had to do this seriously. Well, at least, half seriously. He wanted to give her hot. But how?

He could give her Laramie. Laramie was perpetually hot, with his burning intensity. When he was Laramie, he just let himself quietly smolder. Jed knew Kate liked that. She couldn't keep her eyes off of him then.

But, hell, he didn't need Laramie to be hot. All he had to do was think about Kate, think about the way he was going to love her—long and slow and sweet. In just a very short time, he was going to watch her eyes in the morning light as he fit his body together with hers. He was going to watch her beautiful face as he made her shatter around him, as he let himself find his own blessed release in the sweetness of her arms.

And then he was going to do it all over again tonight. And tomorrow night. And the next . . .

Until the shoot ended and they went their separate ways.

Bad thought. Very bad thought. He mentally shoved it far to the bottom of his emotional box and jammed the lid back on.

Think about Kate. Think about slowly sliding in and out of her sweet body.

Yeah, he could definitely do hot.

Jed hooked his thumbs into the waistband of his shorts and slowly turned to face her. He let all of his desire, all of his need simmer in his eyes as he let his gaze travel down her body.

She shivered, and it sure as hell wasn't because she was cold.

He lifted his hands, placing them on his bare chest, above his heart, one on top of the other. And then slowly he separated them, sliding them down his stomach, to the low-slung waistband of his shorts. But he didn't stop there. He kept going, sliding his hands lower, until he was touching himself, until he was covering the hard bulge of his erection.

He could see Kate's chest rise and fall rapidly with each breath she took. He could hear her swallow in the stillness of the room. She watched his hands, her lips slightly parted.

He moved his hands up, then, this time flicking open the button at the waist of his shorts. He found the tiny zipper pull, but didn't pull it down. He stepped forward, right to the edge of the bed, and with his eyes, he invited Kate to do the honors.

She reached out, about to cover his arousal with her palm, but he stopped her. He took only her forefinger and her thumb and positioned them very carefully around the tiny zipper pull, so that she wasn't touching him at all.

Slowly, looking up into his eyes, she pulled it all the

way down. She reached for him again, but he stepped back, slightly shaking his head no. He had to grit his teeth from wanting her to touch him, but this wasn't about him. It was about her. And he was determined to drive her insane, even if he had to go crazy himself to do it.

Still holding her gaze, he brought his hands back to his chest, putting them once again one on top of the other, above his heart. And this time, as he slowly slid his hands down past his stomach, he freed himself and pushed his shorts down his legs.

Kate gazed at him openly, unabashedly, and the heated approval in her eyes made him even hotter, even heavier.

He moved toward her then, and this time, he let her touch.

He closed his eyes as he fell back onto the bed with her, and his entire world shrank. There was only this bed, and Kate. Her hands and mouth on his body, and his hands and mouth on hers.

He inhaled her, tasted, touched, sliding his palms against the perfect smoothness of her skin as she wrapped her fingers around him, as she lowered her head and touched him with her lips, her tongue, her teeth.

The pleasure was completely mind-blowing, completely overwhelming, and he gasped, moments from losing control.

He let her push him back, let her straddle him, felt her slide against him, slick from his kisses and her own desire. The sight of her astride him was enough to make him groan aloud. She leaned forward, and he kissed her breasts hungrily, burying his face in her fullness as she slid on top of him.

"Please say you have a condom," she whispered, kissing his eyes, his mouth, his face.

He did. In his wallet. In his shorts. "Yes." He pointed, unable to find the words.

"I'll get it." She kissed him, and although her climbing off of him left him instantly bereft, he had the pleasure of watching her walk, naked, across the room. And then back toward him.

She held out his shorts, and he fumbled for his wallet, for the condom he'd replaced just last week. He opened the wrapper, and finally, thank God, he was covered.

Jed would have pushed himself up and rolled them both over to nestle between her legs, but she stopped him. She pressed his shoulders firmly back as once again, she sat astride him. Holding his gaze, she reached down between them to touch him, and then slowly brought him deeply inside of her.

The pleasure was so sharp, so sweet, he saw flashes of color and light. And then, just as he was certain he was going to die from the sensation, she began to move. Each stroke contained more pleasure than any one man deserved for an entire lifetime. Each breath he took was a gasp of amazement, each exhale a moan of disbelief as time stretched way out, slowed down, sped up, twisted around.

And then, minutes or hours later—he couldn't say which—his control was completely gone. And as he felt the first powerful surge of his release, he could do little more than breathe her name.

She still held his gaze, and she smiled. He exploded in slow motion, rockets of unbelievable sensation ripping through him, destroying him completely, reducing him to little more than a disconnected collection of tingling atoms and particles.

But with the particles that used to be his ears, he heard her cry out with her own sweet pleasure. And with the atoms that used to be his arms, he felt her shake with her own incredible release.

And as she, too, fell apart, Jed lost himself inside of her. There were no boundaries, no separations. They were truly one.

And the rush of pleasure that brought was so intense, it

roared around him, blasting open the pleasure-proof lock he kept on his box of emotions, bringing a surge of unstoppable tears to his eyes.

Somehow Jed found one of his arms, and he held Kate tightly, pressing her head against his shoulder. And somehow, he got his other hand reconnected to his other arm, and he reached up and wiped his face before she could see him cry.

Sweet God, he needed a drink.

Thirteen

❧ ❧

JAMAAL SAT IN the slave quarters, watching Victor frown as he watched the video playback monitor.

The scene wasn't working.

He didn't know *why* it wasn't. They'd been filming a sequence of scenes here at Brandall Hall for the past four days now, and up to this point, he and Susie had been hitting the ball clear out of the park on almost the first pitch.

They'd been working in chronological order, starting with the scene where Jane tended to Moses' injuries after Reginald Brooks kicked the shit out of him. As Moses hovered near death, Susie—no, he mentally shook his head. He meant *Jane*—risked her own life and reputation by sneaking out of her house at night to nurse him.

There hadn't been a lot of dialogue up to today's scene—just good, solid acting.

But today, Moses had regained consciousness. And Jane had a thing or two to say to him.

Susie, wearing Jane's long skirts, sat next to him, and he self-consciously rearranged the scraps of rags he thought of as his diaper. It was slightly better than a loincloth, but only slightly.

"What are we doing wrong?" she asked him quietly.

Jamaal looked at her. "You don't know, either, huh? I was kind of hoping you had some answers."

She shook her head, chewing worriedly on her thumbnail.

Her father wasn't here watching today, thank God. If he were, Susie's tension level would be through the roof.

Jamaal felt his own frustrations rise. He'd followed his mother's advice, and had been careful not to push Susie into talking about her father. He'd backed way off, hoping that she'd tell him on her own terms.

So far, nothing.

It was driving him freakin' out of his mind.

Across the room, Victor and Kate were listening intently to Jericho. The man wasn't in costume, and he looked wildly out of place in those safari-style cargo shorts he liked to wear, a Stomp T-shirt, and sandals on his feet. He wore his hair down, too, kind of like a beardless Jesus. Or maybe it was the "found heaven" expression he wore on his face these past few days that made him look like the big J.

Jericho and Kate were getting it on. Rocking the old trailer every chance they could get. They were trying their best to be discreet, but the few times they actually *had* shown up in the Grill for dinner over the past few days, they'd only stayed about twenty minutes before one of 'em made some excuse and they both disappeared.

Didn't take much of a genius to figure out what was up with *that*.

Kate was trying her best to look as if she were in control and cool, but more often than not these days, she looked a little shell-shocked.

Jamaal had heard through the 'vine that some disgruntled former employee—now bundled safely away to jail—had spiked Kate's drink with LSD several days back. He couldn't imagine Kate just sitting and chilling and going for the ride. That *had* to have been rough.

But then again, getting together with Jericho had to be an equally unsettling ride for her.

As Jamaal watched, Jericho shifted his weight so that his arm brushed against Kate's. Even just standing there, deep in some technical discussion, Jericho couldn't stand not to be touching the woman.

"They're talking about us," Susie whispered. "Oh, shoot, I wish someone would just tell me what I'm doing wrong."

"We," Jamaal corrected her absently. "It's we, baby. Or maybe it's just me."

Victor was nodding, nodding, nodding, and then all three of them looked directly up at Jamaal and Susie.

"Susie, can I talk to you for a sec?" Victor called.

Flashing Jamaal a worried look, Susie stood up. Jamaal reached for her, catching her hand, breaking his no touching rule for the first time since that night they'd gone up to the pond and skipped stones. "Hey, don't worry. We'll definitely figure out how to make this click." Shit, when he said it like that, he almost believed himself.

But she wasn't buying. She gave him one of her fake-o smiles as she tugged her hand free.

Jamaal kept a close eye on her as Victor began to talk, ready to go over and smack the man—director or not—if it seemed as if he were doing anything to undermine her already shaky self-confidence.

"Mind if I help you try to figure out this scene?"

Jamaal looked up to see Jericho standing next to him.

"I have an idea," Jericho said, sitting down. "If you're interested in trying something . . ."

"Yes. Please. Tell me what we're doing wrong." Jamaal glanced at Jericho but then went back to watching Susie. So far whatever Victor was saying seemed to be okay. She was nodding, Victor was smiling.

"It's not that you're doing something wrong," Jericho explained. "It's more that you're not doing it *right* enough."

"Well, no shit, Sherlock. That sure was helpful."

"On the surface it's all there. The dialogue, the action—the main message of the scene. Jane's worried that Brooks is going to come check on Moses—to see if he's well enough to work in the field, right? She's afraid Moses isn't going to bow his head and say, 'Yes, master,' and that Brooks is going to beat Moses again, because of that. She believes that another severe beating will kill him. But Moses won't bow his head, and he tells her she can't understand what it's like to want something more than life itself—and to know that she'll never have it, never. And you know what he's talking about here, right? In addition to his freedom?"

Jamaal nodded. "He's talking about *Susie—Jane*," he corrected himself quickly. "He wants Jane. He's always wanted Jane, but he knows there's no way in hell he can have her."

Jericho smiled. "So show it. Underneath every line of dialogue, you've got to be thinking, *I want you.* Do you know what your secret desire is during this scene?"

"Secret desire?"

"Every character has an underlying goal, a desire that sometimes isn't revealed through dialogue, that rules everything they say, every movement they make during that scene. And for this scene, Moses' desire is so secret, he may not even be admitting it to himself. But he's there, all alone in that cabin with Jane, and his secret desire is to kiss her. He wants—almost as much as he wants to keep breathing—to catch her mouth with his and plant one on her."

Jamaal looked over at Susie. God, he knew what that felt like.

"Everything you do in this scene," Jericho continued,

"is ruled by your desire to kiss this girl. You have to inch closer—but make it look almost subconscious. You have to watch her mouth, watch her eyes, and then her mouth again. You have to really want her. She's this totally, completely forbidden thing. You know that, but you want her anyway."

Jamaal laughed, a short, almost hysterical sounding burst of air.

"Do you think you can do that?" Jericho asked.

Jamaal nodded, gazing across the room at Susie. She turned away from Victor and looked directly at him, and he felt that now-familiar punched-stomach feeling deep in his gut. "Yeah," he said to Jericho, still holding Susie's gaze. "I think I can probably do that."

Jericho stood up.

"Okay," Victor called. "Let's try this again. Places."

Makeup came and checked that his bandages were in place, then Jamaal lay on the straw pallet that was Moses' sickbed. Susie knelt beside him.

"Ready?" Victor called.

Jamaal looked up at Susie. His secret desire was to kiss her. Damn, this was going to be the easiest piece of acting he'd ever had to do.

In the dim light, her eyes looked liquid blue, and as he watched she took a deep breath, finding the piece of her that was Jane. He did the same, closing his eyes and listening for a moment to the silence of the slave quarters, listening for Moses' voice.

"Rolling."

Jamaal opened his eyes, looking up at Susie. She was Jane, but she was Susie, too—the same way he now was both Moses and Jamaal.

"Speed."

"Action."

She had the first line, the first bit of action as she expertly cut away the bandage to reveal the crisscross of wounds that laced his back, courtesy of makeup. He felt her hands touching his skin, and he looked up at her, letting himself want her.

"He's going to be coming down here soon," she told him in Jane's backwoods southern accent, holding onto his uninjured shoulder as she spread salve on his back. "Brooks is."

He winced, and she stopped for a moment, his pain echoed perfectly in her eyes. "I'm sorry," she whispered.

He looked up at her, at her hand on his bare shoulder, at her eyes, at her mouth, at her eyes again. *I want to kiss you.* He had to moisten his suddenly dry lips. "I'm all right."

She pulled her gaze away from him almost jerkily, and started again with the salve. "When he comes to talk to you, address him as Master B," she said. "Say 'Yes, Master B,' and 'No, Master B.' "

"I can't."

Her eyes were fierce. "You've *got* to." She finished with the salve and wiped her hands on her apron.

He sat up, turning to face her. "I *can't.*"

She looked at him, her eyes suddenly filling with tears. "If he beats you again—and he will if you don't do this— you might die." One tear escaped, rolling down her cheek.

Jamaal reached to wipe it away, but stopped himself, mere inches from her face. No touching. Moses had that rule, too.

"If I bow my head and call Brooks my master," he said quietly, "I *will* die." Just as surely as he was dying by sitting here and not touching her, not kissing her. God, it was killing him.

She wiped her own tear away, even wiped her nose with the back of her hand—a brilliantly realistic touch. But then she reached for his hand, surprising him by taking hold of it, of actually touching him. That wasn't in the blocking.

"Please." She gazed up at him, searching his eyes.

"You're not strong enough to make the trip north yet, and it's going to be at least another two days before Laramie and I finish the hiding place. I know you don't understand this, but it's a miracle you're alive at all. When Brooks beat you, he made your . . . your insides bleed. If he beats you again—"

"And I know *you* don't understand *this*," he interrupted. "You can't understand what it's like to want something more than life itself—and to know that you'll never have it. Never. *Never*." He let his desire and his need consume him, let it color his voice. "I have spent my entire life being told what to say, what to do, what to think. I've been surrounded by a life I can't have, by things I can't have."

Like you. She was gazing up at him, her eyes so wide, her lips slightly parted, it was driving him insane. Her lips looked so soft, so deliciously moist, he could barely remember his name, let alone his lines.

"I can't choose the kind of work I want to do," he continued in Moses' thick accent. "I can't talk when I want, or . . . or walk where I want to . . . walk." *Or kiss your sweet lips.* Somehow she had moved. Or maybe he had, but somehow now, she was close enough to kiss, and his heart was pounding so hard, he could barely hear his own voice. "I can't . . . I can't . . ."

What he couldn't do was stop himself. He leaned down that extra two or three inches, and God, he was kissing her.

She fell into his arms, kissing him back with a passion that would've knocked him off his feet if he'd been standing up.

His first thought was where the hell had she learned to kiss like this? His second was who the hell cared? He was kissing her—finally, finally, *finally* kissing Susie McCoy.

She tasted like root beer, sweet and sharp and perfect.

He could hear the shocked silence in the room as he pulled back. He could see it echoed in Susie's blue eyes.

But he knew that the cameras were still rolling, and he struggled to regain his breath as he set her aside from him. His hands were shaking.

"I couldn't choose my own wife," he told her, his voice thick with a huskiness that acting couldn't re-create. "I can't choose who to love."

Her hands were shaking, too, as she gathered up her ointments and salve. "I can't, either," she said tightly. "But you don't see me lying down and dying." She stood up. "I'll be back later to put on more ointment." She turned away from him but then turned back. "Stay alive. Because as long as you're alive, there's hope."

Jamaal shook his head. "What good is hope going to do for *me*?" he asked softly.

She turned and went out the door.

There was silence as Jamaal watched her go, as his eyes filled with tears.

Slowly, he closed his eyes and turned away.

"Cut," Victor whispered.

The room stayed silent.

Jamaal opened his eyes to see Susie peeking back in the door, her eyes wide. He wiped his face, wishing he could crawl away somewhere and just cry for about two hours.

But still no one moved.

And then Victor cleared his throat. "Well," he finally said.

"Well," Kate echoed weakly.

Jericho laughed aloud. "Well," he said, "That was friggin' *great*!" He turned to Kate. "What do you think? Was it okay for that kiss to be there?"

She chewed her lower lip. "I don't know. I'm going to have to think about it. Let's go with it for now—it's clearly making this scene work, and we can always edit it out." She turned to Victor. "Is that okay with you?"

"Absolutely." Victor clapped his hands. "Let's set up for a different angle. I want to get a close up of that kiss. You kids up for doing that again without a break?"

Jamaal looked at Susie. Her eyes were still wide, but she shrugged. "Sure."

Jamaal cleared his throat. Kiss her again. "Yeah. Sure."

And for the first time in his acting career, he found himself praying they'd screw up—and have to do at least fifteen or twenty takes.

Kate stood behind the camera and watched her lover kiss another woman by the light of a fire.

They were filming the flashback scene—Laramie and his dead wife Sarah's wedding night.

Jed was freshly shaven, his dark hair gleaming and clean, tied neatly back in a ribbon. He was dressed in a dark coat and a snow-white shirt—a far cry from the ill-kempt broken Laramie stumbling drunkenly around the Willet farm in the dark, or even the recently sober, emotionally raw-edged Laramie he played later on in the movie.

Kate had to admit that Naomi Michaelson was a perfect Sarah. With her long golden curls and her sweet face, she was the quintessential demure bride, dressed in a pure white gown.

As Kate watched, Jed gracefully slipped out of his jacket and shirt, then leaned forward, firelight gleaming enticingly on his well-oiled muscles as he kissed Naomi again. No. Wrong. Laramie kissed Sarah. This wasn't real. It only looked real.

As Jed looked deeply into Naomi's eyes, he unfastened the front of her dress, lightly trailing his fingers across the now-exposed tops of her breasts. The look in his eyes was pure desire, and Kate wanted to look away.

It was so realistic. So intense.

So familiar.

Jed kissed the actress again, pulling her down with him onto the floor, out of the shot, leaving the camera to zoom in slowly on the leaping flames.

"Cut, and wrap for the night."

Naomi pushed herself tiredly to her feet, but Jed didn't move until Kate came to look down at him.

"I have got the worst damn headache in the world," he said from his prone position on the floor.

He sat up slowly, moving gingerly, stopping to close his eyes and press his fingers against the bridge of his nose. He looked pale beneath his tan, his face suddenly drawn.

It was remarkable, really. A minute ago he'd been fine—or *acting* fine, Kate realized.

She crouched next to him and pushed his hair back from his face, placing the palm of her hand against his forehead.

He was on fire.

Kate stood up. "Annie!"

Her assistant materialized next to her.

"What's the name of that doctor in town who agreed to be on twenty-four-hour call for a screen credit?" Kate asked.

"Slocum."

"Call Dr. Slocum and have him meet me and Jericho in Jericho's trailer in fifteen minutes."

"Whoa." Jed pulled himself to his feet. "I don't need a doctor."

"You're sick," she told him.

"It's nothing," he protested. "I sometimes get sinus infections. They give me headaches. It's no big deal."

"Didn't you just say it was the worst headache you've ever had in your life? And I assume it didn't start two minutes ago. Why didn't you tell me about it earlier?"

He used his fingers and thumb to apply pressure to his eyebrows. "Because it's no big deal."

"Jed, you're practically white, it feels to me as if you're running a fever of at least a hundred and two and—"

"So what if I've got a little headache? I'm an actor. I can act healthy. It's no big deal."

"Now it's a *little* headache, huh? Were you feeling all right this afternoon, working that scene in the slave quarters, with Susie and Jamaal? Or were you feeling badly then, too?"

He straightened up and smiled, and the lines of fatigue and pain faded from his face. "Look, I'm fine, see?"

"You're *acting* fine."

"Are you sure? How do you know I wasn't just acting sick a second ago?"

Kate stared at him as he headed out of the room, to the area of Brandall Hall they were using as a temporary costume and changing room. She didn't know. Except . . . She chased after him. "Because you're running a fever, that's why."

Jed stepped out of his pants right in the middle of the room, tossing them to a nearby costume assistant. Another was right there, handing him his shorts and T-shirt. He pulled them on. "It just got a little warm in there. Hell, I was playing a love scene with the director's girlfriend—in front of an open fire in the middle of the summer." He lowered his voice. "Not to mention the fact that *you* were watching. That made me sweat a little, too, you know."

Annie appeared at her shoulder. "Dr. Slocum will be right over."

"Call the doctor back, Annie," Jed ordered. "I don't need him."

Kate shook her head at Annie, then followed him out of the plantation hall. The night was uncomfortably humid. It had rained about an hour ago, and steam and mist were actually rising from the still soggy ground. In the dim light, it was spooky.

She caught up to him easily as he headed toward the minivans that would take them back to town.

"I'll feel better after I take a shower," he told her.

"And I'll feel better after the doctor takes a look at you."

He rubbed his forehead. "Kate, damn it—"

"Jed, what exactly is the problem here?"

He spun to face her. "I don't want to be responsible for creating delays in the production schedule!"

He was serious. He was standing there, sick as a dog but determined to go on working because he didn't want to be a burden to the production.

"Oh, Jed," she said softly. "It's not your fault if you're *sick*." She put her arms around him, pulling him close. God, he was hot to the touch. He'd already sweated through the back of his T-shirt. "No one expects you to be able to work while you're running a fever."

"I have to be better than what everyone expects." He pulled back slightly, and she could see the pain from his headache just from looking into his eyes. "I have to be . . ."

For several long seconds, Kate thought that Jed was going to continue, that he was actually going to tell her how he felt. For a moment she thought he was going to be honest, both with himself and with her.

Reality blurred when she was around him. He was such a convincing actor, she never quite knew what was real and what was not.

Did he really feel the intensity she saw when he looked so deeply into her eyes as he made love to her each night? Or was he merely playing the part of a lover—the way he had been with Naomi in front of the camera just minutes ago?

Everything Jed did was all so perfect—too perfect. Far too often, he was just a little too controlled.

Kate believed he was holding back when they made love, that everything he was really feeling was hidden deeply inside of him.

And love was never, ever mentioned.

Of course, she wasn't about to bring up the subject, either, even though—when she let herself think about it—she knew she loved him. He was living energy, pure lightning trapped and shaped into human form. He could say more with one look, one smile than a hundred other men could, even if they started at sunset and talked until dawn. How could she not love him?

But how *could* she love him?

She still didn't know who he was.

He still sometimes slipped into the character of Jericho Beaumont, movie star. Even though he rarely did that while they were alone, it seemed as if he were staying in Laramie's character more and more these days. It was as if he'd realized how much Laramie appealed to her.

As if he thought she wouldn't notice the way he was hiding behind the persona of a fictional man.

Jed hid so much—even from himself. There was so much darkness and pain and anger still inside him, yet ever since that morning he'd told her about his brother's death, he hadn't talked about anything even remotely as personal.

Of course, she was a fine one to talk. He'd asked her—more than once—about eighth grade, and she'd avoided *that* magic trip down memory lane with a vengeance.

Jed looked over to where some of the crew members were coming out of Brandall Hall, and he pulled back, stepping discreetly out of her arms.

"I'll shuffle the schedule around," Kate told him. "We can put off shooting the scenes with you and Susie building the hiding place for Moses. I bet Susie could stand to have a few days off, too."

"All I want is to take a shower, and go to bed. I don't even need any aspirin. All I need is you, a boom box, and a Garth Brooks CD, and I guarantee you, I'll be feeling no pain."

Kate had to laugh. "Jed!" She felt her cheeks start to heat.

Something softened in his eyes as he smiled at her. "How can you still blush after what we've spent the past week doing?"

"Come on," Kate said. "Let's get you home."

Fourteen

❧ ❧

SUSANNAH SLOWLY SLID her window open a crack and put her face close to the screen. "Jamaal."

"Yeah."

"Do me a favor," she breathed almost silently. "Go to the other window and look in—but don't let my father see you. See if he's watching TV."

"Sounds like the TV's on . . ."

"I know. But . . . Just check and see if he's fallen asleep. Please?"

"As you wish."

Jamaal disappeared into the shadows, and Susannah went to stand at her bedroom door, listening intently.

Last night, her father had been restless. He'd kept knocking on her door, asking her questions. Stupid questions about some of the scripts he'd received from her agent—scripts that he wanted her to do, like *Slumberparty Three*.

Jamaal had tapped on the screen while she was talking to her father, and she'd nearly had a heart attack. But her father hadn't heard. And when Susannah had finally been able to close and lock her door, much to her intense frustration, Jamaal was gone.

It was possible that her dad suspected she'd been sneaking out. Or maybe he was just acting weird because her mother had called. He always got even more uptight after talking to Riva on the phone. Of course, she'd called to speak to Susie—not that Susie had gotten a chance to talk.

She heard the sound of Jamaal touching the screen again, and she went back to the window.

"He's not asleep, but whatever's on, he's into watching it," he whispered.

She shouldn't do it. She shouldn't risk sneaking out while her dad was still awake. Especially since she had this gut feeling that he was on to her.

And, God help her, she didn't want to have to face the brunt of his rage. Rage for doing something that she had every right to do. She was nearly sixteen. She should be able to take a walk at night if she wanted to. She shouldn't be stuck in here, hiding and scared like some little helpless kid. She shouldn't be forced to sneak around.

And her need to see Jamaal had grown out of control. She burned to see him, to talk to him. And maybe—please God!—to recreate some of those kisses they'd shared in front of the camera two days ago.

Susannah pushed back the curtain, and silently opened the screen.

She slid out into the night, and Jamaal caught her, holding her tightly as she closed the window. As he lowered her to the ground, Susannah looked up at him.

For a heart-stopping moment his face was a matter of inches from hers. And for a fraction of a second, she knew that this was it. He was going to kiss her again. Not as Moses kissing Jane, but as Jamaal kissing Susie. He was going to kiss her, and hold her close and tell her that he loved her. And, oh, God, she was going to tell him that she loved him, too.

But instead, he stepped back, away from her and made a sound that might've been a laugh. "What was up last night? I came by three times, but you didn't come to the window."

Three times . . . "My dad was . . ." She shook her head, not wanting to talk about her father. "Let's get out of here. Let's go up to the pond."

"No way. The mosquitoes have grown to the size of vultures up there." Jamaal slapped at his arm as he followed her away from the trailers. "It's bad enough away from the water."

"So . . . where do you want to go?"

Susannah held her breath as he didn't answer. His face was in the shadows, so she couldn't read his eyes.

"You know, you did some really incredible acting yesterday," he finally said. They were walking slowly, and they took a right turn, almost automatically, into the churchyard. "I wanted to tell you that last night. Working with you is incredible. And when it clicks—the way it finally did—it's unbelievable."

"I felt the same way," she whispered. "I mean, about working with you."

"I've never lost myself inside a character the way I did in that scene with Moses and Jane," he said. "It was kind of scary, you know? I mean, we're such good friends, but Moses, he's got such a jones for Jane, all of a sudden he's kissing her, and . . . I really hope I didn't scare you or like, freak you out or . . ."

"I wasn't scared." Now was the time. As Jamaal turned to face her, as they stood there in the graveyard, surrounded by shadows and monuments to people long since gone from this earth, Susie knew it was time to tell him that she had loved those kisses. And that she wanted him to kiss her again—for real this time. She took a deep breath and opened her mouth.

But Jamaal wasn't done. "Good, cause I wouldn't want

you to be scared of me, or to, you know, worry that I'm gonna like, just randomly grab you and kiss you and shit, because that was Moses, you know? That wasn't me. Besides, we don't have that kind of relationship. You and me, we're buds, right?"

"Yeah," Susie said. "Right." She kept her voice light, kept a soft, natural smile on her face. It was an award-winning performance, considering that all the hope she'd been carrying around for the past day and a half had just been crushed into a fine powder and now lay in a dusty pile at her feet— along with the shreds of her tender heart. "You and me, we're buds."

Jed awoke to find Kate slipping into bed. "Hey, who's this strange woman in my bed? Oh, it's you—what's-your-name." He kissed her, molding her body against his. "Gee, I almost didn't recognize you—you've been gone for so long."

"I'm sorry I woke you. How are you feeling?" Her smoky voice rasped over him in the darkness. She was soft and warm, and smelled delicious.

He pulled her even closer and kissed her again. "Completely better. Miraculously cured. Whatever that antibiotic was the doctor prescribed for me, it's kicking this thing clear out of my system. When I woke up at noon— without you, might I add, and missing you desperately, might I also add—I could have gotten up and gone to work."

"Ah," Kate said, running her fingers through his hair, a sensation that felt so good, it should have been against the law. "So now the dreaded visit from the doctor was a good thing, huh?"

"Thank you for making me see the doctor," Jed said, and kissed her again. She tasted like coffee and . . . whiskey? He pulled back. "Hey. Have you been partying without me? What time is it, anyway?"

The clock on his bedside table read 12:47.

"Late," she told him. "We wrapped around ten, but then I had to go over the reports. And then there were the dailies. I haven't been watching them lately, and I should be, so when Victor asked me to come along, I went. And afterward, as long as we were at the VFW, we had a drink."

Victor. She'd been out nearly until one, having a drink and watching the dailies—two things Jed either couldn't or wouldn't do—with her ex-husband. And he noticed that she didn't mention the fact that in addition to the day's reports, she no doubt had spent a great deal of time tonight juggling the schedule around for the next few days—all on his account.

"I guess, um, Naomi left today, huh?"

"She's doing a project over in Italy. She stayed here as long as she possibly could. Victor's pretty down."

"So, naturally he tries to cheer himself up by having a drink with you."

Kate shifted over and turned on the light. "Are you jealous?" She gazed at him, a slow smile spreading across her face. "Oh, my God. You're jealous!"

"No, I'm not."

"You are." Her smile spread to a grin. "I'm the one who spent six—or wait, was it seven?—hours watching you fondle some starlet, and *you're* jealous because *I* have a drink with my ex." She laughed, clearly quite pleased. "That's very funny."

Jed pinned her to the bed. "Yeah, like *you* weren't jealous watching that scene? I saw you. I was watching you the entire time out of the corner of my eye. You were standing there like that Amazon Warrior Queen you sometimes pretend to be. You know, real tough, real bitchy, real hard. The Queen of Mean."

"Frau Steinbreaker," she told him.

He laughed. "You have a name for her?"

"She's a part of me that I sometimes use to—"

"Which part of you? Your little toe? You might fool some people, but you'll never fool me again, babe. You're not Frau Steinbreaker. You're Frau Sweetie-pie."

He kissed her again, harder and deeper this time, and she sighed, pulling him closer, intertwining her legs with his. "And damn right I'm jealous," he murmured. "I'm not sharing you with anyone." He kissed her again. "Even when you desert me for hours at a time." He kissed her again. "Even when you hurt my feelings by having a baby-sitter come in and stay with me all day and all night."

Harlan Kincaid had been out in the other room when he'd woken up at noon. The young pastor had stayed with him until after dinner, when Annie had arrived to take over. The fact that Kate didn't trust him enough to leave him alone for a single day had stung bitterly.

She gazed up at him. "I hurt your feelings. Oh, my God."

Jed shook his head, realizing what he'd said. "No, you didn't. Not really. It's no big deal. I was just kidding."

She gently pushed him off of her and sat up. "No, you weren't. I hurt your feelings—and you *told* me."

She kissed him then, so sweetly and softly he nearly melted.

"I'm sorry your feelings were hurt," she continued, "but I had no choice. And in case you didn't notice—I canceled the agreement with Joe Boren, the supervisor who was supposed to come in. I also called the financial backers and recommended that we no longer require intense supervision for you, but they turned me down. They'd agreed to front the money on the condition that you were supervised. I know this frustrates you, but I can see it from their point of view."

Jed gazed at her, feeling a swirl of emotion inside of him. He cautiously tamped it down. "Are you telling me you trust me?"

"I sleep with you every night. Doesn't that imply some kind of trust?"

It did, but he wanted more. He ached from wanting more. He wanted her to tear up that contract addendum. He wanted her to stop the daily searches of his trailer, he didn't want to attend any more mandatory AA meetings. He wanted to sleep in the same trailer that he hung out in. He wanted her to look into his eyes and tell him she had faith in him, that she believed without a doubt that he would continue to triumph over this illness that had claimed his father and mother, and had damaged the rest of his family. He wanted her—this beautiful woman who had once been such a good little Catholic girl—to look him in the eye—he, who had been everything her parents had ever warned her about, who had woken up facedown in the gutter more times than he cared to remember—and say she trusted him completely. In every possible way.

He wanted to forget that despite everything, he still wanted a drink.

But he couldn't forget, and it scared him to death.

He was—dare he say it—happy. His sex life rated a fifty on a scale from one to ten. And unlike some of the other women he'd had relationships with, he liked being with Kate even when they weren't making love. She was his friend. She made him laugh.

But sometimes, even while he was laughing, he felt that familiar, sharp craving for a drink.

"Hey, here's some news you're going to love." Kate sat cross-legged on the bed. "There was a great review of *Mean Time* in *Variety*. And Siskel and Ebert both loved it, too."

Jed blinked. "*Mean Time?* I didn't even know Stan Grogan finished postproduction."

"It was released last week. I can't believe they didn't tell you. Anyway, this article said the reviews and initial box office were so good, they're immediately releasing it to even more theaters."

Jed nodded. "Stan's a good guy. I'm glad the movie's finally seeing the light of day. I thought I did some good work in it, too."

"Yeah, the reviewers agreed. All of 'em said that the movie wasn't perfect, but it didn't matter, because your performance carried it completely."

"That's nice—come here and kiss me."

She did, but then pulled back. "I would've thought you'd be more excited about this."

"Right now I'm much more excited about *this*." He cupped her breast through her pajama top.

She laughed. He loved making her laugh. "I guess you have another headache that needs healing."

"Well, there's the beauty of making love—it makes you feel better even when you don't have a headache."

She laughed again as she helped him take off her pajamas, helped him off with his shorts. And then he lost himself in the softness of her skin as she kissed him, taking him the closest to heaven he'd probably ever get.

She took a condom from under one of the pillows, and she covered him, and he rolled her onto her side, spooning his front to her back, thrusting deeply inside of her. *Yes*.

"I'm so glad you finally came home," he whispered. "It seemed like such a waste to spend the entire day in bed without you."

Kate laughed again, but her laughter soon turned to a sigh of pleasure as he reached to touch her, stroking her with his fingers as well as his body.

"Jericho Beaumont!" The voice that called out his name was about two octaves deeper than Kate's would ever be.

Bang bang bang! A sudden pounding on the door of the trailer made them both freeze. "Unlock this door, you son of a bitch!"

Kate gazed over her shoulder at Jed. "Were we expecting a one A.M. social call from Russell McCoy?"

"Do you think if we ignore him, he'll go away?"

Bang bang bang! "Unlock it *now*, you bastard, before I kick it in!"

Kate couldn't help but laugh. "I think not."

She pulled away from him, and he groaned. "Oh, hell, can't we just tell him to come back in an hour?"

"He doesn't sound like he's got any patience to spare." She was searching the floor for her pajamas, and she tossed him his shorts as well.

Bang bang bang! "Open this door, damn it! Open it now! I know you've got her in there!"

"Who's he looking for?" Kate wondered as she quickly pulled on her pajamas and then her robe. "Maybe he's drunk, and he thinks you've got his ex-wife in here."

Jed slipped on his shorts, and then looked at himself in profile in the mirror on the closet door. "I dunno. Do you think he's going to be able to guess exactly what we were doing?"

Bang bang bang!

Kate laughed. "I'll go see what he wants. You stay here."

"No way." Jed beat her to the door, suddenly dead serious. "You stay back. If he's drunk he could be dangerous."

Bang bang bang! "Open up, goddamn it!"

"Yeah, yeah, yeah," Jed said loudly. "Hang on."

He opened the door, ready for anything. Russell McCoy tried to launch himself into the trailer, intending to push him back or even knock him over.

But Jed made himself into a wall, and McCoy was stopped short still outside the door.

But he wasn't stopped vocally. "Where *is* she? I know you've got her in here, you sick pervert."

"Who exactly are you looking for, Mr. McCoy?" Kate asked coolly.

The man peered in at Kate in confusion. "But—"

McCoy had been drinking. Jed could smell the alcohol on his breath, heavy and sweet. The vein that was bulging on his forehead looked as if it were about to explode.

And if he were going to explode, the best place to do it would be on the road in front of the trailer—not inside, where Kate could be hurt by flying shrapnel. Jed stepped through the door, herding McCoy back onto the street.

A crowd had gathered—cast and crew members who'd been awakened by the shouting. Jed saw Annie, saw her look back at the trailer, and he knew Kate had come outside as well. He didn't glance back. He kept his eyes carefully on Russell McCoy.

"Should I call the police?" Annie asked.

"I don't think that's going to be necessary," Jed said quietly. "What do you say, Russell? I don't know who you're looking for, but unless it's Kate, she's not with me."

"I think we can all go back to bed and mind our own business now." Kate's cool voice allowed no protests or discussions.

But although the crowd began to turn away, they all turned back when Russell McCoy suddenly lost it. "Yes, I want you to call the police! Susie's been sneaking out to meet with you, I *know* she has, and what you've been doing with her is statutory rape!" He lunged forward, but again Jed was ready for it, and he didn't even step back.

Susie?

Jed turned to look at Kate. *Susie?*

"She said you were giving her and that black boy acting lessons, but now I know that was nothing more than a front for some kind of sick clandestine meetings. You seduced her, you depraved son of a bitch. You seduced her, and now she's gone!"

Kate came down the steps. "Mr. McCoy, if Susie's missing, we can help you find her. But I can assure you, there's nothing untoward going on between your daughter and Jericho."

"What kind of producer casts a man like Beaumont in a movie with a child?" McCoy moved surprisingly quickly for such a large man, heading directly toward Kate, but Jed moved even faster. He grabbed the man's shirt and hauled him past Kate and up against the side of the trailer with a crash.

"When I let go of you," he said tightly, getting right into the older man's face, "you're going to take five very large steps into the middle of that street. If you don't, I'm going to beat you within an inch of your life. And if you so much as twitch a finger in Kate's direction ever again, I'm going to beat you within an inch of your life. Have I made myself clear?"

McCoy nodded. Like most bullies, he couldn't abide the thought of violence in which he was the recipient of the pain.

Jed released him, and McCoy stepped back, straightening his clothes and attempting to adjust his dignity. "Call the police, Annie. We'll see what they have to say about these threats to my person. We'll see how lightly they take statutory-rape charges. They'll make you tell me where Susie is."

"Susannah's with me, Mr. McCoy. She's been with me all evening."

Jamaal stepped forward from the crowd. Susie was with him, and she was holding tightly to his hand, looking as if she were about to faint.

"You?" Russell McCoy staggered as if Jamaal had hit him.

The young man squared his shoulders and lifted his chin, a stance that was not ineffective in showing off both his muscles and his cool. "That's right. I suggest you stop hassling Jericho and Kate, and come talk to me about this." He glanced around at the crowd in that regal manner he had down so well. "Privately would probably be best."

"You?" McCoy's voice broke. The look on his face revealed his thoughts as clearly as day. The only thought worse than Susie with a man twenty years her senior was Susie with an African American man. He looked at his daughter, his face turning a darker shade of purple. *"This* is what you've been sneaking out for? You've been screwing this n—"

Jed cut him off, stepping forward and getting right in the man's face again. "Don't say it, you piece of shit! Don't you goddamn dare say it!"

Jamaal seemed to grow another four inches, and his voice dripped venom. "No, Jericho. Let the man finish. I've been looking for a good excuse to kill him."

"I'm sorry." Susie was crying. "Jamaal, oh, God, I'm so sorry."

He put his arm around her. "Hush, baby! I know it's not your fault."

McCoy reached for Susie, pulling her roughly away from Jamaal. "Get your hands off her!"

Jamaal bristled. "You hurt her, motherfucker, I'll break your arm!"

Kate raised her voice. "Please," she said. "Why don't we go into the production office conference room and try to get this straightened out?"

"What's to straighten out?" McCoy spat. "Call the police." He pointed at Jamaal. "I want to see him up on statutory-rape charges."

"I never laid a hand on your daughter," Jamaal said through clenched teeth.

McCoy laughed. "Yeah, right, I believe *that.* You're going to jail, *boy.* Too bad for you, she's underage."

Jed saw the sheriff's car pull up, saw the lawman and his assistant get out and approach the crowd.

"Jamaal hasn't done anything wrong," Susie sobbed. "I

swear it, Daddy. He hasn't touched me. It's all my fault. I'm crazy about him, but he doesn't even think about me that way."

"You go back to the trailer," McCoy ordered her harshly. "I'll deal with you later."

"Susannah, don't you go anywhere you don't want to go," Jamaal said.

"Do what you're told!"

"Daddy, you don't understand!"

"I understand you obviously take after your mother. You're willing to spread your filthy legs and screw anyone who so much as looks at you."

Silence. Dead, complete silence.

Jed didn't think Jamaal could get any bigger or wider, but the young man did both. But when he spoke, his voice was very, very soft. "I'm going to give you exactly three seconds to apologize to your daughter."

"Maybe he's right," Susie interrupted. She turned to her father. "Because you know what? If Jamaal had wanted to, if he'd asked me to, I would've done anything he wanted. *Any*thing. But I didn't get the chance to, because what he said is true. He never even touched me."

"Well, isn't that a pretty acting job?" McCoy would not let up. "You would say anything, wouldn't you, to keep your lover out of jail." He snorted. "First your mother with her spic, and now you with this n—"

Susie hauled back and hit him. She slapped him, a hard, stinging blow across the face that left a red handprint.

McCoy was going to hit her. Jed saw the man's rage clearly in his eyes. But the older man didn't even get a chance to raise his hand because Jamaal saw it, too, and he tackled McCoy, taking him down into the dust.

Susie started crying again, and Kate pulled her into her arms as the sheriff stepped forward.

"I'm gonna count to five, and if y'all haven't separated yourselves, I'm gonna bring you both in," he announced.

Jed grabbed the back of Jamaal's T-shirt and hauled him off of Susie's father.

"What the Sam Hill is this all about?" the sheriff looked around for answers.

"My arm is broken," Russell McCoy sobbed from his prone position in the street. "He broke my arm!"

"I'd love to take credit for it, but you fell on it, asshole." Jamaal spit.

"I want to press charges. Assault and battery. This punk threatened to break my arm, and then he broke it. And statutory rape. He had sexual relations with my fifteen-year-old daughter." McCoy held onto his arm and rocked back and forth.

Susie, Jamaal, Kate, and Annie all started talking at once.

The sheriff took off his glasses and rubbed his weary eyes. He put his glasses on and held up one hand.

As they all fell silent, he turned to his assistant. "Radio for an ambulance for this one," he said, motioning to McCoy, "and take this one," pointing to Jamaal, "into the county facility for safekeeping."

Jamaal exploded. "But I didn't—"

"If you're gonna start shouting, I'm gonna use handcuffs. Now, you just hush up before you make things worse!"

Jamaal shook his head. "*I'm* going to jail. That's just perfect, isn't it? Color of my skin have much to do with this, Sheriff?"

The sheriff looked him straight in the eye. "Here's what I saw. I saw an argument, and then I saw you go for this man. Now, maybe we can all make friends again and have the charges dropped, but until I know what the devil is going on here, I'm gonna do this by the book. I suggest you, you, and you"—he pointed to Kate, Susie, and Jed—"come over to the hospital so that I can get your statements along with Mr. McCoy's. Do you think we can do that without everyone talking all at once?"

Susie, Jamaal, Annie, Kate, and Russell McCoy all started talking.

"Excellent," the sheriff said dryly.

Jed looked up from the magazine he was reading as Kate came out into the hospital lobby. It was seven o'clock in the morning, and she was completely exhausted.

"Well, I think I did it," she said as she sat next to him. "Russell's dropping the assault-and-battery charges in return for a settlement agreement from Jamaal and O'Laughlin Productions. And he's dropped the statutory-rape charges mainly because Susie insisted on having a physical exam, which substantiated her claim that she hasn't been sexually active—because she's still a virgin. But before McCoy passed out, he was *still* being a son of a bitch, saying that didn't prove anything, insinuating that she's been going down on Jamaal. That man is going to be mighty ashamed of himself when he finally sobers up."

"Do you think Susie and Jamaal *were* fooling around?" Jed asked. "When they were doing the scene in the slave quarters, that kiss was pretty explosive. There was about a ton and a half of chemistry there."

"No." Kate shook her head. "They weren't. Jamaal might come across as a smart-ass most of the time, but he swears he never so much as kissed her outside of that one scene. And I believe him. He's not a liar."

"Yeah, his non-liar aura glows pretty damn brightly. Even *I* can see it."

Jed was smiling at her, and Kate couldn't help but smile back. He looked scruffy and rumpled, as if he'd been pulled directly from bed—which had been the case exactly.

This night had turned out to be very different from the way she'd planned.

"Russell was ready to swear out a restraining order keeping Jamaal away from Susie," Kate continued, "but I convinced him not to. I think I have a new future in hostile negotiations, although Jamaal's not too happy with me right now. Part of the settlement deal was that he had to agree to stay away from Susie unless we're shooting a scene with the two of them together. Jamaal dug in his heels at first. I think he was ready to go to jail over this, until Susie begged him to give in." She paused. "Poor kid, this has been total hell for her."

"Talk about restraining orders," Jed said. "She should get one that keeps her father away."

Kate sighed. "Yeah. You know, I talked to her, and she's holding tight to her claim that her father's never hit her, although it seems apparent that he's been doing enough damage with the emotional abuse. She told me Russell makes her feel as if she's not good enough. She says a single day doesn't go by without him mistrusting her in some way, or blaming her, or just making her feel like real crap." Kate paused. "How could someone do that to their own child?"

Jed looked away. "I don't know."

But he did know, Kate realized. He knew probably better than anyone because, as a child, he'd lived it.

She reached over and took his hand, and he looked up at her.

"I still hate him, you know." He was talking about his father. "Sometimes it feels like it's going to burn a hole right through me."

"You're allowed to be angry with him," Kate said softly, her heart in her throat. "I don't even know a fraction of what he did to you, but I know enough to be certain of that."

"But when I get angry, I'm just like him." He stood up suddenly. "How much longer are we going to be here?"

"Susie's going to stay with Annie for a while, at least until we can get in touch with her mother. Annie's in with her right now. As soon as the sheriff tells me Jamaal's been released, then we can go."

"Thank God."

She stood up and put her arms around him, wishing there was some way she could make him believe that even at his worst, he was nothing like his father.

"I have this vivid memory," he said, his face buried in her hair, "of you crawling into my bed. Weren't we in the middle of something really excellent, like watching a movie? No wait, that wasn't it . . ."

"Let me find the sheriff," Kate told him, "and then we'll go home and I'll refresh your memory."

It was then that she saw them. News vans pulling into the parking lot outside the hospital lobby windows. Reporters with cameras piling out of all the vans . . .

"Oh, my God . . ."

Jed turned to look. He swore softly.

"Someone from the crew must've leaked the story." Kate broke away from him and started to pace. "What am I going to say? How are we going to handle this?" She stopped, attempting to fix her hair in the wall mirror.

"Tell 'em the truth—Russell McCoy got shit-faced and lost his mind."

The hospital doors opened, and the first of the reporters swarmed inside. "There he is!"

The lights went on, video cameras started running, and a bunch of microphones were shoved directly into Jed's face.

"How does it feel to be back?" one reporter asked.

"Did you expect *Mean Time* to be such a runaway hit?" asked another.

"Is it true you've been sober for the past year?"

"What do you think about this nickname everyone's calling you— 'The Comeback Kid?' "

Jed looked at Kate. He looked at the cameras. And then he looked at the reporters. "You guys are here for *me*?"

"Are you aware, Mr. Beaumont, that *Mean Time* just opened to the largest weekend box-office draw ever for such a low-budget independent movie?"

"No. That's . . . cool."

"What do you think of the reports of sold-out houses even for matinees, with theater operators having special midnight and two A.M. showings of your movie?"

As Jed smiled, Kate watched him morph into Jericho Beaumont, movie star. He did it so naturally, she was sure she was the only one who noticed. "Hey, guys, this is all news to me," he told them. "I'm sorry, but I'm totally unprepared to answer any questions, although it sure seems like you can answer some of mine."

That got a laugh.

"I'd love to talk to each one of you individually, but you're going to have to wait to set up an appointment with my publicist," he continued.

"Who's your publicist, Jericho?"

Jericho grinned. "I haven't got one yet—that's why you're going to have to wait."

He extracted himself from the mob that had surrounded him, meeting Kate's eyes and gesturing with his head toward the door. He smiled at her, all of his fatigue completely gone, excitement lighting his eyes.

And Kate knew without a doubt that—just like that—Jericho Beaumont was back on top. And Jed's life—as well as her own—was never going to be the same.

Fifteen

❧❧

IT WAS EARLY afternoon before sheer exhaustion hit.

Jed had been doing laps around their New York City hotel suite, but now he sank back onto the couch, surrounded by scripts his agent, Ron Stapleton, had hand delivered.

They'd arrived late last night, at nearly two A.M., and had gotten up mere hours later for an early-morning radio talk show. They'd gone from one interview to the next all morning long, had lunch with an exec from the studio who'd picked up *Mean Time's* distribution, and then been interviewed some more.

Jed was wearing all black—black suit, black shirt, black tie, black shoes. With his long dark, shiny hair down loose around his shoulders and the slightest hint of stubble on his chin, he looked exactly like what he was—a movie star.

But right now he looked like an exhausted movie star. He was still recovering from that nasty sinus infection that had knocked him out only a few days ago.

Still, he managed to smile as she hung up the phone. "They want me to be the next Batman."

"Really?" Kate couldn't keep the surprise out of her

voice. She was surprised he'd even consider taking such an overdone role, not surprised they'd offer it to him.

But surprise was the emotional flavor of the day, that was for sure. In fact, she'd pretty much been in shock since, sitting in the radio station, listening to one of Jed's interviews, she'd heard him matter-of-factly respond to a question about his personal life by stating no, he wasn't currently involved with anyone.

Kate had sat there, totally blown away by the possibility that Jed might've believed what he'd said. For all the physical pleasures and seeming intimacies they shared, he could well consider himself not involved with her.

And that shook her to the core.

Production on *The Promise* was going to be completed in a matter of weeks. Then she would spend her time between Boston and L.A., overseeing postproduction. And Jed would move on to his next project.

This affair of theirs had had an end date right from the start. If Kate had stopped to think about it logically, she would have realized saying good-bye to Jericho was to be expected. What she hadn't expected was to feel so awful.

What was happening here, in New York City, was simply the beginning of the end.

"Do you really want to be Batman?" she asked him carefully, suddenly unable to guess his answer.

He'd spent the entire morning in the spotlight, in Jericho Beaumont mode—smile wide, charisma on stun. She could imagine Jericho accepting the high-profile role, not for the artistic challenge, but because it would propel him back to A-list status instantly.

But he gave her an incredulous look. "No way. The offer's flattering, but no thanks. Not after playing Laramie."

Kate sat down across from him, slipping out of her heels and tucking her feet underneath her skirt. "Jed, I have to ask you something."

Her heart was pounding so loudly, she was certain he could hear it. She sat for a minute looking down at the floor, praying that she wouldn't sound desperate, or possessive, or frightened, but unable to find any words at all.

"I'm a little confused by something you said in your radio interview today." There. That was a good start. It wasn't accusatory. It placed the potential blame on her rather than him. *She* was confused. *She* was the probable cause of the confusion. "I know I've never really asked you for your definition of involved, but . . ." She forced a smile as she looked up at him and tried to make her voice light. "Call me old-fashioned, but when I get to the point in a relationship when I'm sleeping with a man every single night, well, at that time, I pretty much figure we're involved. Rather intensely involved, if you want to know the truth."

"Oh, my God." As Kate watched, a flurry of emotions crossed Jed's face, ending with intense concern. It was pure Laramie. "Have you been walking around since this morning, thinking I don't think we're involved?" He rubbed his forehead as if his head ached. "Kate, my God . . ." He looked up at her. "Why didn't you say something?"

She sat there, wondering if his staggering disbelief was real or just an act, and hating herself for wondering that. "I'm saying something now."

He held her gaze steadily. "I thought I was doing what you wanted by not talking about us—I thought you wouldn't want anyone to know we're together."

He was so sincere. But he'd been sincere during his interview. He was an actor, for crying out loud. Everything he said, every move he made could be just that—an act.

She would never really know for sure.

Not ever.

She should be glad this relationship was destined to end.

"I'm sorry," he continued. "I seriously thought you'd prefer to keep it quiet."

"I did," she said. "I do. I guess, I . . ." He'd completely transformed himself into Laramie—down to the tiredness that lined his face. Kate faltered. Had she ever seen the real Jed? Or had he always just flip-flopped between Jericho and Laramie? "I guess I'm just a little insecure all of a sudden." She tried to smile. "I mean, look at you. Suddenly the tide has turned. You're surrounded by scripts. If you read one you like, the part is yours. You can handpick your next project." She tried to laugh. "I can't threaten to fire you anymore. If I do, you always have the option to go be Batman."

He stood up. "I've got to be at the TV studio in less than three hours for Letterman. If we take a nap now, we can get two solid hours of sleep." He smiled at her. "Well, maybe ninety minutes. What do you say?"

Kate let him take her hand and lead her into the bedroom, knowing she was powerless and pathetic, and that she would agree to be with him, to take whatever he offered for as long as she could have him.

She might have managed to fool him into thinking that she wasn't feeling desperate, but she hadn't fooled herself.

The phone rang.

He'd only been asleep for five minutes. Less. Just long enough for him to feel really bad at being woken up. Kate stirred as he reached for the phone.

"Yeah?"

"Jericho?"

He closed his eyes. It was his agent. Ron. "Yeah."

"God, you sound awful."

"I'm asleep. I *was* asleep."

"Well, wake up. I'm down at the hotel bar, and you'll never guess who's here with me."

Ron took his silence for the surrender it was. "I'm here with Charlee Reed. She wants to talk to you about her next project."

"Holy *shit*!" Jed sat up, head throbbing, but indisputably wide awake.

Kate's eyes opened. "Everything all right?"

On the other end of the phone, Ron laughed. "Get your butt down here, pal, on the double. Don't keep Charlee waiting."

Jericho hung up the phone and climbed out of bed. "Ron has Charlee Reed downstairs. She wants me for her next project."

Kate sat up. "Jed, that's great! Is she directing or just acting?"

"I don't know." Jed searched for his shirt. "Get dressed and come down to the bar with me."

She lay back and stretched. "I need to shower." She smiled sleepily. "I smell like sex."

She looked like some kind of amazing wet dream as she lay there, naked and entangled in the sheets. He wanted to climb back into bed and kiss her until she begged him in her incredible, sexy, breathless voice to press himself deeply inside of her, and carry them both over the edge again.

But that wasn't all that he wanted. He wanted to hold her, just hold her in his arms until all the uncertainty and fearful mistrust he'd seen in her eyes had vanished for good.

What were the odds of that ever happening?

He pulled on his shoes, suddenly dizzy as a wave of fatigue hit him. Damn, he still wasn't over this sinus thing, and the short time he'd slept only made him feel worse. His head was pounding. It was hardly perfect conditions for meeting Hollywood's biggest female star. But he had to take the meeting while he could.

Jed ran a comb through his hair then kissed Kate quickly. "Shower and meet me down there."

Kate cursed herself for being a coward as she peered around a potted plant.

Yes, that was definitely Charlee Reed sitting next to Jed, her trademark red curls cascading gloriously down her back. She was young, talented, smart, and very, very beautiful. She was slim, with the kind of figure that didn't require a bra. And she wasn't wearing one beneath her T-shirt—a fact Kate felt certain Jed hadn't missed.

Charlee Reed had pert athletic breasts—the kind that made Kate feel as if she herself needed a forklift.

As Kate watched from the safety of the potted fern, Jericho—and he was definitely Jericho right now—listened intently to Charlee. Even in repose, he had his charisma set to kill. He looked like a living dream—his hair pulled back into a casual ponytail, dressed in a black shirt that hugged his upper body, his eyelashes four miles long, his cheekbones and lips a work of art. He laughed at something Charlee said, and every woman in the entire bar stopped to look at him. And why not? Kate wasn't the only one who thought Jericho Beaumont was the sexiest man in the universe.

Charlee looked as if she were in complete agreement with the rest of the world's female population. Her chin in her hand, elbow on the table, it was her turn to listen as Jericho spoke. She seemed fascinated by his mouth . . .

This was really stupid.

Standing here like this, hiding behind the fern was stupendously stupid. Kate should walk around the corner and join her lover and his business associates for brunch. Heck, she'd always wanted to meet Charlee Reed herself.

Kate took a deep breath.

And stayed securely behind the fern.

She couldn't do it. She couldn't go in there and sit at that table, and pretend the fact that Charlee was dying to work with Jericho didn't bother her. She couldn't sit there and pretend it didn't matter that Jericho's feelings seemed to be extremely mutual.

It was possible he would go directly from Kate's set to Charlee's set. And straight from Kate's bed to Charlee's.

And she would not sit and pretend to smile at Charlee. It felt far too much as if she were running a relay race, hitting her mark and passing the baton to the next runner in line.

As she watched, Charlee excused herself. She left the table and headed for the ladies' room, heading directly past the fern, close enough for Kate to get a whiff of her perfume. She wore a Gap scent. Ocean. One of Jed's favorites.

Now was the time to go in there and tell him she wouldn't be able to stay—pretend she had too many calls to return back in the room. But before she could extract herself from the fern, he put his head into his hands.

Jericho Beaumont was gone. The man in the chair was exhausted—his energy completely drained.

Kate wasn't close enough to hear their conversation, but Ron reached into the inside pocket of his jacket and extracted . . .

A pill bottle?

He opened it, shook several into Jed's outstretched hand. As Kate watched, Jed washed the pills down with some water.

Kate was aware of Charlee walking back into the bar only from the scent of Ocean that wafted past. She stood there, behind the fern, for a very long time.

Jericho was flying.

Kate sank onto the couch, exhausted, watching him ping-pong around the trailer. He left a message on David's machine, made them both a salad, and ran through his lines for the coming morning, all the while going a thousand miles an hour.

Somehow, despite his intense fatigue, he'd managed to give two hundred percent during the taping of his appearance on Letterman. He was completely on the entire time.

He'd been the perfect guest, funny, bright, and energetic—with a humorous story he'd obviously prepared about the filming of *Mean Time*.

Somehow?

Kate closed her eyes, trying to block the image of Ron reaching into his pocket for a pill bottle and Jed holding out his hand.

Jed had told her on the plane that Charlee Reed had taken time off from her honeymoon to meet with him. She should have felt relieved—the famous actress had just gotten married to English film director Rufus Poole. There had been nothing for Kate to be jealous about.

But that no longer mattered. Nothing mattered—except the fact she'd seen Jed take some kind of pills, pills that had given him a renewed burst of energy.

He sat down next to her now. "You look wiped. We should go to bed."

Kate gazed into his beautiful eyes, and in that moment, she knew that all this time she'd been lying to herself. She loved him. And if she weren't very careful, she would love him so much that she wouldn't be able to breathe. And then she would be doomed. Because how in God's name would she be able to go back to her old mediocre life, the way it was without him, if she let him become as important to her as the very air around her?

"Before we go to bed, I need you to do something for me," she told him, unable to keep her voice from shaking. She pushed herself off of the couch and went into the tiny kitchen, opening the cabinet.

Jed knew what she was getting before she pulled it out. As she turned, she could see disbelief written clearly on his face.

"You want me to take a drug test?" He spoke very softly, but she could see anger in his eyes. Anger, and outrage. And a very, very deep hurt.

She couldn't look at him. "I'm just doing my job. Protecting my movie." And protecting her heart. She needed something to keep some distance between them. "Jed, I saw you with Ron today, down in the bar. I saw him give you some pills."

"Aspirin." He spoke clearly, precisely, calmly, fighting to control his anger. "He gave me *aspirin*."

She clutched the plastic-wrapped test kit. "And I'm supposed to believe that?"

"Yes." Jed laughed in disbelief. "Shit, I thought you were starting to trust me."

"All right," she said. "I trust you. I believe you." She held out the test kit. "Now, go prove me right."

He took the test kit from her hand. But instead of going into the bathroom, he turned and walked out of the trailer.

Jed picked up the shot glass. He inhaled the familiar scent, but didn't bring it to his lips. He wanted to, though.

He couldn't remember the last time he'd wanted a drink this badly.

He'd been sitting here for nearly two hours. Not drinking. He was on top. He shouldn't be feeling like this.

The drug test kit was on the bar, and he picked it up and took it with him as he left the whiskey on the counter and went out the door.

It was after midnight, and the streets were empty. Most of the lights in the motel and the trailers next to it were off.

Kate's light was still on.

She was sitting at the kitchen table when he came in. Her eyes were red, as if she'd been crying.

He'd come back to tell her he couldn't stand her mistrust another moment longer. He knew it wasn't fair of him to give her an ultimatum. But he simply couldn't handle it anymore. Sooner or later, she was going to have to trust him. And he was intending to demand that it be now.

But Jed knew the moment he walked in, there was no

way in hell he would willingly end their love affair. Whether she trusted him or not, he still wanted her. Whether she trusted him or not, he ached for her touch, for her smile, for the incredible feeling he got when he gazed into her eyes.

"Are you all right?" she asked.

"Yeah." He was so tired, he was swaying on his feet. All he wanted was to crawl into bed with her and hold her. But first he had something to do.

He went into the bathroom and filled the test kit. He brought it out and put it in the refrigerator. "You can send that to the lab in the morning."

She didn't say a word.

Kate stared at the drug test kit Jed had filled and sealed and stored overnight in the refrigerator.

She couldn't send it to the lab. She took it and headed for the bathroom, intending to flush away her chance of ever knowing if Jed really had slipped while away from her in New York. She honestly didn't want to know.

"What are you doing?"

Jed was standing in the doorway.

"Um . . ." She'd thought he was listening to music with his headphones on.

"You were going to throw that away, weren't you?"

Kate couldn't meet his eyes. "I don't need to send this out. I know it's . . . clean."

"That's bullshit," he said quietly. "You really are a lousy liar. You don't want to send it, not because you think it's clean, but because you think I was on something yesterday."

She didn't answer. She couldn't answer. He was right.

Jed took it from her hands, and went to the telephone. He gazed at her emotionlessly as he dialed and waited for the line to be picked up.

"Yeah, Annie." His voice was flat. "I got a urine sample

that needs to go to the lab. Can you get over here and take care of this right away?" He paused. "Good. I'll leave it in the fridge. Make sure Kate gets the results ASAP."

He hung up the phone.

"I'm sorry," she whispered.

"I'm going over to the set early, to work on this morning's scene with Susie. You better come along, because God knows what I'll take while you're not looking."

"If they catch us, they'll probably kill us." Laramie and Jane worked to secure a hiding place for Moses in the foundation of his burned-out plantation house.

Jane barely even glanced up. "Then, we better make sure they don't catch us."

The camera's focus was on Susie as the two actors performed the scene for what felt like the thousandth time that day.

Jed, completely Laramie, laughed softly. "Sometimes I wonder how you could possibly be Sarah's sister. She was afraid of everything, but you've got so much fight in you . . . Sarah couldn't even fight to stay alive when she caught the fever." He paused, and when he spoke again, his voice was rough with emotion. "She didn't want to live after the baby died."

Susie was looking up at him, emotion brimming in her eyes.

Annie touched Kate's shoulder, motioning for her to follow her. Moving soundlessly, they backed far enough from the camera to talk.

"There's a call for Jericho," Annie told her, holding out the cell phone, her hand over the receiver. "A woman named Laura Price has called five times, and she says she's just going to keep calling until she speaks to either Jericho or you."

Kate took the phone. "What's this about?"

Annie shrugged. "She says she's David Stern's sister-in-law? I tried to get her to leave a message, but she wouldn't. She's definitely postal."

Kate put the phone to her ear. "Ms. Price? This is Kate O'Laughlin. How can I help you?"

"Jericho called last night, but we didn't get the message until this morning," the woman sounded extremely upset, her voice wobbling. "Alison's beside herself because nobody thought to call him to let him know."

"Let him know *what*?"

"David's dead."

Jane turned away from Laramie. "Maybe I won't marry anyone. Maybe I'll talk you into taking me west, and I'll dress in pants and paint a mustache under my nose and live like a man. I'll strike it rich panning for some of that California gold."

Laramie laughed. It was real laughter, and the sensation stopped him. The only times he'd laughed like that since Sarah died were when he was with Jane. Jed let all that show on his face as he spoke. "Sarah used to talk about you all the time."

"She did?"

"Yes, ma'am. She used to tell me she was glad you were so much younger than she was. She'd laugh and say that if you weren't just a little girl, I would've fallen in love with the younger Willet sister instead of her. I always thought she was crazy."

At least he did before he met Jane. Laramie didn't say the words aloud, but he let them linger in his eyes.

"I miss her," Jane whispered.

"I do, too."

"And . . . cut!"

Jed smiled at Susie. "Batting a thousand today, huh?"

Her answering smile was slightly strained. Damn, she was doing a remarkable job, considering the pressure she was under from her father. Jamaal was miserable, too.

The tension on the set had skyrocketed over the past few days.

And his own personal bullshit with Kate—the fact that she didn't trust him—was only making things worse.

He rolled his head, trying to loosen up his neck, as the camera was reset for a different angle, as the lights and reflectors were being repositioned. He could see Kate and Victor, off to the side, in a huddle.

Kate looked upset. But that was her expression du jour these days. She looked up, directly at him, and the first thing he thought was, dear God, what's happened now?

"Jed, can you come here?" she called as Victor turned away.

"Hold up, people," Victor called. "A change in plans."

"Wait," Jed said to Victor. "We're not going to do my close-ups now? What's going on?"

"Change in plans. Talk to Kate." The director took off his glasses and wiped the lenses with the bottom edge of his T-shirt. "Susie, can I have you for a minute, please?"

"I'm ready to do this now," Jed protested as Kate led him away from the set, toward the edge of the nearby woods.

As she turned to face him, he saw that she was crying.

"Whoa," Jed said. "Kate, I know the past few days have been tough, but—"

"They're going to get even tougher," she told him. "I have some very bad news."

"My urine didn't test clean? It's gotta be a mistake. A lab mix-up, because I swear to you, I didn't—"

"Sit down." She pulled him down with her, right there in the cut grass. She was wearing shorts that weren't made for sitting in any kind of grass, but she didn't seem to care. She held onto his hand, and when he looked into her eyes, he knew that whatever this was, it was going to be really, really bad.

"Is it my sister?" he asked quietly. "Did her goddamn drunk of a husband finally kill her?"

She shook her head. "No."

"Who, then?"

"David."

David. He nodded. *David*. Around him the world stood absolutely still. The relentless hum of the locusts faded away. Even the sun's rays seemed to lose their strength as time just hung. "Is he . . . ?"

Kate's beautiful blue eyes were filled with sorrow. "He died three days ago, Jed."

"*Three* days?" He took a deep breath. But it was shocking how much the simple act of drawing in air could hurt, so he began breathing shallowly. He pulled his hand away from hers, suddenly unable to bear the gentleness of her touch. "How?"

"You knew he was working up at the state prison."

Jed nodded.

"One of the prisoners lost his temper during some kind of therapy session, and threw David against the wall. He hit wrong, and his neck was broken. Just like that. They put him on some kind of a lung machine, because he couldn't breathe for himself, but . . . complications occurred and he died a day later."

He nodded again.

David was dead. Jed had been in New York, turning cartwheels over his good fortune, and David had already been cold and *dead*.

Grief rose in his chest, a powerful wave of emotion so strong, he knew if he let even the smallest bit escape, he'd drown. He stomped it back, feeling it pushing against him, pressure building. He forced it back, forced it away, sealing it up and slamming home the bolt to keep it locked up.

God help him, God help him . . .

"Alison's sister feels awful that she didn't call you before this. When she saw your name and number in David's book, she didn't believe he really knew you. But when you called and left a message on the answering machine . . ."

The sky was so blue, it hurt his eyes. Jed stared up at it. Pain no longer meant anything to him. He was completely, totally, blessedly, painlessly numb.

"The funeral's late this afternoon," Kate said quietly. "I've already chartered a flight that'll get us to Alabama in time. A helicopter's coming in an hour to pick us up and take us to the airport."

"An hour," Jed echoed, turning to look at her. "Then, there's time for my reaction shots."

Kate gazed at him, and he could see her surprise. Even her tear-filled eyes and slightly red nose didn't detract from her incredible loveliness, he noted dispassionately.

"Jed," she said. "We'll get your reaction shots some other time."

"But I want to do it now." He stood up. "If we do it now, we won't have to screw around with continuity. I want to get it over with."

"Jed, God, it's okay if you cry."

Something twisted inside of him. Maybe she was right, but he couldn't risk finding out. He couldn't risk falling apart. What if he broke down, and couldn't get himself back to his careful state of control? God help him, he'd have to start drinking again, if only to re-achieve this numbness and false sense of calm.

No, it definitely wasn't okay if he cried.

"It won't take long," he said, and went back onto the set.

Sixteen

❧ ❧

"**T**HIS IS BULLSHIT," Jamaal said.

"I agree." Victor sat down in his director's chair.

"What does the Pit Bull think? That I'm going to try to get down with his daughter right here, in front of the camera? Are we really supposed to just do this scene, no real rehearsal? No discussion?"

"Obviously, there's going to have to be some discussion, but McCoy's being a real bastard. You're not allowed to speak to Susie directly. Anything you say has to go through me—if that isn't the stupidest thing you've ever heard in your life." Victor lifted his glasses and rubbed his eyes. "It's been worse with Kate gone again. Annie's overwhelmed. She still hasn't been able to reach Susie's mother. And apparently McCoy's hassling Annie, too, demanding that Susie come back to her own trailer." He sighed. "Christ, what a mess."

Jamaal took a deep breath. "Victor, you gotta help me, man. For a week now, I haven't gotten close enough to Susie to even say like, how are you doing? I just want to be able to look her in the eye and ask her if she's all right."

Damn, what he really wanted to do was pull her aside

301

and ask if she'd meant what she'd said to her father—all
that stuff about being crazy about Jamaal, and willing to
do whatever, whenever. If it was true, thank God he hadn't
known. It had been hard enough to ignore his own desires.
If he'd had to fight hers as well . . .

The assistant director stepped forward. "Annie just
pulled up with Susie McCoy. The father's right behind
them."

"Thanks, Frank." Victor looked at Jamaal. "Just don't
antagonize McCoy, all right?"

Jamaal didn't answer. Susie was coming in the door,
wearing that long dress of Jane's. It had to be hot as hell
with all that fabric around her, and she looked exhausted
as well as uncomfortable. Her eyes found his instantly, but
then she quickly looked away.

Come on, Jamaal urged her silently. *At least* look *at me.*

But she didn't. And Jamaal found himself looking directly into Russell McCoy's eyes.

If looks could kill, Jamaal would be little more than a
drying bloodstain on the floor. "Hey," he said. "Mr. Susannah's Father. How's it hanging, bro?"

"Don't," Victor muttered.

"Hey, I'm just being friendly. Can't I be friendly?"

"No." Victor stood up. "Let's get started. Do we all
know where we are here? It's toward the end of the movie,
Jane and Laramie have built this hiding place in the ruins
of his burned-out plantation house. They've spirited
Moses away from Reginald Brooks's slave quarters, and
he's been in here, hiding for nearly a week. Because she's
afraid she's being watched, Jane hasn't been able to come
out to see him—until now. She's bringing him clothes and
money and more food, and she's here to tell him he's
going to leave tonight. And as much as she wants him to be
safe, part of her doesn't want him to go. And Moses,
you're feeling the same thing."

"Personally, I have reached the ultimately perfect

groove to play this character," Jamaal said. "I am *completely* in tune with his pain."

Susie was standing mere feet away from him, but she still wouldn't even meet his eyes.

"Any questions?" Victor asked.

"Yeah," Jamaal said. "In order to play *this* scene, I need to know: what was the decision about that earlier scene? You know, the one we did in the slave quarters. Did you guys decide to leave in that—"

Kiss. He was going to say kiss, but Susie was looking straight at him now, her eyes wide. She shook her head very slightly, glancing quickly over her shoulder at her father.

Shit.

Victor cleared his throat. "Actually, no," he said, smart enough to be able to talk around it. "Kate talked to the writer, and between the three of us, we decided to cut that out. The scene's just as intense, but the consensus was that it seriously changed the focus of their relationship. We thought it would be more poignant for these characters' feelings to be implied, never confronted."

"So it never happened," Jamaal said.

Susie glanced up at him again, and this time, he was ready for it. He turned his back to her watching father, and mouthed, "Are you okay?"

Her eyes filled with tears.

Shit.

Susie turned to Victor. "Please, can we just run the scene?"

Victor glanced at Jamaal. "Yeah. Remember, I want a really tight two-shot, so make sure you get close together."

The scene started with Susie coming inside. She backed off, and Jamaal faded into the shadows.

"This is a run-through," Victor said, "but—just for the hell of it—let's roll film."

As Jamaal watched, Susie's father stepped toward her.

He could see her shoulders tighten, feel her increased tension from all the way across the room.

"Anyone who's not actor or crew, please stay ten feet behind the camera," the assistant director droned. He looked pointedly at Russell McCoy, who backed off before he could speak his poison into his daughter's ear.

"Settle."

"Rolling."

Shit. What was his first line?

"Speed."

"Action."

Susie took a beat, then came in from behind the camera, carrying a bundle from props, and setting it down on one of the barrels. "Moses?" She turned around, looking for him in the dimness. "Are you here?"

"You don't really think I'd leave without saying good-bye." He spoke from the shadows.

"I think you should do whatever it takes to reach freedom—including leave without saying good-bye if need be." She paused. "Laramie's set to take you north tonight."

He stepped out, into the light. "What about you?"

She turned away, pretending to be busy with the bundle she'd brought. "What do you mean, what about me?"

"If you stay here, your brothers will make you marry Brooks."

Susie turned and looked at him then, and her eyes looked so weary. Her soul looked bruised. How much of that was acting, and how much was real?

Shit, the line was still his. And Victor had wanted a tight two-shot. They were still too far apart for that.

"Maybe you should come north, too," he whispered, shifting toward her. He was close enough now to smell her perfume, to see every freckle on her nose, to be able to lean forward and brush her lips with his . . .

She was looking up into his eyes now. "Now, *there's* a fine dream." Her voice caught.

Think about Moses' secret desire. It's the last time he's going to see Jane, most likely for the rest of his life. These next few minutes were going to be his last possible opportunity to tell her that he loved her. Jamaal could relate. Damn, considering that he didn't have a clue when next he was going to see Susie, he could *really* relate . . .

He had to swallow the lump in his throat before he could speak. "I'll never forget you."

She turned back to the bundle. "I'm doing this for purely selfish reasons—not for your gratitude."

"My gratitude is all that I'm free to give you." He paused. "I have a wife and son waiting for me up in Boston."

She froze, then glanced back over her shoulder at him. "I didn't know that."

"I was told I had to marry, and was sent to lie with a girl I've seen only a few times since. She bore my child—when I left I couldn't leave either of them behind. They made it north, I didn't. But now she's waiting—this stranger who was chosen for me." He reached out and very lightly touched her hair. "Don't let 'em choose for you, Miss Jane." He ad-libbed then, hoping she would get his message. "Don't let *anyone* choose for you."

She turned toward him then, all but throwing herself into his arms. Her action was not in the script, but Jamaal didn't care. He held onto her just as tightly, knowing that all too soon he'd have to let her go.

"I've got to see you," he whispered almost soundlessly into Susie's ear. "Just tell me when and where, and I'll be there."

"I can't," she breathed.

She pulled away. "There's money, food, and clothing in the bag. Go with God."

With a swirl of her skirt, she was gone.

"And . . . cut. That was great, but let's go back and do it again. Moses, get closer to her next time. Jane—you're backing away. Keep it tight."

Jamaal looked across the room at Susie. She met his eyes only briefly before she looked away.

Jed had wandered away while Kate was on the phone, and he now stood outside Grady Falls's only bar.

As she watched from the steps of the production office, he stood there on the sidewalk, like a kid drawn to the window of a candy store.

He'd turned himself into a zombie. She'd held his hand on the charter flight to Alabama. She'd held his hand during David's funeral. She'd held him in her arms every night that had followed, waiting for him to release just a little of his grief.

But he didn't cry.

Sometimes he was so tuned out, she was tempted to check and see if he was still breathing.

When they'd returned to Grady Falls, he'd insisted on getting back to work right away. His performances were brilliant, loaded with emotion and a sensitivity that surpassed everything she'd ever seen him do.

But Jed's performances didn't end when the assistant director yelled cut. They continued when he left the set. He was acting all of the time, she realized. Even when they were alone, even in bed at night.

He didn't look up as she approached. Not until she spoke. "Jed."

He didn't seem surprised to see her there. It was going on five days now, and he didn't seem to feel anything at all.

"There was a message for you in the production office," she told him, watching his eyes. "Alison called. I think she was making sure you're okay."

Still nothing.

"I would've thought it would be the other way around,"

Kate continued, ruthlessly trying to raise *some* kind of re-action. "That you would've called her first. Considering she's the one who's pregnant and all alone."

"Yeah," he said. "Yeah, I should've called her."

He glanced up. Pastor Kincaid was heading toward them, several of the girls from the church youth group in tow.

"Jericho. Miss Kate," he greeted them, his southern manners impeccable. "How are you?"

His words and his concern were aimed at Jed.

Jed smiled, morphing into Jericho, complete with a hint of sadness in his eyes. It was scary to watch. "I'm doing okay," he told the pastor.

"I'm here, if you ever want to talk," the pastor said.

"I appreciate that," Jericho told him. "But I'm fine."

Kate had watched him slip into this character often fol-lowing David's funeral. But it wasn't real. He was an in-credibly talented actor, but he *wasn't* fine. Inside, he was letting himself feel nothing.

And Kate was certain that although she loved him, there could be no way on earth that he loved her. How could he, when he was so careful to keep himself dis-tanced from any and all emotions?

He could *act* like he loved her, and in the course of his performance, he could create feelings for himself similar to love. But since he was only acting, he was completely in control. He would never truly be swept up. He might never feel grief and pain, but he would also never feel blazingly intense joy.

Unless . . . somehow she could force his hand, force an emotional release.

They walked to the trailer in silence. Once inside, Jed picked up his script and sat down.

Kate took it from his hands. "We need to talk about David."

A muscle jumped in his jaw, and she felt the faintest stirring of hope. But then he gave her Jericho, the same way he'd pulled him out for Pastor Kincaid. "Kate, I know that you're worried I'm going lose it and—I don't know, maybe start drinking again but—"

"I want to know what you're going to do, now that you don't have David to talk to."

"I'm not going to drink. I'm . . . not."

He was giving her Jericho's sincere look. She wasn't buying. "Instead you're just going to stand outside the bar? Or maybe you'll go in, have 'em pour you a shot so you can smell it?"

He shook his head. "No, I'm gonna try not to . . . No."

"Do you even know that just a few minutes ago, you were staring at the door to the bar, like it was the gate to the Emerald City?"

His eyes went blank.

Kate laid all of her cards out on the table. "Jed, I'm worried because you're holding everything inside. Your best friend died. You're supposed to be angry. You need to grieve. It's only going to hurt you if you don't let yourself feel something."

He didn't speak, didn't move.

"I once had something really bad happen to me," Kate whispered, praying that he could hear her, because she didn't think she could tell him this twice. "And I didn't talk about it for nearly ten years. And for all that time, nearly an entire decade, I let it eat away at me."

"Eighth grade," he said. He was listening, thank God. "Please, God, don't tell me you were raped."

Kate shook her head. "I wasn't. I was . . . assaulted, I guess you'd call it, for lack of a better word. It was more emotional than physical, but I *was* only in eighth grade, I was just a kid, and . . ." She looked down at her hands, held tightly clenched in front of her. "I was at a party. It was my friend Nancy's thirteenth birthday. Her older brother Doug and some of his friends were there, and they brought us out onto the driveway to check out Ben

D'Adario's new car. We got in, and everyone was laughing and, well, flirting. These were high school boys, and we were flattered and impressed by their attention.

"But then I looked up, and I realized I was the only girl left in the car. I was in the backseat, with a boy on either side of me, and Ben pulled out of the driveway. At first I was like, 'Come on, you guys.' I thought they'd take me around the block, but they didn't. They kept going. Some-one gave me a beer, but I didn't drink it. They were start-ing to scare me—some of the things they were saying, the language they were using, talking about sex, about body parts. Tits. They kept making references to tits. God, I hated that word. I still hate it."

She stood up, unable to sit still, unable to talk about this with Jed watching her. "Doug spilled his beer down my shirt. He started wiping it away, touching me, and I knew he'd done it on purpose. The other boys were laughing, like it was the funniest thing in the world. The other boy sitting next to me—I didn't know his name—he starting pulling up my shirt, saying that I had to take it off or I'd catch a cold. He thought he was so clever. And I couldn't stop them. Their hands were all over me. Even between my legs.

"I was fighting by then, and crying, but they were so much bigger than me—and they were just laughing. They yanked my shirt up over my head so I couldn't see, and somehow they got my bra unfastened, and I was fighting and trying to cover myself and all I could hear was this *laughter* and—"

Kate closed her eyes, their voices still echoing in her head, even after all this time.

"Ben was the only one who had a soul. Or maybe he was just afraid of getting into trouble, I don't know. But he stopped the car on the side of the road, and pulled me away from Doug and the other two. They were still laughing and saying how I wanted it, how I'd been asking for it, just by walking around and sticking out my chest.

"I was crying so hard by then I couldn't see, but I ran. As soon as Ben pulled me free and my feet hit the ground, I was out of there. I was close to four miles from my house, but I didn't stop running until I got home. I took a shower, and I washed that beer off me, but I couldn't wash away the feel of those hands or the sound of that laughter."

Jed touched her shoulders, coming up behind her to slip his arms around her. "I'm so sorry," he whispered.

"I didn't tell anyone," she told him. "I was so ashamed. And I thought if I told, people would blame me. I thought they would think Doug was right, that I'd asked for it, as if I'd somehow had control over the fact that I'd matured so fast. I lived with the shame—shame that I shouldn't have felt—for *years*, because I didn't talk about it. There were times that I thought it was eating me alive. And I'm still . . . not entirely okay, even after all this time. It's still really hard for me to talk about it." She turned to face him. "You need to talk about David, about what you're feeling. I know you're very angry, but you're not letting any of it out." She'd lost him. She saw it in his eyes before he moved even one muscle. She'd brought him halfway back to life for a moment with her story, but now he was gone again. "Don't hurt yourself that way. *David* wouldn't want you to do that. Please," she begged him. "Talk to me."

"I can't." He turned away. "I'm sorry."

As Kate watched, he went into the bathroom. She heard the door shut and the shower go on.

No, she hadn't lost him. It wasn't possible to lose something she'd never really had. "I'm sorry, too," she whispered.

"Lookit, I've made my decision about the end of the movie," Victor told Kate as the camera was reset. "I've rewritten the last four scenes myself and—"

"What?" Kate felt herself start to unravel.

"It's no big deal. It wasn't working for me to have Reginald Brooks win in the end. So after Moses is caught and he's being brought back for the second time, Jane and Laramie intercept the wagon and overpower the driver. It's kind of fun. It's kind of a chase scene, and there's even a little bit of humor in it and—"

"No! *Absolutely not!*" She was shouting so loud, she could see his hair move. All around the set, heads were turning. She saw Jed step toward her. She snatched the script from the script supervisor and smacked it against her hand for emphasis. "This is the story I wrote! And *this* is the way this story ends. It's not about chase scenes or cheap laughs. It's about love and sacrifice. It's about Moses being caught again, and Jane being willing to give up her entire life, willing to marry Brooks, a man she knows is a beast, to save the life of the man—this slave— that she loves. And it's about Laramie having come alive enough again to sacrifice the land he loves so much, the land he's promised his father he'd never sell, the land where he first met Sarah, the land where in his dreams her ghost still walks—because he knows that land will buy both Jane and Moses their freedom. He knows Brooks wants the land that badly.

"Brooks doesn't win, you idiot! *Laramie* wins, because he steps toward the future and finally separates himself from the past. He wins because *he gets his life back!*"

Silence.

It was silent on the entire set, except for her own ragged breathing.

Victor finally spoke. *"You* wrote this script?"

Kate exploded again. "God help me! Out of everything I've just said, that's the one thing you have to focus on? Yes. *Yes,* Victor, I wrote this script."

"But I've read some of your scripts and . . ." Whatever

he was going to say, he wisely didn't say it. "Well, I'm impressed, but I still don't like the ending. Look, just read through the scenes I wrote—"

"No. The entire story drives to this ending. *My* ending. This is not up for discussion, this is not up for change!"

"Kate." Jed was beside her. "Maybe now isn't the right time to—"

She spun to face him. "What do *you* know about when it's the right time and when it's not? For you, it's never the right time. God forbid *you* ever let yourself get angry! But I *am* angry, goddamn it, and I don't care if everyone on this set knows it! In fact, I *want* them to know it! And I'm going to have this out with Victor right here and right now, so just *back off*."

She turned back to Victor. "Here's the deal. You shoot the ending to this movie the way it was written. If you don't want to do that—"

"I really don't."

"Fine. Then, I'm going to have to fire you."

Victor looked like a fish, his mouth opened in shock. "You can't do that. We're a week and a half away from being done! Who are you going to get to direct at this point?"

"I'll do it myself," Kate bluffed. "You found it easy enough to step into *my* shoes and rewrite the ending. I'm sure I can do the same and direct the last few scenes, no problem."

She could feel Jed beside her, his tension almost palpable. But when he spoke, his voice was even. Of course. He was always trying to keep things calm, always trying to keep the peace. "Kate, stop and think. What you're saying could kill this project right now."

Kate ignored him, focusing all of her energy on staring Victor down.

"How could you want to change my ending?" she said softly now. "How could you do to me the exact same thing that was done to you during *Teardrop Twenty*? *The Promise* isn't a movie about justice, Victor. Don't try to make it something it's not. And don't get frightened because there're no chase scenes or explosions at the end. Please trust me and do this my way."

Silence.

Something shifted in his eyes. "Or you'll fire me."

Kate nodded, dead serious. "Yes." It was true. She would rather kill the project than settle for some cheap, fake ending.

She looked over at Jed, and realized she was not going to settle, across the board. She wanted it all.

Or she wanted nothing.

Seventeen

❧ ❧

JED WAS ALONE.

For the first time in months, he was completely alone.

When they'd finished filming, early in the evening, he'd searched for Kate, but she'd left the set.

Without him.

Annie was gone, and Victor was, too. There was no one of authority on the set.

So Jed walked back to his trailer. Alone.

It was quiet inside. It was spooky, the fading light throwing odd shadows around.

He turned on all the lights.

The silence was overwhelming, and he switched on the boom box, and one of Kate's CD's came on. Garth Brooks. He switched it off and went into the shower.

But Kate wasn't there when he got out.

And she *still* wasn't there, waiting for him at eight o'clock, outside the church where his AA meeting was held.

He tried not to want a drink, tried not to feel anything at all.

He headed over to the Grill for dinner, but Kate wasn't there, either.

But Annie was.

He wended his way through the crowded room, not even bothering to stop and get a tray. She was sitting alone, and didn't seem surprised to see him.

"I'm starting to get really worried about Kate," he said, not even bothering to say hello. "Have you seen her?"

"She's in the production office," Annie informed him. "I was about to head over to your trailer—she asked me to give you a message. I stopped by earlier, but you weren't there."

"I was at a meeting." Something major must've come up. Maybe Victor had reconsidered. He'd given in that afternoon, when faced with Kate's crazy threats. But maybe now he was having second thoughts.

Annie pushed a tendril of curly red hair behind her ear. "She asked me to tell you that you're on your own until the end of the shoot."

Jed stared. "What?"

Her thin lips curled up into one of her rare smiles. "You heard me. I think she figured she had so much luck throwing her weight around with Victor today that she was willing to face the financial backers' wrath over *you* if and when it came. But we've only got ten more days. It'll all be over before we know it—and certainly before the backers know what's going on down here."

"I'm . . . ?"

"You're on your own," Annie told him again. "Lordy, Lordy, you're free at last."

Jed knew he should feel happy. Kate finally trusted him. At least he thought this meant Kate finally trusted him. But it had been so long since he'd let himself feel anything, all he felt was numb.

And if having Kate's trust meant losing her arms around him at night, well, damn, he didn't think he wanted it.

* * *

Kate was miserable.

Victor poured himself another glass of wine. "You weren't really going to fire me, were you?"

Kate sat with her head on her arms on top of the conference table. "Yes."

"If this movie is a complete failure at the box office, it's going to be totally your fault." He took a sip of wine. "You know that, right? I'm going to make sure everyone knows I wanted to change the end to make it more commercially viable."

"Everyone knows, Victor. They were all there on set this afternoon, listening to me scream."

"But if the movie's a success," he pointed out, "I'll get all the credit. And believe me, I won't even mention the incident in my Oscar speech."

"Yeah, but you better believe I'll mention it in *mine*."

Victor laughed and refilled her glass of wine.

"I can't believe you wrote that script. You *really* wrote that script?"

"Yes."

"Without any help?"

"That's right."

"I'm impressed." He took another sip of wine. "And proud of you."

Kate managed a wan smile. "Thanks."

It was nearly eleven o'clock. She tried to imagine what Jed was doing. And then she tried to make herself not care. She groaned.

"Look, if you're this miserable," Victor said, "go be with Jericho. What good is punishing yourself?"

Kate lifted her head. "I'm not punishing myself. I'm being kind to myself. I don't need him. I won't let myself need him."

"Well, if you can really figure out how to do that, write a book. It'll sell faster than you can say 'Times List.' "

"I knew it was going to end," she said, as much to convince herself as to convince Victor. "It was inevitable. The shoot's almost over, it's not as if I ever thought we had any kind of a future. All I did was end it a little bit sooner than I'd expected. I got all I hoped for out of him, anyway—a brilliant performance. I'd have been a fool to want anything more." But she had been a fool. God, she'd been *such* a fool . . .

"Gee, and I thought you cut my leash because you trusted me. Instead I have to find out through eavesdropping that you're ending our relationship?"

Kate turned to see Jed standing in the door.

Victor stood up. "And . . . I'm outta here."

Kate waited until the door to the outer office closed behind Victor. "Are you angry with me?" she asked hopefully.

He was. She could see that he was, but as usual, he was refusing to feel it. He came into the room and sat down across from her at the conference table. "I don't know what I am."

Her hope died. "Yeah, that was a big part of my problem."

"There's ten more days," he said quietly. "If you were planning to end things between us after the shoot, why not stick to your original plan? I want those ten days, Kate." He took a deep breath. "I want more than that, but if that's all you can give me . . ."

She fought the urge to cry. "You want . . . more?"

He looked exhausted and empty, and it was the emptiness that broke her heart as he steadily met her gaze. "Yeah. I guess I was kind of hoping . . . I don't know, that . . . I guess that it wouldn't have to end."

"Do you honestly think that we could sustain a long-distance relationship that's based on sex?"

He looked down at the table. "Is that really all you think our relationship is based on?" he asked carefully.

"Yes."

He looked up at her, his voice still so matter-of-fact.

"Wow, I wish you'd told me sooner, because I definitely don't feel that way."

Feel. The word shouldn't be in his working vocabulary. Kate closed her eyes, praying that the emotion and anger boiling inside of her wouldn't make her say something stupid. "How *do* you feel?"

"I, um . . ." He cleared his throat. "I thought you knew. I mean, I thought you loved me, too."

Kate didn't say anything. She couldn't say anything, for fear that she was going to lose the red wine churning in her stomach.

"I do, you know," he told her. "Love you. I know I'm screwing this up and saying it really badly, but . . . There it is."

"Actually," she said, "the dialogue was quite convincing—the hesitation, the humbleness. Another stellar performance. So what's supposed to happen now? A Hollywood happy ending? You say the three magic words, and I'm supposed to just believe you and fall into your arms?"

Her words were hurting him—she could see it in his face. Except, it was all part of the act. There were tears in his eyes, but they—like his words—were no more real than the glycerin some actors used.

"Kate, I know you love me, too."

"How can I?" she asked. "When you won't let me know who you really are? I thought I knew, but . . ." She stood up, reaching for the glass in front of her, topping it off from the nearly empty bottle of wine. She slid it across the table, toward him, and some of the wine sloshed over the sides. "Here. You might as well start drinking again. At least if you drink, you'll feel shame. That's got to be better than the *nothing* that you let yourself feel now."

He stood, too, and as she watched, he struggled to keep his voice even. "Kate—"

"Save the acting for the final scenes of the movie, Jed, because, frankly, I just don't care anymore."

Kate thought that maybe, *maybe* that one was going to do it, but instead, he turned and walked away.

And she knew, for her own sake, for her own peace, her own sanity, that she'd done the right thing.

But knowing that didn't stop her heart from breaking.

Susie was crying.

At first Jed thought the sound was his mind playing tricks on him.

It had been five days since Kate had set him free. Five days filled with an urge to drink—a craving that was nothing compared to how badly he missed Kate.

Kate—who didn't trust him, but who simply had stopped caring.

Three weeks ago, even before *Mean Time* hit big, he'd truly had it all. He'd been too stupid to realize it—like most things in his life, he hadn't figured out its importance until it was gone.

Kate had loved him. She'd loved him from the start. That first time they'd made love may have truly been just sex for her, but after that . . . He knew despite her past, she was too much of a good girl to indulge herself in a relationship based purely on the physical. And if that weren't enough proof, well, he'd seen her love for him in her eyes. She was a lousy actress. She couldn't hide the truth if her life had depended on it.

But now she wouldn't so much as stand still to talk to him. In fact, she'd flown back to Boston the day after they'd broken up. Annie had told him there was business she had to take care of—something with one of her office supply stores. They were sending the dailies up to her, though, and she was in touch 24/7, by phone.

But today she was coming back.

So although it was entirely possible Jed had finally

snapped, the almost silent sound of weeping coming from the rear of the costumer's trailer was not the voice of one of the demons who lived in his head.

It was, instead, Susie McCoy.

She was sitting, huddled against the back wall, behind one of the clothes racks.

"I'm sorry," she said as he pushed aside the clothing and looked down at her. "I started, and now I can't stop."

Jed sat down beside her, letting the curtain of clothing close again, hiding them from the rest of the world. "I know what you mean," he told her. "I've always been afraid of that myself."

"I can't stand it anymore. I want this to be over, but at the same time, I don't."

He nodded. "Yeah, I'm with you there, too." He leaned his head against the wall and closed his eyes. "But if you don't stop crying, you'll have nothing to give for the scene this afternoon."

They were filming one of *The Promise*'s most emotional scenes today—the scene from the beginning of the movie, where Moses was up for sale on the block. Both Jane and Laramie were to look at Moses standing there, and see their own lives wrapped in figurative chains. It was going to be a tough scene to shoot. His stomach started churning, just thinking about it.

"I haven't seen him in days." She was talking about Jamaal. "And he's leaving tomorrow. All I want to do is talk to him, just talk, but if I even say one word outside the scripted dialogue, my father'll press charges for his broken arm and Jamaal will go to jail."

"I could see how it might cause a lot of trouble," Jed said, "but jail?"

She nodded. "Jamaal's got a police record—from years ago, when he got tapped to join a gang, before his mother moved them out of New York City. My father said since he wasn't a first-time offender, Jamaal would probably end up doing time."

"And . . . you believe your father?"

Susie wiped her eyes. "I called my lawyer, and he said if it went to trial and Jamaal lost, he could be facing three to five years." Her chin quivered. "He's been sending me notes, trying to get me to meet him, but I can't. Because my father will do it. He'll press charges. I *do* believe that." She started to cry again. "I haven't even seen him in a week."

God, what a mess. "Has Annie or Kate had any luck getting in touch with your mother?"

"No."

"I'm sorry," Jed said softly.

"He always focuses on the mistakes," she said, almost to herself. "He never tells me when I do okay."

She was talking about her father now.

"Sometimes I feel like I'm going to throw up from all the pressure inside," she whispered. "But when I was with Jamaal, he could make me laugh, and I would stop feeling sick. When I was with him, I didn't feel too short or too fat or too skinny or too stupid or not stupid enough, or whatever my father was currently finding wrong with me. My father never says 'good job, you were great.' It's always, 'Too bad you aren't taller.' Or, 'I guess they can make you look better in makeup.' *God.* But when I was with Jamaal, when he looked at me, I could see my reflection in his eyes, and you know what? I looked okay."

"You *are* okay," Jed told her. "Hell, you're so much better than okay, it's not funny."

"Jamaal and I were just friends," she told him. Her tears had finally stopped, but she looked exhausted. "But now my father's gone and blown everything out of proportion. Jamaal probably wants to tell me he doesn't want anything else to do with me, and I don't blame him."

"Well, I can't speak for Jamaal, but—"

"But you can speak *to* him." Susie looked at him. "Will you talk to him for me? Tell him that I'm not going to talk to him because I don't want him to go to jail. Will you tell him that? Please, Jericho?"

"Yeah, I'll talk to him." Jed turned to look down at her. "I don't suppose you'd want to do me a favor and talk to Kate for me?" She was coming back today. His stomach churned again.

Susie gazed innocently up at him. "I will if you want . . ."

He forced a smile. "Nah, I'm kidding. Bad joke." That was one thing he was going to have to do for himself. Even if it killed him.

Jamaal was in hell.

This was the scene he'd been dreading most since he'd accepted this part in this film. He was standing on the block, striped nearly naked, save for a very small strip of fabric that covered his privates, and the chains that bound his hands and feet.

He'd tried to imagine how humiliating it would feel to be up here—a beast of burden for sale. He knew there'd be plenty of extras for the crowd scene, and he'd braced himself to face their staring, curious eyes.

But now that he was here, none of that mattered.

Jamaal was only aware of one pair of eyes—Susie's. And while she was forced to gaze at him from the distance as they shot the scene again and again and again from all different angles, she always looked away in between shots.

Jericho had told him that the Pit Bull had terrorized her into believing if she so much as spoke to Jamaal, he'd end up going to jail.

He could feel the Pit Bull watching him, feel his own rage and helplessness increasing with every heartbeat. He was just as chained as Moses was, because he knew if he approached Susie, she would probably run away.

He'd called his mother last night. She'd listened and sympathized, the way she always did. But she'd asked him why? Why would he fight so hard to be friends with a girl whose father was backward enough to use the N-word?

Jamaal had friends—good friends—who used the word all the time. It was always 'this niggah' and 'that niggah.' But the word took on an entirely different meaning when coming out of the mouth of a man like Russell McCoy. And Jamaal, he just plain hated it, whoever was using it, brother or no.

But even though he didn't tell her, he knew the answer to his mother's question.

He didn't just want to be friends with Susannah McCoy. He was completely in love with the girl.

And Russell McCoy be damned. There was no way in hell Jamaal was going to go another day without telling her so.

The camera was rolling, tracking Susie as she moved forward, closer to the platform upon which Jamaal stood. The camera was going to dolly around behind her and get an over-the-shoulder shot of him, but right now, its focus was on Susie. He knew that he should stay in character, that he should stare straight ahead, that he shouldn't look down at her, shouldn't . . .

But he *did* look down, straight down into her eyes. She was close enough now for him to see she was crying, her chest heaving with each breath she took. And he knew her well enough to know those weren't all Jane's tears. They were Susie's, too.

Jamaal felt his own eyes fill as he pulled his gaze back up, just in time, before the camera caught him. He felt one tear escape, sliding down his cheek as he stared off at the distant horizon.

"Cut."

It was the word he was waiting to hear. There was about an eight-foot drop from the platform to the ground below, but somehow he managed to land on his feet, chains and all, right beside Susie.

It was the last thing she was expecting, and for a half a second, she just stared at him, shocked.

He took her arm. "Susannah—"

She pulled away. "No!"

The slave chains he was wearing were authentic—they weren't designed to win races in, not by any means. "Get these off of me!"

The props assistant sprang to it, but not before the Pit Bull staggered toward him. "You stay away from her! I'm warning you!"

Jamaal stood tall, squaring his shoulders as he glared down at the shorter man. "If I have to go to jail for simply talking to Susannah, so be it." The last of his chains fell off, and he stepped clear of the pile.

She stood there, watching him, tears streaming down her face. She was ready to pick up her skirts and run like hell, if she had to.

Jamaal knew she didn't have to. He was hoping he could convince her of that, too.

He held out his hand to her, slowly, carefully. "Come on," he said gently, moving toward her inch by inch. "We need to talk."

"I can't talk to you."

"Yes, you can." He looked at the Pit Bull. "Susannah and I are going to step right over here, where you can see us, and we're going to have a little chat. That's all. Just an exchange of words. You can call the sheriff if you want, but last time I checked, talking wasn't a crime."

He was close enough to Susie now to take her hand. He gently pulled her back with him, far enough away from the others to talk privately.

The Pit Bull hadn't moved. Jericho, bless him, had intercepted the man. Jamaal could see the older actor talking, keeping the Pit Bull distracted.

"I'm sorry," Susie whispered. "This is all my fault."

He didn't release her hand. Instead he intertwined her fingers with his. "You don't really believe that, do you, baby?" Damn, he'd missed her so much. Just being with her, just being able to look into her eyes while she talked to him . . .

She closed her eyes. "You must think I'm so stupid . . ."

"What I think is, as much as I don't like your father's methods, I can relate to what he's feeling, because I love you, too."

Her eyes opened, a flash of blue surprise.

"You love me . . . the way my father loves me . . . ?"

Jamaal had to laugh at that. "Not even close. I could be arrested for some of the ways I want to love you. I've been trying hard to be cool about it, but . . ." He took a deep breath. "It wouldn't matter so much if you were twenty and I was twenty-three, but you're only *fifteen*. I can't touch you, for fear I'll lose control—and I'm doubly scared to death now I know this thing I'm feeling is something you feel, too. And if you keep looking at me like that, I'm going to *have* to kiss you, and your father will give birth to a Tyrannosaurus rex."

She was smiling at him. Not one of her little, fake-o, pretend smiles, but a huge, beautiful smile that lit her entire face, even though her eyes still shimmered with tears.

"I can't help it," she said. "I love you, too, but I was afraid that—"

"No," Jamaal interrupted her, gently squeezing her hand. "You don't have to be afraid, ever again."

Russell McCoy was drunk.

Jed stood in front of him, and he could smell the alcohol on the man's breath.

He was drunk, and fighting to hold back tears. "Riva left," he whispered. "First Riva, and now Susie. Susie's going to leave me, too. I know it."

The man was scared to death. It was his fear—fear and alcohol—that made him so damned mean.

"Russell, you've got to stop drinking," Jed said evenly. "Every father's daughter leaves them. It's what happens when you have kids. They grow up. But they don't leave you permanently, unless you do something stupid like spend the rest of your life too drunk to think clearly. When was the last time you told Susie that you love her?"

McCoy shook his head. "I don't remember."

"No kidding. And would you be amazed to find out that Susie doesn't remember, either? But she *does* remember you telling her over and over again how she's not good enough. It's a miracle she hasn't had the court appoint her mother full custody. It wouldn't take much for her to do that, you know."

The man started to cry.

"I know Jamaal Hawkes scares you to death," Jed continued, "but look at your kid. Look at that smile. I haven't seen her smile like that in weeks. Jamaal makes her happy. She's not doing anything wrong by being with him. And if you took the time to talk to him, you'd realize that he's a good person."

"She's only fifteen, and Jesus, he's *black*!"

"She's not looking to marry him." Jed could see Victor out of the corner of his eye. The camera had been reset. He could tell from the director's stance that they were ready to go. It was his turn in front of the camera. His stomach rolled. "Susie's the sweetest, kindest, *smartest* girl I've ever met. If you love her—"

"I do."

"Then, you should reward her with your trust. She's certainly earned it. And that's what love is built on. Without trust, there's nothing there to hold on to." Damn, listen to him. He sounded like David. He was spouting psychobabble—to a drunk, to boot.

But his words were true. God knows he'd spent a lot of

time these past few days thinking it through. His own life was in shambles because of a lack of trust. Kate hadn't trusted him. But he should've been able to live with that. After all, just as Susie had earned her father's trust, Jed had earned the entire world's *mis*trust.

But Kate couldn't live with *his* mistrust of her. He was carrying this ball of pain inside him, unable to cut it loose, for fear it would consume him. He was unable to trust that Kate and her sweet love could help him work through his anger and grief. Instead, he numbed himself, hiding behind the empty facade of the characters he played.

"Lately I don't know what she wants," Russell told him tearily. "I thought she wanted the criticism. When she was younger, it used to upset her, the way everyone always told her how perfect she was. She liked the criticism I gave her. She liked to think she could do better, but she doesn't seem to want that anymore."

"I'll tell you what Susie wants. She wants her father to give her a hug and tell her she's okay. She wants her father to shake Jamaal's hand and see *not* the color of his skin, but a young man who cares very deeply for his daughter. She wants her father to be sober, and she wants her father's trust." Jed could see Kate, standing next to Victor. *Kate*. She was back. His heart instantly lodged in his throat. "There," he said to McCoy. "I've told you what she wants. Now you know. You can either use it, or be a jackass and ignore it. Your choice."

As he spoke the words, Jed knew *he* was the jackass. He'd known all along what Kate wanted. She wanted Jed Beaumont. Not Jericho. Not Laramie. Just Jed.

McCoy started toward Jamaal and Susie, and as Jed watched, Susie moved protectively in front of Jamaal. But then Jamaal moved in front of Susie.

"I'm going to take your daughter to dinner tonight," Jamaal told McCoy. He was standing there, almost entirely naked, but completely in command.

McCoy nodded, a jerky movement with his head. "You touch her, and I'll kill you."

Jamaal nodded, too. "*You* touch her, and I'll kill *you*."

Russell McCoy looked at his daughter. "I love you enough to pray this won't last."

Jed shook his head. It wasn't perfect, but it certainly was a start.

Eighteen

KATE TRIED TO back away, but Jed had already seen her.

He'd been talking to Russell McCoy, and it looked as if—miraculous as it might seem—he'd negotiated some sort of peace treaty between McCoy, Susie, and Jamaal. In fact, Susie looked happier than she had in weeks.

As Jed came toward her, Kate flipped nervously through the papers on her clipboard. God, she'd almost forgotten how impossibly good-looking he was, even dressed as the drunken Laramie, with his hair dull and matted, with three-day-old stubble on his face.

"Hey," he said with one of his rueful half smiles. "It's me. I'm here. How was Boston?"

"One of my stores burned down."

"Oh, hell, I didn't realize that. I hope no one was hurt."

Kate shook her head. "One of the firefighters suffered smoke inhalation, but she's going to be okay."

"I missed you," Jed said. He swallowed, as if he were nervous. Jed nervous? It didn't seem possible. But his eyes looked . . . scared. He couldn't seem to look directly at her.

Kate looked across the set. "I think Victor's ready for you. You better . . . Go." She glanced at him and forced a smile.

"This is, um . . ." Jed swallowed again. "This is a particularly tough scene for me." He laughed, but it didn't quite touch his eyes. "I've been dreading it for the past few weeks." He drew in a deep breath. "It's just a series of close-ups, I know, but well, *you* know what Laramie's feeling here, right? It's some pretty intense stuff. He's coming face-to-face with his despair—the same despair he drinks to avoid. Suddenly it's all right there, this hopelessness, right in his face, unavoidable and . . ." He actually had tears in his eyes. "Christ, look at me. I'm already scared to death because, you know, I've got all this stuff of my own, about . . . about David and everything, stuff I've been working overtime to keep from coming face-to-face with."

Kate could barely breathe. Jed had just told her he was afraid. He'd just been honest with her, admitting he'd been avoiding all of the emotions he'd felt when David died.

"If I . . ." He paused, moistening his lips nervously. "If I, like, lose it, will you, um . . . will you help me?"

"Of course I will," she whispered.

"I mean, I know I can do it on my own. It's not like I'm going to self-destruct or something if you're not there to save the day, but—"

"I'm here."

"Thanks," he said. "Thanks." He actually managed to hold her gaze for three seconds before turning and walking away.

I'm here.

He'd said that to her as he'd approached. *It's me. I'm here.*

Kate exhaled swiftly, making a sound that was almost a laugh. *It's me. I'm here.*

She'd just been talking to the real Jed Beaumont. The

one who'd gone into deep hiding upon David's death. The one she'd thought she'd never really known.

But she did know him. She knew him well.

He'd held her in his arms the night she'd had the spiked iced tea. He'd held her in his arms plenty of times since then, too, as they made love, and then talked long into the night. He'd fixed her salad, and had helped her run errands. He'd met her gaze across the crowd at the Grill, telling her with just one crooked smile that paradise was waiting back in his trailer.

He'd also come into the conference room; told her he loved her, and that he didn't want their relationship to end when this movie finished production.

And she'd sent him away.

Victor called action on the set, and in the dusty clearing in front of the town hall, where the slaves were being auctioned, the camera tracked Jed as he moved with the deliberate care of a slightly inebriated man.

Kate moved to the video monitor. There was a video camera that taped all they were getting on film, so that Victor and the actors could immediately see how each scene looked.

As the camera moved in closer and closer on Jed's face, he looked up at Moses, standing there in chains. He stumbled, falling to his knees, and the camera followed him down.

Kate could see revulsion cross Laramie's face, his shame at being part of a society that catered to such barbaric practices. Then she could see recognition. This wasn't just any slave. This was Moses. Then came bleakness. His own realization that he was as bound to sorrow—deep, *deep* sorrow—and the whiskey that numbed it, as Moses was bound by his chains.

He told all that to the camera without saying a single word.

Tears brimmed in his eyes, and Victor called to cut.

The crew efficiently brought the camera back to the starting point, but Jed didn't move. He knelt in the dust, his head bowed.

Kate moved toward him, but Victor got there first. "I don't think you're going to be able to do that any better, but I know how you like to take at least two or three takes, so if you want to, we're set to go again. Unless you want to take a break?"

Jed looked up, looked over at Kate, and gave her one of his heartbreakingly poignant half smiles. "I think I'm . . ." He nodded, his voice completely matter-of-fact. "Yeah, I'm, um, I'm going to throw up now."

Kate grabbed him, and hauled him to his feet. "Town hall basement," she told him, and he ran toward the brick building, taking the stairs down three at a time. The door to the men's room was swinging when Kate got there, and she stood for several long moments outside of it.

"Jed?" She pushed the door open and peeked inside.

He was sitting on the floor inside one of the stalls.

She knelt next to him. "Should I get a car and drive you home?"

He pushed his hair up and out of his eyes. His hand was shaking, and his face was gray. "It's not much like a home without you there."

"I'll stay with you for a while," she said quietly.

"Will you . . ." He had to start over. "Will you stay longer than awhile if tell you that I feel . . ." His eyes filled with tears, and he squeezed his eyes shut, resting his head back against the metal walls of the stall. "I feel really, *really* angry that David's dead."

Kate's heart was in her throat. "It's okay to be angry."

One tear and then another escaped from beneath his eyelashes. "No," he said, quietly. "If there's one thing I've learned, it's that it's not okay."

"What's *not* okay is to hold it inside the way you do."

He opened his eyes and looked at her. "My father killed

my mother," he said with almost no inflection in his voice. "He got drunk, and he got angry and he hit her, and then she was dead."

Kate put her arms around him. "Oh, Jed, you're not like him."

He held her tightly. "David used to say that, too. Oh, God, I don't want him to be dead."

He was crying. He was finally crying.

Kate sat in the men's room, just holding him, and crying, too.

Kate was still in the trailer when Jed got out of the shower.

He couldn't remember the last time he'd felt this tired. This drained.

He couldn't remember the last time he'd let himself cry when he wasn't in front of a camera.

She'd had dinner sent over from the Grill, and it was out on the table. "Are you hungry?"

He sat on the couch. "No, I'm . . . too nervous to be hungry."

"Nervous?"

"I'm trying to figure out the best way to ask you to spend the night."

She sat down across from him.

"I'm figuring my best bet would be to use a blunt, honest approach. The truth, and nothing but the truth."

Kate nodded. "I'm fond of the truth."

"Okay." He took a deep breath and exhaled quickly. "Here's the truth. I've got a lot of crap to work out here," he told her. "I'm probably going to need to be in therapy until the day I die. I'm never going to be very good at just . . . talking about how I feel. Most of the time I don't even know how the hell I feel. But I know when I'm with you, I actually like myself. For the first time in my life, I don't have to pretend to be someone else."

She was quiet, just watching him.

So he kept going. The truth. "I want to work with you again, Kate. I want to be part of your next project. I don't even care what it is. Hell, I'll go to Boston and stock your store's shelves with paper clips as long as you're working next to me. I want you around, 24/7—except this time I'm thinking twenty-four hours a day, seven *decades*. See, I figured the best way to ask you to spend the night might be to go big, and ask you to spend the rest of your life with me."

"Jed—"

He shook his head. "Better let me finish, because there's more truth you need to hear." He looked her straight in the eye and gave her Jed Beaumont, no trimmings, no frills. "I know I'm not the easiest person in the world to live with. And I can't guarantee that I won't slip back into any old bad habits. I know you still don't really trust me, but I don't resent that. Really. I don't blame you—I'm okay with it. I'll just keep on working to reestablish myself as someone worthy of your trust. I'm going to join AA again—really go for it, stick with it. David wanted me to get back into it. It's a present I've decided to give myself, in his name.

"Meanwhile, I'll keep trying to be honest with you and tell you how I feel. But the truth is, there's really only one promise that I can make you, and it's that I'll love you forever."

Kate was silent.

"So, okay," Jed said. "Maybe it's not such a good deal for you and—"

"Are you going to ask me to stay? Because if you ask me, I'll give you an answer."

"Will you—"

"Yes."

"—marry me?"

From across the trailer, Kate smiled at him. "Definitely, yes," she whispered again.

He smiled, too, feeling his eyes fill with tears. He kissed her, and for the first time since he could remember, he didn't try to contain and stifle everything he was feeling. Terror. He was definitely feeling terror. But it was joyful terror, like having the best party of his life while teetering at the edge of a cliff.

"I love you, Jed Beaumont," Kate whispered, and he knew at the moment that that cliff was nothing to fear. Because with Kate in his arms, he could fly.

Jamaal stood behind the camera and watched as Jericho and Susie filmed the very last scene in the movie. Laramie was saying good-bye to Jane—ready to take Moses, now a free man, north to Boston.

Jamaal wasn't in this scene. He had wrapped earlier this morning and had been officially released. His suitcase was packed, and his plane ticket to New York was in his pocket. One of the gofers was ready to take him to the airport, but there was still a little time before he absolutely had to leave.

And he hadn't said good-bye to Susie yet.

She and Jericho had about four more days of work. Jamaal would've loved to stick around and just watch, because, damn, they were good.

And the last thing he wanted to do was walk away from Susie now that her father had finally taken the first steps toward being human again.

The man was a tyrant to start with, but he'd truly loved his wife. And when she'd left him, he'd crumbled. He'd started drinking heavily. And he'd become even harsher and more cruel in his dealings with his daughter.

But he was ready to change. He'd taken a big step by agreeing to go into counseling just last night.

No, Jamaal didn't want to leave. But he had to.

His agent had set up a meeting in New York with a director who was interested in casting him in a suspense drama about a medical student who uncovered some funky goings-on at a teaching hospital. It was a good part. Susie had thought so, too. It was, she'd pointed out, a part that had nothing to do with the color of his skin.

He'd had dinner with her last night, just as he'd told the Pit Bull he would. It had been amazing to sit there in the light, to not have to sneak around and hide.

They'd gone for a walk afterward, and he'd talked non-stop the entire time—because he knew if he stopped talking, he'd kiss the girl. And he was scared to death that once he started kissing her, he'd completely lose control. And if *that* happened, he didn't doubt for a single moment that Russell would come after him with a shotgun.

But now he knew that if he didn't get a chance to kiss her good-bye, he'd be cursing himself for being a fool for the rest of his life.

As the camera rolled, Jericho picked up a duffle bag and swung it over his shoulder. "Promise me," he said to Susie—to *Jane*. "No taking in any runaways while I'm gone."

"I promise you," she said, "that I won't get caught."

He looked at her, long and steady. "That wasn't what I asked."

"But it *was* my answer."

Another long look. "Go with God."

"You, too."

He turned to leave, but then turned back, subtle emotions playing across his face. "When I come back, you'll be a little bit older."

The look in his eyes loaded his words with meaning. Jane nodded, the look in *her* eyes telling him that she fully understood. "I will be."

"Wait for me," he said quietly.

"I will."

He smiled then. "Good." And he turned around to walk

away. The camera moved up close behind Susie, as she watched him head down the dusty road.

"Laramie!"

He turned, and she ran toward him, the camera following. He dropped his bag, and she threw herself into his arms. Damn, it was powerful. And if Jamaal didn't know both Susie and Jericho so well, he'd be feeling a whole lot more than these little weird twinges of jealousy, that was for sure.

The camera moved in tight on their embrace, and Susie—Jane—gazed up at Laramie. "Some people's second best can be better than most people's first choice," she whispered.

In the video monitor, Jamaal could see that Jericho had tears in his eyes. Damn, he was good. Slowly, he closed his eyes and gently brushed his lips against Susie's. *Jane's,* he told himself. Those were Jane's lips he was kissing. But, damn, that was some sweet, purely romantic kiss. And it was obvious that for Laramie, Jane was *not* his second choice.

Jane touched Laramie's face, searched his eyes. "Please hurry home."

Laramie smiled. "I will."

He set her down, picked up his bag, and continued on his way.

"And . . . cut!"

Jamaal had tears in his own eyes, and he quickly wiped them away as Susie came toward him.

"Hi."

"Man," he said. "That really rocked."

"Will you sit with me at the premiere?" she asked.

"Will you *go* with me to the premiere?" he countered. "As my date?"

Her eyes were actually shining. "Yes."

"That's not going to be for a while," he said.

"Will you call me after you meet with this director?" she asked.

Annie appeared alongside them. "Jamaal, if you don't leave soon, you're going to miss your flight."

He looked into Susie's eyes. "Yes, I'll call you." He took her hand, leading her to where the car was waiting. "I'll call you all the time. Every day, if you want."

"I want."

The driver started the engine. *Shit.* He had four million things to say to her . . . "I love you."

There were tears in her eyes. "I love you, too."

He pulled her close, and she clung to him. "Your father is going to try to tell you that this wasn't real—that it was just a crush." He pulled her chin up so that she had to look at him. "Don't believe him, okay? Because this *is* real."

Jamaal kissed her. He knew the Pit Bull was watching, but he didn't give a damn. She tasted like magic and hope and the power of love.

"It's real," he whispered again. "Don't forget that."

"I won't." She smiled. "I promise."

There was a state police cruiser outside of Jed's trailer, along with the county sheriff's marked car.

His first thought was that Russell McCoy had done something stupid again. His second thought was this had nothing to do with McCoy—these cars were parked in front of *his* trailer.

"Where's Kate?" he asked one of the gaffers who was standing in the crowd, looking on. "Is Kate all right?"

"I think she's on her way over."

Jed pushed his way through to the front, where Ethan and Nate were standing with the sheriff and a state trooper who was wearing mirrored aviator sunglasses. "What's going on?"

"You're in deep trouble, that's what's going on." The sheriff clearly wasn't here to sign up for Jed's fan club.

Nate stepped forward looking apologetic. "I'm sorry, Jericho. We were told to call in the police."

"Why?"

"Please step forward and place your hands against the side of the trailer, Mr. Beaumont," the sunglasses said to him.

"Why? Are you arresting me? Nate, what the hell is this about?"

"Cocaine, Jericho."

Ethan chipped in. "A *lot* of it."

"We found it in your trailer. Just out on the table."

"Half used—lines still on a mirror."

"Mr. Beaumont, please step forward and—"

"It's not mine. If it *was* mine, I wouldn't be stupid enough to leave it out. Didn't you call Kate?" Jed asked the security guards. They were supposed to call Kate first, before calling in the authorities.

"We did," Nate told him.

Jed's heart sank. They'd called Kate, and she'd told them to call the police.

The sunglasses was getting peeved. "Mr. Beaumont, I'm going to ask you for a second time to step toward the trailer and place your hands—"

"I don't think that'll be necessary." Kate made her entrance like European royalty. Or like a fresh breeze sweeping across a stagnant swamp. She took in Jed, the trooper, the sheriff, and Nate and Ethan with a single glance, settling on Nate. "Why wasn't I called *before* the police?"

"We couldn't get in touch with you and—"

Kate turned briskly to the sheriff. "Tom. This is all a mistake."

"Ma'am." He touched his hat. "A substantial amount of cocaine was found in Jericho's trailer this afternoon. I'm afraid it's too much to simply let him off with a warning. We've got to bring him in."

"The drugs aren't his," she said.

Jed's knees felt weak. He hadn't even opened his

mouth to deny anything in her presence, and already she
believed he was innocent.

"Jericho's been clean for this entire shoot," Kate said. "I
have records of tests we ran for drug and alcohol use that you
can use to verify that. And—just for your information—he's
been clean for more than five years."

The sheriff shifted his weight. "However, the cocaine
was found in his trailer."

"Tom, come on. Someone else put it there. Jericho told
me he never used cocaine, not even during the height of
his substance abuse."

The sheriff was skeptical. "You're going on something
Beaumont told you?"

"Yes." Kate turned to Jed. "Are the drugs yours?"

"No." Jed had to smile at her. Even if the sheriff and the
trooper didn't believe him, even if they wound up drag-
ging him to the police station and holding him on possession charges, it didn't matter, because *Kate* believed him.

She turned to the sheriff. "The drugs aren't his."

He crossed his arms. "And someone just put that much
cocaine in his trailer?"

"It happens often enough on movie sets, unfortunately,"
Kate told him. "Overexuberant fans imagine that they're
leaving gifts. And don't forget what happened with that
gofer and the LSD." She took a deep breath and smiled.
"I'd appreciate it if you could properly dispose of the cocaine. And thank you for coming out here so promptly."

Neither the sheriff nor trooper-man were about to let
themselves be so easily dismissed. "I still think we
better—"

Jed interrupted him. "Tom, Nate and Ethan said the
stuff was out on the table—some of it was used. How
about I take another drug test? You can take it over to the
lab. That'll tell you whether or not I was the one who used
that cocaine."

The sheriff glanced at the trooper. "Well . . . I guess that *would* show . . ."

The trooper nodded. "That works for me. But you better not plan on going anywhere until the test results are in."

Jed nodded. "That's fair.

"There're kits inside." Kate's smile was tight. "You want to come make sure Jericho doesn't cheat?"

"Absolutely." The trooper followed them into the trailer.

Kate's movements were almost jerky as she took the test kit down from the kitchen cabinet. She was mad, Jed realized as she placed it in his hand. She was PO'd that he had to do this.

But it was over then, and the sheriff and trooper pulled away, finally leaving him alone in the trailer with Kate.

"If you were anyone else, you wouldn't have had to prove that those drugs weren't yours," she said tightly. "God, it's so unfair—it makes me so *angry!*"

"It's okay to be angry." He pulled her into his arms. "But it's also okay that they don't trust me."

There were tears in her eyes. "I'm so sorry about this. If I hadn't forced you to sign that contract addendum . . ."

Jed kissed her. "I love that contract addendum," he told her. "Signing that was the smartest thing I've ever done." He kissed her again, marveling at how soft her mouth was, marveling that she had actually agreed to marry him. *She* was marrying *him*. He was definitely getting away with something here.

"It's so unfair," she said again.

It was, but it was entirely in his favor.

"I love you," he said. "When you stood up for me like that, I was . . . I was honored." He felt like crying, and for once he didn't fight it. He just let his eyes fill with tears, let her see how moved he was.

Kate touched his face, her own eyes looking decidedly

moist. She kissed him, and he pulled her closer and kissed her yet again, unable, as always, to get enough of her.

It didn't even help knowing that she was his forever.

Epilogue

❧ ❧

T HE ROOM WAS packed.

Kate recognized nearly all the faces in the crowd. The complete production staff from *The Promise* was there, as well as the postproduction staff. She saw Victor, his arm around some new young flavor of the month. Susie and Jamaal were sitting in the front row, holding hands, grinning at each other. Jamaal had come all the way from New York, taking time off from his latest movie. Even Alison Stern had flown out for the occasion, her brand-new baby in a front pack, seven-year-old Kenny beside her.

Kate looked at Jed and smiled as he moved toward the podium. He was nervous. Not that he looked it. But she knew because he'd admitted it to her in the car on the way over.

This wasn't the Academy Awards. It wasn't even *The Promise*'s premiere. They were all going to have to get together again in two weeks to kick off the release of her movie. *Their* movie. Thanks to brilliant performances by Jed and Susie and Jamaal, and a postproduction team that worked eighteen-hour days to get the film ready to go, the movie was set to open in every major market, right before

Christmas. It was going to be big. And Kate was betting it was going to sweep the Oscar nominations.

She was going to enjoy watching her husband's acceptance speech for the Best Actor award, but even that wouldn't top the achievement award he was receiving tonight.

He tapped once on the microphone, to see if it was on. The audience quieted, and he spoke.

"My name is Jed Beaumont, and I'm an alcoholic. It's been exactly six years since I've had a drink . . ."

He met her eyes then, and smiled as applause thundered though the church basement.

Yeah, the Oscars were going to be fun, but they weren't going to be any better than this.

I love you, Kate mouthed to him, and his smile got even wider. He nodded. He knew. The same way she knew he loved her, too. 24/7.

Read on for an exciting preview of

FLASHPOINT
by Suzanne Brockmann

Published by Ballantine Books
in April 2004.

Before tonight, the closest Tess Bailey had come to a strip
club was on TV, where beautiful women danced seductively in
G-strings, taut young body parts bouncing and gleaming from
a stage that sparkled and flashed.

In the Gentlemen's Den, thousands of miles from
Hollywood in a rundown neighborhood north of Washington,
D.C., the mirror ball was broken, and the aging stripper on the
sagging makeshift stage looked tired and cold.

"Whoops." Nash turned his back to the noisy room, carefully keeping his face in the shadows. "That's Gus Mondelay
sitting with Decker," he told Tess.

Diego Nash had the kind of face that stood out in a crowd.
And Nash obviously didn't want Mondelay—whoever he was
—to see him.

Tess followed him back toward the bar, away from the table
where Lawrence Decker, Nash's long-time Agency partner,
was working undercover.

She bumped into someone. "Excuse me—"

Oh my God! The waitresses weren't wearing any shirts.
The Gentlemen's Den wasn't just a strip club, it was also a
topless bar. She grabbed Nash's hand and dragged him down
the passageway that led to the pay phone and the restrooms. It
was dark back there, with the added bonus of nary a half-
naked woman in sight.

She had to say it. "This *was* just a rumor—"

He pinned her up against the wall and nuzzled her neck, his
arms braced on either side of her. She was only stunned for
about two seconds before she realized that two men had staggered out of the men's room. This was just another way for
Nash to hide his face.

She pretended that she was only pretending to melt as he kissed her throat and jawline, as he waited until Drunk and Drunker pushed past them before he spoke, his breath warm against her ear. "There were at least four shooters set up and waiting out front in the parking lot. And those were just the ones I spotted as we were walking in."

The light in the parking lot had been dismal. Tess's concentration had alternated between her attempts not to catch her foot in a pothole and fall on her face, the two biker types who appeared to be having, quite literally, a pissing contest, and the unbelievable fact that she was out in the real world with the legendary Diego Nash.

They were now alone in the hallway, but Nash hadn't moved out of whispering range. He was standing so close that Tess's nose was inches from the collar of his expensive shirt. He smelled outrageously good. "Who's Gus Mondelay?" she asked.

"An informant," he said tersely, the muscle jumping in the side of his perfect jaw. "He's on the Agency payroll, but lately I've been wondering . . . " He shook his head. "It fits that he's here, now. He'd enjoy watching Deck get gunned down." The smile he gave her was grim. "Thanks for having the presence of mind to call me."

Tess still couldn't believe the conversation she'd overheard just over an hour ago at Agency Headquarters.

A rumor had come in that Lawrence Decker's cover had been blown, and that there was an ambush being set to kill him. The Agency's night-shift support staff had attempted to contact him, but had been able to do little more than leave a message on his voice mail.

No one in the office had bothered to get in touch with Diego Nash.

"Nash isn't working this case with Decker," Suellen Foster had informed Tess. "Besides, it's just a rumor."

Nash was more than Decker's partner. He was Decker's friend. Tess had called him even as she ran for the parking lot.

"So what do we do?" Tess asked now, looking up at Nash.

He had eyes the color of melted chocolate—warm eyes that held a perpetual glint of amusement whenever he came into the office in HQ and flirted with the mostly female support staff. He liked to perch on the edge of Tess's desk in particular, and the other Agency analysts and staffers teased her about his attention. They also warned her of the dangers of dating a field agent, particularly one like Diego Nash, who had a serious 007 complex.

As if she needed their warning.

Nash sat on her desk because he liked her little bowl of lemon mints, and because she called him "tall, dark, and egotistical" right to his perfect cheekbones, and refused to take him seriously.

Right now, though, she was in his world, and she was taking him extremely seriously.

Right now his usually warm eyes were cold and almost flat-looking, as if part of him were a million miles away.

"*We* do nothing," Nash told Tess now. "*You* go home."

"I can help."

He'd already dismissed her. "You'll help more by leaving."

"I've done the training," she informed him, blocking his route back to the bar. "I've got an application in for a field agent position. It's just a matter of time before—"

Nash shook his head. "They're not going to take you. They're never going to take you. Look, Bailey, thanks for the ride, but—"

"Tess," she said. He had a habit of calling the support staff by their last names, but tonight she was here, in the field. "And they are too going to take me. Brian Underwood told me—"

"Brian Underwood was stringing you along because he was afraid you would quit and he needs you on support. You'll excuse me if I table this discussion on your lack of promotability and start focusing on the fact that my partner is about to—"

"I can get a message to Decker," Tess pointed out. "No one in that bar has ever seen me before."

Nash laughed in her face. "Yeah, what? Are you going to walk over to him with your freckles and your Sunday church picnic clothes . . . ?"

"These aren't Sunday church picnic clothes!" They were

running-into-work-on-a-Friday-night-at-10:30-to-pick-up-a-file clothes. Jeans. Sneakers. T-shirt.

T-shirt . . .

Tess looked back down the hall toward the bar, toward the ordering station where the waitresses came to pick up drinks and drop off empty glasses.

"You stand out in this shithole as much as I do wearing this suit," Nash told her. "More. If you walk up to Decker looking the way you're looking . . . "

There was a stack of small serving trays, right there, by the bartender's cash register.

"He's my friend, too," Tess said. "He needs to be warned, and I can do it."

"No." Finality rang in his voice. "Just walk out the front door, Bailey, get back into your car and—"

Tess took off her T-shirt, unhooked her bra, peeled it down her arms, and handed them both to him.

"What message should I give him?" she asked.

Nash looked at her, looked at the shirt and wispy lace of bra dangling from his hand, looked at her again.

Looked at her. "Jeez, Bailey."

Tess felt the heat in her cheeks as clearly as she felt the coolness from the air conditioning against her bare back and shoulders.

"What should I tell him?" she asked Nash again.

"Damn," he said, laughing a little bit. "Okay. O-*kay*." He stuffed her clothes into his jacket pocket. "Except you still look like a Sunday school teacher."

Tess gave him a disbelieving look and an outraged noise. "I do *not*." For God's sake, she was standing here half naked—

But he reached for her, unfastening the top button of her jeans and unzipping them.

"Hey!" She tried to pull back, but he caught her.

"Don't you watch MTV?" he asked, folding her pants down so that they were more like hip huggers, his fingers warm against her skin.

Her belly button was showing now, as well as the top of her panties, the zipper of her jeans precariously half-pulled down. "Yeah, in all my limitless free time."

"You could use some lipstick." Nash stepped back and looked at her critically, then, with both hands, completely messed up her short hair. He stepped back and looked again. "That's a little better."

Gee, thanks. "Message?" she said.

"Just tell him to stay put for now. They're not going to hit him inside," Nash said. "Don't tell him that, he knows. That's what I'm telling *you,* you understand?"

Tess nodded.

"I'm going to make a perimeter circuit of this place," he continued. "I'll meet you right back here—no, in the ladies' room—in ten minutes. Give the message to Deck, be brief, don't blow it by trying to tell him too much, then get your ass in the ladies' room, and stay there until I'm back. Is that clear?"

Tess nodded again. She'd never seen this Nash before— this order-barking, cold-bloodedly decisive commander. She'd never seen the Nash he'd become in the car, on the way over here, before either. After she'd made that first phone call, she'd picked him up downtown. She'd told him again as they'd headed to the Gentlemen's Den, in greater detail, all that she'd overheard. He'd gotten very quiet, very grim, when his attempts to reach Decker on his cell phone had failed.

He'd been scared, she'd realized as she'd glanced at him. He had been genuinely frightened that they were too late, that the hit had already gone down, that his partner—his friend—was already dead.

When they got here and the parking lot was quiet, when they walked inside and spotted Decker still alive and breathing, there had been a fraction of a second in which Tess had been sure Nash was going to faint from relief.

It was eye-opening. It was possible that Diego Nash was human after all.

Tess gave him one last smile, then headed down that hall, toward one of those little serving trays on the bar. God, she was about to walk into a room filled with drunken men, with her breasts bare and her pants halfway down her butt. Still, it couldn't possibly be worse than that supercritical once-over Nash had given her.

"Tess." He caught her arm, and she looked back at him. "Be careful," he said.

She nodded again. "You, too."

He smiled then—a flash of straight white teeth. "Deck's going to shit monkeys when he sees you."

With that, he was gone.

Tess grabbed the tray from the bar and pushed her way out into the crowd.

Something was wrong.

Decker read it in Gus Mondelay's eyes, in the way the heavyset man was sitting across from him at the table.

Mondelay gestured for Decker to come closer—it was the only way to be heard over the loud music. "Tim must be running late."

Jesus, Mondelay had a worse than usual case of dog breath tonight.

"I'm in no hurry," Decker said, leaning back again in his seat. Air. Please God, give him some air.

Gus Mondelay had come into contact with the Freedom Network while serving eighteen months in Wallens Ridge Prison for possession of an illegal firearm. The group's name made them sound brave and flag-wavingly patriotic, but they were really just more bubbas—the Agency nickname for homegrown terrorists with racist, neo-Nazi leanings and a fierce hatred for the federal government. And for all agents of the federal government.

Such as Decker.

Even though Deck's speciality was with terrorist cells of the foreign persuasion, he'd been introduced to informant Gus Mondelay when the man had coughed up what seemed to be evidence that these particular bubbas and al-Qaeda were working in tandem.

Those insane-sounding allegations could not be taken lightly, even though Deck himself couldn't make sense of the scenario. If there was anyone the bubbas hated more than the federal agents, it was foreigners. Although the two groups certainly may have found common ground in their hatred of Israel.

Dougie Brendon, the newly appointed Agency director,

had assigned Decker to Gus Mondelay. Deck was to use Mondelay to try to work his way deeper into the Freedom Network, with the goal of being present at one of the meetings with members of the alleged al-Qaeda cell.

So far all Mondelay had provided him with were leads that had gone nowhere.

Mondelay made the come-closer-to-talk gesture again. "I'm going to give Tim a call, see what's holding him up," he said as he pried his cell phone out of his pants pocket.

Decker watched as the other man keyed in a speed-dial number, then held his phone to his face, plugging his other ear with one knockwurst-size finger. Yeah, that would help him hear over the music.

Mondelay sat back in his chair as whoever he was calling picked up. Decker couldn't hear him, but he could read lips. He turned his head so that Mondelay was right at the edge of his field of vision.

What the fuck is taking so long? Pause, then, *No way, asshole, you were supposeda call me. I bin sitting here for almost an hour now waiting for the fucking goat head.*

Huh?

Fuck you, too, douchebag. Mondelay hung up his phone, leaned toward Decker. "I got the locale wrong," he said. "Tim and the others are over at the Bull Run. It was my mistake. Tim says we should come on over. Join them there."

No. There was no way in hell that Mondelay had been talking to Tim Ebersole, Freedom Network leader. Decker had heard him on the phone with Tim in the past, and it had been all "Yes, sir," and "Right away, sir." "Let me kiss your ass, sir," not "Fuck you, too, douchebag."

Something was rotten in the Gentlemen's Den—something besides Mondelay's toxic breath, that was.

Mondelay wasn't waiting on any goat head. He was waiting for the *go ahead.* The son of a bitch was setting Decker up.

Mondelay began the lengthy process of pushing his huge frame up and out of the seat.

"You boys aren't leaving, are you?"

Decker looked up and directly into the eyes of Tess Bailey, the pretty young computer specialist from the Agency support office.

But okay, no. Truth be told, the first place he looked wasn't into her eyes.

She'd moved to D.C. a few years ago, from somewhere in the Midwest. Kansas, maybe. A small town, she'd told them once when Nash had asked. Her father was a librarian.

Funny he should remember that fact about her right now.

Because, holy crap, Toto, Tess Bailey didn't look like she was in small-town Kansas anymore.

"There's a lady over at the bar who wants to buy your next round," Tess told him, as she shouted to be heard over the music, as he struggled to drag his eyes up to her face.

Nash. The fact that she was here and half-naked—no, forget the half-naked part, although, Jesus, that was kind of hard to do when she was standing there half-fricking-naked —had to mean that Nash was here, too. And if Nash was here, that meant Decker was right, and he was about to be executed. Or kidnapped.

He glanced at Mondelay, at the nervous energy that seemed to surround the big man. No, he got it right the first time. Mondelay was setting him up to be hit.

Son of a bitch.

"She said you were cute," Tess was shouting at Decker, trying desperately for eye contact. He gave it to her. Mostly. "She's over there, in the back." She pointed toward the bar with one arm, using the other to hold her tray up against her chest, which made it a little bit easier to pay attention to what she was saying, despite the fact that it still didn't make any sense. Cute? *Who* was in the back of the bar?

Nash, obviously.

"So what can I get you?" Tess asked, all cheery smile and adorable freckled nose, and extremely bare breasts beneath that tray she was clutching to herself.

"We're on our way out," Mondelay informed her.

"Free drinks," Tess said enticingly. "You should sit back down and stay a while." She looked pointedly at Deck.

A message from Nash. "I'll have another beer," Decker shouted up at her with a nod of confirmation.

Mondelay laughed his disbelief. "I thought you wanted to meet Tim."

Decker made himself smile up at the man who'd set him

up to be killed. Two pals, out making the rounds of the strip clubs. "Yeah, I do."

"Well, they're waiting for us now."

"That's good," Decker said. "We don't want to look too eager, right?" He looked at Tess again. "Make it imported."

Mondelay looked at her, too, narrowing his eyes slightly —a sign that he was probably thinking. "You're new here, aren't you?"

"He'll have another beer, too," Decker dismissed Tess, hoping she'd take the hint and disappear, fast.

Mondelay was in one hell of a hurry to leave, but he was never in too much of a hurry not to harass a waitress when he had the chance. He caught the bottom of her tray. Pulled it down. "You need to work on your all-over tan."

"Yeah," she said, cool as could be. "I know."

"Let her get those beers," Decker said.

"I'd throw her a bang," Mondelay said as if Tess weren't even standing there. "Wouldn't you?"

Deck had been trying to pretend that a woman who was pole-dancing on the other side of the bar had caught his full attention, but now he was forced to look up and appraise Tess, whom he knew had a photo of her two little nieces in a frame on her desk along with a plastic action figure of Buffy the Vampire Slayer. Nash had asked her about it once, and she'd told them Buffy represented both female empowerment and the fact that most people had inner depths not obviously apparent to the casual observer.

Decker felt a hot rush of anger at Nash, who, no doubt, had been taking his flirtation with Tess to the next level when the call came in that Decker needed assistance. He wasn't sure what pissed him off more—the fact that Nash had sent Tess in here without her shirt, or that Nash was sleeping with her.

"Yeah," he said now to Mondelay, since they'd been talking about the waitresses in these bars like this all week. He gave Tess a smile that he hoped she'd read as an apology for the entire male population. "I would also send her flowers, afterward."

"Tell me, hon, do women really go for that sentimental bullshit?" Mondelay asked Tess.

"Nah," she said. "What we really love is being objectified, used, and cast aside. Why else would I have gotten a job here? I mean, aside from the incredible health plan and the awesome 401K."

Decker laughed as she tugged her tray free, and headed toward the bar.

He watched her go, aware of the attention she was getting from the other lowlifes in the bar, noting the soft curve of her waist, and the way that, although she wasn't very tall, she carried herself as if she stood head and shoulders above the crowd. He was also aware that it had been a very long time since he'd sent a woman flowers.

They were in some serious shit here. Whoever set up this ambush had paramilitary training.

There were too many shooters set in position around the building. He couldn't take them all out.

Well, he could. The setup was professional, but the shooters were all amateurs. He could take them all out, one by one by one. And like the first two on the roof, most of them wouldn't even hear him coming.

But Jimmy Nash's hands were already shaking from clearing that roof. A cigarette would've helped, but last time he'd quit, he'd sworn it was for good.

He washed his hands in the sink in the men's, trying, through sheer force of will, to make them stop trembling.

It was that awful picture he had in his head of Decker gunned down in the parking lot that steadied him and made his heart stop hammering damn near out of his chest.

He'd do anything for Deck.

They'd been Agency partners longer than most marriages lasted these days. Seven years. Who'd have believed *that* was possible? Two fucked-up, angry men, one of them—him—accustomed to working alone, first cousin to the devil, and the other a freaking Boy Scout, a former Navy SEAL . . .

When Tess had called him tonight and told him what she'd overheard, that HQ essentially knew Decker was being targeted and that they weren't busting their asses to keep it from happening . . .

The new Agency director, Doug-the-Prick Brendon, hadn't tried to hide his intense dislike of "Diego" Nash, and therefore Decker by association. But this was going too far.

Jimmy used his wet hands to push his hair back from his face, forcing himself to meet his eyes in the mirror.

Murderous eyes.

After he got Decker safely out of here, he was going to hunt down Dougie Brendon, and . . .

"And spend the rest of your life in jail?" Jimmy could practically hear Deck's even voice.

"First they'd have to catch me," he pointed out. And they wouldn't. He'd made a vow, a long time ago, to do whatever he had to do never to get locked up again.

"There are other ways to blow off steam." How many times had Decker said those exact words to him?

Other ways . . .

Like Tess Bailey.

Who was waiting for him in the ladies' room. Who was unbelievably hot. Who liked him—really liked him—he'd seen it in her eyes. She pretended to have a cold-day-in-July attitude when he flirted with her in the office. But Jimmy saw beyond it, and he knew with just a little more charm, and a little bit of well-placed pressure, she'd be giving him a very brightly lit green light.

Tonight.

He'd let Decker handle Doug Brendon.

Jimmy would handle Tess.

He smiled at the pun as he opened the men's room door and went out into the hallway. He pushed open the ladies' room door, expecting to see her, live and in person. But she wasn't there. *Shit.* He checked the stalls—all empty.

It sobered him fast and he stopped thinking about the latter part of the evening, instead focusing on here and now, on finding Tess.

He spotted her right away as he went back into the hall. She was standing at the bar. What the Jesus God was she doing there? But then he knew. Decker and Mondelay had ordered drinks.

And he hadn't been specific enough in his instructions, assuming "get your ass in the ladies' room" meant just that, not "get your ass in the ladies' room after you fill their drink order."

The biggest problem with her standing at the bar was not the fact that she was bare-breasted and surrounded by drunken and leering men.

No, the biggest problem was that she was surrounded by other bare-breasted women—i.e. the real waitstaff of the Gentlemen's Den. Who were going to wonder what Tess was doing cheating them out of their hard-earned tips.

And sure enough, as Jimmy watched, an older woman with long golden curls, who looked an awful lot like the masthead of an old sailing ship—those things had to be implants—tapped Tess on the shoulder.

He couldn't possibly hear U.S.S. Bitch-on-Wheels from this distance. Her face was at the wrong angle for him to read her lips, but her body language was clear. "Who the hell are *you*?"

Time for a little secondary rescue.

He took off his jacket and tossed it into the corner. No one in this dive so much as owned a suit, and his was ruined anyway. He snatched off his tie, too, loosened his collar, and rolled up his sleeves as he pushed his way through the crowd and over to the bar.

"Oh, here he is now," Tess was saying to Miss Masthead as he moved into earshot. She smiled at him, which was distracting as hell, because, like most hetero men, he'd been trained to pick up a strong, positive message from the glorious combination of naked breasts and a warm, welcoming smile. He forced himself to focus on what she was saying.

"I was just telling Crystal about the practical joke, you know," Tess said, crossing her arms in front of her, "that we're playing on your cousin?"

Well, how about that? She didn't need rescuing. The Masthead—Crystal—didn't look like the type to swallow, but she'd done just that with Tess's story.

"Honey, give her a little something extra," Tess told him, "because she did, you know, lose that tip she would have gotten."

Jimmy dug into his pocket for his billfold, and pulled out two twenty-dollar bills.

Tess reached for a third, taking the money from his hands and handing it to her brand-new best friend. "Will you get those two beers for me?" she asked Crystal.

The waitress did better than that—she went back behind the bar to fetch 'em herself.

Tess turned to Jimmy, who took the opportunity to put his arm around her—she had, after all, called him honey. He was just being a good team player and following her lead, letting that smooth skin slide beneath his fingers.

"Thanks." She lowered her voice, turning in closer to him, using him as a way to hide herself—from the rest of the crowd at least. "May I have my shirt back?"

"Whoops," he said. Her shirt was in the pocket of his jacket, which was somewhere on the floor by the rest rooms. That is, if someone hadn't already found it and taken it home.

"Whoops?" she repeated, looking up at him, fire in her eyes.

As Jimmy stared down at her, she pressed even closer. Which might've kept him from looking, but sure as hell sent his other senses into a dance of joy. It was as if they shared the same shirt—she was so soft and warm and alive. He wanted her with a sudden sharpness that triggered an equally powerful realization. It was so strong it nearly made him stagger.

He didn't deserve her.

He had no right even to touch her. Not with these hands.

"Are you all right?" Tess whispered.

Caught in a weird time warp, Jimmy looked down into her eyes. They were light brown—a nothing-special color as far as eyes went—but he'd always been drawn to the intelligence and warmth he could see in them. He realized now, in this odd, lingering moment of clarity, that Tess's eyes were beautiful. *She* was beautiful.

An angel come to save him . . .

"I'm fine," he said, because she was looking at him as if he'd lost it. Crap, maybe he had for a minute there. "Really. Sorry." He kissed her, just a quick press of his lips against hers, because he didn't know how else to erase the worry from her eyes.

It worked to distract her—God knows it did a similar trick on him.

He wanted to kiss her again, longer, deeper—a real touch-the-tonsils, full firework-inducing event, but he didn't. He'd save that for later.

And Decker always said he had no willpower.

He looked out at the crowd, trying to get a read on who was shit-faced drunk—who would best serve as a catalyst for part two of tonight's fun.

"Did you find a way to get Decker out of here?" Tess asked. He could see that he'd managed completely to confuse her. She was back to folding her arms across her chest.

"Yeah, I cleared the roof." He wondered if she had any idea what that meant. He glanced back at the room. There was a man in a green T-shirt who was so tanked his own buddies' laughter was starting to piss him off.

But Tess obviously didn't understand any of what he'd said. "The roof? How . . . ?"

"I called for some help with our extraction." Jimmy explained the easy part. "We'll be flying Deck out of here—a chopper's coming to pick us up, but first we need a little diversion. Have you ever been in a bar fight?"

Tess shook her head.

"Well, you're about to be. If we get separated, keep to the edge of the room. Keep your back to the wall, watch for flying objects and be ready to duck. Work your way around to that exit sign, and . . . Heads up," he interrupted himself.

Because here came ol' Gus, right on cue, searching for Tess, wondering what the fuck was taking so long with their beers, impatient to send Decker to the parking lot where he'd be filled with holes, where he'd gasp out the last breath of his life in the gravel.

And here came Deck, right behind him, the only real gentleman in this den of bottom feeders, ready to jump on Gus's back if he so much as looked cross-eyed at cute little Tess Bailey from support.

"When I knock over that guy sitting there with the black T-shirt that says 'Badass,' " Nash instructed her, meeting his partner's gaze from across the room just as Gus spotted him with Tess. Gus reacted, reaching inside of his baseball jacket either for his cell phone or a weapon—it didn't really matter which because he was so slo-o-o-w, and Deck was already on top of both it and him. "Lean over the bar and shout to your girlfriend Crystal that she should call 911, that someone in the crowd has a gun. On your mark, get set . . ."

Fifteen feet away, Decker brought Gus Mondelay to his knees and then to the floor, which was a damn good thing, because if it had been Nash taking him down, he would have snapped the motherfucker's neck.

". . . Go!"